The Cupel Recruits
by
Susan L. Willshire

WOLF PAW MEDIA

Boulder, Colorado - Orlando, Florida

Cover art by Kate Wyman, based upon concept by the author

Printed in the United States of America

Wolf Paw Media

3415 W. Lake Mary Blvd. #950879

Lake Mary, Florida 32795, USA

wolfpawmedia.com

The characters and events in this book, living and dead, are works of fiction. Any similarity to real persons, living or dead, is not intended by the author and is coincidence.

ISBN: 978-0-615-39736-8

Printed in the United States of America

<u>Prologue</u>

"I am engineering a solution," Stone said to Wood as he handed him the disk.

"The new recruits?" Wood guessed. Wood turned the case over in his hands nervously and swallowed hard as he felt a constriction in his throat.

"Yes," replied Stone with heaviness in his voice, "They arrive tomorrow." He stared at Wood unflinchingly, closely watching his colleague for any signs of reaction that might tell their fate. He was hoping to learn more than he was privy to through nonverbal clues, but Wood's experience won out and revealed nothing more, though both already knew the situation to be grave. Wood had no intention of making it worse or rattling his coworkers.

"Will she be pleased?" Wood asked flatly. His question really required no response. It was merely a test, as all of life is; He already knew the answer as he had pulled the files from Stone's system in the late hours the night before.

"I believe so," Stone responded sincerely, "These clips show their capabilities. I heard they were hand-picked for a complementary skill set and amazing aptitude. There are three connectors and two legacies in this batch."

"Two legacies. Hmmm. I thought there were four connectors-what happened?"

"The fourth wasn't ready. I studied her quite carefully," Stone responded. He felt the weight of his decision. They didn't leave a team member behind lightly, but he'd spent hours and hours watching her surveillance tapes and felt she simply wasn't ready.

"She'll be left behind alone? That will be rough." Wood stood pensive for a moment, but was abruptly jolted to attention when Ruth Fielding entered the room. Ruth was 5'5" and petite, but walked with the authority of a drill sergeant. Her grey hair shone an iridescent white offsetting her crisp blue eyes, which somehow were warm while conveying a laser intelligence.

"You're too recently back," Ruth said quietly to Wood. Stone pretended not to hear. "There is no room for sentiment right now. I've been guilty of it before myself, because I know they get to you sometimes with the amount of surveillance we do, but there's a time and a place." She stepped toward the vast computer system embedded in the wall and switched on the viewing software. Speaking more loudly so Stone could hear also, she instructed:

"And we did pull two legacies in one batch once, long before either of you were born," she smiled to herself remembering the lessons of long ago, "and you should see how that class turned out. Ancient history now, though."

On the surveillance screen appeared a beautiful woman, about 28, with long, black hair, green eyes and a stellar smile. People often spoke to Lela like she was dumb, which amused her. Sometimes she would play along so as not to hurt their feelings. If they did it in a condescending way, however, she could cut them with an insightful comment as easily as look at them. Fortunately, today was not such a day. Ruth watched Lela on the screen for about 10 seconds,

"You're right, she's not ready," she said directly to Stone. He breathed an inward sigh of relief, simultaneously grateful for her assessment and amazed that she could conclude in 10 seconds what he had spent hundreds of hours stretched over months to conclude. Well, he was only a Circle 2, so that was to be expected. No one really knew what circle Ruth was- she would never confirm, but he and the other young ones guessed it to be around 20. She knew it all, they said. And she did.

<u>Chapter 1</u>

Lela parked the car on the curb in her parent's familiar neighborhood, just a few blocks away from the house. Cruising by, her brother's car and his fiancée's car were already in the driveway, so she kept going until parking was available. It was one of those neighborhoods full of charm and large on walking or biking to various shoppes, fruit stands, and bakeries. Her mother loved it because she could walk out daily and easily gather fresh ingredients for a meal without a large trip to the grocery store. Lela and her brother, Gabriel, loved it because they had fond memories of growing up there in an era where they had the illusion of safety and the naiveté of youth was permitted to persist, unlike today. Normally, Lela might have viewed the occasion as one to be disgruntled with "the alleged fiancée", as she referred to her in her own mind, but being grateful for a short walk in the neighborhood outweighed her annoyance on this day.

She paused at the corner, remembering the beauty salon that had gone out of business and the space that sat empty for a few years until the neighborhood built up enough to attract a few larger chains. At that moment, her phone rang for at least the hundredth time that day.

"Aquila," Lela said in a drone.

"Ms. Aquila, this is Captain Willingham. Just wanted to let you know I emailed you the final instructions for your team's security protocols for tomorrow."

"Thanks, Captain. I'm happy to say that's the last item on your list," she reported as she checked an item from a multipage checklist. "See you tomorrow." Breezing into Starbucks, she rattled off her usual order as if on autopilot, "Chai Latte with skim milk, please." Staring out the window, her mind began racing through that long to-do list for the event she was organizing the next day. Without her notice, an athletic-looking man one might call distinguished-looking were he a bit older stood less than a foot away and was staring at her intently. Her thoughts interrupted, she silently gave him a quick glance wondering why he was encroaching on her personal space.

"God marked you," he stated flatly. He reminded her of someone. She laughed a quiet, awkward laugh that was more out of nervousness than out of humor and took half a step back. He stared at her seriously, picked up his coffee from the counter and walked out without a word. She relaxed, listening to the smooth sounds of Dean Martin as she waited for her order. Humming along under her breath, under the loud whir of the espresso machine, she amused no one but herself. Coffee in hand, she walked the blocks to her parent's home thinking once again of all that she had to do the next day. This really wasn't the most convenient time for a family dinner, but as she and Gabriel grew older, they seemed to be less frequent, maybe once a month. 'Family comes first' she reminded herself. Work would always be there; their parents, sadly, would not.

Three more calls arrived during Lela's short walk to her family home. She checked off each of the items- territory map displays, mineral samples, and the schedule for tours of the new scientific facility- in order. As she walked up the stone pavers through the front garden, she saw Gabriel sitting on the front porch, sipping a tall iced tea.

"Wow, you look like Dad when we were little," she truthfully teased her brother. Gabriel was about 6' 0" tall, had brown hair with subtle caramel highlights where the sun hit naturally at the part, and an easy grin that had always made him the one with the charm. Lela wasn't really introverted so much as a bit hesitant. Once she knew people, she was warm and open. Gabriel, extroverted and popular, seemed even more-so because he, too, was a scientist. Her somewhat quiet nature tended to blend well in the scientific community, but Gabriel stood out like a rock star. They were both brilliant, but he received more public accolade since he was a more affable interview. Lela had always liked having Gabriel there to take the spotlight so she would not feel the burn of its' glare. He wore khaki pants and a plain white shirt with the arms rolled up to contrast his tan arms, unbuttoned to reveal the white ribbed tank underneath due to the heat.

"I think it's the 40's outfit," she giggled, hugging her brother and sitting down on the step next to him. Without realizing it, they sat in identical posture, elbows on knees, and each held a drink in their right hand. It was a picture their mother would have cherished: two grown siblings genuinely caring for each other. Teen years of bickering had been replaced with mutual respect.

"I'm on the front porch and it's hot," he jokingly defended, "Besides, Gretchen doesn't mind. She likes to get dressed up and go swing dancing."

"Of course she does," Lela responded.

"Be nice today," he warned, in a subtly more serious tone. Gabriel knew his sister was slower to warm up to people, but would not allow his fiancée to be uncomfortable as a result of it. At 33, he felt it had taken him a long time to find the woman he wanted to marry and he had no intentions of anything jeopardizing that.

"I will," she conceded, tipping back the last of her latte and shaking the empty cup. They wordlessly arose and headed into the house.

Once the front door opened, the warm smells of Dad's barbeque chicken and Mom's baked goods filled the house.

"There she is!" their Mom exclaimed as both parents rushed her like a defensive line going for the quarterback. Crushed with their affection, Lela wriggled from their hugs after a moment and removed her shoes and over shirt, tossing her purse on the green lumpy chair in the corner.

The television was on and tuned to 'Phillip Harriman: Master Psychic.'

"Oh, Mom's watching the witch doctor show again," Gabriel announced loudly and everyone paused to watch as the host delivered messages from beyond the grave to the grieving family on the screen as they sniffled and huddled together.

"Oh, I just had it on because Daddy and Gretchen were out back with the grill. But he's not a witch doctor. You know, last week, he did one of those celebrity readings and told Shayna Falon where her family had left some stock certificates hidden. Sure enough, he was right," Mrs. Aquila responded.

"And the rich get richer," Mr. Aquila offered.

"Oh, please, that is sooo fake," Gabriel contributed. Gretchen observed silently, trying to learn all the family dynamics that would affect the lives of her and her son for years to come. Lela's phone rang again and she glanced at the display before clicking the caller to pass to voice mail. Surely, one hour of uninterrupted time wasn't too much to ask.

"Actually, Mom," Lela added, "you'll be happy to know the Governor gave me a "gift" of a reading with this guy as a "reward" for all the work I've been doing on the project. He's a really spiritual guy and believes in all that stuff, does trips to remote corners of the world to cleanse his soul and all that. So, I have to use it, since they're friends and he'll know if I don't, but I figure I'll just ask whatever questions you want me to, since you're into this stuff."

"Oh, honey, that's so exciting. You really should be more open-minded. We've always raised you kids to be accepting of all religions and points of view."

"Religions, yes, Mom, but witchdoctorey, come on!" Gabriel retorted.

Mrs. Aquila casually turned off the television and all knew that was the end of the discussion.

"We're almost ready to eat," their Mom stated as she turned back to her cutting of salad at the counter. Lela and Gabriel reverted to well-worn roles, she setting the dishes at the table and him pouring the drinks into glasses.

"Can I do anything to help?" Gretchen asked.

"No, we got it," Lela replied quickly. Gretchen fidgeted a bit nervously with her soon-to-be in-laws, without a task to do.

"I could use some help with these mushrooms," Mrs. Aquila offered and Gretchen brightened, cheerfully picking up the task. Lela's phone rang again and, after viewing the display, she passed the caller to voice mail.

"I hope you know you're not bringing that thing to the dinner table," Mrs. Aquila advised. Lela laughed and placed it on the buffet behind her chair.

"Oh, two feet away, that helps," her mother teased, then turned her attention to Gretchen as all were seated, "So, where is little Caleb today?"

"He's with his grandparents. They had tickets to the zoo," Gretchen replied.

"I hate to see animals in captivity," Lela said in earnest, grabbing a roll from the center basket. Gabriel nudged at her under the table and beseeched with his eyes for a more amiable exchange. "But I'm sure he'll have a great time," she added for her brother's benefit.

Mrs. Aquila looked pointedly at Lela. 'Mom look number 4' they called it as kids, when they knew she was displeased. Gabriel smirked at Lela a bit, half gloating as the victor of parental approval and half in empathy.

"Lela, are you dating anyone these days?" her mother asked, knowing the answer.

"No, mother," Lela, getting the point, added quickly, smiling, "but there was a really dreamy guy back at Starbucks; I can run and fetch him if you like." She struck a pose half-raised from her chair as if to run.

"Please do," her Mom said with a definitive bite of salad and a hint of a smile at the corners of her mouth. Mrs. Aquila was a person who laughed with her eyes, knew her mind, and took pride in a task well done. Lela thought that was the end of it and relaxed back into her chair, but her escape was only momentary.

"Whatever happened to James Matthews?" Mrs. Aquila asked. Lela breathed deeply.

"Working overseas, I think," she said curtly and shoved a too-large large bite of barbeque chicken in her mouth.

"Oh, that's attractive," their Dad teased.

"I thought the military men *liked* the more down-to-earth girls who can shovel food in at the rate of a sailor. Isn't that right, Dad?" Gabriel asked, since his Dad had been in the military and he had not.

"Why, yes, Son," their Dad answered in mock exaggeration, "while in foxholes, we would frequently discuss our desire to have a woman who could out-eat us, out-curse us, beat us in an arm-wrestle, you name it." Finished chewing by this point, Lela tried to deflect jokingly,

"My dream: to win over any old military man who'll have me!"

"What's wrong with military men?" her Dad asked more seriously.

"Nothing, Daddy, but you were only in for 6 years. You've been a scientist for the last 26. I just think I'd find someone more my speed in my own field."

"Beggars can't be choosers," Gabriel added, grinning from ear to ear, and Lela plopped her cucumber, which neither of them liked, onto his plate with a gallant gesture of her wrist.

"Regardless of what he's doing, I just think James Matthews was always the nicest young man," their mother prodded. "Have you spoken to him lately?"

"We email some," Lela kept her answer short as she grew tired of this line of questioning.

"So, I heard you have a big project launching tomorrow," Gretchen changed the subject. Lela was grateful for the save, but surprised at her rescuer. She'd take it, though, and gave Gretchen a brief look of almost-sisterly acceptance.

"Yes!" Lela launched, figuring if she grabbed the topic enthusiastically, maybe the transfer of focus would be complete. She gave extra detail, to prompt questions in this direction, "We are launching an African relief project in conjunction with the governments of the African nations to arrange corporate sponsorship of provinces, to build schools, roads and bridges, improve drinking water, and make sure each area can build jobs around their natural resources or skills of the region. Our government has offered steep tax cuts for the corporations willing to do this, so it's really a win-win situation for everyone. The project accountability council makes sure that the dollars go directly to improvements in each region, and by limiting each corporation to one region, we ensure no monopolies or hoarding of resources result," she summarized.

"I think it's all about greed and air space," Mr. Aquila added.

"Dad, why would you offer to help with the project if that's what you think?" Lela prodded in a concerned tone.

"Because we need the air space?" he replied, half jokingly. "Look, I'm not for corporate greed, and I wouldn't have agreed to work on the project if you didn't put the oversight measures into place, but at the end of the day there's a lot of good to come out of this and I really am proud of your work on it."

"Speaking of the project, I have a couple things I need to show you quick before tomorrow, L," Gabriel said to his sister.

"Sure," she said, sliding her chair away from the table.

"Oh, don't think you two are running off to hunker in that laboratory for hours without cleaning up first!" Mrs. Aquila reprimanded, "And you're limited to a half hour tonight. We still have dessert." Wordlessly, everyone under the age of 50 began cleaning up as Mr. and Mrs. Aquila retired to the music room for a post-dinner date with the piano. As Lela wiped the table, she glanced at her brother and Gretchen at the sink. They clearly had a system for dish duty and it seemed to work well. Gabriel absentmindedly touched the small of Gretchen's back and continued drying. Lela realized at that moment that his brother must really love this virtual stranger and considered how different his life would be from his bachelor days. Her cell phone rang and "SEC" appeared on the display in an array of pale blue illumination.

"I've gotta take this," she reported as she swept into the anteroom and shut the door.

"Anything to get out of dishes!" Gabriel shouted after her in feigned dismay.

"Yes, Madame Secretary," Lela waited patiently for the forthcoming instructions. Late-night calls were not uncommon, particularly the night before a major project launch with heavy press coverage.

"Ms. Aquila, is everything set for tomorrow? My admin said she did not receive confirmation from the venue and I'm concerned they may not have the preparations in place."

"I received a second confirmation from them today. They are aware we need the podium area set up in accordance with the security layout Captain Willingham delivered. Rooftop patrols go in place at 4 am and they will start setting up the aesthetic aspects at 6am," Lela responded. She had felt more like an event coordinator than a scientist over the past few months, but the energy and healthcare impacts of this project related so closely to her work, she had to be sure it was executed properly.

"Excellent. I'll see you in the morning." and with that, Madame was gone.

"Yup, goodbye! Have a good evening! Glad this will help your candidate get reelected," she said into the dead receiver and shook her head at the abruptness that passed for conversation among the politicos. Like most people, she had never really liked politicians, but recognized the need for them. Up close, she had been able to witness the mixed motives of most of them, but was stunned to discover she found among them a man of vision, conviction and inspiration in the current Governor. Though his staff wasn't much different than any other, he stood out as an example in the state, galvanized people in tough times, helped the poor - everything a good leader is supposed to do. Governor Buck J. Jacob was rumored to be a Presidential nominee in the next election.

Lela returned to the kitchen to find it completely clean: all dishes in the dishwasher, large pots in the drying rack, everything else already washed and dried, neatly away, with a glisten of freshly-wiped counters reflecting the light from the street lamps outside through the long kitchen window. It smelled of bleach. Mom's kitchen, she thought to herself. The piano in the distant corner of the house bellowed forth some boisterous ragtime, beckoning her to join in the fun. Turning the corner into the music room, she was surprised to see that it was Gretchen at the bench and not her mother. 'Wow, she's really good', Lela thought to herself. She decided not to interrupt with talk of the lab visit until later- everyone looked too peaceful. Gabriel and Mr. Aquila sat in chairs on either side of a Victorian end table holding a tiffany-style lamp, sipping their coffees, while Mrs. Aquila sat on the red velvet chaise, head back, eyes closed, legs crossed at the ankle, tapping her top foot in gentle rhythm to the music. The house was filled with so much positive energy that it seemed to glow and spread the energy outward to the world in an effort to uplift humanity. Lela and Gabriel's childhood home experienced the same doldrums of suburban life, teen angst, occasional financial strife as any normal American home, but it always seemed to shine more brightly than most. As Lela listened to the closing chorus, she couldn't help but appreciate the momentary respite from her own hectic life. Had she known what was to come, she would have appreciated the moment even more than she did.

Chapter 2

Gabriel awoke early, before the alarm went off, and watched Gretchen sleeping peacefully for a casual time before jumping out of bed. She had squinched herself into a semi-ball and was holding tightly to the sheets in a fist below her cheek, as if afraid they would leave her. Though she looked very glamorous with make-up, Gabriel liked her without it, since he could see the sheer smattering of freckles across her nose, which were not normally visible. He also liked her hair completely messy- the more sticking up the better. Since he had guarded himself so long against this level of closeness, these intimate details were still new to him and carried with them a sense of privilege for being the man who gets to be with her.

Somehow feeling him watching her, Gretchen slowly opened her eyes to see him just a few inches from her face and a wide smile lingered across her teeth while she coyly rubbed her eyes. Reaching out to smooth out his hair, she spoke softly so as not to awake the very walls of the house, or Caleb.

"Gabriel Aquila up before necessary? I haven't seen that since Christmas."

"I had that weird light lake dream again. Besides, it feels a little like Christmas today," Gabriel replied, "We've worked on this project so long that to have the big unveiling is exciting." He reached over and scooped her close to him, holding on with a reassuring amount of pressure. Gretchen thought to herself how that was the move that always made her feel safe, like everything would be all right, when there were days when life was sure to be difficult, days unlike today. "Don't get me wrong," he continued," scientifically there are some interesting aspects to it, and I think based on some new findings that there may be even more, but it's not the slickest thing I've ever worked on. But, to see Lela so happy, and all the political people and that actor that's onboard the project, it's definitely higher profile than I'm used to and I think that's fun. Ya know, the team dynamics." He wasn't sure if she understood, but she did. "Plus, to feel like we're really going to do some good for once."

"Is that why you reopened your old lab at your parent's house, to get more time in?" she asked.

"Partially," he responded," since it's so close to work, I can just swing by before or after, or during lunch. Also, to get away from prying eyes," he confided. Gretchen looked at him seriously, but could not pursue any details that moment.

"Mom, I hear you guys. Can I come in?" a small voice somehow managed to bellow from the hallway. Gretchen breathed the last peaceful sigh of a mother who had too few moments of tranquility, like most mothers, and rose to put on her robe. Gabriel sprawled out to take up the space she'd left on the bed, including using all the pillows at once with his own sigh, but his was one of deep satisfaction. He loved the family feeling that was in this house now, a stark contrast to the clinical feel of it before Gretchen and Caleb moved in.

"You, bet, Cay-Cay" Gabriel answered. Caleb ran in and jumped on the bed with the full speed and force available to his 7-year-old body," Good morning!" he shouted, hugging them both.

"Good morning, Caleb," Gretchen responded, breathing in the baby-shampoo smell of her son's hair wistfully. 'The only thing about him that's still a baby' she thought silently. He was already dressed in his karate uniform, though his belt test was not until 3:30 that day

"Are you planning on wearing that to school?" she asked playfully.

"Yep! I'm gonna warm it up so it's all ready," he replied optimistically.

"I still wish we could come to the kickoff event," she said as an aside to Gabriel.

"Are you kidding?" he asked, mirroring her playful tone, as he picked Caleb up and wrestled him while tickling, "and make this guy wait 6 months until the next test?" Caleb giggled and wriggled, pushing with all his might on Gabriel's chest, but could not get away. "Well, you better go eat your oatmeal if you want to be strong for your test today," Gabriel relinquished.

"Yeah! I'm gonna be the strongest!" Caleb shouted backward while running out of the room at full speed.

"I'm glad we decided to move the houses together last month rather than wait for the wedding. I know it's a short time, but I wouldn't have wanted to wait anymore," Gabriel said to Gretchen, grabbing her hand as they walked toward the kitchen.

"Me neither," she echoed, "Oh, and remind me about that paperwork this weekend." Flipping on the small kitchen television, hoping to catch the weather, the top story of the day centered on the project launch. TV crews were already onsite, showing the setup of the podium and seating areas that Lela had assured Madame Secretary would begin at 6am. It had. The television crews showed only the same still shot over and over of the new command center atop Moss's hill. The event was planned so that the kickoff festivities, tents, and speeches would all occur in the flat land at the base of the hill, with the new command center shining in the distance. Then the science teams would caravan up the hill, ceremoniously cut the ribbon across the front door, and allow the media and outsiders the very first glimpse of the new facility. A bit dramatic for the tastes of most of the science team, but the usual PR hype with which the rest were accustomed.

When Lela arrived on the scene at 6:30, a surprising amount had already been done. 'Not too complicated to set up some chairs, I guess' she thought to herself. Her gaze was immediately drawn to the soldiers flanking the small valley area on the rooftops of the surrounding buildings. From a security perspective, it was a good location. Behind the podium was the hill, and the entrance to the small valley area was controllable with a degree of ease. The winding path up the hill to the new facility followed the curve of the mountain and was the only real open access point. Since the security team had the new facility locked down, there was no real risk there either. Unless someone cared enough to come by air up the side of the mountain, and this project was nowhere near big enough to generate that kind of interest, Madame and Captain Willingham should be satisfied. 'Speak of the Devil' Lela thought.

"Ms. Aquila, may I see the checklist?" Madame "greeted". Lela wordlessly handed her the clipboard. "The buses aren't here yet, why are they checked off?" Madame asked sharply. As Lela began to reply, Madame continued, "Luxury buses 1-4 are for the core team, seating in order of importance of course, and the standard buses after that are for the media, the friends with money we've invited and any other leachlings still lying about." Lela saw Madame take a breath and launched in:

"Yes, Madame, the buses are in fact here. Captain Willingham asked that we line them in order down Flag Street so they would not interfere with visibility for his teams in any way."

"Fine, just have them pull around right when the Governor finishes his speech so we can keep things moving. Events like this are all about momentum," she said in an instructional tone.

"Yes, Madame Secretary," Lela replied, suddenly feeling uncharacteristically weary. Lela spotted her father standing in a small circle of colleagues near the rear of the seating area. "Please excuse me, I'm going to check on the science team," Lela fished for an out.

"Fine," Madame retorted and thrust the clipboard back at Lela. Walking across the field, Lela surveyed the area once more to be sure everything appeared in order. A sole man sat in a chair in the middle of the seating area, scribbling notes furiously into an expensive leather folio. In a suit and tie, he removed his suit jacket and laid it neatly on the chair next to him. Lela's keen sense of observation noticed the top of a tattoo peeking above his starched collar below the bottom of his perfectly manicured haircut. He appeared an academic, but something in his manner seemed familiar. 'Probably a plant by Captain Willingham' she mused to herself. 'I've probably met the guy before. Either that or he's just the most eager beaver in the village.' Reaching her father and his circle of colleagues, Lela noticed they were discussing the wall of exhibits prepared by the PR team.

"Lela, they did an excellent job with these exhibits, very accurate with the topography and mineral compositions," Mr. Aquila complimented.

"Madame's work, Dad," Lela smiled.

"Oh, Madame knows technical requirements now, does she?" Mr. Aquila asked, knowing Lela was the one who had to provide all the detail to make the documents accurate, "Her formatting idea maybe," he conceded that small element to highlight the fact that the real work was done by his daughter. "Lela, this is Enam Bamidele, my esteemed colleague and good friend."

"It's a pleasure, Mr. Bamidele- after so much email correspondence I am happy to finally meet you in person," she smiled at the tall man, immediately admiring the sincere and pleasant aura about him.

"Actually, Miss Lela, we have met before, when your father and I worked together in Mexico, but you may not remember, being only three at the time." He pulled out a stack of pictures from his shirt pocket he was kind enough to bring for Lela to see pictures of the mysterious "life in Mexico" period she'd heard so little about. Taking the photos by the edges, Lela thoughtfully examined the young, 2-dimensional versions of her parents. In the last, she was eating an ice cream cone at her mother's knee while her parents laughed heartily with Enam Bamidele over some now-forgotten amusement; Gabriel hung from a tree in the background. She held the photos out to return to Enam Bamidele but he waived his hands in protest.

"No, no, Miss Lela, I brought those for you." She thanked him as her mother rejoined the group after a brief absence. Lela glanced at her mother, who looked briefly at the rooftops, then at the seated man with the leather folio, then to Lela. She gave Lela a fake smile and Lela looked at her questioningly, to which her mother's look replied 'later'. One beauty of family was the ability to communicate nonverbally. With no pockets or briefcase, Lela carefully clipped the photos under the large stack of papers on her clipboard.

As 9 am approached, the tents and seating area filled up quickly and the small valley was alive with conversation. Non-VIP media was held back to a point 200 feet beyond the event area bordered by barricades while media with a VIP pass could access beyond that point. In the distance, farther back from the base of the hill, the array of TV trucks and media vehicles were all corralled into one region so as not to be disruptive to the participants and guests. It took an hour and fifteen minutes to get through the introductions, presentment of the science team, presentment of the political team and presentment of the African stakeholders whose goal was to convey the difference this project would make in the everyday lives of the people in their country. Madame Secretary shot Lela a dissatisfied look, since the Governor's speech was to begin one hour into the event, promptly at 10am. 'How am I supposed to control exactly how long each of these people speaks?' Lela thought to herself. She'd given them each their time limit. Beyond that, what was she supposed to do, go tackle them off the stage if they ran over? 'Madame probably would have preferred that' Lela thought. Glancing next to her brother as the sentiments of project importance continued, Gabriel gave her an unobtrusive wink from his chair in the science row to the left of the podium. Though he was facing the entire audience, it was so quick as to be almost imperceptible so Lela doubted anyone noticed.

Next Madame Secretary took the podium to share her own thoughts on the project, smoothly veiling her real purpose of simply introducing the Governor.

"The importance of this project to both the region and to the corporate sponsors cannot be minimized, " she said with all the sugary sweetness of a salesman trying to seal a deal, " and, I would like to add that this project is of such personal importance to me," Madame breathed deeply and blinked back "tears", "that I will forever be indebted, with unending gratitude," she paused for effect and her voice shook slightly, "to all those that have worked so hard to make this a reality. To the science and political teams, to the real heroes, who have invested in the project by generously allocating their corporate sponsorship to help the world. I'd also like to acknowledge especially Mr. Jack Reedson who took time from filming his latest film, Thermopyle, to join us!" Madame Secretary shouted unnecessarily into the microphone. The crowd applauded, a large contingent in the rear of the seating area boisterously cheering. 'Probably the ones who came just to see him' Lela thought cynically.

Jack Reedson rose halfway from his chair to Madame's left, giving a perfunctory wave and wry smile. He was the least hammy actor Lela had ever seen and his sincerity in motive was evident during the planning stages of the project. He quietly put forth solid ideas among the scientists, careful to not invoke a "just an actor" rebuff from them. Over the long months, he had won their admiration and confidence with his subtle style. There was only one actor on the stage at that moment and it wasn't Jack Reedson. When the crowd died down, Madame continued beaming and piling on the praise for various other project participants of value to her. 'Where's my shovel?' Lela thought. Of course, no mention was made of Lela specifically. From Madame's perspective, she'd been included when she had acknowledged "the science team".

"And finally, I'd like to acknowledge our most important visionary toward the success of this project, Governor Buck J. Jacob!" Madame clapped a slightly uplifted, exaggerated clap to encourage the crowd to applaud, which was unnecessary. The entire crowd, not just the rear contingent, was quickly on its feet and applauding at a deafening level that rivaled an NFL stadium. The beloved leader smiled and waved gently in a feeble attempt to quiet them. Behind him, his wife, Jillian, and four-year-old daughter, Phoebe, sat smiling, dressed conservatively in navy blue. Phoebe's legs swung from the chair adorned with white patent leather Mary Jane shoes, completing the picturesque political family. The Governor's unsuccessful concessions to the applauding crowd continued for 3 more minutes before the crowd would be seated, ready to gobble up his wisdom. His speech was no longer than it needed to be, motivational and eloquent. Before Governor Jacob even concluded, the applause began. It built until his last word when the sound erupted into a roaring rampage of clapping.

As the crowd finished cheering and disbanded, small groups sprinkled the grassy area between the seating area and the line of buses. The vehicles had now pulled around to be lined up at the base of the hill path about 150 yards away. No one rushed, since they knew the core project teams would be boarding first and proceed before they could follow to the grand unveiling of the command center. They chatted about current events, caught up with colleagues and gathered food and drink from the small kiosks standing around the area.

Lela thought to herself how hungry she was, but brushed off the thought as an impossibility. 'I'll have to sneak away after the ribbon cutting' she thought realistically. Bus numbers had been pre-assigned to the core team to speed the transition and each member was now making their way to their own bus number.

Lela stopped next to Bus #1, holding the core team members, and took a mental inventory of The Governor, Madame, the science team, including her Dad, Brother, Mr. Enam Bamidele and her mother, traveling up as a visitor with Mr. Aquila and Gabriel. Lela also spotted the small team from the United Nations, most of who were speaking to the Bus 1 African visitors, except Jasmine Free who had eyes for Gabriel throughout the entire project. Lela admired her brother's ability to deftly deal with her advances without hurting her feelings. Lela's handling of this situation usually amounted to something like "no thanks, creep" so her brother's soft touch was an example to be emulated in Lela's eyes. As they were boarding the bus, Madame pulled Lela aside,

"Lela, Captain Willingham is waving from across the field. It doesn't seem urgent or he'd have a runner sent, but we should see what he wants." Lela's heart sank as she immediately knew "we" meant her. Seeing her face drop a bit and not appreciating the fact that a small moment of victory on the triumphant ride up the hill would be missed, Madame posited her solution in annoyance, "Oh, don't worry, you can just follow in bus 3 or 4. You won't miss the ribbon-cutting or anything."

"I'll take care of it," Lela advised without intonation. Madame turned and boarded the bus, thinking no further of it. Lela began walking back toward the seating area as Bus #1 pulled away for its victory lap without her. As she reached the edge of the row of chairs holding a few stragglers still seated, she glanced longingly back over her shoulder at the bus pulling up the hill like the little engine that could toward the beautiful white and glass building at the top. When it was about 1/3 of the way up, Bus #2 began to pull away. She was halfway through the seating area at this point and quickened her step toward Captain Willingham who was still about 50 feet away so she'd be sure to make one of the remaining core buses. It was bad enough she'd been ousted from her coveted position, she didn't want to have to ride with the general event attendants.

Passing by the still-seated gentleman with the leather portfolio, he looked up and locked eyes with Lela. His eyes were as green as grass, a fact that escaped Lela's attention earlier since he was continually looking down to write. As he held her gaze, Lela heard a loud noise behind her. Startled, she glanced back to see Bus 1 a little more than halfway up the hill now, with Bus 2 still lagging behind it, hitting into the interior side of the mountain with a loud crashing of metal. She had no time to process or even to think before the bus turned sharply away from the interior collision and instead cut to the left. Lela watched in horror as the bus barreled straight through the guardrail and off the side of the mountain. She cried out to the heavens, or no one, and fell to the ground, knocking several chairs around her over as her legs gave out beneath her. She didn't register the arms around her shoulders, or Captain Willingham running by with a batch of soldiers, or the media outside the barricades who had caught all this on camera because of their better angle from the distance, as they pushed forward and ran up the hill to not miss a moment of the tragedy recorded on film, or even her own hysterical sobs. Lela registered none of this. She was in shock.

Chapter 3

Wood and Stone happily ended their surveillance shift, handing off to Kennedy and King. After executing handoff procedures precisely and double checking the status list as per protocol, they practically ran from the room.

"I like surveillance because we get to learn so much, but I'm also glad when it's over," Wood said, rubbing the back of his neck. Stone nodded in assent as they walked down the long corridor. Halfway down the hallway, they passed a display screen about 3 feet high by 5 feet long, set at eye level, embedded in the wall and bordered in a steel-colored material. Usually, the hall display board would contain a list of briefing locations for the day, any bullet points authorized for mass distribution and major upcoming project milestone dates. As they passed, they noticed it listed only one item in giant characters that filled the screen : "95.3%" and the border was ringed in amber light. Both shot each other a glance and faint attempt at a smile.

"So that's what an alert looks like," Stone mumbled under his breath.

"Guess so," responded Wood. Since neither of them had seen a live one before, their gaze lingered a few moments longer than necessary, as if absorbing the image. "We must've passed 95% just after we started our shift." They turned into the common eating area, pausing for only a few moments to refuel before continuing on to the training room. As it would be a long day, both should have been eating extra heavy since they may not have another opportunity for 8 hours or more, but this turned out to be a challenge for Wood, who grabbed a small muffin, a banana and a juice, hardly a meal for a long day. Stone observed his friend's light meal and banged with a fist dramatically on his own abdominals.

"Steel, I tell you," he smiled, trying to alleviate his friends anxiety, "I even ate on day 1 here!" he boasted.

"You were the only one in your training team who did," Wood affirmed.

At that moment, Saraceni walked in, falling in behind Wood and Stone at the food area. He was well advanced in rank from them, Circle 13, and a quiet, contemplative man by nature. Most would think someone with a more open nature might have been a natural choice to receive the assignment as trainer to "the critical class" as the junior staff had started referring to that day's arrivals, but Saraceni's outstanding knowledge, dogmatic execution and legendary stoicism had won out. A few senior leaders in Circles 16-20 questioned the choice, but in the end they agreed that though he wasn't as advanced as the higher circle staff, or as adept at the long-range planning and development associated with those circles, he was a better trainer for a short-term assignment such as this. Saraceni had a way of making things equally clear to an audience of varied backgrounds and education levels. Senior leaders did not usually have to encounter brand new recruits, but for an occasional few moments. They were used to a much more advanced team by the time a team member would advance enough to be trained by a level 16-20. They could do it, but not as well as Saraceni, who frequently indoctrinated new recruits. Of course, certain subjects were taught by the masters of each subject area. No one, not even Saraceni with his rapid learning, could know every topic of the complex infrastructure well enough to be the best choice to teach it.

"Good morning, gentlemen," Saraceni addressed Wood and Stone, "Will you be performing the final check on my training room this morning?"

"Yes, sir," they replied in unison.

"Excellent," Saraceni responded, "If you wouldn't mind, could you please each try out the sensory awareness platform yourselves? It seemed to be underperforming yesterday and I would like to be sure it's running clean. We're going to have a tight enough schedule on this one; we can't afford any technical delays that could have been avoided."

"Certainly, sir," they responded. Saraceni still felt uncomfortable with all the "sirs" from the junior staff, but Ruth Fielding had explained that certain customs are really more for the benefit of the recruits at the lower levels than for the senior staff themselves. She had explained that a sense of familiarity helped people adjust until they passed level 5, after which some of these unnecessary elements were halted. So, Saraceni endured despite his own personal preferences. He reflected on Wood and Stone and remembered how he himself had felt at Circle 2: Somewhat confused, somewhat excited, eager to contribute and slightly fearful of failure.

"Would you like to listen in on the briefing today?" Saraceni asked. Wood and Stone both brightened noticeably and looked at each other to confirm their good fortune.

"Yes, sir," they replied, but this time with noticeable enthusiasm. Though Circle 2's were not usually included, Saraceni felt a desire to motivate these two young men that reminded him so much of an earlier self. In addition, he thought the move was strategic since he would rely on Wood and Stone heavily for administrative and technical support in the coming weeks. Due to the accelerated pace, he would have to delegate some tasks that he would normally perform himself, and their improved understanding could only help.

"Needless to say, if I allow you to participate, the details cannot be discussed outside of the core project team. We wouldn't want to distract any of the parallel operational teams from their subtasks as we will rely on them to be complete in our final week."

"Of course," Wood acknowledged quickly and Stone nodded.

"Excellent, I'll pick you up on my way to the briefing," Saraceni advised and abruptly departed, glancing at his watch. Energized by their enthusiasm, Wood and Stone practically raced to the training room to complete the final check so they would be sure no unfinished task would interfere with their ability to listen in on the briefing. Surveying the training room, clipboard in hand, Wood noted the setup of the room was set to "Configuration 1": A traditional configuration, this, too echoed the comfort of past experiences for the recruits, though it was not the most efficient. The room consisted of one large table at the front of the room, a display module with an array of controls, and 6 tables arranged 3 on the left and 3 on the right with 2 chairs at each. Training teams generally consisted of 12 recruits. Arranged in semicircles on the right and left sides of theses tables, on the outer perimeter of the room, stood multiple platforms set to meet a variety of requirements. The sensory awareness platform resided at the front left position. Setting the clipboard down, Wood removed the 2 chairs from the back right table and stored them in the adjoining anteroom.

"What are you doing?" queried Stone. Wood walked to him, picking up the clipboard on the way, and tipped it casually in Stone's direction so he could see the instruction as listed.

"It says to remove those 2 chairs. This class will have only 10," Wood commented, shrugging his shoulders with a half-raised eyebrow.

"I hate that eyebrow thing," Stone informed.

"I know," Wood grinned. "Have you ever heard of a class of 10?"

"No, but I'm sure it's one more thing they did 'before our time'," Stone mused dismissively. Since the checklist was complete, he walked stridently to the sensory awareness platform and turned it on. "I hate this thing. You first." In response, Wood jumped up onto the platform, turned to face his partner and did a little tap dance. Stone sighed quietly. Usually he enjoyed Wood's jovial nature, but found it difficult when he was battling his own anxiety as he had been all day.

"Ready?" Stone prompted.

"Yeah," Wood answered, his jokester tone leveling out to denote the nature of the task. Stone selected "arrival intro test 1" on the monitor and pressed 'run'. Wood immediately felt a sensation of flying and reported. Next he felt a sensation of walking and reported. Next he saw a blue bird flying through the room. "Blue bird," he informed Stone, who marked down each response diligently. "Bell ringing" he continued. The test continued for approximately 20 minutes through cold, heat, pain, nausea, hunger, satiety, etc. as well as a series of visual images and sounds. As the test ended, Wood stepped off the platform and sat down in the closest chair, feeling a little dizzy and disoriented.

"Want some water?" Stone offered.

"Yeah," Wood answered, resting his heard downward in his hands on the desk for a moment in an effort to not take in any additional visual stimuli. Once a few moments of recovery had passed, Wood's head emerged from its shelter as tentatively as a turtle head pushing out for a view.

"My turn," Stone announced, setting the clipboard on the table to the right of Wood. Knowing his friend had even a worse reaction to the test than his own, Wood suggested that one test was enough. The platform had performed adequately.

"No, Saraceni said for each of us to test it," Stone deflected the shirking of duty, "Thanks, though." With that, the pair repeated the test and recorded the results. Following his test, as Stone sat sipping water, he looked around the room observing the additional oddities of the training environment. In the right rear corner of the room stood a large orb perched on a pedestal, glowing the same amber color as the border to the hallway display. Customarily, the orb glowed a light iridescent blue, so the change did capture his attention. Lining the back wall were seven paintings arranged in a progression according to when they were painted. The earliest was an early cave drawing and the last was a 20th century modern piece. The most notable was the middle painting, which Stone guessed was from a middle era and clearly European. The vibrant colors and elaborate detail matched the gold gilded Louis XIV-style frame that encircled it. The frame complemented the gold, blues and red tones of the painting. The detail was amazingly accurate to what Stone now knew of the nature of the universe-impressive considering the time from which it came. Saraceni's head appeared in the swiftly opened door and alerted:

"It's time." Wood and Stone fell in swiftly and silently behind him and the three made their way down the corridor to the adjacent wing where the briefing was to be held. Turning into the room, Saraceni pointed to two chairs against the back wall in the corner and his gaze directed Wood and Stone to sit as part of that linear row, which they did. Saraceni took a chair as part of the 8-circled concentric configuration around the center podium. Once the remaining seats were filled and the briefing start time arrived, all grew silent and directed their attention forward without any instruction.

"Good morning, colleagues," Ruth Fielding began when all had arrived, "for the minutes, this is briefing 12873, subject matter: status update on training class titled 'Molior'. Instructor, project manager, senior project manager and project Champion all present. She looked pointedly at each: Saraceni, Kuminsky, and Hallowell respectively. She was, of course, the Champion herself. Wood and Stone looked at one another with the naming of the training class. 'Did they name all training classes?' they wondered. Perhaps it was one of the behind-the-scenes items reserved to senior leaders.

"Agenda item number 1: reduction of class training time. Saraceni?" Ruth looked expectantly at Saraceni.

Saraceni cleared his throat and commenced, "Gap analysis is complete. Revised training times by objective are listed in exhibit 128." Saraceni moved his hand along the flat surface of his table, tapping accordingly where necessary so the exhibit appeared on each surface of the octagonal display at the center of the room. All could see regardless of vantage point, but also transparent so a view of the opposing side of the room was not obscured. He highlighted each training objective down the page as he spoke, "As you can see, each objective's target time has been reduced as much as possible within the limits of our resources and preserving the minimal amount of sleep needed by the recruits. I have inserted three somewhat longer staging periods to promote absorption at equal intervals throughout the process, the last one being 2 days before the final mission to ensure maximum alertness and energy for final task execution. With this revised schedule, the training may be completed in 4.5 weeks as opposed to 8, with some compromise of quality acknowledged on items 4, 12, and 16."

"That's the shortest we can get it to?" Ruth asked seriously.

"To be sure they can actually achieve the mission, yes." Saraceni confirmed, aware this was not welcome news to his colleagues. He had reworked the training objectives and training agenda three times just to get it down to this, so he knew there was nowhere else from which to shave time. Ruth stared at exhibit 128 pensively, fairly certain of the answer to her following question.

"Hallowell, as senior project manager, can you advise when we will reach 100%?" Ruth asked.

"Since we have multiple moving parts: a progressive algorithm, a new scenario that has never been run even in the test environment and the beginning effects of decoherence which can only be approximated, we can only estimate with a 92% degree of confidence, but we put it at five weeks, " Elizabeth Hallowell responded. Seeing the tepid response from her colleagues, she nervously tucked both pieces of hair, which dangled, framing her face, behind her ears and continued, "Of course, we will be looking for every possible opportunity between now and then to delay the progression and increase our certainty in the estimate. We will be reprojecting every 38 hours until the mission is complete, providing real-time updates to this team via alerts," she concluded.

"Okay." Ruth Fielding acquiesced, "We'll add the projected time to the master monitoring display and keep it current so all eyes are on the prize. End of the day, though, Elizabeth, we need more time, so finding some countermeasures would really be helpful." Elizabeth nodded and made some notes as if she were adding something of this well-known fact to her report. Wood and Stone perceived a seriousness they had never encountered in their senior leaders and fidgeted accordingly while remaining riveted on the briefing.

"Agenda item 2: risk mitigation steps. Kuminsky?" Ruth prompted.

"All risk mitigation steps have been executed on schedule as per the last update," Kuminsky began, "with one notable addition. Surveillance indicated one recruit in this series," he paused glancing at his sheet to confirm the name, "a Lela Aquila, as not yet ready. Though she was not elemental to the 10 of the Molior class, her removal from one of the other classes in this series does constitute a risk mitigation step due to its impact on the overall configuration of the larger incoming team."

'So, they do use all those hours of surveillance data' Stone thought to himself. He realized at that moment the importance of the work he had been doing, though he sometimes thought of it as "grunt work" or "busywork". They had been told in training that there really is no unimportant work, but he did not believe the overarching importance of each person's contribution, no matter how small, until this very moment. Wood also reflected internally that his measurements of incremental performance gains on the platforms' performance times might actually end up being a few days aggregate difference. With the time window so narrow, that, too, could make a difference, he thought.

"For the minutes, please mark all risk mitigation steps complete as of today's date," Ruth instructed loudly.

"Lastly, what about attacks- have the number continue to increase?" Ruth asked.

Saraceni jumped in, since his crew had been monitoring the increase in attacks very closely, "They have continued to increase," he relayed, "but their strategy still appears to be more broad, not focused on our priority targets." The remaining items in the briefing were fairly routine in comparison, and as the team marched through them in promulgated order they concluded that all major milestones of the project were on schedule and they were ready for the arrival of the new training series, and most importantly, for the arrival of training class Molior. A few moments shy of the conclusion of the briefing, Kennedy entered the room unscheduled. All eyes turned from the octagonal display to the door.

"Excuse me, E. Fielding, but you asked to be informed immediately according to your instructions for the surveillance team, "Kennedy broached cautiously. As a Circle 2 also, he felt no more comfortable in this audience than Wood or Stone did.

"Yes, yes," Ruth encouraged him gently. "What news do you bring?"

"There's been an accident," Kennedy responded.

Chapter 4

Lela gave up on her feeble attempts at sleep at 5:42 am and shuffled her slippers along the hardwood floor via dragging motion as she moved from the bedroom to the sofa in the living room. She flopped down as if the 50 foot journey had sapped every ounce of available strength. She flipped on CNN out of habit and stared at the screen vaguely digesting the morning's news. Lela pulled her slippered feet up onto the sofa and curled into a ball under a fleece blanket still there from the day before.

Today was three days from the date of the accident. "Wednesday" Lela muttered to herself, not feeling as if it mattered but her brain pushing forward through the logic as a computer trying to finish an already-running program, "No, Thursday," she corrected herself. Once through the financial news, the coverage returned to news of the accident and the same "iconic" shot of the bus going through the guardrail and over the edge. Lela pounced on the remote and hit 'last' to change the channel before she heard one word of the news coverage. A reality show appeared and Lela stared blankly as the participants argued. "Now I know why people like this stuff," she continued muttering to herself, "you don't really have to think." Realizing what she was doing, Lela added, "and now I'm talking to myself" and turned off the television in disgust.

She shuffled to the kitchen and opened the refrigerator. The large appliance was packed full of covered dishes from friends, neighbors, family acquaintances. There was barely any room left. "Why do people always want to feed you?" Lela asked herself, "as if I could eat." But, for the first time in 3 days, Lela *was* slightly hungry. Eventually the body would win out over the apathy and today was the day. "Still talking to yourself," she chided as she poured some orange juice and ate two bites of cold spaghetti. Her stomach rejoiced at the heaviness of it and she added two more bites before returning the casserole dish to the fridge and throwing the fork in the sink. Taking her orange juice with her, Lela shuffled to her reading chair in her office and flopped there, staring out the window for 15 minutes while sipping her juice like a small child. Today was the day of the funeral and part of Lela didn't care, but her responsible nature took over by default as she realized she wanted to make sure there was a nice service for her family.

Lela abruptly switched into a very efficient mode, thinking of what needed to be done, distracting herself from distracting herself. She noticed a blinking light on the answering machine on the edge of her desk and reached long in a contorted fashion in order to hit play without having to actually arise from the chair. Three messages of condolence from friends, each one sounding a little more concerned. She hadn't spoken to a single soul except her best friend since the accident; avoiding everyone and not returning calls was certainly allowed. She hid in her room the days before as her best friend, Bianca, made apologies, accepted flowers and covered dishes, made funeral arrangements, basically took care of everything. Of course, Lela was presented with a series of choices that she cared nothing about- flowers, casket styles and responded to most by just pointing at one picture or another that Bianca presented to her. Mr. Aquila's company had a grief assistance group that had offered to manage most of the details, and Lela gratefully let them, keeping her involvement to a bare minimum through the conduit of Bianca.

The messages continued with one from one of her parent's closest friends, another man Mr. Aquila used to work with, Mr. Charles, "Lela, hello, this is Peter Charles. I know I left a message yesterday, honey, but I really do need to speak with you before the service. It's very important. Mrs. Charles and I also wanted you to know that if you need anything, to please just call us. Anything at all." Lela felt guilty for not calling him back yesterday, knowing that he, too, was under great duress from the loss of his closest friends. Lela began searching the room for the cordless phone as the final message played, "Lela, hi, it's James. Bianca called me. I'm so sorry," he sounded very upset, "I'm scheduled to arrive at 10 am and I'll call Bianca and find out where to meet up with you guys to go to the service. Um, call me if there's anything I can do or bring that would help." Lela stood frozen and stared at the phone. She hadn't seen James Matthews in about 18 months and suddenly felt slightly more peaceful just knowing he would be there. She dialed Mr. Charles and, after apologizing, agreed to meet him at the funeral home a full hour before the service. He was reluctant to talk over the phone and insisted that he needed to speak to her in person.

Lela selected a black suit from her cedar closet, picking the one she liked the least as she planned to give it to charity after today. She knew she could not bear ever wearing it again. Bianca had arrived and sat on the bed as Lela got ready.

"Don't worry, L, everything is set for today," Bianca offered sympathetically.

"Thanks, Bee," Lela responded half-heartedly as she combed her hair. As Lela rummaged through her make-up bag for Chap Stick, Bianca offered more advice just to keep the conversation going. She knew Lela well enough to know there was nothing she could say or do that would make today any easier, but just being there was a commitment to their friendship that was really more like a sisterhood.

"No eye make-up today, hon, you'll just cry it off," Bianca reminded.

"I don't cry in front of people," Lela's rote reply expressed her long-standing rule.

"I know, L, but Ecclesiastes- there's a time and place. You're certainly allowed to cry today." Bianca put her arm around her friend's shoulder. Lela just set her jaw stubbornly. She was trying not to cry even then. Today would be hard. The doorbell rang and Bianca moved toward the door. The bell jolted Lela out of her half-dazed state and it was the first time that day she thought of Gretchen and Caleb.

"Bianca, I forgot to tell Gretchen to meet us here," Lela started to get upset that her forgetfulness might add to Gretchen's distress.

"I took care of it yesterday when you first mentioned it," Bianca responded as she walked out of the room to answer the front door. Lela heard the faint mutterings of two voices and, though muffled and distant, she instantly knew James was there. She sat motionless on her bed and felt the mixed feelings triggered by his presence. She was so grateful to have him there; he always made her feel safe somehow, but she also was nervous to see him after so long and had been somewhat angry with him for his limited contact, as if she didn't matter to him at all. She took a deep breath and hoisted herself off the bed with all energy, as if her body weighed a ton.

As soon as Lela saw James, it was like no time had passed at all. She hugged him a hug that both wished could last forever and immediately felt a little lighter. James touched her hair briefly and then abruptly took one large step backward. He didn't want to add in any way to her emotional distress, so reminded himself not to crowd her, though he wanted to. Lela looked at him strangely and turned to Bianca.

"What time do we have to leave?" she queried.

"To get there an hour early, about 10 minutes or so. Oh look, Gretchen just pulled up. I'll go see if I can help her." Lela and James stood alone in the room and she stared at the floor.

"I'm so sorry, Lela. I just can't believe they're gone. I meant to come home at Christmas. I just wish I was here for a happier occasion," he said. Lela felt a flash of anger at him 'yeah, me, too' she thought to herself, but that paled in comparison to the gratitude she felt for him being there and she raised her eyes to meet his and kept herself from crying or showing emotion.

"I'm just glad you're here," Lela affirmed. Bianca reentered, followed by Gretchen and Caleb. Gretchen's eyes looked hollow and her hand held Caleb's tiny hand as he rolled in behind her like a wagon she was pulling. Caleb, who Lela had always seen a happy, playful boy, was silent. Lela suddenly was more upset at seeing them upset, as if she could keep herself in control so long as no one was around, but being confronted with the ghostly shell of Gretchen and knowing that she must look the same, she had to admit that none of them would ever be the same again. She turned away abruptly and picked up her bag.

"Well, we'd better get going," Lela said. Gretchen wondered at that moment if Lela even wanted her there. Maybe she shouldn't have come. The invitation to drive over came from Bianca after all; maybe she was just being nice. She missed Gabriel, who always served as the intermediary in situations like this with his family.

"We can follow in our car," Gretchen offered, suddenly feeling once again like an outsider. It was important to Lela that they all go together. This was the only person on the planet that felt even a shred of the grief she was feeling and, for that, she felt closer to Gretchen.

"We have plenty of room," Lela replied, grabbing her keys. James took them from her wordlessly and locked the door as the pseudo-family made their way to the car. James opened the doors and put each passenger in. Adjusting the seat back to accommodate his long legs, he bashed into Bianca seated behind him.

"Sorry, Bianca," he offered. Rubbing her knees at the site of impact, Bianca shook her head and tried to lighten the mood slightly.

"You've always been jealous of me being closer to Lela than you. Now I see your plan to get me out of the picture."

"I was never jealous of you, Bee, just all the guys circling," James joked sincerely.

"Whatever," Lela said barely audibly, staring out the window. She didn't have the energy to debate his misconceptions today. They arrived at the funeral home and though it was early, Lela spotted a handful of her parent's friends gathered on the front steps as well as a few of her own and Gretchen's parents. They stood in a circle, talking quietly and appearing somber as the occasion prompted. As the group exited the car and walked toward them, the gaggle on the steps broke up and looked toward them with concerned faces. Gretchen's parents immediately went to Gretchen and Caleb and the boy seemed to brighten a bit as he was lifted by his Grandfather.

"Granddaddy!" Caleb nestled his face in the man's neck and let himself be carried, which he had not been for the last few years. James walked next to Lela and, as if to brace herself, she hooked her arm into his and held tight. To the outside eye, he appeared more like a boyfriend than a friend. Odd, Lela thought, considering she wasn't even sure some of the time if he even wanted to be friends. His sporadic communication certainly left room for doubt.

Mr. Charles broke away and approached Lela, "How are you, Lela? Is there anything we can do for you?" he asked again, concerned.

"No thank you. I'm fine, "she lied. Noticing James was still attached to her she added, "Mr. Charles, this is my good friend, James Matthews." Not wanting to unhook his right arm from Lela's, James nodded instead of shaking hands and said,

"It's nice to meet you." This greeting felt wrong under the circumstances, but James knew not what to say as there was really no way to say 'I wish I didn't have to meet you like this.'

"I met you once when you two graduated from college, though there were so many people, I'm sure you don't remember," Mr. Charles confirmed. "Please, call me Peter. Lela, I must speak with you alone for a few moments." He motioned toward a bench on the lawn away from the others.

"Certainly, but anything you have to say to me you can say in front of James," she said while taking a step, James still by her side, toward the bench.

"Not this," Peter Charles said, touching her arm gently and darting James an apologetic look. Lela thought nothing of it and released James, giving him a quick nod of affirmation that it was okay. Mr. Charles and Lela sat on the bench and he looked serious. 'Well, at least there's no more bad news,' Lela thought, knowing she was already at the very bottom.

"Lela, I'm sorry we don't have more time to talk. I was trying to reach you so I could do this better, but please just hear what I have to say now and know that I will provide you a more complete explanation later and you can ask any questions you want," he launched into a pre-prepared speech that rang like one. Getting a bit nervous, Lela looked at him skeptically sideways. He continued, "I know you haven't cared much about the arrangements, but I've worked with your father's employer to make sure the service will be a suitable remembrance."

"Bianca took care of most of it, but I did make some selections," she offered, wondering if he was upset with her for not being more involved.

"That's fine. Please, don't worry. You both did an excellent job. I just wanted you to know before the service begins that there were a few aspects of the arrangements that I had to make as Bianca wouldn't be aware of them."

"Okay," Lela replied in a hesitant tone, her open gaze clearly conveying that she didn't know where this conversation was going.

"Lela, there will be two flags presented to you today. One for your father's service," he paused, "and one for your mother's." She looked at him confused.

"My mother's? What are you talking about? My Dad was in for 6 years, but my Mom never served."

"As I said, I know it's confusing, and I will explain it all to you later, but they both served until the day they died." Lela was stunned and thoughts raced as to what more he could possibly share that could explain why her parents hid this for all these years. Still not having the energy for any more than just getting through the day, she said,

"Um, sure. Well, I guess we'll talk about it later."

"One more thing, Lela, I'm sorry to put this burden on you, but I wanted you to know the truth. We can't let people know they were both part of a military science operation until three days ago, especially not until the accident investigation is concluded. If anyone asks why there are two flags, please confirm your Dad's earlier service and say that your Mom served in her youth, as if everyone knows that. Just make it sound like it was long ago."

"Okay," she answered and looked across the lawn at James, who knew from the look on her face that something was wrong. 'Investigation?' she thought to herself, and turned to Mr. Charles more forcefully, "Are you telling me that this wasn't an accident?" her tone was serious. He put an arm around her shoulder, partly to comfort her and partly to keep her quieter,

"We don't know anything yet, but I do need time to look into it. Could be yes, or could be no- there were many prominent people on that bus. It may have nothing to do with your parents." Lela swallowed hard and nodded.

"Okay. Well, we'd better be getting inside," she said and made her way up the lawn, back to James, and then up the steps. As she shook hands with people and absentmindedly received condolences, she noticed some of her and Gabriel's childhood friends as well an assemblage of quasi-distant relatives and acquaintances. A few remaining people from the project were there, like Captain Willingham. The clipboard man with the green eyes was with the Captain and Lela turned to him.

"Lela, this is Brett Davies," Captain Willingham attempted the introduction.

"Thank you for your help the other day," Lela said, and shook his hand firmly instead of the half-hearted handshake she'd been delivering all day. Knowing her well and perceiving the slight difference, James bristled but did not speak. Were it any other occasion, he would have distanced this guy from her.

"My condolences for your loss," Brett answered briefly and they parted.

As Lela entered the funeral home, she felt overwhelmed by the scene of flowers, pictures and crying family. She pulled harder on James' arm and, approaching the family row, suddenly began looking for Gretchen. Gretchen stood in the aisle by her parents with Caleb once again holding her hand. She shifted uncomfortably, not really sure where to sit. Her parents had kept a few seats open next to them, about two-thirds of the way back. Lela strode directly to Gretchen and pulled her toward the front,

"You two sit in the family row," Lela said firmly, seating Gretchen and Caleb in her own row on the other side of James, who hadn't even asked where he belonged. It was assumed between the two, if only for today. Lela listened throughout the service, intent not to cry, but could not help remain fixated on the two flags representing her parents. 'There are triangles of fabric where my parents should be,' she thought, 'and why didn't they tell me?' She wondered if Gabriel had known.

Chapter 5

Gabriel awoke and felt very strange. His body felt like he had a hangover, but without the hangover or headache, as if getting ready to get the flu, three days prior, where he didn't really feel poorly yet or know why, just odd. He sat up slowly and looked around the room; It appeared like a very modern-style hotel room. For a moment, he thought- Am I on a business trip? What city am I in? Was the bus accident a very vivid dream? As his clarity progressed, he was very sure it was no dream, or even nightmare. Anxiety on the edge of fear did a dance in the space within his chest behind his heart. Instantly his thoughts turned to his parents and the near-fear turned to borderline panic. He tried to leave the room, but could not. The door was locked.

As soon as he tried the door handle, the frame around the door illuminated and a slow, soft chime began at intervals of thirty seconds. After a few moments, the chiming stopped, the door frame deluminated and the door opened. Gabriel stood ready for a fight, not sure what to expect or who would kidnap him and hold him hostage like this. A well-dressed man seemingly not much older than himself appeared in the doorway. Gabriel examined him closely. He had dark hair, a European look, and the frame of a man that was lean but strong, like a cyclist. He did not appear unfriendly, but did not smile readily either. Careworn- that was Gabriel's first impression of Saraceni. Something in his air immediately let Gabriel know this was no enemy and he relaxed from a fighting stance.

"Are my parents okay?" Gabriel asked hurriedly.

"Yes. You will see your father soon." Saraceni tried to ease his panic. This wasn't the first time he'd had this type of conversation. 'Though it may be the last' Saraceni pondered to himself.

"Why not my mother? Is she injured?" challenged Gabriel.

"She is fine, but it will be longer before you see her." Saraceni knew what Gabriel would ask next, yet waited for him to digest rather than preemptively answering the question.

"Why? I want to see her now!" Gabriel's upset grew and his thoughts raced, "and how am I unharmed? We went off that cliff! What kind of medical team could have me here without a scratch? I don't remember hitting the ground. Did we hit the ground?" Gabriel paced back and forth in the small studio suite like a caged animal as he fired off questions. Saraceni walked to the refrigerator, handed Gabriel a bottled water and emitted a calm, even tone in response to the rapid-fire inquiry,

"I know you want answers, and you will have them, in time. There's an order to things." Inside, Saraceni too felt impatient to hurry this along. The deadline loomed and getting these people into training mode was priority one, but if the transitions were handled poorly, it would slow them up for weeks. 'Small time invested now yields large payoffs in operational speed later on' he reminded himself with the words of Ruth Fielding. He continued to Gabriel, "If you are hungry, there is plenty of food in here, but I'd encourage you not to eat too much today, or you may not be able to keep it down. Just go slow."

"I'm not hungry," answered Gabriel quietly.

"I'll be back shortly to take you to a room where you can learn more. Until then, please try to rest a bit." Saraceni turned to leave, but Gabriel's voice halted him.

"I need to call me fiancée. I need to let her know I'm alive."

"We'll discuss this after I return to collect you." Saraceni was careful to neither affirm nor deny the request. He left. Gabriel felt like he should be angry, but had trouble actually becoming angry at Saraceni. It was as if the man were a member of his own family and Gabriel knew deep down that he was just doing what was best.

Saraceni repeated strikingly similar conversations nine more times and gave his recruits a bit of time to think before returning to collect them. This way, they would be ready to absorb information when entering the training room and would have already worked through their immediate emotional responses. It would be a day of extreme ups and downs for them, he knew, so he aimed to make it as smooth as possible. He knew other instructors were that moment doing the same for the other classes that had arrived that day, but his ten were his main concern. The others were certainly important, but his ten recruits would be deciding all their fates, other new recruits included.

Gabriel was the tenth recruit Saraceni collected. It would have been more efficient to have junior team members walk the recruits to the training room, but that wasn't how it was done. The members of Molior would have exposure only to Saraceni until after they passed their sensory acclimation test-couldn't have muddled interactions all over the place if they were miscalibrated in some way.

The two men silently walked down a different hallway to get to the training room than the one Wood and Stone had used the day before. The training room entry on the east side was used by project team members, Circle 2 and above. All recruits were not designated a Circle by default throughout their training and restricted to quarters and common areas in the west side of the facility. They did not have access to the same news, warnings, people or areas as everyone else. They had limited access to the outside world as well-only under controlled conditions. Basically, they were sequestered until their training was complete. Saraceni walked more slowly than usual as Gabriel still seemed out of sorts.

Upon entering the training room, Gabriel saw nine other people standing and conversing quietly in the room, eight of whom were from the Bus 1 accident, one man he had never seen before and one of the eight who was his father.

"Dad!" he shouted and hugged his father, "Have you seen Mom?" he asked.

"No, son, but they claim she is fine." Mr. Aquila attempted to reassure his son though he himself felt unsure. Mr. Bamidele stood next to his long-time friend and shook Gabriel's hand with affection driven by familiarity.

"Are you well, Gabriel?" Enam Bamidele inquired. He noticed Gabriel did not have his usual charismatic shine emanating from within. Simultaneously, Gabriel noticed Enam's usually clear, dark, African skin seemed splotchy and almost pale, if that was possible.

"I'm alright. What happened? I remember going off the cliff, but I don't remember hitting or anything." Gabriel rubbed his temple in an effort to recover the lost memory. The one person in the room, besides Saraceni, who was not on Bus 1 jumped into the conversation.

"You people keep talking about a cliff. What cliff? I don't remember anything at all." George offered. He was a man of about twenty-six and dressed more formally, in brown pants and a tweed vest, not like the rest of the recruits clothing, more like Saraceni himself.

"Do we all have memory loss?" Gabriel asked Saraceni directly.

"Yes, though most of you very little," Saraceni followed the training rules when answering the question: 'Always answer truthfully. If unable to answer truthfully without disturbing the training order, then do not answer the question.' The rules had been created to preserve the integrity of the higher purpose while promoting the steepest learning curve possible. Too much information too soon would only confuse the recruits and consequently disrupt their larger mission. Lies, of course, though more convenient, would undermine trust and were against the order.

"If you will all please be seated, I will try to explain things to you and answer as many questions as possible." Saraceni continued. The group moved slowly, warily, and reluctantly to their seats. If any had felt better, there would likely have been challenge to Saraceni at this point. Gabriel moved to sit by his father.

"Gabriel, please sit in this chair next to Juliet. It's best for learning if you don't sit by your father," Saraceni motioned to the back left table, whereas Mr. Aquila sat at the second table on the right. Gabriel complied with a look across his shoulder to his father as Enam Bamidele instead sat next to his familiar friend, Alexander Aquila. Gabriel nodded out of polite habit to Juliet, who he had seen in passing on the day of the accident, but never actually met. Juliet Avignon had dark red hair, dark brown eyes and a dark, brooding mood on that day. She stared straight ahead at Saraceni, anxious to know what he could possibly share that would make this bizarre experience make any sense.

"Let's start with questions until they get us into trouble. Then we'll switch to a format more...structured." Saraceni began the formal teaching of the Molior class.

"Where is everyone else from the bus? Are they okay?" Enam punted the first question.

"Many of them are here, at this facility, and those who are, you will see in time," Saraceni paused so they would not be shocked. "Some did not make it."

"How could <u>some</u> not make it?" Gabriel chided, "Either we went off the cliff and died or we didn't, right? No one could have survived that."

"Some are here and some are not," Saraceni responded.

"So some are dead and some are not?" Juliet inserted her question with a level gaze.

"Yes," Saraceni answered her slowly.

"Are we the dead ones?" asked a voice from the front right table of the room. It belonged to Kyle Chambers, the youngest of the crew, at sixteen. He nervously ran his hand through his chin-length brown hair. The entire room was silent for a moment as the team pondered the question only a couple of them had even considered. Juliet shot Kyle a look, letting him know she was thinking the same thing. As a scientist, she had long-ago abandoned the notions of angels in robes and a bright white light.

"You are not dead," Saraceni affirmed.

"Then how do you explain us being here, if we did go off the cliff?" Juliet retorted.

"Your bodies in their present state are the result of an amazing amount of work by a large team of people with whom I work. Your bodies will not be 100% functional for at least a month, during which time you must be carefully monitored, protected from infection, tested and developed. During this time, you must be here and cannot leave or the outside influences will disrupt the process." Saraceni knew from long experience what question would be next.

"When can we contact our families and let them know we are alright?" The question was proffered by David Running Wolf, who sat at the front left table in front of a blonde British woman, Jane Grey Windsor. Saraceni thought carefully before responding as this area of training was a delicate, and unpopular, one.

"You will be able to contact your families on a limited basis in your third week of training, but not before then," Saraceni responded carefully. Unhappy, David Running Wolf stood up. He was a large man, at least 6'4" with long black hair and strong arms that were tense as if this pacifist might hit Saraceni.

"They'll think we're dead! I have children!" David pleaded. Gabriel's thoughts turned to Caleb, who was to be his own son officially in just a few short weeks, but already was in every other way.

"It is a consequence of having your present life, I'm afraid," came Saraceni's rebuff, "I am sorry."

"You keep saying "training", what do you mean "training", what are we being "trained" in?" asked Alexander Aquila inquisitively. Saraceni's answer to this question was well-rehearsed to the point of memorization, and so he replied:

"Since we have given you this life, and you must be sheltered for the benefit of your bodies, you will also be trained for the benefit of your minds and souls. It is our sincere hope that after you learn all that we have to teach you, you will want to use this knowledge for the good of yourselves, your loved ones and the world in general."

"The world in general?" Juliet ventured, "You really think you can teach us something that will benefit the whole world?" Saraceni did not flinch and his certainty permeated the room like a drop of dye spreading out in a bowl of water.

" 'Never doubt that a small group of thoughtful, committed citizens can change the world; indeed, it's the only thing that ever has.' Quote compliments of Margaret Mead. And, yes, I do think we have much information that would be a treasure to inquisitive minds such as those in this group." Saraceni concluded. At this point, he also knew what the next question would be. It was human nature to resist authority, after all, though the thought of himself or their workgroup as authority slightly amused the instructor.

"And what if we don't want to?" Jane asked while folding her hands with finality on the table in front of her. Again, Saraceni's response was pat:

"We will not force you to participate in training, but if you leave right now, you will die. I can tell you that if you do learn what we have to teach, you will absolutely be able to help those you love most in the world in a very meaningful way. This I promise you." And so the gauntlet was thrown. Anyone who did not buy into the concept of the training heart and soul would be resistant and jeopardize the mission, so voluntary acceptance of each team member was absolutely critical. The room remained silent.

"Okay, then, I think we have ourselves a training class," Saraceni boomed with a solitary clap of his hands in the space in front of him. The dramatic gesture was not really his personal style, but had been shown in data analysis of prior classes to increase the firmness of commitment by 23%, so he did it. They needed every possible edge, even if he personally disliked the tactics at times.

"Please take a short break and have some water from the tray in the back of the room and we will continue," said Saraceni. The class milled about, glancing at the features of the room, sipping water and looking at one another skeptically. They were bought in just enough to not leave, but little more at this point. It was already late in the afternoon. Molior should have been hungry by this point, but they were not. After about 20 minutes, they noticed Saraceni turning the power on to a machine in the front left of the room and pressing some buttons, so the class gradually returned to their seats. Saraceni went to the door, receiving a rolling bin from a pair of hands belonging to an unseen visitor. Gabriel craned his neck in an attempt to see the faceless minion, but to no avail. Saraceni wheeled the bin behind a screen near the machine and faced the class.

"This device is called a sensory awareness platform. It will measure the ability of your bodies to respond to a variety of stimuli. A test for each of you is necessary to ensure your bodies are operating properly and prepared for steps in the coming weeks. It is not a comfortable test. Nausea is fairly common. Should you feel ill, there is a bin behind this soundproof screen. Who would like to go first?" Saraceni saw an opportunity to give the recruits some control over their own destiny by picking the order, so he liked to provide freedoms whenever possible. David Running Wolf stood up immediately. 'The bravest' Saraceni thought to himself at the speed of David's ascension.

Running Wolf proceeded through the test as Wood and Stone had the day before, but without the benefit of experience, and remained stoic throughout the process. He correctly identified each experience and, thus, passed the test. He became ill immediately following and dove behind the screen, emerging shaky and somewhat green. And so it proceeded through the remainder of the recruits. Near identical experiences, except George, who did not become ill, just slightly queasy, and Jane Gray Windsor, who did not pass the test.

"It's not uncommon with more petite frames to require subtle recalibration," Saraceni informed her when she failed. "Jane, please remain here and I will see you to our medical team for attention. The rest of you are free to return to your rooms. Your doors are no longer locked, so you have access to the common area for your team, but your quadrant is still closed from the rest of the facility, so please note the doors at each end of the master hallway are locked. I know this has been a long and difficult day. I encourage you all to get some rest. I'll see you in the morning."

The recruits, still tired and now queasy, returned to their rooms on shaky legs. Gabriel walked with his father and Enam down the hall toward their rooms.

"Dad, I have a lot I think we should all discuss, but I'm so exhausted. Can you wake me up as soon as you get up in the morning and we can all discuss before this "training" class starts again tomorrow? " Gabriel asked with the heavy eyelids of a newborn child. Gabriel knew his father naturally awoke very early, so they should have some time to talk then.

"Yes, Gabriel, I think that's a good idea. Normally, I don't think we would sleep, but my body is tired as if I've been up for two days," Alexander Aquila replied.

"Mine, too," agreed Enam.

"The morning, then" Gabriel affirmed, giving his father a hug. He entered his room and collapsed on the bed fully dressed, asleep within one minute.

Chapter 6

As Gabriel predicted, Alexander Aquila did rise early. Even though he'd been exhausted, his body still was not one to sleep late. He showered quickly, brushed his teeth and donned clothes from the assortment hanging neatly in the closet. The clothes had been there, perfectly his size, but slightly different from his own taste. An array of jeans, slacks, shirts and shoes with no bright colors, no tags, labels or designs, all comfortable, all functional, and a few sets of athletic gear. He didn't really care about the lack of selection much, but just noticed in the inquisitive way that was his trademark.

After hanging his robe neatly back in the closet, closing the door and making the bed, Alexander turned his attention to the window. He examined the frame and the seals. There was no way to open the window and the construction appeared to enter directly into the wall for some depth. If the glass had been set into a window frame resting in the opening, it would have been fairly easy to chisel along the edge with a knife or some implement and remove the window. This, however, was not the case. He put the nearest dark mahogany chair in front of the door to his room and climbed up on the bed to check out the ventilation system. It was barely large enough for a cat, much less a person. 'Not even one of the smaller females' he thought, dismayed. There was no crawl space outside of the ventilation system either; the ceiling tiles were only a few inches below the subfloor of the floor above them. He knocked above his head on the subfloor of the room above him. It appeared to be something similar to concrete, maybe a bit thinner.

Removing the chair from against the door and replacing it at the small matching desk in the alcove area of his suite, which was identical to the suite of every other recruit, Mr. Aquila left his room and ventured out into the hallway. Assuming they had cameras in the common areas, he wanted to check things out without appearing to be looking for an escape route. He could hear mild stirrings in the quadrant of running showers, muffled voices and the whirr of a coffee machine down the hall with the occasional splunk of dropping water. A few others were starting to rise and prepare for their day. George emerged from his room across the hall from Mr. Aquila's.

"Good morning," George said, barely awake, moving on autopilot toward the cafeteria for some coffee. While each room had a refrigerator for drinks and snacks, they did not have their own microwaves or coffee pots. The recruits had to eat in the common area for their main meals. George turned the corner into the cafeteria, disappearing from Alexander's sight and the hallway was once again empty. To Alexander's left stood about four or five steel doors before the door leading to the training room. To his right was a long hallway. These doors were not all being used as living quarters. In fact, they seemed to be spaced to one vacant suite between each occupied suite.

Fortunately, Gabriel's room lay at the very end of the hallway, just prior to the opposing door. Gabriel moved down the hallway, looking at the floor boards and ceiling structure subtly as he walked. There were no additional vents in the hallway and the general construction seemed to mirror what he had found in his room. At the end of the hallway, he stood by Gabriel's door and cocked his head, for the benefit of any rolling cameras he was clearly listening to see if his son was awake yet. The interior was silent.

The door at the end of the hallway swung open and a man carrying a tray of baked goods entered. Alexander didn't jump even an inch, though he was startled.

"Good morning," said Stone to Mr. Aquila with a small nod. The door swung shut and Alexander heard a lock reengage when it did. His other question had been answered.

"Good morning," Alexander replied politely as Stone quickly moved past him toward the cafeteria. Not knowing who this new person was or if he was sent to check on them, Mr. Aquila knocked loudly on Gabriel's door. "Gabriel, time to get up," Alexander said in a moderately loud voice. He had not intended to wake his son up this early, though it was not very early. He had wanted to allow him to sleep as long as possible, but…plans change. Gabriel's sleepy face appeared at the door and pushed it wide for his father to enter.

"Gabriel, get ready and I'll get Enam and be back in ten minutes." Gabriel nodded wordlessly and returned to the depths of his room. Mr. Aquila gathered Enam from his room and returned in ten minutes as promised. The door shut behind them.

"We were just told by that new fellow that we have about twenty more minutes to eat breakfast. Most of our class is in the cafeteria already, so we had better speak quickly," Enam informed Gabriel as he sat in the chair at the desk while Alexander and Gabriel sat on the sleek bed, facing him.

"I checked this place out. Looks pretty tight structurally. I think we could get out one of the end doors pretty easily if we wanted, but no telling what's on the other side. We've only seen two people, and there are ten of us." Mr. Aquila summarized.

"So we're looking for a way out? " Gabriel asked, "Does that mean we don't believe what they're saying about dying?"

"It just means we're assessing all our options," Mr. Aquila replied, patting Gabriel on the shoulder like when he was thirteen.

"Well, do you actually think we'd die if we left? Sounds pretty implausible." Gabriel looked between his father and Enam expectantly.

"Well, we have no evidence that this story of some medical miracle is true," Mr. Aquila began, but was cut off by his dark friend.

"I'm not sure, Alexander, we should at least consider it a possibility," Enam stated. Considering the alternative was death, Gabriel thought considering it a possibility was at least a given.

"Well, of course, we need to gather information. I'm just saying I haven't seen one single thing to make me think that's true. I mean, we don't have memories, we don't really know what happened with the bus. Hell, maybe it turned into a plane and flew us away for all we know. We may not have been harmed at all," Gabriel said.

"Maybe not," said Enam, raising the side of his shirt to reveal obliques in good shape for a man of his age, "but I used to have a long scar here from the war and it's gone. The skin seems so smooth, like maybe they used a high-yield human growth hormone for burn victims or something. I'm just saying something must've happened to us, even if we don't know yet exactly what it was." Gabriel and Alexander Aquila looked at each other seriously, carefully digesting this new piece of information.

"Well, they're obviously part of a pretty upscale think-tank. I've never seen anything like that sensory acclimation test, and Enam and I have both worked on some pretty high-level projects," Alexander added.

"We'd better get with the others. We'll talk more later. On breaks, let's split up and each talk to three of the others in detail and see how much information we can gather," Enam concluded.

The three men joined their newfound colleagues and ate quickly, enjoying the brief meal for its stark contrast to the uncomfortable eating of the day before. Without a look or any coy smile, Juliet handed Gabriel an orange juice. A drop of condensation fell from the carton onto the table. Though nothing like her, the mere action somehow reminded Gabriel of Gretchen and he wondered how she was doing. 'She must be worried sick that I'm missing', he thought to himself. He hoped she would keep the wedding plans going so they could get married on schedule. He hated the thought of pushing it back because of this, whatever *this* was exactly. 'So you steal a bus full primarily of scientists, plus a few random folks who were mixed in' he thought. His first thought was that it must be a weapons project. Why else all the cloak and dagger? He'd never worked on a weapons project in his life, and he absolutely refused to start now. 'The first sign that we're being used for a harmful purpose, I am NOT participating,' he promised himself. Gabriel would sit in his room alone for the next four weeks before doing anything that might do harm.

David Running Wolf sat alone eating breakfast of eggs, bacon and bagel at the adjacent table and was thinking the same thing. An MIT graduate, he'd turned down many lucrative jobs in bioweapons design to continue working on genetic mapping and testing. His work allowed pregnant mothers to be aware of markers for certain illnesses and conditions early enough to take preventive action, like beginning vitamin therapies or medication to ensure a healthy child.

The man Mr. Aquila had seen in the hallway earlier appeared at the door to the cafeteria accompanied by another, taller man that had the look of a soldier. Stone spoke, since they had seen him bringing in trays of food and were no doubt more comfortable with him.

"It's time for class, everyone," he said and started to clear the tables. The recruits cleared their tables quickly and began clearing the room and heading down the hallway to the training room. The last to exit, Juliet, dropped her tray. Wood rushed to help her pick it up.

"Are you shaky at all?" he asked, still on the watch for medical side effects of the day before.

"No, just a damn klutz," Juliet responded. She left the room and jogged a bit to catch up with the tail end of her class. Wood watched her go.

"She's not even a Circle One yet, my friend, as in off limits," Stone said to Wood. Wood's voice responded about a half octave above his normal decibel,

"I know." When Stone and Wood entered the training room, all recruits were already sitting and Saraceni stood at the front of the room. Saraceni addressed them as they entered.

"Gentlemen, thank you for your assistance. Team, I'd like to introduce you to two men who will be assisting us throughout your training experience, Wood and Stone."

"Who's who?" Juliet asked Saraceni, glancing back at the two men. 'The one is clearly the brawn of the outfit, but why the muscle? Do they think we're going to make a run for it?' she thought to herself.

"On the left is Wood and on the right is Stone," Saraceni answered.

Juliet summed the two up to herself. 'So, the slightly shorter one is Wood . He seems smart and alert. The other one is harder to read, but they're clearly friends as well as coworkers,' she thought.

"Now that the introductions have been made," Saraceni slightly raised his voice to regain the attention to the front of the room, "we will commence our lesson for today. We have a lot of material to move through in the next few weeks, so I will be moving at a quick pace, summarizing some pretty large areas of study and have a specific order of approach. This may not fit with your questions. I'll make every effort to answer them, but we will have occasions where we have to parking lot them to revisit later or where we just have to move on. I'm saying this to acknowledge that there is a much deeper layer to this subject matter and you will likely want to learn it at that level of detail in the future, but for now, think of this as an overview class."

"An overview of what- what's the subject matter?" Gabriel asked, eyeing Saraceni intently for signs of lying.

"Let's call it 'Nature of the Universe 101', for now. Today's a pretty basic day, foundational information, so let's begin," came Saraceni's reply.

Gabriel's gaze remained on Saraceni like a laser, but could find no signs that Saraceni was hiding a weapons program or something equally dubious. The class looked at each other measuring reactions to this.

"So, you mean like how the universe was created and all that?" asked Kyle Chambers, the sixteen-year-old.

"Among other things," Saraceni confirmed.

"Most of us are scientists. We know this already. Or at least have pretty definite opinions of our own, I imagine," David Running Wolf observed.

"Oh do you?" answered Saraceni, "I don't deal in opinions in here. I deal in fact, but we are not starting with how it all began, we are instead going to start with what it is, the basic nature of the universe. Much of what we discuss here is not as much for you to *learn*, but to relearn- to take what you already know and put it in the proper context."

"So what is the universe?" asked Saraceni. The room was silent for about ten seconds before a voice ventured to enter the discussion.

"A collection of planets and other astronomical occurrences, like black holes," answered Kyle.

"In part. So, what are those things called at a simple level?"

"Matter," offered Jane Gray Windsor

"Right, mostly, but is it correct to say the universe is matter? What else is it?" Saraceni continued.

"Space," added George.

"In part, what else is it?" Saraceni looked at the class wondering who would get the closest answer. None of them would get the whole answer, of course, but conceptual thinking showed promise and he tracked his recruit's participation carefully.

"An interaction of matter, space and time..." Gabriel began and then paused

"Good, they interact- for what purpose?" Saraceni walked toward Gabriel at the back table with enthusiasm, as if to encourage his thinking with proximity, offering some of his own energy.

"To further life?" Gabriel answered.

"Okay, let's assume it's to further life. Why? Why further life? What difference does it make?" Saraceni asked.

"Well, if we don't further life, we don't exist. Our species doesn't continue, or any other species, for that matter," Kyle responded again from the front of the room. Saraceni backed up to be more inclusive.

"For that matter," Saraceni laughed, "excellent double entendre, Kyle, but what does it matter if life continues. Who cares?"

"We do," Enam replied, "People...and animals, too, I guess. We care if we live."

"Okay, so we care now that the universe is here," Saraceni prompted, "but if we have matter, space and time interacting to promote life, what would have been the initial goal of their interaction?" he asked.

"You mean when created? I thought you said we weren't going to talk about how the universe was created today?" Juliet challenged.

"That's right, Juliet, we'll talk about *how* it was created another day, but we are discussing *why* it was created, which is key to understanding the nature of it- how it works, its purpose." Saraceni paused and could see Juliet's wheels turning. "So, I repeat, what's the goal of that interaction?"

"You mean God's plan?" it was the first dialogue in two days from Chandra Wells, a woman in her early thirties who sat at the front right table next to Kyle. Chandra had minored in religious studies, so her response was not surprising to Saraceni, but he wanted to avoid religious doctrine at this point. With her finally speaking that left only one recruit in the room, Jack Reedson, the actor, who had not spoken yet.

"Chandra, we need to table any discussion of God for the moment, but assuming that you, and anyone else who wants to operate on that premise internally, wants to do so, then try to answer the next layer down- *if* there were a God, putting aside which God and whose God, but assuming it's irrelevant which God we're talking about, however you think of it, what might His purpose be?"

"To create life," David repeated.

"So the universe is an interaction of matter, space and time for the purpose of creating life?" Saraceni hoped restating the amalgamated concept might demonstrate its inadequacy. "But why? Is anything missing from that definition?'

Alexander had an epiphany and couldn't believe he hadn't said it earlier. He'd spent an entire conference in Copenhagen discussing just this concept.

"Information!" Alexander revealed.

"Excellent," Saraceni rewarded, "can you summarize in a way that can be understood by the non-scientists in the room?" Alexander thought for a moment. It was his nature to think in terms of formulas and the math of it. To translate it into layman's terms wasn't as easy as keeping it in mathematical terms. He stumbled at the start.

"Well, information processing is occurring all the time. Every particle-electrons, photons, they are all processing information all the time. The basic unit of information being the bit, or binary digit, which gives a choice between two alternatives, um, so, then in quantum physics the particles information-processing is counted in qubits, meaning a particle can be in a yes state and a no state at the same time," Aquila was still struggling to find the right words, but improving.

Saraceni interrupted, "Simpler."

"Well, it's like every particle in existence at every moment has two choices. It can act in a way to say "yes" or to say "no" to any potential action, or question, or....command. But, quantum physics says that a particle can answer "yes" and "no" at the same time, so it expands the possibilities exponentially as to how it can process information."

"You mean like it answers itself "yes" and goes in one direction and then at the same time answers itself "no" and then it's answering any question with all possible answers at one time?" asked Chandra

"Basically," Alexander answered

"Why? What's the advantage to that?" she asked.

"Efficiency," Juliet responded, "If you were trying to answer a bunch of questions, it's faster to answer all the potentials at once. Like if someone asks you which way you wanted to take to the airport and your answer was "it depends". If you said" If we're leaving Saturday morning, I'd like to take the interstate and then they asked, well, what if we leave Wednesday morning and then you'd say you wanted to take the back way. You would have answered the question more thoroughly and conveyed more information concisely if, when they first answered the question, you had responded 'If we leave on a weekday, the back way, but if we leave on the weekend, the interstate would be fastest'."

"So the universe cares about how efficiently we answer questions? You're saying God cares how much information we gather?" Chandra asked Juliet, still not sure she was following. Saraceni now took back control of the class, having let them develop the idea naturally to this point.

"Yes, whoever designed the universe cared about how we gather information. Since the universe itself is in fact a quantum computer where each particle carries and transmits information, information-processing does seem to be one purpose."

"Wait, now the universe is a computer?" Jane asked," You're saying we live inside an actual computer, like the one in my office? What are you talking about?" Being an anthropologist, Jane did have a scientific mind, but not as strong a physics background as some others in the class.

"Not like the one in your office. The universe is organic, but if you examine those organic components, they comprise every necessary element for a computer, which is really just a machine for processing information. So, the universe is as you know it, organic, with chemicals, lightning, particles, many types of waves (radio waves, ultraviolet rays, etc.) but the properties of all those things provide the foundation for what is actually an amazingly powerful computer. Think about any computer: It needs instructions or a system on how to process, or code, like DNA or the Krebs cycle or any other multiple coding instructions we see in nature. It needs a mechanism to transmit information, multiple ways of getting it around, like - electrical conductivity, the principles of harmonics and frequency, and finally somewhere to store the data when it's finished processing, like all the billions of particles in our universe, each of which stores, carries and transmits information. Think back to your own life, haven't you ever heard a neurologist say the brain is really just a computer, with neurotransmitters, connections, storage capacity, and more processing capability than you even use. That is a microcosm of what I'm talking about on a much larger scale. All the properties of the universe function like a computer like a brain does, but much more broadly." Saraceni glanced around the room to be sure his recruits appeared to be following before continuing.

"So, putting all this together, the universe is an interaction of matter, space and time for the purpose of creating life to process and transmit information at a rate exponential to anything that could be achieved artificially."

"So, people don't have real lives, their lives are just illusory to keep them processing information?" Jane continued.

"No. People have real lives, and they go on living them, but through that process an underlying purpose is the gathering and transmission of information. Again, the principle is efficiency. Any engineer will tell you that it's a basic principle to make as many elements of your design do double or triple duty as possible. So, a person can have one purpose, to live their life, as well as a second purpose, to gather and transmit information while doing so. The two are not mutually exclusive. Haven't you all felt at times that your life served a greater purpose or design?" Saraceni paused in his explanation and then finished, "As I said, I'm simply reframing what you already know."

"Assuming that's true," Juliet began," why does the universe need all this information and why does it have to be processed exponentially fast?"

"I'm sorry to say we have to table that question for two days from now, when you're ready to hear the answer," Saraceni disappointed the group.

A rap at the door drew Saraceni's attention. He strode over and once again spoke with an unseen visitor.

"Everyone, we're going to take a five minute break. I'll be right back," and with that, he was gone, leaving the recruits to think about what they had just synthesized.

Chapter 7

A week had passed since the funeral and Lela was doing a very good impression of someone returning to their normal life. She had found it surprisingly easy, in fact, especially since she had spent the week largely alone. A stark contrast to the constant activity surrounding her in the few days before the funeral, it was as if a light switch had been turned off and everyone from the outside world simply stopped speaking to her. "Giving her space" she presumed. Bianca had gone away on business, a trip she had already pushed back a few days. James had returned to his duty station and she hadn't heard from him since, not surprising given their awkward goodbye. They never seemed to leave things on a definitive note, like there was a giant invisible cartoon bubble over his head that read "to be continued…". Even Mr. and Mrs. Charles had become instantly unavailable. So, she was on her own. At least she was used to that, though she was used to having her family there when she did need them, though it was more often a situation of wanting their company than needing it.

Lela had continued to stay at her house and had not yet ventured over to her parent's house since the day they died. At least by Gretchen and Gabriel living together, she wouldn't have to pack up Gabriel's house, too. It was Gretchen's now and Lela would allow her to deal with his belongings as she saw fit. Anything else would be intrusive. She had received two calls from her parent's lawyer. That was the funny thing about the world: mortgages, property insurance, and other such practicalities left little room for grief. So, Lela was returning to work and moving into cleanup mode on all those practical details suffocating her thoughts at night.

She wore a dark grey wrap dress with professional accessories, but nothing too flashy. She still felt as if bright colors would be disrespectful, though there were no official rules on it. It was just her own personal discomfort that governed her selections. Despite her efforts to look plain, she was still stunning and did fulfill her true aim, to appear capable to the new project team members arriving that day- Yet another aspect of the world that would not wait for her to catch her breath. Lela grabbed her keys and grey patent leather laptop case while holding a letter to mail between her teeth as she picked up 3 boxes with a prong-like finger arrangement on her free hand. She pulled the door swiftly behind her with her foot and scurried quickly out of the way so it could lock properly without her involvement.

Lela drove up the mountain road to the sparkling new project facility and saw the temporary patch on the break in the guardrail along the mountainside road. She felt nauseated and gripped by grief rising up in the form of a huge lump in her throat. She focused on the road ahead, trying hard not to look at the guardrail or the view over the side and forced herself to take deep, even breaths. If she had to come here every day, she thought, she'd have to quit her job. She had discussed this with the new Secretary, replacing Madame, and the two concluded Lela should accompany the core team to Africa and work from there starting next week. If not for this development, she could not have continued. It was hard enough without driving this road every day.

The new Secretary, Mr. Pfister, must have been watching for her because he greeted her as soon as she entered the building. At that moment, it struck her that she'd never seen the finished interior. She had seen the structure, yes, but not with all the phones, equipment, decorations and people. Bright flowers in glass vases were evenly spaced down a long table against the wall in the entry alcove, with large glass walls behind. A beautiful, tapestry-style rug combined with the flowers to provide some symmetry to the space and avoid the clinical feel which would have otherwise prevailed. It really had turned out well, and within budget. As soon as they exited the alcove, however, it was clean glass lines and white walls, with the occasional generic print artwork to break up the landscape. They obviously ran out of decorating money after twenty feet, not uncommon on a government project, but the difference stood out. She was also struck by the bright line contrast between Mr. Pfister, and his predecessor. Madame Secretary, as Lela called her, was cold and shallow to the core. Mr.Pfister immediately took her coat and offered to get her a coffee. Though his nurturing qualities were no doubt enhanced by the circumstances, his behavior was still something that never would have even occurred to Madame. Lela felt slightly guilty for being glad that she was gone. She didn't want the woman dead, of course, but off the project certainly did make her life easier, hence the guilty mixed feelings.

"I'm sorry the Governor cannot be here," Mr. Pfister apologized, "As you can imagine, she is very busy trying to transition the many gaps left by Governor Jacob. It would be a big job for any new Governor coming on board, but his shoes are twice as large to fill as anyone else's ."

"They certainly are," Lela agreed somberly. She had liked the Governor very much and could already tell that Mr. Pfister's sincerity would allow her to respect him as they worked together. He had garnered an office on-site, though he would only be there half the time until the project was completed. He took Lela's coat and, hanging it on the hook on the back of his office door, closed the door to the outside world. Lela sat at the small round table with four chairs instead of the two chairs facing his desk so they might spread out the project plan and discuss the excavation site with charts and maps fully in view. As she spread out the materials, she noticed the faces of three beaming children imprisoned behind a glass picture frame on Pfister's desk. Pictures colored by little hands adorned just one small corner of his wall space, one of the beach and one of the planet Earth, with its green continents and blue oceans done in the brightest Crayola shades and "For Daddy" written in pink marker.

"I'd like to get a full hour with the new geologist sometime today, if that's alright and with our local political liaison as well. Is Willingham still on board for security?" she asked, making notes on the project plan as they spoke.

"He's still on point," Pfister responded," but I'm not sure he's going to Africa still. He's needed here to continue to address....matters." Pfister carefully chose his words.

"You mean because of the accident, he has to stay and deal with the investigation?" Lela cut to the chase so they could move on.

"Yes," Pfister confirmed.

"Okay, I'll have to get some time on his calendar tomorrow and find out what the plan is," she made notes as she spoke.

"Do you feel fully up to speed on the project?" she asked Pfister with genuine concern for his comfort level.

"I read all the materials and the binder you and Mr. Aquila put together." He paused, realizing his gaffe and watched her with trepidation for signs of upset. None appeared, though she felt an internal pang, so he continued, "I do have some questions, but I think we can address them in the briefing with the whole team, so everyone can benefit from the answers. That way, you don't have to repeat yourself."

Lela was again struck by his sensitivity and appreciated the efforts. It did feel good to move into the familiar swing of day to day tactics and she could see how comforting it could be to immerse oneself in work. That would be her plan, in the short-term anyway, to become a workaholic.

Lela and Pfister met with the broader project team, a collection of twelve individuals, in the large conference room situated to the left of the entrance to the building. The room had been designed so that the conference room would be inviting and impressive to visitors, with large picture windows and a beautiful mountain view. Lela saw only the terracotta chasm where her family had died. She hoped that would change in time.

The only other remaining member of the original project team was Tina Vail, chief medical officer. Lela didn't know her very well, but felt bonded upon shaking her hand again at this remeeting since they both had to deal with the remnants of a team now gone. For someone without many female friends, Lela had bonded more in one week with the women around her-Gretchen, Bianca, Tina, than she would have expected. Maybe when it comes down to it, the bonds of sisterhood do count for something. Moving through the briefing, they established their timeline, schedule for specific deliverables, and the responsibilities of each team member at the base camp in Africa. For things to proceed on schedule, they would need to clearly establish the boundaries for each district for corporate sponsorship as well as document natural resources in each region to be sure the local economy remained balanced and one district was not zoned in a way to usurp all the resources from the others. The corporate sponsors had already commenced their own surveillance and were already lobbying for specific areas that accommodated the needs of their true motives. Lela's jaded thoughts intruded, 'They're not there simply to be philanthropists, of course, or to help the local residents, but to try to further their own corporate agenda. ' She figured she could use their greed to have them help the local communities, whether that was their true intent or not. About half the corporations had applied early and already been selected for sponsorship, but about half the slots were still open and companies still being reviewed for their worthiness. Pfister would be overseeing most of that onshore, but Lela would certainly have a say. He had expressed a willingness to be much more receptive to her input than Madame ever would have considered. Lela felt grateful for a more collaborative work environment and felt her skills were more appreciated, plus the fact that the project seemed less tense now. She didn't think she could have dealt with another dramatic temperament on top of everything else.

As the sun set over the mountain, Lela's hybrid 4 wheel drive SUV descended after a long day. From here, the twinkling lights of the small town below seemed like tiny crystals of promise, each representing a family preparing dinner, or watching TV together. Lela pulled into her parent's driveway and noticed the intense darkness of the lot. No tiny crystals of promise here- her mother's ritual of turning the lights on at dark would no longer be followed. Lela reminded herself to program the lights while she was there. The last thing she needed was a break in. Exiting the car, she removed the empty boxes from the back and made her way to the front door. Another moment of truth, Lela turned the key in the lock, took a deep breath and entered.

She wasn't sure what she had expected, maybe for it to smell musty, or to be dusty, or look different, but it did not. Everything seemed exactly the same, as if her parents might return at any moment from a brief run to the grocery store. She knew she needed to look for certain documents in her parent's office, and pulled the list their lawyer had emailed her from her sleek grey bag. She started toward the office, but stopped at the piano room, as if she could still hear the music playing from the last night they had all been here together. She immediately turned on the stereo and moved the dial to the hardest rock station, as if to drown out the soft piano music in her head with something that more matched her heart. Before the metal could erase the memories entirely, though, she suddenly recalled her discussion with Gabriel the last night they all spent here. It had occurred in his laboratory and it suddenly occurred to her that it might be relevant to the next day's events. She dropped the boxes and darted to his laboratory.

Lela quickly began sifting through the disorganized mess that was Gabriel's desk. For someone that was otherwise very organized, his desktop always appeared a myriad of folders, scraps of paper, sticky notes, pictures and diagrams. She slid everything aside until she found what she was looking for- the blue folder with the yellow stripe he had been holding when they spoke that night. She recalled his concerns:

"Lela, I found some data I think you should look at," he held the blue folder in his hand, running his fingers perpendicular along the edge, "I think we should do some additional tests on this mineral." Gabriel had said. They had agreed to discuss it in detail the next day, a discussion that never came. Lela opened the folder and saw some of Gabriel's hand-written notes. It was fortunate she was one of the few people who could actually decipher his handwriting. The notes didn't make much sense to her and the basic geological report was not in the folder. She'd have to hunt for it, she decided, but it was already nearing eight o'clock and she hadn't even started on the list for the lawyer. First things first, keep the house running for now and start working on the estate. She did clear Gabriel's desk, shoving a small mineral sample in its tiny plastic home in her purse, and collected all Gabriel's files and papers, putting them all in the safe. Somehow this made her feel better. First, nothing could happen to them; they would be protected. Second, the desk appeared organized and she felt like she was doing a favor for her brother. Ironic since he wouldn't have cared at all had he been alive.

Her parents' office was the exact opposite, a perfectly clear and ordered desk with stapler and other office accessories at perfect right angles. The files and bins of old documents were perfectly labeled using a professional label maker. Lela's mother was one of the most efficient people she'd ever known. It struck her in that moment that it was odd how she had never noticed how militaristic her mother was in her thinking and approach to things. Somewhere deep inside she'd really not been surprised when Mr. Charles told her that her parents were both still active military. Though on the surface it seemed shocking, it resonated at a subconscious level. Lela was able to quickly gather the documents needed by the lawyer.

Out of the corner of her eye, Lela noticed a large star in the mix of notes on the desk calendar that covered nearly the entire surface of the desk. The star was in red pen and colored in extensively, as if someone had doodled while on a telephone call and recolored its interior until it was dark and pressed into the paper more than any other notes for the month. The star was on the day of her family's death and it said "The Day" under it. Lela got a chill and had a bad feeling the moment she saw it.

'Well, it's not surprising they would note it; it was the kickoff day for the project.' she thought to herself. Yet, somewhere down deep, maybe in the same cavern that housed her true knowledge of her parent's vocation, Lela knew that was wrong. The project was big to her, and her Dad and brother were helping, but it certainly wasn't the biggest thing going on in her parents' life. It would be noteworthy on their calendar, but not a focal point. Within the same square, under the star and "The Day", it said "see also Dossler Case". The format appeared to be to some reference material, maybe a legal case. She wrote the words on a sticky note and stuck it to her own laptop inside her bag so that she could research it later. With a final backward glance to the star, Lela turned off the interior lights, set the timer for the exterior ones, and exited the house.

She awoke the next day with "Dossler Case" on her mind and she lay awake in bed staring at a stuffed wolf carelessly thrown among the pillows she had cast aside from her bed to the floor to climb in the night before. The wolf was cocked half upside down, one ear pressed against the wall and staring at her with a dopey grin. He'd been a Christmas gift when she was eleven, and suddenly reminded her of a warm family Christmas. She arose, picked up Johann the wolf and carried him with her to the next room, the first time he'd been anywhere but the bed or the floor in years. He was no doubt excited by his field trip.

She sat Johann on her desk and stared at his one brown eye and one blue as she dialed the phone to the investigator whose card had been thrust at her the day of the accident. She hadn't even reached out to accept it; the green eyed man with her, 'Brett', she corrected herself, had taken it from the investigator and put it in her bag, telling her it would be there later when she needed it. Due to the profile of the case, it ended up at the D.A.s office, though it otherwise would never have been routed there. The D.A. assigned was Felix Lee, an experienced investigator who was the "always gets his man" type. If they'd been living in the forties this guy would've been the one with the trench coat.

"We're looking into multiple avenues," he informed her, "but so far we see nothing to suggest there was anything intentional going on here."

"Way to be noncommittal," she responded. Lela's frustration with lack of answers was apparent. She really just wanted to know how this could happen to her family, but came across as venomous, "Mr. Lee, if you can't do your job, I assure you the new Governor will find someone who can," she barked into the receiver. As soon as she hung up, she regretted it. She was not a very religious person, but the faith she did have guided her to know that God would not take her entire family without something more to it. Mr. Lee was doing his best to get to the truth. If that truth was that this was intentional, then whoever was responsible would pay, she thought. Johann's cocked head mocked her.

"I know," she said to the personified stuffing.

Chapter 8

Still disgruntled and still carrying Johann around her own house by one worn front paw the next morning, Lela decided to check her email to see if James had responded. He seemed to be her haven whenever she felt really lost, and reaching out to him did seem to make her feel better even if the topics were just light banter most of the time.

He had responded, but upon opening the email, Lela was disappointed to see two short lines. "I hope you are doing better. Glad Bianca will be coming back next week." She clicked it closed without any further discussion. "Whatever," she said aloud. Johann the Wolf readily agreed with her assessment, as she expected him to. Already frustrated with the prior conversation with Investigator Felix Lee, now compounded by the fact that James didn't seem to care, Lela felt desperate for answers, for some kind of forward movement out of the way she'd been feeling for days- In short, for hope.

She spied on the desk the card Governor Buck J. Jacob had given her "Phillip Harriman: Master Psychic". 'Well, dead people are this man's business, right, so maybe I should at least try talking to him' she thought. She was surprised how easily she was given an appointment for late that afternoon, since this man was supposedly heavily sought after by celebrities and booked months in advance. 'Probably all PR' she thought to herself 'he probably works out of some strip center near the airport.'

She was surprised by two things in Phillip Harriman's office. First of all, it was an older Victorian house in the antique district, very nicely furnished, yet warm and comforting in its feel. Secondly, that it contained religious icons from every major religion as well as artwork centered on angels, tranquility and some modern art. There were crystals placed subtly in the four corners of each room, on beautiful pedestals and colored with lights, so they appeared much more decoration than purposeful. Otherwise, the home appeared as any home, with a nice living room, a couple sitting rooms and an office that looked like it could have as easily belonged to a therapist or lawyer.

Phillip Harriman himself was no surprise as she had seen him before on her mother's television, but his demeanor was much more affable and relaxed in person than when he was onstage. Phillip was about twenty-nine or so, but carried himself like a man of fifty. He had an air of wisdom and comfort with his place in the world beyond his years. He wore dark jeans and a long-sleeved maroon shirt with orange swirls subtly overlaid, like something a loyal surfer would wear. On his left wrist he wore a cancer bracelet and saw Lela eyeing it.

"It's for my mom," he said, gesturing to the bracelet. "She went to the next world last year."

"I'm sorry," Lela said, shaking his hand, "I'm Lela Aquila."

"It's nice to meet you, Ms. Aquila. Buck told me you'd be coming, or I told him, I can't remember." Phillip responded.

"You told him?" she asked

"Perhaps. I did see you in some of my readings for him. I think it's why he wanted you to come, to see if you could trigger any better detail on what I was seeing," he responded.

"What did you see me doing?" she asked.

"Readings are confidential, Ms. Aquila, and though he's no longer here with us, he does still exist, so the confidentiality holds," he said with a smile and an ease far surpassing her own on the topic of death. "Please, have a seat. May I get you a drink?" he offered.

"No thank you," she declined

"I'm sorry to hear about your family, Ms. Aquila, I know it must have been quite a shock," he began.

"Yes, it was," she cautiously ventured out, "I was….hoping you might be able to help me better understand what happened." Phillip closed his eyes and concentrated, breathing evenly and Lela heard a grandfather clock ticking in the next room. She remained silent for what seemed a long time, but was really less than a minute.

"To improve our frequency, you have three choices, we can either hold hands," (he could see from the look on her face this was not her first choice. Lela did not hide her distaste well in any occasion, and this was no exception) "… which some people feel more comfortable with after they know me as a friend a little better," he quickly added, "or you can hold a large clear crystal, or you can place your hands face down on the table and I can work around them," he concluded. Lela liked the idea of keeping her hands to herself, so she opted to hold the crystal as she could hold it in her lap and keep her body coiled together. Phillip handed her a clear crystal about four inches by two inches and she held it tightly clasped between both hands.

"Please close your eyes and breathe evenly and think about the questions that you have and the free flow of information providing answers to those questions. Take as long as you like, and not until you're ready do you open your eyes."

Lela followed his instructions and after a few moments she opened her eyes. Phillip sat in a chair across from her with no obstructions between them and he himself had his eyes closed and was rubbing his thumbs against his fingers on both hands as if he were feeling a fabric. She wondered how long he'd stay like that when he interrupted her thoughts

"Stay focused, I'm getting to your wavelength. It's…different than most others. I'm almost there." Another moment passed and he opened his eyes suddenly and appeared very clear and directed, as when a radio scanning finally gets to the next station. "You're marked." he proclaimed.

"Some guy told me that a couple weeks ago. I thought maybe he was joking about my beauty mark, but he really wasn't the joking type," she advised, rubbing her cheek.

"No," Phillip corrected," he meant marked."

"What do you mean marked?" she asked, uncomfortable talking about herself when she really only wanted information about her family's death.

"For a higher purpose. Some people come into this world marked. We all have purpose, of course, but some people have a critical mission in this lifetime and it's easy to see by those who know what they're looking for."

"How do they see it?" she asked, curious but skeptical at the same time.

"A combination of factors," he replied, "For one, you have a gold aura, and then you have a different frequency than most, a higher one, that's why I had trouble finding yours. I was looking too low at first."

'Gold aura, right' she thought to herself and wondered why she had come. How could she leave without insulting this man? She couldn't, she realized, and out of respect for Governor Buck Jacob, she remained, but expected this man could be of little help. 'What was I thinking?' came her internal reprimand.

"Please, concentrate on your questions," he pulled her back to attention and she obeyed, clasping the crystal a little tighter and allowing her brain to sift through images of the bus crash, her parent's house, the funeral. Her hands began to feel warm and she swore she felt a slight vibration in the crystal, but rationalized she imagined it.

"Your brother left you something," Phillip began, "in a blue and yellow folder, but it's locked away. You need a key." That got Lela's attention and she leaned forward.

"Yes, I saw that," she confirmed.

"You know, there are more papers that go with that, in another location, but you'll have them in a few days," he continued, "and your parents left you something too."

"I didn't see anything when I looked in their office, well, nothing they'd left, just a note on a calendar," she denied.

"No, not the star, they left something specifically for you, not just something you happened to see. Does their house have an upstairs?" he queried.

"Yes," she answered.

"It's in the yellow room, upstairs, in the back of the house," he paused, "Did that used to be your nursery?" he asked.

"Yes," she again confirmed, and the crystal in her hand became very warm now and its vibration intensified.

"What is it you most want to know?" he asked. Lela hesitated and then came clean with this stranger about the largest question in her life.

"Was the bus incident intentional?"she began, "I mean, did someone plan to kill the people on that bus, and were they after my parents?"

"It's hard to see," he said, "there's something in the way. It wasn't an outright murder, but there is an impression of some type of intent to it." Phillip tried to focus in more specifically on the empty gap in his vision, but the harder he tried to open the gap, the more elusive it seemed. Lela's hands started burning and a vibrational pain shot up her left arm like a sharp muscle pain. She dropped the crystal and grabbed her left wrist with her right hand.

"Ow!" she cried out. Phillip looked at her warily.

"That hurt?" he asked almost accusatorily, out of surprise. No client had ever had a painful experience in his care, though he'd heard of his colleagues trying some more advanced divination techniques having similar experiences.

"Yes!" she replied, continuing to rub her arm up to the elbow. It would hurt for two days, as it turned out. She'd been shocked by a socket helping her Dad install a lamp at the age of ten, and the aftereffect felt similar. Phillip leaned down and retrieved the crystal from the ground. It was still fairly hot and he held it briefly and absorbed its remaining warmth, but it was cooling and no longer vibrating in his hands. He rolled it between his hands and stared off to vacant space to his left.

"You have another gem with you," he declared and looked directly at Lela, "like a ring or necklace with an unusual stone maybe," he scanned her body for the item he was looking for.

"No," Lela denied, "I'm not even wearing any jewelry today. I felt too crappy to care," she continued bluntly. Phillip concentrated and appeared as if he might be listening to a song playing quietly in another room.

"No, it's here. It's small, but it's here. A rock or gem. Your brother gave it to you," he corrected her. Lela suddenly recalled the small piece of mineral she had taken from Gabriel's office, in its tiny plastic cage in her purse. She retrieved it and produced it to Phillip who examined it carefully. He held it and closed his eyes, focusing on the mineral.

"I can't get anything off of this. It's been altered in some way. We need one in its raw form, not treated or scanned or changed in any way," he told Lela.

"Why?" Lela asked.

"I'm not sure, but it's important. And...this is why you had the reaction with the crystal. This mineral interacted with it and basically acted like an amplifier. I didn't know you had it with you," he suggested, to be sure she knew his process was not the cause of the mishap.

"I'd forgotten about it entirely," Lela revealed, "not that I would have even thought to mention it had I remembered."

"You need to return with more of this in its natural state. I think it will help us see more clearly and that I may be able to see the cause of the bus accident," Phillip didn't realize he was dangling a diamond carrot to Lela. She knew she would wonder her entire life what happened to cause the bus to go over the guardrail and any clues, no matter how small, would be a great help with that.

"I'm going to where it's mined. I can bring a piece back," she offered.

"I see you in the northern part of Africa," he said.

"Yes," she confirmed.

"Look deeper," he said. "Does that mean anything to you?"

"When the team is mining?" she inquired.

"I'm not sure, I just get 'look deeper'. Well, you'll call me when it's time and we'll continue. I'm sorry I couldn't see more today," Phillip sincerely apologized. He knew there were no guarantees with an ability such as his, but he did truly feel like he was letting people down sometimes, like a singer who gave a concert and only played their newest songs and none of their well-loved hits. Lela thanked Phillip and shook his hand and turned to go, still rotating her left arm back and forth a bit.

"Ms. Aquila," Phillip interrupted her departure, "He can't always communicate with you when he wants to."

Lela knew instantly that he was referring to James and also knew somewhere in her gut that he was right. She gave a half hearted smile and nodded in assent and left

As she left out the front door, she walked across the Victorian wraparound porch with multiple rocking chairs and began to descend the steps. She had not seen a hidden figure rocking to her left.

"What a racket," Brett announced, his green eyes piercing her solitary thoughts in a way that was accidentally intrusive, "Let me guess, come back with even more money and I'll be able to see everything for you."

"I didn't pay him anything," Lela countered, defensive and a bit insulted, "He is a friend of the Governor's and I came by to see him regarding a conversation the Governor and I had before he passed." The statement was accurate, though incomplete, but Lela didn't owe anything to this man and his invasion into her privacy was not appreciated.

"Mr. Davies," Lela emphasized the formality as a reminder not to be overly familiar without invitation, "I do appreciate your assistance on the day of the accident, er, incident, but your commentary is neither required nor appreciated." Brett could tell he'd offended her and was dismayed at his gaffe. His intent had been to be charming, but he came off as cocky. Still, he would not backpedal and appear weak.

"Well, it's your time, Ms. Aquila," he mirrored her formality, "Still, I'd bet he's a snake oil salesman after something." Lela couldn't help but think to herself that he had asked for some of the mineral, but, of course, did not share that information with Brett.

"And, are you following me? I mean, what are you doing here if you're obviously not here to see Phillip Harriman?" she asked.

"I've been assigned to you while they're doing the investigation, just in case what happened to your family was not an accident. We can't afford to risk you being hurt," he advised.

"Captain Willingham assigned you to me?" she asked, indignant. Brett laughed gently.

"No, Ms. Aquila, I do not work for Captain Willingham. I was a Captain about eight years ago. I'm here at the request of General Charles."

"*General* Charles," Lela repeated, absorbing the title of her father's closest friend, "Look, I appreciate the babysitting offer, but I can take care of myself. I leave for Africa tomorrow, anyway, so you're off the hook."

"With all respect," Brett countered, "my presence is required or you will be placed into federal protective custody, so you need to get used to it. I'm here more as a favor to a friend than in an official capacity, so think of me as a tourist added to your crew. My ticket for tomorrow's flight is already booked."

"Great," Lela concluded and could tell from the look on his face that this was not a battle she would win.

Chapter 9

Ruth Fielding stopped Saraceni just outside the training room.

"How are they doing?" she asked. Catching a quick briefing in the hallway often gave her information the team was too guarded to reveal in an official briefing, so she did it often. Saraceni was used to this and always left ten minutes early for the training room in case he was stopped on the way.

"Pretty well," he responded. "They seem to be a pretty good group. Nothing revolutionary so far that makes me see why they are the Molior class, but it's early."

"Maybe today's test results will yield something," Ruth hoped.

"As soon as they analyze their results and we begin the teambuilding exercise, I will have Wood or Stone reprint their results from Platform 2 and run them to the senior leadership committee for full review," he confirmed.

"Excellent, and Saraceni, if you need any additional resources, any at all, you let me know. We don't want you to be underwater on this one and not speak up," she instructed supportively. Saraceni was slightly embarrassed. His one major weakness in his work style was a reluctance to request additional help. He preferred to gut it out and make up for lost time alone. He knew she was right. She was always right.

When Saraceni entered the training room, most of the class was grouped along the back wall, discussing the paintings. He'd never had a class hold a seminar on the artwork before. He walked up behind them quietly and without notice.

"They all have similar themes," George observed.

"People talking to God," Chandra interjected.

"How is this one people talking to God?" Juliet asked, pointing to the first prehistoric painting. "It's people reaching up to this circle with lines beneath it. That looks like the sun. They're probably sun-worshippers or something."

"God was frequently represented in art as the center, or the sun," Chandra responded.

"Look, you can't impose your beliefs on everyone. Look at this modern one, it has stars and animals. No God." Juliet held her hands up displaying their emptiness. The class noticed Saraceni's presence and looked at him expectantly.

"I'm no art critic," Saraceni said, and walked toward the front of the room. Molior followed and took their seats.

"So, yesterday we learned the basics of the outer universe. Today we're going to explore the basics of the inner universe." Saraceni moved quickly to Platform 2 and turned on the machine. The class groaned. "No, no, none of the other tests carry the same discomfort as the sensory acclimation test. I am sorry that was required."

The class perked up a bit. "This machine records, sequences and analyzes your DNA and prints out a report you will be using for an important exercise today. So, let's get the tests completed and then I'll explain what you will be doing with them," Saraceni communicated. "David, while we are conducting the tests, which are very brief, can you please explain this to the class?". Saraceni dropped a file folder in front of David. Running Wolf opened the folder, and despite his extensive genetics background, was slightly puzzled by what he saw.

"Well, it looks like the Pheres software results, but much more complicated. There are sequences here I've never seen before," he looked at Saraceni like a baby bird waiting for its worm, but it wasn't feeding time yet. Saraceni reassured his pupil, but wanted the class to begin their thinking process while he was running the test.

"Please just explain the basics of what you do know and then I'll bat clean up," Saraceni urged. Part of Molior's development process was about developing confidence in their own ability to analyze and execute. While they should look to him for guidance, if they became overly dependent, it could hamper their ultimate mission performance. "Kyle, let's start with your test and just work our way down the right side of the room." David stood up and held up the multicolored chart so the class could see.

"Okay, so this is similar to a DNA program we use back in my lab called Pheres. These colored blocks within the circle represent individual DNA code and then..." he switched charts to show a block presentation in place or a circular presentation, but the same color scheme, "...this one is a different representation of the same information, but the longer, rectangles make it easier to see matching sequences. For example, here is a sequence: green, orange, purple, red, yellow. Um, the key is different on this than what I'm used to, so I can't identify the code, but, see here's a matching sequence."

"So, what's a 'matching sequence', like if they match, does that mean you're in the same family or you have the same hair color or what?" Kyle asked. By now he had returned and Jack was being tested.

"Well, Kyle," David switched back to the circular chart, "genes are grouped here according to function, so items that do similar things are grouped together, like this section might govern the way you look and the adjacent section might govern disease states, so depending where you find a matching sequence would tell you what kind of similarity the match meant between two subjects."

Jack returned to his seat with his printout of results and Juliet took her place at the platform.

"But what if you matched in some gene that wasn't identified yet? I mean, they don't know what they all do, right? Aren't they still figuring out what some of them do?" Kyle asked

"Right," David confirmed, "Actually, that's much of my life's work, figuring out what genes go to what functions or diseases. Actually, only about 5% of our DNA is even functional and only about a fifth of that does any protein-coding, so there really is just a bunch of unknown mixed in there as well, which most think is nonfunctional."

"So matching the unknown junk is a waste of time, and you match the stuff that counts?" Kyle affirmed his understanding.

"We focus on sequencing the known, but also look for hidden clues to the unknown. It's as much luck as science, though," David responded.

"So, what's the rest of it?" Jack Reedson piped up for the first time, "I have a hard time believing it's just there for no reason. Wasn't there a time when we didn't know the function of any of it- we probably thought it was *all* there for no reason."

"Well, there's a debate about that right now among my colleagues. See, DNA wraps around partner proteins to form chromatin, and by looking at the chemical groups on the chromatin, the cells can tell which sections of DNA should be transcribed. So, scientists noticed that the transcribed ones have a chemical mark on them, but then they noticed many more of these chemical marks than there were protein-coding genes, so people started arguing that they must be marking something else, something other than proteins. So, it was suggested that they're a type of RNA, you know how there's messenger RNA, but there are also functional RNAs and then we recently found a new class called microRNAs, and the non-coding or linc RNAs. Well, lincRNAs have always been thought to be an exception, an anomaly, but some of us think they're actually critical components and do perform a specific function. We just don't know what it is yet," David explained.

"Sorry I asked," Jack whispered to Kyle with a raised eyebrow. Kyle smiled, but they both were actually interested.

"So, you think they have a function? I mean personally?" Juliet asked.

"Yes," David admitted.

"Why?" she inquired.

"Because it's consistent across all mammals. Usually genes that aren't needed fall by the wayside. But these are there, and in large numbers-there's like 1600 of these in the genome, and similar in all animals. That suggests to me they serve a vital function because of the consistency," he confessed.

Gabriel, the last of Molior to test on Platform 2, stepped down from the platform and received his printout from Saraceni, who was now turning his attention back to the class. He was pleased they had gotten as far as they did and impressed that David had advanced to this level of understanding.

"Mr. Running Wolf," Saraceni began to take back the reigns of the class, "don't they call that the DNAs dark matter?"

"Yes," David answered, sliding his large frame back into his seat at the table, somewhat grateful to return the class's attention to their teacher.

"So, just to relate this back to what we were discussing yesterday, amongst all the matter and space within the universe, there also exists dark matter out in space. Our geneticist friends are likening these items of unknown function to a similar phenomenon that exists beyond the cellular level. Mr. Aquila, can you briefly describe dark matter in the universe just so we can all stay on the same page?"

Alexander began, but Saraceni cut him off, "I'm sorry, Alexander, but since you were so helpful yesterday explaining quantum information processing, I was hoping the junior Mr. Aquila could assist us today. Gabriel?" Saraceni watched Gabriel intently. This recruit had been quieter than expected and uncharacteristically so for his personality. The leadership paradigm for this team was relying on his charismatic personality and personal leadership style to encourage and motivate the others later during their mission. If he didn't start establishing his role as a lead figure now, the mission could suffer. Saraceni would nudge him out if his shell.

"Dark matter is really an unknown entity in astronomy, but it's hypothesized matter that's not visible, doesn't emit or reflect electromagnetic radiation the way regular matter does, but its' existence is presumed from the gravitational effects we do see on visible matter like galaxies and stars." Gabriel recited it rote. He'd been tested on this many times in college and had it memorized verbatim.

"Good enough for now. Just trying to keep our concepts fresh so we don't have to revisit later," Saraceni said, switching topics. "So- now that you have your results from the Platform 2 genetic testing, you have an assignment to complete with them."

"Mine is shorter than everyone else's," George observed, concerned that he was missing some portions of his printout.

"So is mine," Kyle added.

"Yes, yours are shorter. A section has been removed to....preserve the intent of this exercise." Saraceni was again careful with his words. George and Kyle's sequences were so dense that they would make the exercise too long, so Saraceni had held them back. "It will not alter today's exercise and I will provide them to you on a later training day so you will have a complete report."

"Sounds like they're just trying to make it challenging or something," Jane said to George next to her and he didn't pursue.

"Your assignment is to identify all sequences that you have in common with each other, then count up the colors of the matching sequences, arrange them in descending order from the color of the greatest amount of concordance to the color of the least amount of concordance. Everyone with me so far?" The class nodded and murmured agreement, so he continued, "Once you are that far, Wood here will escort you outside to a training area and you will proceed through the course following the colored markers that correspond to your matching sequences. "

Wood stood up in the back and nodded to the class, acknowledging his participation.

"He will also hand out the gear you will need. You will be given fifteen minutes following Part I of the exercise to change into your athletic clothing before he escorts you outside for Part II," Saraceni concluded.

"I thought we couldn't go outside?" Jane asked, concerned.

"In controlled circumstances, you can. The area is controlled for this exercise," Saraceni responded.

"Controlled- how can they keep germs from being in the air at large?" Juliet asked Gabriel, supposedly sidebar, but Saraceni did hear.

"You were each given additional supplements at breakfast this morning. They were for this purpose," Saraceni informed. Juliet looked down, realizing she had overstepped her bounds. Saraceni turned to leave, but turned back abruptly, "and…there will be a reward if you reach the end of the assignment correctly and within the time limit," he added. With that, he left, and the class knew that but for Wood escorting them outside, they were on their own.

"So, what's the best way to approach matching up our sequences?" Chandra asked David.

"I always just match them one at a time, line by line. It's the most foolproof, but that will take forever with ten of us to examine," he answered. They all began standing in a huddled group and holding their sheets side by side. It would be hard to look at all the pages lined up visually, and the potential for error or missed identical sequences would be great.

"We should call bingo," Gabriel announced.

"Bingo?" Enam looked at him as if he were crazy.

"Yeah. One person reads out theirs in order and if we find a matching sequence, we each mark it off on our sheets. Then, the next person calls off only their sequences that didn't match. Then we continue with each of us and it should get progressively shorter for each person, rather than taking the full amount of time times ten. It's the shortest path that still covers every permutation without potential for a miss," he explained.

"Sounds reasonable to me," his father supported, "Can anyone think of a better way?" They all glanced around and no one came forth, so the consensus became solidified. Since it was his idea, Gabriel began and Molior intently marked their sheets accordingly. They went around the room, one by one, calling the remaining unmarked sequences, until they had moved all the way around the room from the back left table where Gabriel sat, to the second and last table on the right, where his father sat. To be sure they did not follow sequences that only a few of the classmates had in common, they went through each sequence and the class raised their hand if they had it marked. They highlighted only the ones where all ten of them raised their hands, which were greater in number than expected. David Running Wolf was instantly concerned.

"The odds of us having this much in common at random are astronomical," he informed the class, some of who already shared in this assessment.

"So a bus of genetically aligned freaks crashed?" Jane added with slight sarcasm. "Sounds like we were all drawn to the location, or the project or something, but by what?"

"It is strange," Enam agreed, "but we'd better figure out why we are so similar later. We're on a deadline." Wood agreed with Enam's gentle reminder and noted the time, advising the class they had fifteen minutes to change and return before the clock would start again. They were slightly ahead of pace on the time the project team had estimated behind the scenes and he hoped they could close out the day with a success. It would certainly improve morale throughout all the quadrants if word got out that the class was performing on task so far.

Wood escorted the athletically-outfitted team outside and they relished in the experience of fresh air and sunshine. They walked quickly, but took in all that was around them, appreciating the nature in stark contrast to their sleek and modern, but bland, accommodations. Wood led the class down a sidewalk that ended and turned into a dirt path, down a small hill between towering pine trees. Flowers were splayed out at the base of the trees like sprinkles on top of ice cream. Jack Reedson breathed in the fresh scent of pine and flowers, tipping his head back slightly, jutting the chin of his chiseled jaw upward. The handsome actor was clearly the outdoor type and felt like he was coming home to be entering the wilderness. The sky looked like a painting, colors more alive than he had ever remembered seeing. 'Too much time in LA' he chided himself.

"Is it me or does the refraction here seem like we're at a very high altitude?" Alexander asked Enam as they walked.

"It does have that clearer look to it, but the air seems heavier than high altitude, at least as heavy as sea level, if not slightly more dense. It seems so easy to breathe- we can't be at a high elevation," Enam responded.

"We were in the mountains. Maybe they didn't take us far," Gabriel added. Twenty marching sneakered feet sang in unison for another 100 yards and the group came to a halt.

"This is the beginning of your exercise range. Please follow the colored markers as fast as you can based on the matching DNA sequences that you found," Wood said. "Good luck," he spoke more directly to Juliet than the others, but did include the whole team. She looked down at her feet and then back up at Wood briefly, watching his square shoulders walk the path back toward the grouping of buildings they had just left. She flicked her head around quickly, her red ponytail hitting the side of her face with a thwap only she could hear.

"We could make a run for it," Juliet suggested as soon as he was out of earshot.

"And go where?" Jane responded. Her deferential demeanor made her the least inclined for survival skills.

"Away from here," Juliet countered, "I'm tired of playing guinea pig."

"What about the immunity mixture they gave us. I'm sure it doesn't last indefinitely," Alexander said.

"And if those are just scare tactics to keep us here?" Juliet challenged.

"And if they're not?" George jumped in, surprising everyone since he had been avoiding confrontation. The countenance of his smaller frame was not challenging in any way and he shoved his hands in the pockets of his shorts.

"Look, I believe they have done some medical work on us. I had a long scar that is now gone and…I have noticed some other changes as well. We don't have time to stand here arguing, we're on a deadline. I, for one, am not eager to find out if that deadline relates to how long our bodies can last out here." Enam authoritatively retrieved the group sequencing results that David had been carrying and, reading them, began in the direction of the first color marker, "Whoever is coming with me, let's go. Anyone else, good luck," and he walked away without looking back.

David was the first to follow him, followed by Gabriel, Alexander and George. After a moment's pause, Jack, Jane and Chandra quickly followed suit. Chandra pulled a hat from her backpack with a ladylike maneuver and shielded herself from the intense sun as all proper southern girls had been taught to do. She loved her perfect cocoa skin and did not want it marred by sun damage. Juliet and Kyle remained at the crossroads of the paths and silently communicated their doubt to one another.

"If you want to go, we could try it together," Juliet offered, suddenly feeling the weight of responsibility as if she were a big sister. This would be easier if someone older than sixteen were the one to stay behind. Then, she'd have no sense of personal accountability for swaying the decision. True, he was very smart and sixteen is certainly a capable age, but not quite as independent as if he'd been say, twenty.

"Do you think we could make it?" he asked, looking at the rugged terrain around them that stretched as far as they could see. There were no towns or roads visible nearby, just dense forest and rocky, rolling hills. The rest of

Molior were getting almost out of earshot at this point, half of them around the bend already and out of sight. Juliet looked at them grow smaller as they left and saw Chandra and Jack, the last in the gaggle, glance back over their shoulders at them.

"I mean, I know I could get us out of here if it were just the terrain we were dealing with, the survival aspect of it, but I really don't know on the medical angle. If they're right, we may not last out here." Kyle weighed her words in his mind and thought of the pros and cons of the decision. He cracked his knuckles three times and pushed his chin-length hair once again back from his face.

"It seems too big a risk," he concluded with an even stare. "I mean, if we're wrong, we die, but if we're right, we get out of here a few weeks ahead of when they say."

"*If* they're being truthful," Juliet also weighed. "If not, we may be prisoners and may not get a chance like this again." That actually solidified Kyle's position.

"If they were really concerned about keeping us prisoner, they wouldn't let us out here unsupervised. Besides, I like what we're learning here and Saraceni said we'll be able to help people when we're finished." He began to walk backward in the direction the rest of the group had gone, facing her, but picking up his pace as the distance grew. "Come on!" He turned and faced forward, beginning a light jog to catch up.

Juliet sighed and took four even, heavy steps at a measured pace before increasing to a jog to catch up with him, an easy task for her. He hadn't convinced her entirely, but he'd raised enough doubt that she didn't have the conviction to proceed alone. If only Gabriel or David had stayed, she thought. Looks like the sixteen-year-old didn't need her to be responsible for him after all. He took responsibility for them both. They caught up with the remainder of the group just as they completed the first leg and made the turn to the second. They knew they had been in Part II for seventeen minutes now, but didn't know what finish time was considered success, so they just pushed at maximum pace. Alexander and Jane were out of breath already. After three and a half hours of following the twists and turns of markers through the woods, they realized knowing the full length of their journey would have been better to pace themselves. How long could they continue at maximum pace before some of them started hitting the wall and could not continue?

"How much farther?" Chandra asked Enam, gasping for breath and fanning herself with a manicured hand. Seeing her distress, David stopped short as they arrived at the next marker and stood in a clearing by a river. He pulled his own long black hair in a sweaty pile away from his neck.

"OK, let's all take another five here." They opened their backpacks and each consumed some water and something akin to a protein bar, though it tasted much worse. David retrieved the map back from Enam and examined it carefully.

"Looks like we are a little more than three quarters of the way done; It can't be too much farther now," David declared. He looked at the marker ahead of them, which was blue, the next color they were to follow. He noticed the next several colors were blue, five blues in a row, in fact. "We've got a really long string of blues here at the end. I don't think we've seen that much of the same color in a row so far."

"By the river, there's a marker with two long blue lines," Gabriel pointed to a marker about fifty feet to the right of the blue marker that stood before them and about twenty feet closer to the river, right near it. The marker before them led down another path.

"But our blocks in the sequence aren't any longer," George pointed out.

"But there's a bunch in a row, so that could imply a longer line, if you connected them," Gabriel said. The rest of the team listened to the exchange while guzzling water.

"None of the others required any connecting, though. It's been my experience you follow the existing pattern," George answered, but he saw Gabriel's logic and really was on the fence.

"I think we have to put it to a vote," Alexander offered. "Whatever we do, we must do as a team, we can't have only half of us showing up and half of us lost." With that, they took a vote and the shorter, single blue marker won out over the river way. Hoisting their backpacks atop their backs once more, the team trudged on for another hour and twenty minutes before finally reaching Saraceni at the end point of their journey. A boat dock along the river to his left stood empty.

"Congratulations, team! You made it within the time limit!" The team all removed their packs and a few lay on the ground at his feet. "Though just barely. I'm surprised you didn't take the boat. You'd have been here an hour ago."

"The boat?" Jack queried.

"The river path! I'm sorry," George apologized to the group at large, but more pointedly to Gabriel as he had tried to convince them to go that way.

"Don't be. We took a vote," Gabriel encouraged truthfully, "and we still made it in time, so we didn't miss our reward or anything."

"What is our reward?" Kyle asked Saraceni.

"Let's ride the transport back to base camp and then I'll share it with you."

Gabriel sat alone in his room later that night after they had all returned for showers, food and rest. They were reporting one at a time for their "reward" per Saraceni's instructions and Gabriel, noticing the clock read his designated time of 7:30, strolled with stiff muscles beginning to be sore to meet Saraceni in the training room. They made their way from there down a long hallway, passing a monitor that Gabriel noted read "96.4%". He intended to discuss it with his father later and made sure to remember the number. Arriving at their destination, Saraceni and Gabriel entered the surveillance room and encountered a man and woman whom Gabriel had not yet met. Kennedy and King rose from their seats, grateful for the interruption to their surveillance duty, and excused themselves.

"So my reward is taking over work from those two? I'm not sure I'd have marched all day if I'd known that was it," Gabriel joked, a bit of his regular personality returning as his comfort grew with both his teacher and his new surroundings.

"No," said Saraceni turning on the monitor, "as we discussed in class, you cannot communicate with your loved ones until later in your training, but due to your performance today, we will allow you limited observation rights. Gabriel saw Lela on the monitor. It appeared late at night, and she was in her home office on the phone discussing leaving for Africa the next day. Gabriel was glad to see her but his guarded suspicion returned upon realizing that these people had planted cameras in his sister's house.

"You have illegal cameras in my sister's house? Why?" Gabriel's voice rose.

"It will be part of your training, Gabriel. It's not to her detriment, I assure you. I told you that you would have the opportunity to help your loved ones, and you shall. We need surveillance in order for that to occur." Gabriel was still skeptical and somewhat angry, but his heart strings won out in the short term and the ethical debate could ensue later.

"Do you have Gretchen too?" he asked quietly. The monitor switched to show Gretchen's room. She lay in bed staring at the ceiling, her face barely visible in the dim light, but clearly thinking heavily was the source of her insomnia. Gabriel wished he were there to ease her troubled thoughts and felt a pile of contradictions at once: sad and upset at seeing his sister and Gretchen and missing them, feeling the loss of his normal life in the midst of this temporary insanity, and also a sense of accomplishment at the learning their training class was doing and the successful completion of the assignment. Saraceni knew this and, like all his moves, calculated the level of adaptation he was achieving with his team that day. This was just a fraction of how overwhelmed they would feel before their final mission was complete. Getting them used to it was simply another step in the process.

Chapter 10

Lela had been a passenger on Flight 1562 to Dubasi, Africa for over six hours already. Brett Davies slept to her right. She'd already read her project notes and made as much additional headway as possible on her laptop. Without the luxury of keeping busy, her thoughts began to wander back to the conversation with Phillip Harriman. She withdrew the small plastic container of the mineral, whose temporary unofficial name was dumortierite light since it appeared to be similar to dumortierite, but a much paler bluish-purple with a crystalline structure more like an amethyst than the rock-like appearance of dumortierite. Until the official name was given by the geological department, they couldn't really call it that, but she tired of calling it "the mineral", so DL for short worked well. She turned the mineral in the sun and watched as light played on the light and dark purple tones. The object split the light into multiple parts and a series of geometric octagons danced on the back of the seat in front of Brett and on her food tray.

Brett awoke for the first time during the long flight and stretched, hitting his hand on the low cabin above.

"What time is it?" he asked groggily.

"Almost four," Lela answered still lazily staring at the dancing pattern of the mineral.

"Wow, I was really out. I guess I was more tired than I realized. Man, am I hungry; I can't believe I missed food service." Lela withdrew the chips and crackers from her airline snack box, which was too large to finish, and held them out to Brett as an offer to abate his hunger. He thanked her and selected the peanut butter crackers as the more filling option.

"So, that's the mineral they found in some of the zones?" he asked.

"One of 'em. There are a lot of natural resources we need to log," she replied.

"Is that one of the top priorities on this trip?" Brett was just making conversation, but was also curious on her view of their itinerary in terms of priority.

"Absolutely. We need to finish getting the land surveyed and catalogue all the natural resources. This will protect against allegations that the corporations are here merely to raze the land, which of course some of them are, so it's also for us to use as a hammer when they try and protect these villages. Then we also need to find sponsors still for the as-yet-unassigned zones."

"How do you find the sponsors?" he asked

"Pfister's job mostly now. Before, everyone was eager to be on the Governor Jacob bandwagon, but I'm not sure if this new Governor has the same political capital, so I don't know if we'll see interest decline."

"Probably," he assessed truthfully.

"Yeah, but I will also be on calls with Pfister this week to work out the maximization of our project money and volunteers. I figure if we get the schools and clinics going first, and focus the healthcare work on HIV and malaria prevention where it can have the most impact, plus nutrition, of course, then we may be able to quickly demonstrate the project's impact and use that to garner more sponsors."

"Is that the full extent of the project?"

"No, we would like to tackle housing so these villages aren't made only of tin, cardboard and mud, but that will take longer. We can't afford to wait until we dig in on the housing problem to get more corporations on board, so we'll really have to play up the PR value of the schools and clinics." She paused and thought reflectively before continuing, "At the end of the day, we just want these people to know they matter and are empowered to change the future of their community. They have the most amazing community spirit, but it's largely the education and money to do it that is lacking."

"Wow, I can see why you're so passionate about this project. Seems like you could really make a difference if all goes as planned."

"I hope so."

As they descended enough to see the landscape for the first time, both Brett and Lela were enthralled by its beauty. From the air, the lush green landscape adorned with bright floral arrangements seemed like a paradise.

"The rainforest is amazing. I don't think I've ever seen anything like it." Brett murmured.

"Me neither. How beautiful."

Once landed, however, the view changed. On the ride from the airport to the base camp village of Svikiro, Lela was upset to see poverty all around her. Small boys chased after their vehicle waving their arms frantically.

"It's different seeing it in person than on TV or in a newspaper," she confided to Brett.

"Yeah," he agreed, taking in the deplorable conditions. Gunfire broke out nearby. In reflexive fashion, Brett grabbed Lela and, turning them both, tackled her to the floor of the bus. The bus itself sped up to full speed, whisking them down a dirt road off of the main road. The driver rocketed through twists and turns on the off-road trail, bouncing all the bus passengers into the air and into the floor repeatedly. Bags fell from the racks overhead, but no one moved to retrieve them. They stayed where they fell, in many cases on top of the passengers. The gunfire grew more distant.

"Stay here,'" Brett said emphatically to Lela as he was the first to pop up to a standing position. He snaked his way in the lowest posture possible to the rear window of the bus, drawing his 9mm glock along the way. By the time he reached the back window, the gunfire had faded to the point of being barely audible.

"Okay, everyone," he announced, "I think it's safe to return to your seats now, but still say low and be prepared to hit the floor again if necessary." Lela and Brett returned to their seat, but Brett required they switch positions and that she sit on the interior and he by the window.

"This area was supposed to be clear," he fumed, "I am so pissed off at the advanced team right now."

"Well, they're not psychic," Lela reminded him, "from what I've read, this sort of thing happens all the time down here." He was amazed at how calm she was and sure that meant one of two things: either the feelings of danger really hadn't hit her yet and she'd react later, or she was so heavily in grief mode that she genuinely didn't care if she died. Brett looked at her for a long moment, her black hair falling across her expressionless face and her jaw was set squarely. He assessed her stature to be more in the category of holding back and was glad. That meant she did care, but would react later. Lela felt his gaze lingering too long and began to feel uncomfortable.

"You know, I'm starting to really not like buses," she said, "I knew something bad would happen." Across the bus aisle from Lela was one of their African guides.

"If you think bad things will happen, they will happen," the guide instructed her in a very thick accent. This was beyond the guidance than she was looking for, but since she didn't want to appear rude, she gave him a weak smile.

"Did Phillip Harriman tell you that?" Brett joked in a whisper. Lela's smile broke from a weak, faint one to a broad, genuine one.

"No, smartass, but I didn't ask either. Maybe I should have."

"What did he tell you?" Brett asked

"That I'd be coming to Africa," she began.

"No news there. I'm sure that was in the papers," Brett deflected.

"AND …" she continued, emphasizing playfully that he cut her off, "that the mineral is important. He wants to see a sample of it." Lela caught herself. She did not intend to reveal information to anyone, especially someone she'd known such a short time. It was not her nature. "And some other pretty specific things," she continued more vaguely, "and lastly, that I'd be saddled with a smartass babysitter who couldn't wait to get away from me because I caused him all sorts of grief."

"See, I told you he was faking!" This time it was Brett who feared he had spoken too much, so he added, "I'm no smartass." The bus pulled into the campsite and the passengers began to depart, picking up their toppled bags along the way. Each person was only allowed two bags- one duffel and one backpack, so it was not a large undertaking. The underneath storage area housed their gear and equipment, both medical and scientific. Immediately upon disembarking, Lela changed into her hiking shoes, hung her mosquito netting and stowed her duffel bag in her tent. They had pre-assigned the camp areas (housing, medical tent, science tent, food tent, cooking area, etc.), so the team already knew exactly where they were to go. The first few hours had been designated as time to get settled and unpacked. They would meet as a group for dinner at seven o'clock and then begin their first full day of project work in the morning. She liberally applied insect repellant, grabbed three bottles of water and, jamming them into her backpack, began to walk away from the camp.

"Where are you going?" Brett asked.

"Exploring a few areas that seemed questionable on the geology maps," she replied, slightly resentful of the question, but given the incident on the way over, she understood his question.

"Jumping right in? Not even a few minutes to get settled?" he asked.

"Don't need 'em. I'm as settled as I plan to be." She sensed an endless series of questions and felt her time slipping away. "Brett, I mean, Mr. Davies, we already agreed that if I stayed within the second ring of the perimeter, I don't have to advise on my every sneeze and step. I may not have been to Africa before, but I did do large portions of my field work for my PhD in a similar environment. I'm not used to five star accommodations."

"First of all, please drop the 'Mr. Davies' treatment. Brett is fine. Secondly, yes, we did agree, but you need to at least let me know what quadrant you'll be in. If you go missing, I don't feel like searching four times longer than I have to in order to find you." She knew he was right and paused a moment before acquiescing.

"Quadrant 2, Zone 8, actually," she said and turned quickly and began walking northeast. In less than a minute, she was no longer visible through the dense vegetation.

"Women," Brett muttered again to himself and then turned to his own tasks of unpacking and debriefing the local security detachment embedded amongst their crew.

Lela stopped after an hour in a small clearing with a fractional window of sun shining down. She'd learned not to stop under the large trees whenever possible lest unwelcome things, like snakes, scorpions or tarantula drop on her from above. This vegetation proved more difficult as clear patches without any tree cover overhead were few and far between. She crouched down, enjoying a large drink of cold water from her canteen. She took a few extra sips since she didn't intend to stop again until she arrived near the river. Lela pulled out the waterproofed map of the area and double-checked her position. As far as she could tell, she was still on the right path. She pulled out her compass to again double-check. Typical scientist, double-check everything.

Placing her canteen and map once again into her black and orange backpack, she brushed some ants from it, swung it onto her back, continued again down the trail. Her legs were sticky with dirt and bits of grass attached to them. She scratched an itch on her right calf and noticed a giant mosquito bite there. "Already" she said to herself under her breath. The trail was fairly clear, but occasionally, when she reached an area where the vegetation had already overgrown the path, Lela would withdraw the small machete from her waist and clear the way. They'd be using this trail a lot in the next few weeks, so she would cut it a little wider than necessary for just her to get through whenever time allowed. After another half hour, Lela felt the air become even more moist, as if that was possible, and knew she was nearing the river. Within another five minutes, she began to hear its roar. The thunderous rushing of a large volume of water was loud enough that she would have had to shout were anyone with her by the time she reached the water's edge.

Lela immediately went to the cliff face, just to the left of the river where the reports said the strongest concentration of the dumortierite light, or DL as she called it, was found. The reports indicated only a small amount of DL found, but the per-square-inch concentration of the mineral to the sample indicated a dense pattern. She could see where they had taken the sample from the cliff's edge. Just a small area, it was clear that the surveillance team collected the bare minimum and moved on, since they had to gather samples from over 100 places in this entire region in short order. She intended to be more thorough and followed the edge of the cliff to the left from that point of sample withdraw, away from the river. The vegetation was quickly in the way, grown thickly against the face of the rock. She wrestled with the vines, cutting them away to reveal another ten feet of the rock.

Lela was breathing hard from the exertion, but enjoyed the labor of it. Physical work was much more distracting than mental work and she began to get into a rhythm as she continued to clear another few feet. Surely enough, the vein of mineral was widening as she moved left and the color getting more rich and vibrant than the half-rock, half-mineral sections by the river. She could see the mineral clearly on its own now. Continuing another few feet, the vegetation grew twice as thick. Lela's arms were cut up past the edge of her gloves by this point. She would have brought different tools had she known this would be her task, but she pressed on with the insufficient small machete instead of waiting to return tomorrow. Anyone else would have given up already.

Clearing away the thickest part of the vegetation, Lela no longer felt the leverage of her machete against the rock in the next step. She changed her angle to cut inward and downward instead of outward and upward, which required more strength without a fulcrum. As she pulled the long strings of vines and tropical cover away, a break in the cliff face appeared, only about three feet wide, but seeming quite deep. Lela took a long branch and reached it into the opening, swirling it around, trying to scrape up against the sides to dislodge any animal residents and to judge the way it opened up inside. Judging it safe enough to just stick her head in, Lela did just that and was amazed by what she saw. First of all, there was plenty of light, which she had not expected. The small crevice led to a large cavern behind the cliff face, which had a giant golden beam of sunlight streaming in from a wide opening about three quarters of the way up the mountainside on the opposing side of the cavern. The sunbeam opened up as the cavern did, so it was small and laser focused at the apex, and became wider and more diffuse where it hit the floor. Seeing everything plainly and sensing no danger, Lela drew her arms in close to her body, making her way carefully across the jagged rocks of the crevice until she reached the smooth rocks and an open area just beyond. Once fully in, her vantage point changed and her eyes grew wide.

The entire cavern was covered with the DL mineral, practically every face was made of it. She felt as if she were herself sitting in the center of a giant geode. Sitting on a rock and finishing the second half of her water from her first canteen, Lela gazed at the sunlight dancing on the DL, and the small octagonal shapes all over the floor. 'Just like on the airplane, but a thousand times bigger!' she thought to herself and smiled. Sitting on that rock, an amazing sense of peace washed over Lela and she basked in it as an alligator sits in the sun. As she breathed in and out, her breathing itself became very even and her chest felt light, almost giddy. Her thoughts came to her as if they were almost reflexive, 'Don't tell anyone about this place, not yet.'

Chapter 11

Gabriel burst into his father's room early the next morning.

"By the time I was finished with Saraceni in the monitoring room last night, and visited medical, you were asleep," Gabriel explained.

"Like now?" his father joked, throwing the covers aside. Alexander swung his legs to the floor quickly and stared alertly at his son, "Everything okay?"

"You mean, as okay as it can be here? Yeah, but they let me watch surveillance on Lela last night. Do you think she's in danger? I swear, I'm a calm person, but if these people do anything to her, or Gretchen, or Caleb, I don't know who I'll become."

"I saw her too," Alexander confirmed. He squinted his eyes as he did in stressed concentration and tapped his thumb repeatedly on the bed. "She seemed alright, but I definitely don't like them recording her like that, and I let Saraceni know about it."

"What did he say?" Gabriel asked.

"Same old you'll understand in time rap," Alexander responded. He was making his bed with hospital corners and neatly tucked his slippers under the front right corner of the bed.

"You and your nervous energy, Dad." Gabriel handed his father a pillow, "She was talking about flying to Africa the next morning when I saw her. She seemed very tired- physically okay, but...not herself."

"I saw her on the plane to Africa, talking to that Brett Davies guy. She didn't seem too tired, but she mentioned seeing that Phillip Harriman. Your Mom'll be jealous."

"She actually went to see him? I'm shocked." Gabriel responded. "She must've been going for Governor Jacob. I haven't seen him here. I wonder if he's one of the ones who died."

"I wish I knew. I'm used to having more information. This place is pretty hard to bear in that regard, but somehow I still feel more at ease here than I should."

"Most of the time," Gabriel agreed, pushing aside the olive-toned curtain to look out the window. He had ceased pacing like a caged animal since the outdoor excursion; it was just what he, and many of the others needed, basic outdoor exertion. Today would be another long day in their seats in the training room, but since many were sore from the day before, Molior didn't mind as much.

Later that morning, in the training room, Gabriel entered and heard David's voice booming at Saraceni about the surveillance.

"I don't understand why you need to monitor my family. Are you planning on blackmailing us? I'm not building any weapons, even if you hold my family hostage." Murmurs of assent came from many recruits.

"We are not blackmailing you and we are not hurting your families," Saraceni said flatly, obviously offended at the accusation. It was the first time he had appeared more like a regular person and less like some Socratic model.

"Then why tape them?" Juliet asked.

"We don't tape them. You view them in real time. And we do it so you can see that they are fine and to help you learn," Saraceni responded.

"What can we learn from watching our families doing dishes?" Juliet countered.

"It can't be in real time," Gabriel challenged, and Saraceni looked weary, "My Dad and I visited you in the monitoring room an hour apart, but it was night at first and then the middle of the day an hour later. That's not possible."

"Time is a slippery concept," Saraceni began. The door swung open quickly and Ruth Fielding breezed in. The class was caught off guard and took their seats. Wood and Stone immediately stood up and began collecting papers from the work bench in front of them, expecting to be called away.

"Good morning, recruits. I am Ruth Fielding. I work here and help prepare your curriculum," she explained while putting down her files and water on the table at the front of the room. Saraceni looked at her quizzically and Ruth's eyes conveyed that she had everything under control.

"Ruth Fielding runs this facility," Saraceni added for the benefit of his recruits, who didn't know what they were in for.

"Time is a slippery concept? Is that the topic of today's lecture?" Ruth looked at the class, not Saraceni. They all looked at her, clearly conveying they didn't know the topic of today's lecture. "Oh, I see. Well, perhaps before you stage a mutiny you should try to put aside your emotions and visit the subject matter as a clinical observer. Perhaps you might learn something." Kyle stared at his feet and shuffled them on the floor. Jane Grey Windsor intently took notes, as if staring at the paper would allow her to escape scrutiny. The rest of the class remained silent. All felt like they were in 5th grade again.

"Mr. Saraceni, the project team could use your services. I think I will teach today." Saraceni nodded slightly, picked up his things and walked slowly past her to exit, glancing over his shoulder at the startled look on his recruits faces. He motioned to Wood to join him and he moved to follow. Ruth caught Saraceni's arm and whispered to him so no one else could hear, "The Dark Janae attacks have broken into new territory, and with a greater rate of success. I need you to coach Hallowell and her teams." Saraceni nodded and he and Wood filed out of the room. Stone retook his seat. He'd never seen Ruth Fielding teach a class before, and he was enthralled at the idea of what he might witness. Her actual teaching style and personality might be visible to him. Surely this would make him a sought-after storyteller among the Circle 2's. Ruth removed her suit jacket and hung it neatly on the back of a chair. She pushed a wisp of silver bangs away from her forehead and assessed the class. She'd read all their profiles and seen surveillance on all of them. She knew them better than they knew themselves, literally.

"So, the linear concept of time.... a slippery concept indeed. If we say it is today here, and it is tomorrow in Tokyo right now, is that an impossibility? Isn't point of view involved? Is time objective? Gabriel?" her laser focus was sharp and she started in more quickly than Saraceni would have. The class perceived the difference and shifted to a more business-like mode.

"Time is objective and subjective," Gabriel concluded after a moment's thought.

"How is it objective? Are you sure?" Ruth prompted.

"Yes, I mean, regardless of point of view of where someone is physically located, even the old astronaut example, there's still some core true time that remains constantly moving forward. Even assuming that we as humans don't measure it perfectly, or even properly, the reality of "real" time is still present."

"And what if time doesn't really progress, or it doesn't really move in the direction it seems to, how would we know?' Ruth asked, jarring awake the analytical minds of her students-for-a-day. "Anyone?"

"Like we're all under some mass delusion that we all perceive time to progress the same way, but it doesn't?" Kyle asked. His vernacular seemed to adapt to that of the group at an exponential rate.

"Hypothetically." The corners of Ruth's mouth turned slightly up as she amused herself with her own internal monologue. She often had two or three trains of thought progressing simultaneously, which is why teaching was not a comfortable fit for her anymore. Recruits minds were so linear it was confining to the advanced Circles.

"Not a mass delusion," Enam Bamidele corrected, "but we're all subject to the same thermodynamic reactions so we experience what they call the "psychological arrow of time". It's like one of the physical laws, where chemicals reactions only work in one direction, but not in the reverse. We experience time the way we do because our brains are wired to experience it that way."

"Yes, psychologically, we order things to make sense of them," Jane added as the resident anthropologist.

"You can't be saying that time itself is just a psychological trick. I hate to break it to you, but there exist reams of scientific data that refute that," Gabriel added.

"Yes," Ruth agreed, "based on the principals of the universe that go along with that scientific data, and before we begin, I'm not suggesting that time moves backwards, but let us just theorize for a few moments." All nodded agreement.

"Let us suppose you are moving along a wire across the universe, and the person next to you is moving along another wire in a different direction with a shorter initial path. Since we know from our astronomer friends that the universe is expanding at an exponential rate, depending on where you started and where they started, your positions in the universe, if you are moving along your wire as the universe is expanding, could not the initial shorter journey become the longer one as you are making it?" she asked.

"You mean like if I started walking on a boardwalk out toward the ocean, but they were building the boardwalk as I walked so I ended up walking farther than I initially intended to?" Juliet asked, demonstrating her grasp of the concept.

"That works fine for a boardwalk," Gabriel challenged, looking to his right at Juliet in a collegial peer debate, "but for that to occur on the scale of the universe's fabric of space-time, we don't live that long. For us to actually feel the impact of the universe's expansion at the level of our own perceptions, even assuming," he stared pointedly at Ruth Fielding indicating his skepticism of the concept, "that *hypothetically* that was possible, we'd have to live aeons. It would never be perceptible to a species that lives like 70 or 80 years."

"What if you didn't have to stay on the same path, but could jump from your wire to someone else's ? If their path was much longer and you jumped to it, wouldn't you then feel the difference in time quite abruptly" Ruth continued the hypothetical example.

"That's not allowed," Gabriel refuted. "You can't just jump to someone else's reality. And even if you could, they'd be in the same boat as you, so it still wouldn't make a difference."

"Define 'same boat'," Ruth pressed, forcing Gabriel to reanalyze his last statement.

"Assuming," he conceded, "that they were of the same matter, time and dimension as you to begin with."

"So you think you can't jump to someone else's wire? What about another wire of your own, paths stemming out before you like the spokes of a wheel?"

"Maybe from one initial starting point, there are multiple possibilities, but once you're on a spoke, you can't just jump to another spoke, not where time is involved," Gabriel maintained. He knew theoretically one could move along a thread of time, not across.

"If you were small and physically on the spoke of a wheel, like a bug or something, you could just jump to the next spoke," Chandra aimed her comment at Gabriel.

"Yes, but that's in physical space, not in space-time." Gabriel countered.

"Well, why couldn't you- where time's involved, I mean, hypothetically?" she glanced hesitantly at Ruth to see if she was on the right track.

"Within a universe, time does not work that way. It would break the laws of physics," David spoke up for the first time since his outburst. Ruth intervened.

"To keep us from going down a rat hole, please allow me to change the example.

Imagine you have one man who starts walking at the North Pole along the surface of the Earth and walks any longitudinal line straight to the South Pole (ignore that there is water in the way for now). His journey would be very long, one step at a time, and at the end, you would ask him if he walked a straight path, what would he reply? "

"Most people would reply yes," Enam contributed.

"And would they be right?" Ruth prompted

"No," Kyle answered, "I mean, he must've walked around some rocks, or deviated to find somewhere to sleep, so it wouldn't be exactly straight."

"Certainly, but that's not exactly where I'm headed. I mean, assuming we gave him a compass, a GPS, everything he needed and told him he would be awarded 1 million dollars if he walks an exact straight line to the South Pole, and he walks down the seven degree East longitude line- when he arrives, would he be paid?" Ruth queried.

"No," answered Alexander, "whoever was on the hook to pay him would tell him he didn't walk a straight line because of the curvature of the Earth."

"Well, he can't help that, what's he supposed to do, burrow through the crust?" Juliet retorted.

"Then, to clarify, if we had a second, impartial observer located at the Earth's core, and the Earth were invisible, and she watched the man walk down the seven degree longitude line, it would be clear his path was not a straight one because of vantage point," Ruth advised.

"So, you want us to see that we aren't moving straight through time though we think we are because the fabric of space-time is curved," Gabriel concluded.

"Precisely," Ruth praised him with her affirmation.

"Are you trying to say we can time travel by cutting a corner of the curve or something?" Kyle asked.

"No. A universe is finite in space and time and time travel is impossible within it. For you, Einstein proved that. I'm merely stating that your perception will vary due to the perceived expansion and contraction of the universe."

"Perceived expansion and contraction? So, now you're saying it doesn't really expand and contract, we just think it does?" Gabriel asked.

"Hypothetically, Gabriel, for now. Let us suppose that man is walking North to South Pole on a sphere, but he's doing it on a surface that's expanding as he walks, I think the prevailing scientific example is a balloon. Like an ant walking the side of a balloon as it blows up, he'd begin thinking he was not very far from his destination, yet surprise would ensue when suddenly it was getting very late and he still had not arrived. The poor little ant man would be wondering what on earth is going on! Now let's say, he's not walking the edge of the balloon, but a slice out of it, like a cross section that's like walking on a piece of fabric. Since he's walking a straight line either way, in 2-dimensional fashion, he wouldn't know the difference because flat seems flat to him. Is everyone following to this point?"

Ruth paused and looked around the class. All were nodding, some more clearly and in some she perceived hesitancy, so she decided to expand her example.

"Now, let's say the size of the universe is not the entire sphere, but just that cross-section, so if he is in the cross-section in a slice that's near the North Pole, it will be a smaller circle than if he were in a cross-section that was cut at the equator. If we don't view this from down in the muck of it, but instead detract ourselves from the man and look at the cross-sections, it appears to be expanding and contracting because the fabric sheet, your plane of universe, starts out at a single point at the North pole, then expands to its largest diameter at the center of the sphere, then contracts progressively again down to a single point at the South pole location. Then it all repeats until you are back at the North Pole again. You seem like you are getting somewhere, but you are really just moving in circles!!"

Ruth paused and poured herself a tall glass of cold water from a nearby pitcher. As if on cue, many members of the class recalled their own thirst and took drinks from their own water bottles. Stone retrieved some additional bottles from a nearby refrigerator and passed them out to the class. Ruth was providing the class digestion time and she did not want to be the next one to speak. George was the first to break the silence. He adjusted his vest, pulling it down flat across his stomach and smoothing his hand over the buttons as if trying to recall a long-forgotten memory, "That's why when people talk about the universe ending when it contracts down to a single point, it really can't, any more than one could fall off the edge of the earth by standing at the South Pole. It's just where he is standing at that moment, temporary, not the full reality."

"So you're really saying time is circular?" Gabriel stared intently at Ruth, fully comprehending where she had led them.

"Yes. The Alpha and the Omega. A point at the beginning and at the end. They are one and the same," Ruth confirmed.

"So the future is the past and the past is the future?" Julia asked skeptically.

"Basically," Ruth confirmed, "but there is some additional complexity. Think of many of your religious texts- they frequently alternate between present and future tense in the original versions, converted to present tense only in the translations."

"So we're not talking Groundhog's Day here?" Kyle asked.

"I'm sorry, Kyle?" the wise elder asked.

~ 97 ~

"You know, the same events over and over again?" Ruth chuckled.

"Oh. No, Kyle. It's more like each time you complete a cycle back to your starting point, you are "promoted" for lack of a better English word, to a new concentric circle of fabric, keeping our same visual analogy. It exists beyond the perimeter of the old one."

"So you're stomping all over the people that are in the one smaller than yours, the one you just came out of?" Kyle asked. Ruth laughed even louder this time.

"Not stomping on them! You're in the same space as them and, as such, you perceive their boundaries, but since you exist in boundaries that are broader than theirs, a wider concentric circle so to speak, they can't perceive your boundaries, because they can only see to the edge of their own."

"So when you loop around and you're all back at that one point at the 'North Pole' place, which it sounds like is very full, how do you know which ring to get on, so you're on the right circle? I mean, what if you picked the wrong one?" Kyle asked, fascinated with the teenage curiosity allowed to him.

"Do you have to tell your cells how to divide? Or to tell your body how to age?" Ruth responded rhetorically, "Your path is programmed into your very DNA, just as those characteristics are. The dark matter in your DNA, that large percentage for which no one seems to know the purpose, is actually the programming for your soul. It is embedded and has a soul map to follow, to know how to proceed, build and advance your being, just the way your cells have the double helix structure as their map for physical development."

"The maps we followed in the woods? You're saying those were actual instructions for our souls?" Jack Reedson was taken aback by the notion.

"Yes. And what beautiful souls they are."

Chapter 12

Lela moved through the camp at a quickened pace. If she could get through the required tasks for the day, she hoped to get back to the cavern and explore a bit more. She longed to test some basic mineral properties with the volume of the mineral there, as opposed to using a tiny sample in a lab. It had been a full week since setting up camp and each day she hoped to return, but the project requirements were extensive and the needs of the team great.

Today alone Lela had to meet with the volunteer team captains on the anti-malarial and HIV education plans, hold a two hour conference call with Pfister and the corporate sponsors for their first weekly update, meet with the survey team, check on the progress of the recording of the local resources, and tour some potential additional sponsors around the camp.

The chief volunteer project lead was Tina Vail, the Medical Director, who had worked with non-profit organizations for years. On a project this small, each person had to wear many hats. Her talents would have drawn a large salary from the private sector, but she chose instead to live off of rice and vegetables the majority of her life and contribute her talents to the advancement of causes she deemed worthwhile.

"Hi, Tina!" Lela greeted her enthusiastically. She had developed a quick respect for the woman over the last week and was amazed by what Tina could accomplish in the span of a single day. Clearly, she had successfully managed troop movements for a number of initiatives. In the volunteer tent, the volunteers, mostly young adults in their late teens and early twenties, bustled around Tina packing supplies in boxes including water test kits, medication, books, and clothing.

"Hi. We're going to load up the truck and head out to the Gumubades Village in just a bit. Care to come? They've set up the clinic already and have almost all the materials to start on the school," Tina informed Lela. Her small frame and short, light brown hair were set off with long khaki shorts, hiking boots and a beige linen blouse, already quite dirty though it was not yet nine in the morning. She wiped her hands on her shorts and mud smudged across them as well.

"I wish I could," Lela conveyed truthfully, "but I'm stuck here today doing more administrative tasks."

"Fun! At least you have that Brett Davies to keep an eye on you. What a sweetheart." Lela laughed to herself at the idea of someone perceiving Brett as a sweetheart. He was many things, but she didn't think the "sweetheart type" was one of them. Two volunteers, a boy and a girl in their early twenties, walked up to Tina and waited for an opportunity to ask a question. Both had dark brown hair and eyes and deep tans obviously achieved through months of field work. Their affable manner and hardworking approach endeared them to Lela immediately and she had a strong impression of them as trustworthy. If she needed volunteers to assist on her expeditions, she'd surely request the pair, she thought to herself.

"Lela, I'd like to introduce you to Brian and Rachel, a brother-sister team from Florida who are twice as productive as most volunteers at their stage, I think because they're used to the heat!"

"Nice to meet you," Rachel said, with a quiet nod from her older brother. Lela immediately thought of Gabriel. Had they ever been that young? Seven years ago for her, it may as well have been seven decades ago for how it felt to Lela. In fact, the single last week at the camp had already felt like a month, since they had accomplished so much already.

"You as well. Well, I can clearly see you have questions for Tina, and I'm expected by the survey team. Please excuse me," Lela waved goodbye. "I hope we can work together soon," she added, and Rachel smiled.

Lela walked across the camp, between the tents, dodging chickens along the way. They ran around the camp freely and often got underfoot as a result. She passed the food service tent and saw Brett Davies eating breakfast alone. A large smile emerged from his face and he waved, motioning her over. Lela glanced at her watch, observing she had a few minutes before she was due at the survey tent.

"Just having breakfast now? Must be nice to sleep late," Lela teased.

"Yes, I'm just a real slacker," Brett responded, but he had dark circles under his eyes and didn't look like he had slept in at all.

"Prowling around till all hours?" Lela guessed.

"No way! I'm afraid of the animals." Brett deflected, "Are you hungry?"

"I ate already. Some of us work for a living." She laughed over her shoulder as she walked out.

"Maybe dinner then!" he shouted after her.

The survey tent was by far the neatest in the camp. Every item was stored in a waterproof container, clearly labeled and color coded. The containers were so numerous that the tent itself felt like a tiny castle of colored plastic. The master assignment whiteboard held a grid of black tape and names assigned to every task while the survey locations appeared in precise, capital letters written in black marker. The king of this castle and its architect was Mako Yoshikew, a clean-shaven, perfectly manicured geologist with perfect posture and a perfect eye for rock formations regardless of the surrounding terrain. He was well-traveled, well-spoken and meticulous about his work. Mako's Lancelot appeared in the form of Lance Lawrence, a laid-back Texan whose lack of structure annoyed Mako, but whose skills otherwise made up for it.

"Hey, Mako." Lela stood at the doorway to the tent until instructed to enter.

"Please, enter, Miss Aquila," Mako advised.

"Mornin' Miss Lela," Lance echoed with a single wave of his hand.

"Good morning," Lela observed the assignment board in detail, extrapolating from it much of the information she would need for her weekly briefing with Pfister and the sponsors. Sneaking a peek at the map with zones cordoned off in red marker, Lela made specific note of the zone containing the cliff face near the river. She recalled carefully re-covering the entrance with vegetation as she left, but the clearing of the entire cliff face leading up to it would likely be noticed anyway by anyone with an ounce of skill. Unless they sent interns, it would surely be discovered.

"Why is Zone 6 blank for an assignment?" she asked

"We are short-staffed and it's the easiest, so I was hoping someone would volunteer for a double load," Mako shrugged his shoulders and looked with consternation at the board. "It is not looking promising, though, considering the width of the survey areas." Lela immediately saw an opportunity to buy some more time before the inevitable sharing of her cavern.

"Tell you what," she began," I'm no geologist, but I had some other resource mapping to do over in Zone 8 anyway. How about I do the preliminary review for Zone 8 and you could put the Zone 8 team on Zone 6?" Mako looked skeptical.

"Hmmm, that's an awful lot of work for just one person. I don't think you could manage it," he replied.

"I can take two interns with me. That's three people, and with me coordinating, I'll make sure the reports are accurate. Since it's just the preliminary review, we can just note the items for the second team to then focus on. The area would still have a high-skill team looking at it before we're through," she argued convincingly.

"Two interns? Well, that would alleviate our short-handedness problem. If you could certify the results yourself, then I agree it is a viable solution." Lela smiled. Lance looked at her sideways, but said nothing. Mako delivered to Lela his very detailed weekly briefing in a glossy, bound folder. He had inserted charts and graphs showing the trends for week one. "These aren't very impressive now, but as we accumulate more data, the week-over-week trends should really stand out in this format."

"They're great, Mako, thank you." She glanced at her watch and rushed off. Mako quickly became engrossed under the microscope and Lance rushed ahead of her to withdraw the curtain to the tent, sweeping his arm out beside himself in a grand gesture. Lela laughed and bid farewell.

"Later. I'll be eager to hear your findings by the river over in the East 40," he said with a wink and was gone in a flash behind the tent flap. Lela's smile vanished from her face and she stood seriously for a moment contemplating whether Lance might already know she had a significant finding in Zone 8.

"Suspect, maybe. Know, no" she concluded, talking to herself again in the middle of the jungle. She moved through the remainder of her rounds, gathering the status of the other resources found, the general welfare of all team members. The medical officer advised there were two sick already, but they had both been in Mexico prior and appeared to be suffering from digestive symptoms, so they would simply be monitored. Lela returned to her own tent and assembled the materials just in time for the conference call with Pfister, another side effect of the week one start-up timeline. Lela preferred to have updates ready well in advance, and would be requiring updates by end of day the day prior in the future, but many of the team leaders were also scrambling to get their tent posts up and running and Lela did not want to further stress them with an aggressive deadline.

The conference call began smoothly enough, with routine updates, but for the agenda item covering the sharing of found resources, the sponsors became much more animated, demanding to know which zones had the greatest potential.

"How soon can you relay a full assessment of the natural resources?" Richard Currier asked in a sharp tone. He was the VP in charge of this project for one of their largest sponsors, Fabricorp Hulix, a technology start-up who had not disintegrated with the depression they called a recession.

"Mr. Currier, as explained in the initial overview, a full assessment will not be available for several weeks. However, we do expect to have some preliminary findings available for presentation three weeks from today," she reported.

"Several weeks!" he blew up. "In our world, things move in minutes, not hours, or days, and certainly not weeks!"

"I understand the need for information, but the project team does need adequate time to do the job justice," Lela maintained in a very even and pleasant tone.

"If you cut quality to 80%, how much faster can you deliver? We have products to get in the pipeline."

"80% quality?" she began.

"80/20 rule! My God, hasn't anyone there been to business school?" His impatience began to rattle Lela at this point. She was not really to 100% performance yet, and after seeming much better since being in Africa, she felt the thinness of her emotional state in the face of Currier. As if sensing this, Pfister jumped in to assist.

"Mr. Currier, I do recognize you have a corporate agenda, but this is primarily a humanitarian and scientific expedition. Much of our team is comprised of volunteers. Perhaps in the next few weeks we could focus with our respective marketing departments here on the mainland to be sure to maximize the public relations value of your sponsorship."

"Damn straight we will, and if there aren't enough boots on the ground with the volunteers, we'll start shipping over our own people. We need results and I can't hold up a multi-million dollar project launch while they're down there singing kumbaya around the campfire."

Lela had regained her composure and continued her attempts to win Currier over, "I assure you, Mr. Currier, completing our tasks on schedule is our number one priority. If you'll examine the zip file I sent via email, the document is marked "timeline" and you'll see we are running on schedule."

"Who set this timeline? I've launched entire companies faster than this," he asked rhetorically.

Somehow, Lela and Pfister made it through the remainder of the conference call. In the end, her notepad was covered in notes of takeaways, interim deliverables, additional updates needed, and notes to herself regarding improving the format of her presentation materials to anticipate the level of scrutiny that would clearly be forthcoming. Mako Yoshikew's charts would certainly add value, she thought gratefully. The dark-haired beauty would not be looking forward to these weekly update calls. Not even able to look at the materials any more today, she cast them aside in disgust and sat back in her chair, feeling her body relax for the first time in the last two hours. The constant tension had given her a back and neck ache and she stood up and stretched.

On top of the filing cabinet, she noticed her personal file box and recalled the blue and yellow folder she had brought from home within its borders. Already emotionally raw, she felt a lump in her throat upon seeing Gabriel's chicken scratch on the page. On the plane trip, she had tried to consolidate her thoughts into an outline format she could follow, and she used colored, self-adhesive tabs to mark key pages in his composition book. As he had mentioned to her the night before his and their parent's death, Gabriel had noticed some interesting properties to the DL mineral. He had made a partial list of his ideas, and only because Lela was so familiar with his way of thinking was she able to follow his train of thought. These notes would have been useless to anyone but her or Gabriel. 'Or maybe Dad' she thought to herself. She noticed CAF for the second time scrawled in the margin. She had registered it mentally the first time she saw it on the plane, but she failed to write any notes on it because she had not noticed the repetition. She flipped through, looking for any more appearances. 'CAF?' she thought. California? The Central Analytical Facility at University of Alabama? Compressed Air Foam? Crunched Article File? The possibilities flooded her brain like a waterfall.

"Probably cafeteria," she said aloud, mocking her brother jokingly as she continued to flip through the pages. When Gabriel was a teenager, Lela frequently joked that he had a one-track mind- not for sex, like most teenage boys, but for food. On one car trip to go surfing, they'd had to stop five times for food to appease Gabriel's stomach, and that was after he'd polished off everything in the cooler. He did grow seven inches that year, she recalled fondly. Finally, on the third from the last page, she saw a slightly modified version: "CaF?"

"Calcium Flouride!" she realized and made a note to research further. Hearing team members outside making their way to dinner, she herself became the one focusing on food. Yet another night she'd run out of time before making it to the cavern, she thought. She suddenly felt emotionally exhausted and wasn't sure she wanted to eat with the others. As if on cue, Brett appeared in the doorway.

"I think we agreed to dinner, right?" he began in an upbeat tine, but quickly realized her demeanor was very different from their morning exchange. Lela rose and returned the yellow and blue file folder to its' rightful place with the heavy movements of a grieving person. She turned to face Brett.

"Is there any news on the investigation?" she asked. Brett adjusted his own countenance to match hers, reflexively. He had been trained to mirror subjects and it had almost become second nature now.

"It's underway. We should have more information soon," he responded.

She closed the distance between them and spoke quietly, "Can you do me a favor?"

"If I am able," Brett's tone conveyed a sincerity that betrayed his feelings.

"If you find out anything, will you tell me, even if it's not cleared yet?"

"Okay," he agreed, hoping he wouldn't have to operate without clearance for the first time in his career.

"Promise?" she pressed. Her light green eyes were still a bit watery and beseeched him.

"I promise, Lela."

Chapter 13

"It feels so nice to have some downtime," Chandra said to the others as they stood outside in the small courtyard surrounded by a four foot concrete wall. Juliet, Gabriel and Jack all stood in a row next to Chandra, leaning forward against the wall and staring out at the landscape as the sun started its slow descent of muted colors in the sky.

"I've never been in any sort of training program where you only have two or three hours each day to yourself. It's intense," Juliet commiserated.

"You should try filming a movie," Jack teased. "You only get six or seven hours sleep time, that's it."

"Only 'cause you're the star!" Chandra said, framing the sky boldly with her hands as if putting his name up in lights. Jack turned red.

"How can you be so easily embarrassed when you're an actor?" she teased.

"It's not about me. I mean, it is, but it's this abstract concept of me. Like, "me"- the product. Not, "me"- the person. Actually, they mostly don't even look at me like a real person."

"Is that why you got involved with the Africa project?" Juliet asked.

"Partly," he replied.

Just beyond the wall were the paths heading to the woods straight ahead, but off to the left was another path heading to an open field with a track and obstacle course.

"It's just great to be outside. After learning about the nature of my soul all day, I can tell you, I feel like running. Anybody wanna do the course with me?" Gabriel asked his teammates.

"Are we allowed over there?"

"We were allowed all the way out in the woods. That's just a few feet past the patio!" Gabriel reassured. He hopped the wall deftly and turned back to the others, "Loser has to do my genetics assignment!" he joked and took off.

"I'll race you for your soul map" Juliet joked and Chandra looked at her disconcertingly. The three quickly followed Gabriel and in a few short minutes, all stood expectantly at the start of the obstacle course. They had changed into casual clothes following class, but not athletic gear. Gabriel, Juliet and Chandra all had on sneakers, but Jack had worn hiking sandals and was at a decided disadvantage. The foursome began cursory stretches, just enough not to get hurt, when they saw Wood walking across the grass toward them. They stopped their stretching and watched his approach. He carried water bottles and a small bag.

"Does Saraceni know you're out here?" Wood inquired before he even reached them.

Gabriel responded for the group: "He said we could go to any area to which we had access. This is just a few feet beyond a waist-high wall, so I assumed that wasn't actually expected to be a barrier. Besides, we need exercise. We sit inside all day!"

"I remember," Wood muttered, pulling a bottle from the small sack he carried.

"You were a trainee?" Juliet asked, curious to learn more about Wood.

"A recruit, yes, but that's not why I'm here," Wood replied. Gabriel noted the use of the word "recruit" instead of "trainee" and made a mental note to discuss with his father and Enam. "I came here to bring you medication, since I saw you outside. You're lucky I saw you."

"I thought that was just the first time we came outside," Juliet answered.

"No, it's every time. Just for a while, until you....acclimate," he looked pointedly at Gabriel, "but that is why you are not supposed to go beyond the wall without informing someone."

"Sorry, we really thought it was okay," Juliet smiled at him warmly and he acquiesced through silence. They each took the pill quickly with a swig of water and resumed their stretching. "So, can you join us?" Wood didn't know if this was prohibited or not. He stood for a pensive moment and then concluded that there should be no conflict of interest. He, too, needed exercise after all. He'd not spent so much time sitting in one place as in the training room since he himself was a recruit.

The five flew from the starting point like horses out of their gates at the Kentucky Derby. They ran a long stretch down a gently sloping hill before reaching the first obstacle. Gabriel felt the cooler evening air fill his lungs refreshingly and breathed deeply in and out as he ran, enjoying the soft orange and pink color in the sky. Returning from his distraction, he tackled the first obstacle, hearing the breathing pace of a competitor close on his heels. Wood, as it turned out. The two men grabbed the ropes one after another, hands flying quickly past one another with the rhythm of a boxer. Jack, Juliet and Chandra were all behind them by a short distance and Gabriel noted how fast the women were. On the next turn, Wood passed Gabriel and left him behind by at least ten feet. Chandra, who had run track in college, caught up and ran pace with Gabriel, followed by Jack and Juliet not too far behind. The four were still running a fairly tight formation as they did legwork and Chandra pulled ahead slightly due to her smaller feet and dancer's agility, but Gabriel soon caught up and was running by her side. Wood had pulled significantly ahead and disappeared behind a short thicket of bushes, emerging out from the other side and running back in their direction down a parallel path to their right. He passed Gabriel and Chandra and slapped hands with Chandra in passing, as athletes will out of habit. Jack had just cleared the legwork and began his next stretch of run when Juliet began the legwork. As Wood approached Juliet, she glanced, losing sight of her intricate stepping and tripped. She fell hard, one foot still hooked in the apparatus and then pulled her leg out, lying motionless for a moment. She sprawled thinking only of what a loud thud she had made and nothing else for a moment or two. Wood arrived at her side, kneeling on the ground beside her, and put his hand behind her head, checking her pupils for dilation level.

"I told you I'm a klutz," she smiled briefly at him before realizing the intensity of the pain in her leg, thus vanquishing her smile. She winced and closed her eyes for a moment. The other team members fell in quickly beside Wood.

"Juliet, are you alright?" Chandra exclaimed. Juliet opened her eyes and sat up.

"I'm fine, I'm fine," she assured, "just clumsy. Have I wowed you enough with my athletic prowess?" she asked.

"Yeah, it's getting dark anyway," Gabriel noted the orange glow growing more and more faint with every passing moment. Chandra assisted Juliet in rising to her feet. Wood looked at Juliet's slight limp and realized his own error in judgment.

"Yeah, we'd better get in. If any of you get hurt, there will be hell to pay," he said. He observed as her limp improved with each step. 'Tough to shake that off so quickly' he thought to himself.

"But it's okay for you to get hurt?" Juliet asked him jokingly.

"I'm not one of you." His tone was even.

"So that makes you expendable?" she pursued.

"More so than you. Look, I'm not supposed to talk about this stuff." He trotted ahead and opened a swinging section of the wall with an unfamiliar, almost invisible locking mechanism. The group paused on the patio as the last bit of light disappeared completely from the sky and they were enveloped in darkness and an abundance of stars that could only be seen in the country. 'Low light pollution' Gabriel again noted mentally, figuring they must be at least a distance of 100 miles or more from any major urban area. Three shooting stars struck through the sky, one leaving a purplish trail behind it. All were enraptured with the sight, and in another moment, another one went by.

"We need to get in," Wood concluded and ushered them along.

"What a beautiful meteor shower!" Chandra exclaimed, "Looks like Jack's not the only star around here," she teased.

The complement, including Wood, returned to the common area of the media room, grabbed some chips and sodas from the bar-like counter next to the stereo and flopped on the two semicircular sofas, facing one another. Juliet crossed her ankle over her knee, rubbing it absentmindedly, then removed her shoe and put her foot up on the coffee table in front of her, sinking back into the soft cushions as they enveloped her. Wood sat next to her, falling in naturally with the group, thoughts of any lines between them lost along with the last light of the faded sunset. All remained silent for two or three minutes as they turned over the events of the day in their mind and enjoyed the brief respite. Gabriel was slightly annoyed when Chandra broke the silence and kept with his head back and eyes closed.

"So, if our soul maps' matching was right, how is that possible? I mean, if they're programmed right into our bodies the way Ruth Fielding said."

"It's more like your soul is independent and your body overlays it, getting instructions from the DNA on how it should act in that body. So, as the DNA instructs your molecules to build the body out through mitosis, it instructs the soul to build out with the map it should follow while in that body," Wood clarified. He knew he hadn't gone beyond what Ruth had said, just summarized.

"So our path is predestined as much as our eye or hair color?" Chandra asked.

"Sure, but with some option of variability, like how your nutrition and environment also plays a role in your body's development." he replied. Gabriel's head arose and his eyes opened.

"The care and feeding of my soul," he mused under his breath, but all could hear.

"Potential," Wood confirmed. "Still up to everyone to reach it. And, believe me, not everyone does."

"I never thought I'd say this in my life, but I'm so tired of learning," Jack declared decidedly and flipped on the stereo while browsing through the video games nearby. Mostly math puzzles and flight training, he observed. Nothing fantastical, which was his preference. He reluctantly returned to the sofa, still having energy to burn since their exercise was unfortunately cut short. Chandra popped up and began dancing . She held out her hand to Jack in a sisterly fashion.

"C'mon Jack, I saw you dance in 'Film Noir'." He shook his head.

"That was a stunt double," he bantered.

"They showed your face!" she retorted.

"Creative editing?" he tried a second avoidance.

"Get your ass out here," she directed, and he complied. The remainder stayed seated, Juliet because her leg still hurt.

"Real men don't dance. Hollywood over there is just too nice to say no," Gabriel said loudly, so Jack could hear his ribbing, though he did not mean it. Wood laughed heartily, for the first time in weeks. He, too, needed this respite from the pressure they had been under.

"Is there any alcohol around? This feels like a small party," Juliet asked Wood.

"No, not here," he replied very adamantly.

"You mean because we're in training?" she asked.

"I mean here at all. It weakens the mind and poisons the body," he informed.

"It's not allowed at all?" she asked.

"It's not really a prohibition. Let's just say it's not desired at all," he explained. She and Gabriel looked at one another in disbelief. She'd never been a big drinker anyway, but found it odd to have an entire community of people where it was a nonissue. The song ended and Chandra and Jack, as if someone turned off their power switches, felt their energy drained by the slow song that followed. Chandra turned off the stereo.

"We'd better crash. It's almost lights-out." The group broke up and moved toward their rooms. Juliet, still slowed by her hobbled foot, was the slowest. As soon as she cleared the room, Wood used his key and turned off the lights to the common area except for a small side lamp. He and Juliet turned in opposite directions down the hallway, as he returned to his world and she to hers.

"Goodnight," he said under the cover of darkness, knowing they would return to their previous roles in the morning.

****

"Good morning," Wood said to a groggy Gabriel in the kitchen the next morning.

"Good God, man, weren't you just here?" Gabriel asked and Juliet and Jack laughed. Stone looked at Wood inquisitively but did not comment on the exchange.

"Saraceni said you should report to the patio for class this morning. Class will be held outside today, since you all seem to like it out there," Stone advised. David Running Wolf stared blankly, but the five from the prior night exchanged glances.

"Fresh air will be nice," David said, missing the jab. Molior assembled on the patio, where a simple white board and some comfortable chairs had been arranged. Saraceni was drawing a grid of 0's and 1's on the whiteboard, showing possible combinations of zeroes and ones in a four digit number progression, for demonstrative purposes: 0001, 0011, 0111, 1111, 0110, 0101, 1001, 1010, 1110, 1100, 1000, 0000. Wood walked to Saraceni at the board and stood silently shifting his weight from foot to foot, waiting to be addressed. After a few moments, he broke the silence.

"You asked to see me?" he broached tentatively.

"Yes, I was wondering if you gathered any useful information from your extra time spent with the recruits yesterday?" Saraceni asked.

"Actually yes, sir," Wood began in a very formal tone, "Gabriel is starting to demonstrate signs of his expected leadership role. Also, I'm not sure, but I think George may be starting to recover his memory. I'll be watching him closely over the next few days." Saraceni nodded assent as he put down the whiteboard marker he'd been using and, with that, Wood turned on a quick heel and made his way to his empty chair next to Stone in the back.

"That wasn't that bad," Stone confirmed. Wood nodded and raised his eyebrows, grateful for the light treatment.

Saraceni easily garnered the attention of Molior and began his lesson with little introduction. "Today we're going to continue with our discussion of quantum computing. Through our discussion, we established the ability of a quantum bit, or qubit, to be in superposition, that is, in a state of 0 or 1 or anything in between all at once. This allows massive, nonlinear calculations exponentially faster than in a traditional computer. However, entanglement is also required to achieve these calculations. I'm not doing all the talking today. Who has heard of entanglement?"

A few hands rose including, surprisingly, George's.

"George?"

"Einstein referred to a concept he called "spooky action at a distance", which today is commonly referred to in scientific circles as entanglement, and it's just that - entangling two particles in a way where they continue to interact with one another across any distance, even across galaxies."

"That is spooky," Jane added.

"Yeah, real trip for Einstein," Juliet agreed.

Saraceni expounded on the concept , "So, using one of a variety of methods, which we'll discuss in a moment, particles are entangled and thereafter, until disrupted, communicate with and behave in a way tied to one another. What "disrupts"?" Saraceni waited patiently, but no one volunteered. "George? Juliet? Gabriel?" but each looked at him blankly.

"Observation! That's the hitch, we can gather amazing information by seeing how they interact, but observation breaks the entanglement. Cryptography is a good example-that's how you can tell when your security has been broken. If the particles aren't still entangled when they reach the other end, if someone tapped in along the way, it would have "halted" before end state and you'd be able to see exactly how far it got before halting, before some third party interfered. See, the 0s and 1s are encoded with the properties of photons, like spin. If someone intercepts a photon-based message, the spins change and the receiver knows the message has been compromised."

Saraceni continued and the class watched him attentively, focusing on his every word, "So, how do we get around this problem of using qubits for quantum computing if they breaks down in quantum decoherence (basically like a program halting) when observed? Turns out, to come at it in a sideways fashion. The trick is not to measure it until just the right moment and in just the right manner. By performing a very weak measurement, then when the particle is only partially collapsed, one alters certain properties of the particle and performs the same weak measurements again, thus returning the particle to its original state before it decoheres. This concept hinges upon the fact that there is not a distinct line between the quantum world and the classical world, and rather plays on the grey area between."

Alexander jumped into the conversation. His sheer enthusiasm was evident, "I read about this! See, classical particles behave one way, in accordance with classical physics. Quantum particles behave in very different ways that from our traditional experience seem virtually impossible. In many ways, they have more wave-like properties and can exist in many places at once."

"Well, classical principals have already been shown not to hold at the mesoscopic level," his good friend Enam joined in.

"Yes. Your scientific community has only begun to scratch the surface of the value of distant particles speaking to one another. The potential is enormous." Saraceni was glad to see the class not only absorbed the concepts, but also seemed genuinely excited.

"But also scary- didn't the idea that distant particles could basically 'talk' to each other really trouble Einstein?" Kyle asked. Juliet and Gabriel exchanged an odd look.

"Yes, but Einstein didn't know everything we know today," Saraceni answered.

"For example?" Juliet probed.

"For example…that we can control the entanglement. So, let's talk about how you'd actually build a quantum computer, to control that entanglement in a way that you harness the computing capability without releasing uncontrollable scenarios." Saraceni uncapped his marker and began drawing once again on the flip chart. He was no artist in this venue. "So if I gave you an assignment to build a quantum computer, where would you start?" he asked the class.

"I knew it!" George cried out "that's why we're here, isn't it? You want this team to build a quantum computer!"

"This is all still learning at this point," Saraceni answered. He waited patiently once again for his question to be answered. Alexander was the first to offer a suggestion:

"Well, I'd start by reviewing the approaches tried so far and what's worked," Alexander offered.

"Why bother? They've only got up to a 32-qubit computer and you need that times like a thousand, at least, to do any meaningful computing. From what I've read, that's at least ten years away, probably longer," Juliet contributed, twirling her hair absentmindedly around a finger, splitting the ends. Wood watched Saraceni's face for signs of displeasure at her pessimism.

Saraceni responded evenly, "Humor me- where would you begin?"

"Well, I think they started by a molecule and using lasers to entangle," Alexander recalled. Gabriel was next to break his silence. He knew more on this topic than he was letting on, observing the dynamics keenly, still trying to ascertain the true mission of this facility.

"And then nuclear resonance imaging, using magnets, they program with radiofrequency pulses. A tiny test tube filled with special molecules placed inside the machine while scientists use radiofrequency pulses as software to alter the atomic spins," Gabriel explained. .

"But I heard that's all irrelevant now, the newest quantum computer is 32 qubits and is using electric current for entanglement. It even solved a Sudoku puzzle and some other basic calculations," Enam recalled.

George was pensive, "They're coming at it wrong. Taking baby steps. They're acting like the end-state goal is to factor some huge number or something. That's a nice parlor trick, but that's not the real value to quantum computing."

"Then what is, in your opinion?" Juliet asked, wondering why George had been hiding this level of knowledge he clearly possesses.

He responded matter-of-factly, "To create a quantum simulation algorithm. Because any physical process, any could theoretically be modeled by a quantum computer. In fact, so well that you couldn't tell the design you built from the original. I guess unless you wanted to and figured a way to, but otherwise they'd be indistinguishable. But you are obviously needing wayyyy more than 32 qubits, or 138, or even 1000 times that many to achieve something the size of a state."

"What about the size of a planet, a galaxy, or a universe, could that even be possible?" Kyle asked. Saraceni was glad the youngest team member was participating. The other members respecting him as an equal participant was vital.

"Well, how would we as scientists be able to create something that big when it's so much larger than ourselves? We would be strictly limited in our ability to program and work on it just due to sheer size. Even if every person on the planet programmed qubits all day long for a living, you wouldn't have the man power to do it," Alexander offered, from his vast experience on large projects with serious resource limitations.

Gabriel countered his father, "Unless you could build it to be self-programming, or self-building at some point."

"But then you lose control," Enam warned.

"Well, you're in control of the self-building software, right?" Gabriel responded.

"How would you turn it off if you didn't like how it was building, or needed to make a correction?" Juliet asked.

A large, loud beacon sounding like a tornado siren screeched out from the building. Wood and Stone jumped up. Saraceni knocked over the whiteboard as he spun about. "The general alarm!" he cried out. "Get them inside!" he said to Stone and Wood. The recruits were on their feet in seconds. Staring out over the half wall of the patio, running bodies streamed across the field in colored groupings. Ten or fifteen teams of twelve people, Gabriel estimated, each in a different color of matching athletic wear. They ran up the hill, appearing like little ants, or an advancing army. The group had their ears covered with double hands.

"Back to your rooms! Stone, Wood, they are restricted to the quadrant-INSIDE- until further notice. Go with them and stay in the empty rooms on the floor until I come for you. You're not to leave the quadrant either!" Saraceni shouted over the siren. Stone and Wood waved the team in. Gabriel grabbed his father, to make sure he accompanied them, when both froze. Looking over the wall, they saw Mrs. Aquila running across the field in turquoise athletic wear. The fact that she was still a distance runner showed today.

"Mom! MOM!" Gabriel yelled, but she did not hear and kept running up the hill with her team.

"Her team lead has her, Gabriel-NOW!" Stone barked, holding the door off the patio open as members of Molior streamed inside. With one reluctant backward glance toward his wife, Alexander Aquila dragged his son inside the door, which slammed shut and automatically bolted as storm shutters descended over the windows. The hopeful rays of radiant sunshine were replaced by a solitary fluorescent bulb in the hallway.

Chapter 14

As teams of recruits raced up the hill, Saraceni hurdled the concrete wall surrounding the patio with the skill of an Olympic athlete, flicked his security badge past the scanner, and entered the building of the adjacent wing through the side door. He raced through the corridor, cut through a laboratory, raced through a second corridor, cut through the art gallery and burst into the briefing room. Ruth Fielding and three other council members were already there, huddled over the main conference table with Elizabeth Hallowell, the main project manager, and Kuminsky, her #2.

All looked distressed and Saraceni's concern grew as he drew within earshot. Zeb Gata, a contemporary of Ruth's, barked commands to a few of Hallowell's team members as he pulled up the alert detail on the screen. Three scattered. The rest remained.

"97.4%!"

"Yes, Sir, it's raised exponentially since yesterday, and a full half percent in the last hour." Hallowell responded, her voice cracking.

"What happened to four and a half weeks?"

"Decoherence accelerated."

"Obviously, " he stopped, closed his eyes, bowed his head and breathed deeply for a full fifteen seconds before continuing in a much more directed tone. "Okay. We must assess, decide, execute, remediate. Assess: What has caused this accelerated decoherence?"

"We're not sure," Hallowell delivered reluctantly. "None of our monitoring showed any spikes."

"Okay. Root cause analysis should commence but we may not have time for that, given that at the current rate the world may rip apart in a few hours." He said slightly more agitated. Ruth offered her thoughts:

"While root cause analysis is underway, we should launch any and all countermeasures. If we can't yet stop the advancement, we must counteract it. Hallowell, what has your countermeasures committee come up with?"

"Nothing concrete, ma'am, nothing we're sure will work" Hallowell responded.

"Forget sure! Do we have anything that we have any remote expectation might be of assistance? Has anyone had a single idea?" Ruth pressed.

"The committee had some ideas, but many were theoretical. We didn't even fully vet them all yet since it's only been a week. This wasn't expected so early." Hallowell replied.

"Well get them in here, or there may not be a later," Ruth commanded, pressing her palms flatly against the table in front of her, grey hair abandoning its proper dominion in its neat placement on her head.

"All of them? Some are only circle 4's. We were using it as a learning experience," Hallowell questioned, twisting her fingers together like a small child.

"I don't care if they are still in The Cupel, get them in here," Ruth responded in an even, measured, and very serious tone. Hallowell ran from the room to retrieve her countermeasures committee. Saraceni moved in and began examining the alert detail closely. He was amazed at the interdependencies he saw woven together like a cobweb. The highly capable individuals were often the most frustrated to realize the interdependent nature of their society after being recruits. The Cupel produced such attachment to individualism that it was hard to break later.

Kuminsky reviewed the basic symptoms of decoherence to the shock and amazement of all present. Since this had never before happened in the history of the universe, it was difficult to know how to respond. One man in Hallowell's project team began to cry.

"I know it's difficult," someone near him said.

"Get him out of here," Zeb said quietly to Kuminsky, who quickly ushered the man out.

"What effects are from measurement and what are true effects?" Saraceni asked Ruth and Zeb. Several other council members were arriving.

"We don't know. The project team can't distinguish. Which are the system and which are the surrounding environment?"

"Have you tried the superconducting ring?" an elder on the council asked.

"Not yet," Ruth confirmed, "it's an option, and if we didn't have the seepage problem, we would use it, but in the present state, we just aren't sure what it will do."

"Well, we may soon have no other choice but to give it a whirl," he responded, his leathery hands pulling up a simulation on the detail screen. Simulation scenarios began running one at a time. The results came back one after another: FAILURE! Inconclusive. Inconclusive. FAILURE! FAILURE! FAILURE! FAILURE! The monitor jumped to 97.5%

"See, you can't do a simple reversal of current using the ring because the backward flow won't flow straight back to the original source since the system and environment have shifted. Current just flies randomly all over the place! It may even make the situation worse," Ruth reasoned. "I've been through these scenarios countless times. There is no way to alter the course other than to open a new circle, as we all know, but if we had some countermeasures to not alter the course, but just slow it, that's all we really need!" As if on cue, Hallowell returned with the countermeasures team, about 30 team members from all disciplines and circles.

"We are at 97.5% and progressing at a geometric rate," Zeb announced without sparing a moment, "Has the countermeasures team had any ideas that may be of use?" His manner was so stern and authoritarian that the assemblage cowered in his presence.

Ruth aimed to soften the message to promote idea-sharing, reverting as if by instinct back to the core methods of the facility. Just because Zeb had let panic make him harsh, she could not see valuable minutes lost. "Please, we're looking for any idea at all, even if it's just a scrap, we may be able to build on it." She pleaded with the countermeasures team as she prayed silently to herself, to whoever would listen.

A short girl in the back with wide eyes who looked rather like a startled rabbit stepped forward slightly, shoving her fisted hands deep into the pockets of her sweat jacket.

"Yes?" Ruth prompted gently, fearing if she pushed this girl, she might bolt from the room. She looked at Elizabeth Hallowell as a cue for the girl's name.

"Soo Jin," Elizabeth relayed to Ruth clearly, the only useful information she'd been able to supply so far today.

"Soo Jin," Ruth prodded," do you have an idea?"

"Mikhail had one," she reported, and stepped quickly back to her place. Hallowell spun instantly to a tall, gangly boy of nineteen, also in the back, who was dressed as if he had just returned from a concert. "Mikhail? Did your calculations yield a result?" Hallowell accused. How dare he keep information from her!

"I wasn't sure," he stammered, "it was just an idea I had, but it's probably stupid."

"I said share any ideas! " Hallowell scolded, not realizing her own lack of leadership skills caused this dilemma. Ruth stepped between the two and Hallowell shrunk back next to Saraceni.

"Mikhail, I don't believe we've met." Ruth smiled at him warmly, sweeping her grey hair back from her face to its usual position, "If you had any positive results at all, we could use anything with which to work."

"Well, I noticed when this was originally set up, the team added a conservatism factor for every grid across the entire spectrum," he continued.

"We were told to build in conservatism, to be sure. For safety," Hallowell defended, correctly, as that was the original instruction.

"Right," Mikhail stepped forward to the screen and pulled up a large display of amber grid covering the entire screen, the outline of about a thousand small squares, "but we added .008 for each grid, which is a conservative number, assuming every grid were impacted, but if you think about it, we really only needed to build a buffer at the measurement points. He manipulated the display and about 100 of the squares lit up, or 10% of the surface area of the grid, evenly spaced throughout. "So, we have a buffer of 8.0 built in when, using just the measurement points, the buffer should really be just .8."

"We're 7.2% over! Oh, thank God!" Zeb cried out. Ruth stared at the grid and smiled.

"I don't think I've ever been so happy to find out about an error in all my lives." Ruth said.

"But, the decoherence is still progressing exponentially," Saraceni pointed out. At the present geometric rate, that would set them back to 89.7%, but they'd be right back to this point in about 12 hours.

Mikhail, emboldened by the confirmation of his idea as correct, offered up the real idea he'd held back from Hallowell, "I was thinking. Measurement aggravates, if not directly causes, decoherence, so if we measure at 100 points now, and we stopped measurement, then we could slow the decoherence." The group considered the idea. Zeb walked to the screen and pulled up the critical measurements list as he spoke.

"Well, we can't stop measuring altogether because of The Cupel. That might cause even greater problems." His fingers flew and calculations spewed across at an alarming rate. No one else but Ruth could even follow them that fast. "But.... if we shut off all measurement except for the minimal juncture points, basing on the present decoherence rate and progression factor..." He ran to a notebook on the desk and double-checked using a slide rule. A student in the back chuckled.

"It will still progress, but the slower rate, coupled with the resetting back to 89.7% will buy us three more weeks!" he announced jubilantly. The group cheered and Saraceni exhaled a long sigh and slumped his shoulders in relief. Ruth turned to Saraceni, placing a hand on his shoulder reassuringly.

"Our fate will still rest with you, and Molior, as it has all along, but you will have the time to execute the original plan." The weight of her hand felt like the weight of the world on his shoulders.

Back in the sequestered quadrant, Molior members were piled in the hallway inside the closed door. Kyle and George, who had been the first to run in the door at the sound of the alarm, had been knocked to the floor and were being helped up by the others. Gabriel pounded on the door.

"My mom's out there! What's going on?" he shouted.

"She'll be fine. There's time for them to get inside," Wood reassured, pulling him from the door.

"Then why did the doors bolt and shutters draw down?"

"Precautions. We take no chances here, especially in this quadrant. We try to be safer than we have to be. If you knew the stakes, you'd understand." Wood continued to try to diffuse the situation, but his first thought was that he was notably nowhere near Saraceni's level of communicating.

"Enlighten me!" Gabriel jerked his arm away from Wood's grasp and turned back toward the door. Wood looked at Stone, searching for his affable manner to intercede.

"He can't," Stone confirmed.

"Well somebody better or I'm outta here. I'm tired of all this cloak and dagger, I want some god damned answers," Gabriel continued. His father watched, partially wanting to hold his son back, but also agitated and wanting answers himself. He wanted to see where this would lead.

"You'll get them," Wood was just trying to calm him down at this point, "as soon as Saraceni arrives, he'll explain everything." As he said it, he knew it was a promise he couldn't make for Saraceni, but hoped optimism and faith would be enough. George, who was on his feet again by now, leaned over halfway, hands on his knees.

"George, you look woozy, are you okay?" Chandra asked, kneeling down before him. He looked at her just a few inches from his face, but she became blurry at the edges. Her brow was knitted tightly in concern.

"You look like Sampson's wife." he said, and fell over, holding his head. David Running Wolf rushed to his side, as did Wood and the rest crowded around.

Kyle leaned over with his hands on his knees and also looked woozy.

"Kyle?" Chandra asked . He was breathless and woozy, but responded in a weak voice.

"I'm okay." The group turned their attention back to George.

"You're the doctor, what should we do?" Wood asked David.

"I do genetics research, I don't work in an ER! My M.D. rotations were 12 years ago!" David responded, simultaneously checking George's vital signs and turning him on his back. He opened George's eyes forcibly with his fingers. Juliet took one step in and clutched Wood's arm in desperation.

"Do any of those scanners in the training room do anything useful like medical screening? Will they tell us anything other than DNA minutiae?" Alexander offered.

"Yes!" Stone shouted. "Grab his feet!" The team collectively picked George up by the arms and legs and raced him down the hall to the training room.

"Platform 7!" Wood shouted and the group deposited George's limp form on the platform. Wood booted it up and the orb in the corner began to glow.

"Come on, come on," Jane pleaded with the machine impatiently. The program ran and Stone and Wood huddled together, reading the results.

"Well, is he okay?" Gabriel spoke for the group. Wood and Stone turned and looked slightly more relaxed, but not without concern.

"He is stable," Stone relayed.

"Oh, thank God!" Chandra said, crossing herself. Wood placed a hand on Juliet's shoulder and looked at the rest of the team members solemnly.

"What?" Juliet asked him quietly.

"He's in a coma," Wood reported.

Chapter 15

Lela felt a wave of uncharacteristic anxiety wash over her as she flew back to the States, not due to flying, but because her work had been abruptly interrupted with a demand to fly home. The funding was in jeopardy and she was needed ASAP, that was all Pfister had told her. She had enjoyed the escapism of Africa, ironic given that many wouldn't consider the location she visited a place to escape to. She knew she would have to return and deal with the real world and her life eventually, but she was gradually easing up to it, preparing herself. Suddenly, here it was. It's only six days, she kept reminding herself. At least she had reworked her ticket to not connect through O'Hare- that was a plus since she always got delayed flying through Chicago. Her connection in Dulles allowed her to stretch her legs and get some food so by the time she arrived home she was not completely worn out.

Entering the familiar hallway of her own apartment, she dropped her keys on the hall table and picked up the pile of mail. One of the grad students in the building watered her plants and picked up her mail when she was away- for a fee of course. It used to be her mother or brother that would do these things for her. Since Lela had put all her important mail on hold or e-delivery before leaving, the pile was surprisingly small. She probably would just leave it that way when she returned home- saving trees seemed the right thing to do given the beautiful forests she had just left.

The first thing she did was take a luxuriously long, hot shower. That was one of the few things she really did miss of civilization, feeling truly clean. The hot water danced over her body, and she wished it could wash away all her sorrow and anxiety as easily as the dust of Africa. She relaxed and let her mind wander and suddenly out of nowhere she thought of her family in danger.

"A little late," she mused. She fell into a deep, heavy sleep like children do and awoke the next morning feeling uncharacteristically refreshed. She resolved to do some research on the notes in her mother's office before meeting up with Pfister later in the day. She'd tried to find a "Dossler case" reference on the internet from Africa, assuming it was something easily found, but was dismayed to discover there was no mention of it anywhere, even in the scientific journals.

Pulling up to her parents' house again, this time she was startled. It didn't feel just the same. A for sale sign loomed out front and though she'd contacted the family real estate agent via email, it was different seeing it live and in color. She entered and put on a pot of coffee, and opened most of the ground floor windows, to rid the house of its closed-up smell. Entering the office, she pulled out her notes. Dossler case, red star on the calendar, the mineral. None of this seemed related, yet she was determined to learn anything that might help. She opened the filing cabinet and was not surprised to see the bare minimum files. She knew her mother's system well-current year's records were kept in the filing cabinet throughout the year. Once taxes were filed, every item from the prior year was boxed according to year and each small file box placed in a separate supply room. Looking through the current year files, she saw no mention of a Dossler case. She fired up the computer and hunted for 45 minutes through the files available on the desktop, again to no avail. In light of what Mr. Charles , or, she mentally corrected herself, *General* Charles had told her, it was likely any important computer files of her parents were in another location.

She entered the supply room and saw boxes upon boxes of files, one for each year going back three decades. 'Fun' she thought. She opened the first box and in the front stood a cover page. Each file was listed by name and next to each a "file number" and "master reference number". The first file number was 1, but its master reference number was 886. She quickly assessed that each box could hold approximately 30 files and since there were about thirty boxes, the number implied the master reference numbers corresponded to all files present.

"All I need to do is find the master reference sheet. Thank God my mother was so logical. Well, she'd keep the master in either the first box, or the last." Since there was no master reference sheet in the final box, Lela dug through the dusty piles until she saw box 1, toward the back. Opening the box, she did immediately see the master reference sheet in the front, with every 30 files or so hand written in slightly different ink, felt tip, blue, black, etc. She read each file name on the list and finally, on page 2, approximately halfway down the page, she spotted "Dossler" on the sheet, file number112. 'That means it's about 29 years ago' she thought to herself. She tried box 4, but it ended at file 111, so she jumped to box 5, but found it started at file 113, so she returned to box 4 and went straight to the back, only to confirm that it ended at file 111. File 112 was missing. Noticing the time, she left to meet Pfister and hoped she could prevent the bastard Currier from pulling the funding because they couldn't produce results faster than humanly possible.

At 10 am, Pfister greeted her and briefed her on the way to the conference room.

"Lela, he wants us to produce results faster or he's going to pull all the funding."

"Well, we can only do what is humanly possible. Maybe we can speed up the crops and teleport matter for him while we're at it," she replied. Five hours later they left with the funding retained and a detailed, painstakingly scheduled agreement of deliverables.

Driving down the mountain, she dialed Bianca's familiar number on autopilot.

"Hey, Bianca. I'm only back in the states for a couple days. That Currier jerk threatened to pull all our funding, but Pfister and I fixed it. I'm leaving the office now. Wanna meet up for dinner later?" Lela inquired.

"Yeah. Dandelion Café at six, babe. Oh, and James keeps emailing me asking how you're doing. Why he doesn't just call you is beyond me, but please call him, I beg of you." Bianca responded.

"Unbelievable. He barely cares if I'm alive or dead for months and now it's all, where am I? I'll call him if I have time. Thanks, Bianca. I'll see ya later, just gotta take care of something first." Lela watched the scenery change as her hybrid SUV made its way through town and into the winding streets of the historic district. Pulling up to the antique Victorian home with its' familiar wraparound porch, it seemed a million years since she'd first visited Phillip Harriman's office. She smiled as she thought of her guarded exchange with Brett on the porch, which now seemed odd since he had come to be someone she trusted more than almost anyone else.

In the cocoon of Harriman's office, sitting in a Queen Ann high-backed chair, Lela's relaxed demeanor was a stark contrast to the tension of her first visit. She looked at Phillip more as a person for the first time, and noticed he was a pretty handsome fellow, and his easy manner made him seem almost- dateable. She resolved to introduce him to one of her friends when things calmed down and gratefully accepted tea from him.

"Thank you. Okay, here I am, as requested, with the raw mineral." She plopped a lemon-sized chunk of raw mineral she'd retrieved from the cavern on the carved cherry table. Phillip Harriman pensively lifted the purple gem from its resting place and held it in his hands. Feeling overwhelmed, he quickly replaced the mineral to the table.

"Powerful stuff. Give me a minute." He lifted it again, with both hands, closing his eyes.

"God. I can see everything over there. Your family is fine. They made it to the other side. Gabriel wants to get you a message, but he hasn't learned how yet." Phillip informed. He put down the rock and opened his eyes.

"That mineral sure does act like an amplifier. Everything is much clearer," he added.

Lela struggled for her questions, forming them slowly, "What are you saying, that they're in heaven? And what happened with the accident?"

"I don't have all the answers, Lela. I never think of crossing over as going to heaven because it doesn't come across that way to me, but I don't like to tell people what to think. It was an accident, from our point of view, but really they were called. They have a higher mission and they had to leave here to achieve it, but there was no malice in it." He was clear and thoughtful in his explanation.

"There's a file I was looking for this morning, but couldn't find- any ideas?" she hoped he might have some useful insight.

"This one's different from Gabriel's. Was this your mother's?" he asked.

"Yes," she confirmed.

"Did you ever look in that back yellow room upstairs, the one that used to be a nursery?" he asked.

"No, I forgot," she admitted truthfully, "I'll look. If you say Gabriel is trying to get me a message, what can I do? I mean, I'm not really into that sort of thing, what if he can't get through to me or something because I'm so ...distant?"

"I'd keep some of the mineral with you. It seems to facilitate. And be on the lookout- it should be something very specific, something you would absolutely know is from him. The cavern will be your savior, and Gabriel's. That's all I see." Lela shook his hand and gave him the lump of mineral.

"Thanks, Phillip. You keep this one. I have more and I'll bring some more back from Africa for you." Lela confided openly.

"Thank you, Lela. Safe travels." he responded, walking her out.

After dinner with Bianca, though tired, Lela knew she could not sleep if she did not return to her parent's house to look for the file. Proceeding immediately to the former nursery, she looked around and saw nothing unusual. Sifting through the dresser in the now guest room, she found only clothes and linens, nothing out of the ordinary. The only remnants of the room's life as a former nursery lay in the closet, a disassembled crib and three boxes of baby clothes. One clearly labeled Lela, one clearly labeled Gabriel and a third, smaller box that said "Baby" on it. Then "B.D" and the year. Lela recalled it mentioned once that one of her mother's charity endeavors was to take in a pregnant teenager for about six months, giving her a place to stay until she had the baby and could get back into school. The girl's parents had kicked her out. Lela was reminded of her mother's good heart. The baby was two or three months old when the girl moved out. Lela had no recollection as it was all before she was born. She opened the box and saw a teddy bear and tiny choo choo train outfit on top, with a matching hat.

Digging further into the contents of the box, she found more clothes, some pictures and then a large manila envelope. Opening it, her heart jumped as she realized it contained a file folder. Drawing it out slowly, she stepped from the shadows of the closet into the clear light of the room and read "Baby Girl Dossler" clearly on the tab. Lela sat tentatively on the edge of the bed and gingerly opened the file, still stunned to be learning her parents had secrets from them. The file contained blood work for the infant, a lock of baby hair, and a recently-printed Pheres genetic printout for her DNA. Nothing seemed particularly notable to Lela, no diseases, no anomalies. Clearly, her mother had been researching this child and not just housing the mother. In the bottom right corner of the page, in her mother's handwriting, Lela read "Psalm 139".

She immediately went to her parents' bedroom and pulled her mother's bible from the nightstand on her side of the bed. Psalm 139, underlined in bold red by her mother, were the words:

"For you formed my inward parts; you knitted me together in my mother's womb. I praise you, for I am fearfully and wonderfully made. Wonderful are your works; my soul knows it very well. My frame was not hidden from you, when I was being made in secret, intricately woven in the depths of the earth. Your eyes saw my unformed substance; in your book were written, every one of them, the days that were."

In the underlining, one phrase within the paragraph was underlined twice, whereas the rest was underlined once: "my soul knows it very well,"

Back in Phillip Harriman's office, he held the mineral and focused on his remote viewing techniques. He saw Gabriel sitting next to Mr. Aquila on a semicircular sofa with several others. He couldn't believe how much clearer his visions were with use of the mineral. Phillip watched as the scene unfolded.

Chapter 16

The recruits sat on two semicircular sofas in the common area. Kyle bit his nails as Jane tapped her foot nervously.

It was Jane who finally broke the silence. "When will the doctors be finished with George? Ugh."

"And where's Saraceni?" David added.

"Wood said that Saraceni will be in as soon as he can, that he's with some other team fixing the alarm. He'll be here" Jack reassured, his shoulders set back and square jaw jutting forward slightly.

"Kyle, are you okay? What happened back there?" Chandra queried.

"I just felt like I was gonna pass out, that's all," he replied. "Then my head started hurting really badly. I felt…like I had something I wanted to say, but then it went away. I'm fine." Looking at him, his hair was pushed back from his face for once. A cold sweat had frozen it in place, making his face appear thinner and paler than normal. He did have an odd look, as if he hadn't slept in a thousand years. Kyle's brow was knitted, struggling to remember, yet he could not. The key images were just out of reach.

Wood and Gabriel entered the room and many recruits stood, anticipating the news they would bring.

"How's George?" Jane asked urgently.

Wood delivered the news welcomingly. "He's alright. No change."

"Where is Saraceni, Wood?" Gabriel asked sternly.

"What's wrong?" Gabriel paced the common area and all of Molior could tell that he was upset. Some walked toward him, huddling around, eager for any additional information about the unfathomable events of the day. Others were attentive from their seats.

"What's wrong?" Alexander asked his son. As if on cue, Saraceni entered and immediately registered that something was wrong with his prized training class. Having just come from the briefing room, he, too, looked as tired as Kyle.

Gabriel thought carefully and examined the others. His father paced, clearly rattled by having seen Mrs. Aquila with no opportunity to speak to her. Kyle was biting his nails, while Chandra now tapped her own manicured nails nervously on the countertop. Enam's eyes were closed and he was breathing deeply, clearly calming himself.

Gabriel decided to go on the offense. "Saraceni, what's going on? We know nothing. There are alarms going off- we're powerless to do anything. Now I find in George's room detailed writings that talk all about killing Governor Jacob. How on earth are we to trust you people when we clearly don't even know what's going on? How does George even know who Governor Jacob was? He wasn't even on our bus." Gabriel watched Saraceni like he had cast a line into the deep sea.

Saraceni sat on the sofa edge, rubbing the back of his neck with closed eyes. Again- careworn, weary. The shoulders of Atlas. A full minute passed. Saraceni slowly opened his eyes and clocked Gabriel with a level gaze. The shift in the air was perceptible to all. Finally he spoke.

"Because George is Governor Jacob. Many of us here have lived before. Many times. You even know some of our other names from history," Saraceni said.

Even Juliet was speechless. With no witty comebacks, the group just digested the information.

"Like reincarnation?" Jack was the first to hesitantly break the silence.

"Somewhat, but not exactly like you know it. Again, we merely reframe what you already know into the proper context. You don't die and go to heaven and all that and go back. Not through our process. It's really more medical. We've just perfected body recreation and repair to such a point that it takes many, many cycles for someone here to actually die," Saraceni responded.

Kyle stepped back, blinking a few times, looking like a teen that just learned it was time to be a man.

"I've been here before, too, haven't I? That's why it seems so familiar?" he asked Saraceni.

"Yes, Kyle, you and George have been here before. You were needed and we had to pull you back early." Saraceni put his arm around his longtime friend.

After a pensive moment, Enam, absentmindedly rubbing where his scar used to be, was the next to query, "Then why doesn't George look like Governor Jacob?"

"The first time you are here, you are created in the image of the body of your life, but after you have been here many times, you can choose before you leave which body form you would like to enter when you return. George chose one of his historic forms before he left," Saraceni explained. Gabriel again hesitated before proceeding. He almost wasn't sure he wanted to know the answer to his next question.

"You keep saying "there" and "here". Where are we?" he asked on behalf of the entire group.

"On Earth," Saraceni responded. A long pause ensued.

"Then where *were* we?" Alexander asked hesitantly. Ruth had been standing unnoticed in the doorway for some time. She wouldn't have chosen this path for these recruits. Not this early. Their assimilation was too important, but now Pandora 's Box had been opened.

"Come with me. I must show you," Ruth confided. She turned and walked down the corridor to the training room with the measured steps of a General going into battle . It was not just Ruth's experience through many lifetimes that translated into her calculated demeanor, but a formidable character that had been hers from the beginning. In her youth, she was more energetic and brash, more like Juliet, but no less exceptional. Upon reaching the training room, Ruth stood against the back wall, the warm amber glow of the light from the orb caressing her features and the progression of paintings through time displayed behind her on the wall. Just above her right shoulder clearly displayed on the middle painting was the signature 'Saraceni'. Chandra, who had minored in art with her anthropology degree looked at Saraceni with awe.

"You're *that* Saraceni?" she asked incredulously.

"Art was always a distant second to teaching for me, but I did enjoy it," he responded quietly.

The recruits looked from him and then expectantly at Ruth – reeling from their second shock in as many weeks.

And so Ruth began, "We've been teaching you about quantum universes. Well, we built one. And, like George said, it is an exact copy of this universe, so precise it was hard to even tell them apart at first. We once endangered the Earth to the point of almost blowing it up, and we swore we would never do that again. So, we created a test environment where we could see how things would interact with our environment, without actually risking our environment."

"I remember! There were seven project teams. I was on one and George was on one, and the others!" Kyle exclaimed excitedly.

"The project grew," Ruth continued, "We had perfected genetic engineering, with no real problems. Just meat, after all. We learned about the soul maps and dark matter DNA and we had the idea to do metaphysical engineering to complement the genetic engineering. To engineer the new souls created, and to guide the development of the existing souls so we could progress as a species."

Juliet stared hard at the ground in front of her. She pulled her hair into a tight bunch with one hand, exhaling audibly. She groped for the words she wanted.

"Metaphysical engineering? How did you do it?" Juliet launched.

"We turned the other universe into The Cupel." Ruth responded flatly, providing them time to wrap their brains around each line of her words as she spoke.

"A cupel is a dish in alchemy used to sort the lead from the gold," Kyle explained.

"Correct," Ruth continued, "so we created The Cupel. We conducted surveillance into it and those who are ready are allowed to be born into this world. We don't allow anyone of inferior character, or inferior intellect, or who is not prepared to accept the multiple streams of consciousness required to excel here. We keep our planet and our society clean and safe and on a path of enlightenment by only selecting those worthy to participate in it."

"And you just kill off the rest?" Juliet's voice became shrill.

" Of course not, Juliet," Ruth's tone was calm and motherly. "We try to help and guide people to complete the learning they need before coming here. New souls find our society difficult, too advanced, to function in without sufficient knowledge and skills. So, it's like a teaching tool, from which we take the most valiant and worthy."

"You're playing God," Chandra spat the words out.

"Some have argued that. And we are paying the price. All the religious doctrine you have been taught has come directly from our own, so we believe in a higher being and that we will go on when we die, just like most of you do," Ruth replied.

Kyle added quickly, "But we broke it up-into seven pieces- one for each project, and the languages, too."

"Yes, synthesis of concepts is a critical learning. We broke up all religious learning, and the languages, and all the other knowledge, and gave 1/7 to each project team, to each culture. Your civilization is gradually assimilating it, and when you have, you will have advanced to where we are now. Of course, we'll be farther by then." Ruth explained very clinically, as if giving a lecture. Saraceni noticed the distress on his recruits' faces. He feared they were losing the battle for their hearts, critical to the completion of the mission as any general would relate.

"So other than George and Kyle, we're all from this Cupel, your black box project? Where is it? How do we get back?" Gabriel resumed his role as mouthpiece. Ruth walked to the corner with the globe-sized amber orb behind protective glass.

"It is right here, Gabriel," she said, motioning to the globe-sized orb, "We are the titans. Think about your creation stories. We passed along what we knew, but some of our early teachers tried to explain about our world here, and oral traditions retained some of that, too. Don't you find it odd that religious doctrine has such fantastical stories of giants, magic healing, miracles, people created out of body parts of others- things that might look different from a scientific perspective? No less valid, but just doing double duty, performing two functions- teaching you what we know about God while also teaching what we know of the universe."

"All the knowledge is there. They just haven't put it all together yet, but they will," Kyle added encouragingly. Ruth could see several recruits shaking their heads.

"Think about it- isn't it too coincidental that the very first words in our religious doctrine are "let there be light", followed by a statement that everything started with Adam and Eve. Atom and Eve- a particle and a unit of time? Light + matter + time just happen to be the exact necessary quantum building blocks. And then later, the Quran refers to the perpetual expansion of the heavens. Do the Upanishads not refer to the oneness of all ? That's how we figured it out. It was all there all along, just waiting for us to become evolved enough to read it on the right level," Ruth revealed.

Chandra backed up almost reflexively, shaking her head in disbelief. "This is ridiculous. It can't be true. You're saying everything we know, everyone we know, is in there." She motioned at the orb in disgust. "And you created it. How do we get back?" Saraceni looked at Ruth and Kyle looked down. Gabriel stood in the center of all the Molior recruits, facing Ruth and Saraceni and staring at them. He thought of Gretchen, and Caleb, and Lela.

"We don't." Gabriel said somberly.

Chapter 17

Having successfully assisted Pfister in retaining funding, Lela returned to Africa on the first available flight. Emerging from the building, the heat of the day wrapped around her like a loving snake, the humidity gently pressing in on her in a close way. Her driver had been hired by Brett, who had learned the trusted local networks in a matter of weeks. As they left the city, Lela noticed less people than usual on the streets. Overt calmness permeated the view in a way that signaled not all was alright.

"You need to get on the floorboard for the rest of the journey, Miss Lela. You keep your head down." He gave her a blanket, "and cover up with this, that's what Mr. Brett say." Lela hesitated and then complied. After 20 minutes, she actually began to feel carsick in this position, an experience she had never before felt. Each bounce in the road tempted her stomach to betray itself. Lela resorted to deep, even breaths as a measure of controlling the nausea. Just when she progressed to the point of wondering how much longer she could continue this, she heard the high-pitched squeal of the breaks as the car came to a halt.

The driver seemed all too hurried removing her bags from the trunk and leaving, citing that he had been prepaid as he waved away her attempt at a tip. Already feeling this to be quite strange, Lela spun about to face the camp only to discover it appeared to be empty. She cautiously and quietly walked along the edge of the tents down the main path rather than in the center and made her way back to the cafeteria tent. Empty. Suddenly, almost startling her, Tina emerged crossing the camp diagonally carrying a full plat of water bottles.

"Tina!" Lela shouted at her. Tina recoiled in fear and dropped the water plat, bottles rolling around in the leaves and dirt below.

"Jesus, Lela! You scared the hell out of me!" Tina replied frantically, scrambling to pick the bottles up in haphazard fashion.

"Where is everybody?" Lela queried as she stooped to assist her friend.

"You're back! Come with me-quickly." Lela followed her as the woman raced through the camp, her dirty, khaki pants hanging low on her hips, revealing additional weight lost on an already-thin frame since coming to camp. Was she that thin just a week ago?

"We've been stockpiling food and water. Brett's orders."

"Brett's orders? Since when does he run camp?"

"Since we developed a security crisis. Rebels are making their way through the countryside and aside from some local travelers, we're completely cut off to the west." They arrived at the back tent, one originally used for storage, to find Brett and a handful of soldiers in full gear with guns standing before them. Others stood at the four corners, facing outward, on the lookout for anyone approaching. Unseen, in the surrounding jungle, lookouts responsible for sending back word of any approaching rebel bands were perched. Brett saw Lela and his face contorted in uncommon anger, a rare flash of emotion before his men.

"Damn it! They weren't supposed to bring you here! My message didn't get through!" he said to her, but really to no one.

"No. He said he got your instructions for me to be on the floor of the car," Lela responded.

"Those were the original instructions. I sent word yesterday recanting those and telling him not to bring you here."

"Well, I guess he didn't listen."

"No, that means he never got the message. Our courier to the west must not have been able to get through. I wish these local guys had cell phones."

"Not this far in," the soldier to Brett's left added.

"Where is everybody?" Lela asked.

"Inside," Brett responded, "It's safer to have everyone pulled together to one location." Just then a lookout returned, out of breath. Tina handed him some water, which he quickly downed, gaining enough breath to speak.

"They're headed this way. From the south," he reported.

"Get inside," Brett barked at Lela, "We have to prepare to hold them off out here." Everyone inside has any remaining weapons, so get one and be prepared in case.

"Wait, Brett, this is not the O.K. Corral- we can't just have a showdown. Can't we just escape to the east? There are villages that way."

"With this many people, we'll be too slow. We wouldn't make it more than a few clicks before they catch up. We have the advantage here over terrain we don't know at all. And we can't go north. We'd run into the river. No boats, rapids, we'd never make it to the other side and there's no civilization on this side of it." Lela's nausea from the car, which had never really disappeared, now welled up to the top of her throat again. Could this really be happening? Stunned, she went into the tent, grabbed two knives and sat silently next to the others, watching the doorway, listening intently for any sounds from the distance, any approaching footstep, any voice, any gunfire, but she heard nothing. She looked around at the scared faces of those around her- Mako, Tina, interns Brian and Rachel, little more than children, and the goofy, good-natured Texan, Lance, with all the geologists, medical workers, logistics personnel, all those who were not soldiers and not trained for this sort of situation. Mako clutched a single clear plastic container from his colored castle as if it were a security blanket. The mineral inside it was raw, not even neatly wrapped as was his custom. Lela's nausea quickly subsided and an overwhelming urge moved its way up into her throat. She jumped up and ran for the door.

"Brett! Brett!" she scanned the landscape quickly searching for signs of him. The sentry posted to the tent quickly rounded the corner and put his hand over her mouth.

"We are in silent mode," he whispered to her, "until our scout returns to tell us how much time we have, we have to assume they are close." Lela nodded, his hand still covering her mouth, and he removed it.

"I need to speak to Brett most urgently," she whispered.

"Impossible, Davies is in operational mode now. I can't just pull him back here. Whatever your question is, it'll have to wait." His tone was subtly patronizing, as if to suggest her need to speak to Brett was for comfort.

"Look, I may know of a safe location near here I discovered while resource mapping. So, you get him back here now or you may be deciding we'll all be unnecessarily slaughtered." The young soldier appeared conflicted. "Do you really want that sort of decision on your head at this stage of your career?" she pressed in an emphatic whisper.

The sentry pressed a series of buttons on his walkie-talkie which made no sound but the pressing of buttons. In a moment the device returned one blink of a light.

"He'll be right here," the sentry reported. Lela looked around the still jungle in the minutes before Brett arrived and observed what a beautiful day it would have been had the humans not been warring with one another. The untouched jungle presented a sharp contrast to the areas closer toward town that had been razed. After four minutes that seemed like twenty, Brett arrived.

"Lela, I don't have time for this."

"I know, I know, but I found a cavern when I was exploring. I think we could hide there. It's plenty big enough for all of us," she confided hopefully. Brett considered the suggestion.

"These are local people, Lela. They've grown up here their whole life. The chances that they don't know about that cavern already are very slight."

Lela pressed, knowing deep in her gut that if they didn't go, they would die. Each passing moment she felt it more and more intensely. Death was approaching. She could just go on her own, but leaving all the others behind did not feel right, not when she truly felt they wouldn't make it. She had to convince Brett for all of them to go.

"The only entrance was covered with like fifty years of vegetation. I cut it away myself. And the inside was completely untouched. Full of mineral and no sign of even a single axe mark. If anyone knew it was there, it would have at least been mildly disturbed." Brett sighed as he considered the suggestion.

"Trust me, Brett, I would not suggest it if I didn't think it was our best hope. And, it's to the northeast, we'd be moving away from them at the same time, which would give us time to get there." He looked at her, his keen ability to read people confirming to him that she believed with every ounce of her soul what she was saying. In the end, the real question was: how much did he trust her, this woman he'd known only a short while? Brett turned to the sentry.

"We need a distance estimate right now."

"The scout isn't back yet and we're on radio silence. If we ping him and he's very close to them, it may compromise his position."

"I know that. Ping him once. He'll know what it's for and ping back how many clicks away they are."

"That's not standard protocol, sir. He won't know what we're asking for. We can't rely on that data."

"You're right, but in real operations things don't always go exactly as planned. I trained him myself. It's not the clearest communication, but he'll figure it out. He'll know that's the only question we would be breaking radio silence to ask the man that is the scout. There would be no other logical reason to break radio silence. Send the ping."

"Yes, sir," the sentry withdrew his walkie-talkie once again, adjusted the frequency and sent a single click. The three watched the device for any response. Silence.

"He may be out of range," the sentry commented. Brett did not respond, but remained intent on the device. He glanced at Lela, his mind already thinking through the logistics of their exodus, should they have sufficient time to make one. He withdrew a laminated map from his pack and held it up to Lela, who wordlessly pointed to the location of the cavern. Brett marked the location and calculated the distance and travel time in his head. He examined the perils of two competing routes.

"I cut this path through, it might move faster since it's partially cleared, but it's narrow," she reported.

"This wide valley is open, so not as much cover. Even though it's not as direct, the openness of the terrain will allow a group this size to get there faster than the direct route. Plus, that area's all torn up by animals, not as much work to cover our tracks as the straight route." Their whispering sounded eerie in the silence of the camp, like ghosts talking. Finally, a response from the scout: 4 clicks.

"That's 12 kilometers. It'll be tight, but if we leave right now, I think we'll make it with a little room to spare." He turned to the sentry. "Miller, gather everyone else quietly and return back here in 10 minutes. Lela, we've got to prepare the other civilians." They burst into the tent and witnessed the still-huddled crew waiting in crippled silence. They looked at Brett with hope, instantly gathering from his demeanor that something had changed. They could only hope some good fortune had befallen them.

"Good news, we have an alternate location which we think will be safer than this one, and which the rebels likely don't know about. Bad news, we're out of here in ten minutes and have a trek ahead of us. So, pack water in your packs, and drink at least a liter right now before we leave, eat a protein bar, and take care of any bio needs you have now. We won't be stopping for at least 2 hours. Dress in proper gear and protection; change your shoes if you need to. We need to make good time and we need to move in silence. Any questions?"

"What about the animals?" Rachel asked. She had tended to the animals every day since arriving in camp and the small brow on her thin face furrowed at the thought of them being hurt.

"They stay here," he replied with no shred of sensitivity. "Anything else?" Silence. "Okay, we move out in ten." He exited the tent. Lela moved to Rachel.

"They won't hurt them," she reassured Rachel, "They need milk from them same as we do, so they'll take good care of them, if they even stop here."

The camp members dumped all extraneous items from their packs. The few belongings they had intended to keep with them- a single book, extra clothes, a bit of music, or pictures from home- were hastily dumped into a pile and replaced with extra water bottles and protein bars. As much as each person could carry was stuffed into backpacks. Everything they thought was important no longer was- only survival was. In exactly ten minutes Brett stuck his head in the tent.

"Time," he declared, more quietly than he would have preferred. The members began filing out of the tent and following his hand motion to line up in two lines.

"The path is wide enough for two rows. Try to walk as softly as possible so the tracks we leave are less clear as being fresh. When we get to the clearing, spread out so the tracks are widely dispersed. We'll cover our tracks on the other side and with a little luck, they'll be unable to tell which direction we went after the clearing," he advised. As they set out, with five soldiers on point with guns, two at the halfway point of the line of evacuees, and five at the rear, Brett had an uneasy feeling. He looked at Lela and had an instant recollection of when he first met her in the States. He'd watched her from his seat in the audience, all smiles talking to her father and the other scientists, running across the field, winking at her brother. It all seemed a lifetime ago now. He hadn't seen her truly smile once since that day, and today was no exception. He knew if this plan didn't work no one would be smiling today, or ever again. This wasn't an area of the country where they cared to take prisoners or bothered with ransoms. He knew his enemies well and if they were caught, they would surely be killed.

He heard some noise in the distance. Waving the others on, Brett held four soldiers back with him. The youngest and thinnest, Kye, climbed a tree in moments with the graceful agility of a dancer in an attempt to get a visual. He strained his eyes into slits, peering through the muted green tones of the jungle, but saw nothing. Seventy feet above his team, he withdrew his binoculars and scanned intently. Finally, he saw the rebels, still far off in the distance, but on a path toward the camp. Convinced their own team still maintained the tactical advantage, he began to breathe easier when suddenly he noticed an enormous Anaconda at the other end of the branch on which he sat. Without haste, as if not concerned in the least, the snake made its way toward Kye with a sly smile. He knew sudden movement would provoke the creature to accelerate. Following protocol, keeping one eye on the snake, he snapped twice to his team below. Silently, he looked down at them, at the snake and back again, while assessing if he could withdraw his knife from his waist holster without losing his grip. It was on his inner side, pinned between his body and the tree. To shift to reach it might cost him his life. The snake itself was massive, at least 20 feet long and 2 feet around. Kye's team, including Brett, swiftly arranged themselves in a quadrangle capture position and as the snake reached just a few meters from him, Kye launched himself out of the tree and into the arms of his comrades below. Having done this from only a height of fifty feet, Kye was surprised at the additional force imparted by only an extra 20 feet of height. They all fell to the ground with a thud, but other than basic bumps and bruises all were unharmed. The five quickly jumped to their feet and looked up, scrambling to the side in case the snake might drop itself down on them, but the snake was bored and not overly hungry, so it decided to remain in its haven in the trees, waiting for the next animal to come along. The five double-timed to catch up with the rest of the camp on exodus and reached them just before the entire party reached the clearing.

In the clearing, everyone fanned out as instructed, but remained silent. Lela walked with Tina, Brian, Rachel, Lance and Mako. She noticed the return of the five soldiers and gave small prayer in gratitude that they had returned safely. It was the first time she had prayed since her family had been killed, yet she did not realize it at the time. God has a way of sneaking back into our lives by being there for us, she would think later. She acknowledged Brett with a small nod of her head and a small smile that let him know she was glad he was back. When he looked pleased, somehow her thoughts immediately turned to James. Where was he right now?

As they moved through the valley, all frequently scanned the higher ground, almost in a paranoid way- eyes darting left and right, round and round, looking for the threat that might appear and wipe them out. After twenty minutes or so, they neared the other side of the clearing when suddenly a flare went up back at camp.

"Jesus! How could they be to camp already?" Lance exclaimed with his Texas twang. This was, however, exactly the pace Brett had predicted and he was internally grateful they would be out of the clearing, and out of sight, before the rebels reached the starting point at the other side. If they saw them in open terrain, it would be easy to follow them and there was no way to outpace them, unless the rebel force didn't follow their path directly, but had to at least look for it a bit first.

As the first of the evacuees reached the far edge of the forest, they reassembled into a line to fit within the path toward the river. This path wasn't wide enough for two lines, so they were instructed they would need to start moving double-time at this point. Three soldiers in front set the pace and the whole line followed. The remaining soldiers gathered branches and ground cover to cover their tracks. Lela lingered back to help, but when Brett noticed he marched straight to her.

"Lela! They need you up front! You're the one who knows where this cavern is," he scolded.

"I told them, go to the river, hang a left, not complicated from here," she replied.

"You said you covered it well. We can't risk it. Please." His eyes pleaded with her. He had too much to think about to deal with her stubbornness right now. Why couldn't she realize her obstinacy was her greatest drawback? Lela agreed and disappeared into the brush to catch up with the camp. She reached them easily and made her way toward the front. Miller ran pointe and when she arrived, she passed him up.

"Ma'am, please stay behind the armed detail," he instructed.

"Brett told me you needed me to be up front. You guys should make up your mind."

"He meant the front of them," he nodded toward the line of evacuees, "not in front of us." He affirmed this with slight amusement at the absurdity of this small, unarmed woman running pointe. One of the older people fell to the ground, obviously straining under the pressure of the double-time pace. Miller judged that they could afford to slow for a bit, and reduced the pace. They couldn't stop, but it gave everyone a chance to catch their breath.

Brett and his team completed the ground cover and darted off into the jungle. Knowing they didn't have to stick to the path as the others did, they began a diagonal course through the thick to intercept their group and be there when they arrived at the river. There might be trouble there if any of the rebels did know about the cavern, and they all knew they needed to be ready to fight. The five deftly made their way through the foliage. At this rate, they would catch the group easily. Speed turned out to be their enemy, though. They raced through the trees and around a puddle area when suddenly the first in the group, Kye, descended straight into a vat of quicksand. Instinctively, Kye outstretched his arms sideways to brake his body. The four behind him stopped short immediately and stepped back slightly from the menacing edges of the vat.

Kye knew well enough not to move too much, or to struggle, lest his descent be hastened by his actions. He breathed evenly and shallowly as Brett retrieved a strong branch from nearby. He leaned over extending the branch across the pit for Kye to hold onto. Next, Brett grabbed a second branch to assist pulling Kye out.

"You're not batting a thousand today, man," he said to Kye in a calming tone as he extended the branch to him. Kye did not speak, but upturned the corners of his mouth slightly in an appreciative grimace. He knew, as any trained person would, that his team could not simply pull him straight from the mixture. It was too heavy for that. Instead, he slowly leaned his weight forward in an effort to flatten himself out, as one does when swimming. He used the branch and a newfound hold on the firm edge of ground to slowly and steadily pull himself forward, maneuvering his legs closer to the surface as his angle became less than perpendicular, less than 45 degrees, then closer to 30. It was at this point that he nodded to Brett as the team pulled the branch forward as he held tightly, clawing the firm ground with his other hand and crawling his legs like a gecko until he was free from the pit. His heartbeat returned to normal as he righted himself. His pack was gone, a small price to pay to the jungle.

"That's two," Brett said as they moved out. Kye remained silent, but ran in last position. They reached the team shortly thereafter, who had resumed a double-time pace. Brett noticed first how tired they looked. Some were wheezing and clearly struggling to keep up. Almost all were limping. Brett was immediately struck by their lack of fitness. He wasn't used to civilians in this context and was secretly appalled. The group reached the river and saw the canyon side. The mineral vein was clear back several feet from the river's edge, but Lela had done an excellent job covering the entrance to the cavern. It was so well-concealed that, even in looking for it, Lela had to point out where it was specifically.

She pulled back the coverage and people began filing into the crevice. Brett and his team secured the area and covered their tracks around the trail and the riverside. Two men posted atop the cliff face hid as the first to take guard duty. The elevation provided excellent visibility, but the rocks hid them from approaching rebels.

Inside the cavern, the camp members were amazed at the sparkling beauty of the mineral-covered cavern. Mako smiled as he sat on his one plastic container, which he had elected to carry all the way from camp. Tina handed out provisions and began tending to minor wounds of the others. Moods were so elevated so quickly by having arrived that the noise level rose. Kye, who had entered the cavern to take a headcount, lost his count.

"Quiet, everyone!" he instructed, "They're not far behind us and we still need to maintain silence to stay safe." His words had their desired immediate, sobering effect and the group was silenced. Rachel managed to busy herself with a task in the vicinity of the young soldier.

"You look a mess," she commented, staring at the floor and removing water from the extra packs. She tried to look indifferent, but her voice betrayed her.

"I'm fine," he responded, with no inflection at all. She looked up at Kye, hopeful, searching his face for clues whether he was really in good health. She knew him well enough to realize something was off. He turned, gave her a quick wink, and exited. She smiled very subtly to herself. Lela noticed this exchange, but pretended she did not, since it was clearly intended to be an internal conversation. She strode outside to help gather brush, since she had already found some good sources. The cavern was covered except for the last few palm leaves and just enough space to crawl in.

"It really does look just as well-hidden as before," she commented as Brett walked up alone. Looking at the rock face, he agreed with her assessment. He stuck his head into the cavern and was stunned to not only see sunlight streaming in unexpectedly from the other side, but the remarkable way it spun the lavender mineral into an array of rebounding dots of light enveloping the locale. He suddenly felt they might really escape detection and be able to get out of this situation without a fight. He jumped back out, picked Lela up and spun her around.

"I can't believe you found this place!" he exclaimed genuinely.

"I know!" she replied enthusiastically.

"I can't believe you hid it from everyone," he added more seriously.

"I know," she conceded guiltily. After retreating into the cavern and replacing the coverings, the entire group, sans those on guard duty, crouched in silence in the cavern, awaiting the arrival of the rebel forces. Kye hoped to himself that his luck would hold, feeling as if he'd already used more than his fair share in one day. Rachel slept leaning against his shoulder. She awoke suddenly at the sound of voices shouting outside and clutched Kye's arm reflexively. Everyone remained still.

Chapter 18

The recruits had returned to the common area still shocked by the information that the Cupel had sat silently in the corner of their training room all along. Saraceni and Ruth stood in the training room, staring at the lightly glowing orb in contemplative silence for a full minute after they left.

"Aristotle's coma persists," Ruth acknowledged, "and he is not replaceable."

"I know," Saraceni affirmed. "Should we consider moving him to the main medical facility?"

"We may have to, but the loss of time would be great indeed. I fear it might endanger the mission either way," Ruth replied.

"He's your son- Do you fear for his life?"

"Of course, but the fate of us all rests in the mission. If it's the entire Dryan vs. my son, of course the decision is clear," she responded coolly. After a moment she reflected, "Though I hope it does not come to that." She walked to the window, weighing the variables before them.

"I've never seen the medical team struggle with something so basic as a coma before. Did he mention anything before he left for this lifecycle as Governor Jacob, anything off with his calibrations or his geodesics?" Saraceni queried.

"No," Ruth confirmed, "but I highly suspect it is the decoherence causing the problem, so that wouldn't have shown up that long ago. That's 42 years in The Cupel. Symptoms began recently." Ruth pulled up the master display and began double-checking the decoherence calculations from the last project team meeting. They were correct. It appeared they had slightly over two weeks remaining, which meant the mission should commence in one week. A decision had to be made.

"I have a strong feeling he'll emerge tomorrow. I dreamt it," Ruth advised. Saraceni nodded at the potential good news. Circle 20's were rarely inaccurate in their dream-visions, but where they were, it was attributed to being too close to the subject, so the fact that Aristotle was Ruth's son potentially corrupted her view.

"We'll give it until end of day tomorrow, and if he doesn't emerge, we will have to transport him to the main facility and continue the test runs without him to assess the impact. I just hope the biocentric release will still run with a lesser number of them," Ruth declared emphatically, returning to her usual demeanor. Saraceni nodded encouragingly, but looked down at the soft brown leather of his shoe. Repeated projective tests over the last year had demonstrated the release would not run without all 10 of Molior. They were selected, and some of the younger ones designed, just to provide the combination necessary. Any deviation would not execute the lock and key model they'd built to open it, he thought to himself. Since the outcome would not change, however, he did not share his thoughts with Ruth. She knew this already and she couldn't force George out of the coma, of course. They would just have to wait and see.

****

Back in the training room, the group looked at Kyle as if an alien had landed.

"It's still me, guys; I just didn't have my memory before. It's not like I intentionally deceived you. I didn't know myself." Kyle swiped his hair behind his ear, but his easy grin and carefree posture were gone. He seemed more intense, more measured, more thoughtful. As if he had aged overnight.

"Great, we started with a 16 year old who was like a 24 year old, and now we've got a 16 year old who's like 40." Juliet rolled her eyes and pressed her lips tightly together as she pulled on her red ponytail.

"More like a few hundred years old," Enam corrected. Kyle decided to be forthright, though he could have deflected.

"Our time is not the same as yours, I mean --as in The Cupel. So, more like aeons," Kyle confided.

"How long's an aeon again?" Jack quipped.

"Old as dirt," Chandra said, her Atlanta drawl rolling the southern phrase off her tongue like notes from an instrument.

"So, you were alive when the Earth, I mean The Cupel, was created?" Gabriel asked Kyle directly.

"Yes. George and I were on the original project teams that created the quantum computer and programmed the Cupel," Kyle explained. He sat alone in a chair as the others sat on the two semicircular sofas to his left and right. The sofas were white. His chair was black. The sofas were soft, luxurious fabric. Kyle's chair was hard wood. The room had a feeling of a trial, and the irony of that was not lost on the very old young man. "Well, it appears we have some time," Juliet launched, "Why don't you tell us how the project began? " The others turned to Kyle expectantly.

"Like Ruth explained, our civilization had nearly destroyed itself. We'd come back from it and entered an enlightened era. The moral degradation and criminality that nearly led to our destruction led to a penal colony. We placed the disruptive thinkers there and prevented them from breeding through painless, chemical sterilization. Within a generation they would all be gone, or so we thought."

"How did you choose the people to go there? Was it based on them committing a crime?" Chandra asked.

"Initially, yes," Kyle confirmed, "but later we developed the soul map testing and realized we could sort out those who carried the DNA for disruption, and sent them, too,"

"Sounds unconstitutional," Jane said.

"Sounds evil," Chandra added.

"We don't have the constitution here," Kyle began slowly," our body of law is founded on a set of principles around egalitarianism, but not so much a focus on individual freedom as the U.S. Constitution, though that is one school of thought here."

"So it's more like communism? Pure communism, I mean, though, not Marxism?" Jane's anthropological brain dug to understand this new society within which she found herself.

"It's just totally different. It doesn't really translate. If you combined all the political systems you know, you would get the result. You are asking me to determine which is more important- the note, the musician, the composition, or the instruments? The symphony is the goal so asking to choose between these things is an impossibility."

"But you did," Juliet added, "choose, I mean. You chose to get rid of the so-called disruptive thinkers."

"Yes, and we've enjoyed over a millennium of peace, prosperity and growth because of the choices we made," Kyle defended.

"So peace trumps someone's right to live?" she retorted, escalating in volume. Kyle's tone remained more even.

"Juliet, we did not kill them. We quarantined them and prevented them from reproducing further. Most lived out a perfectly normal life."

"If they were capable of living out a normal life, then why did they have to be quarantined? "

"It was the only way to be sure. You're talking about people with a strong tendency to violence- upheaval. We're talking murder, rape, bombings, making children live in a warzone, intentionally releasing disease and biotoxins- we're talking evil stuff here."

"Right, but you didn't know for sure all those people would behave like that. You chose them based on a predisposition, and that is what I disagree with!"

"C'mon Juliet," Gabriel interceded. She looked at him in surprise, "Are you really saying if we could ensure peace for a millennium by quarantining a few hundred thousand, you wouldn't do it?" Gabriel pressed further, "Think of all the suffering, the millions that die in that space of time and the cruelty endured. If you could erase all that for one generation, you wouldn't do it?" His gaze penetrated hers as if they were siblings. She squinted, considering, then remained silent.

"I know it's difficult. It was for us, too, but it's long since done and I do think it yielded more good than bad," Kyle concluded.

"So no people with the "disruptive thought patterns" still exist?" Mr. Aquila asked.

"Not here." Kyle answered. Gabriel noticed the measured response and, learning from the communication style used by Saraceni and Ruth, decided his next question.

"Then where are they?" he intensely threw the question at Kyle.

"Well, some escaped into The Cupel, after we constructed it, but I'm jumping ahead," he responded.

"Well, get there soon, okay?" Gabriel directed. Jack was walking around the room. Enam got a drink from the wet bar area. Jane Grey Windsor settled for some tea and sat next to Chandra on the sofa, handing her a teacup. She accepted it in picture-perfect finishing school style that would have made her mother proud. She tapped her long fingernail against the delicate saucer, creating a gentle dinging noise each time she did.

"Okay," Kyle continued, "so, while the DTs were all rounded up, our council of elders ruled on a proposal and it was decided that we should take great care not to disrupt our newly-achieved balance. If anything upsets that balance, the system will get out of equilibrium. Some were concerned, however, myself included, that we might implode from the inside societally if we had no avenues for growth, creativity, or expansion. So, we realized we needed a way to test any new ideas and make sure they could be introduced into the system in a way that didn't disrupt the equilibrium. We needed a test environment."

"And the petri dish that was our lives was born," Juliet chimed in.

"Yes, souls were no longer allowed to pass directly into fetuses without screening, implantation, and calibration, so we could control the processes and make sure only the best of the souls were used," Kyle added.

"That's playing God," Chandra reaffirmed her earlier position.

"Chandra," David Running Wolf was the one to jump in this time. Kyle was grateful. He and Gabriel were expected to be the early adopters and, so far, they were proving that to be true. "Is it playing God to screen aging mothers for the genes related to Down's Syndrome, Tay Sachs, Sickle Cell, any of the other diseases we can see the genes for? If we can see them, know they will be bad, and have the ability to control it, why not?" he inquired.

"I guess I'm just more comfortable with the clarity that those genes create those diseases. It's proven. Screening for these soul-genes or whatever they're called sounds more like moral judgment to me," Juliet responded.

"I know it can seem that way, when you haven't fully seen or learned our technology, but it has been just as clearly proven that some of the dark matter DNA in the soul is just as disruptive, just as much a clear clinical anomaly, and the outcomes just as far off of normal and healthy. Have we been wrong so far?" Kyle continued.

"How would we know?" Chandra defended, "Everything has been so secretive, and now you want us to trust you."

"It wasn't secretive because we were deceiving you. It was secretive because it had to be. We've perfected the assimilation process over a millennia. Can you imagine if we brought you in here the first day and told you all of this? Your minds would be so closed to it and then twice as defensive to learning the new information. We've done it. It ends up taking twice as long. Besides, there could be no errors with your class."

"Why? What makes us so special?" Enam asked.

"We have a special purpose. I can't advise on that. It must come from Saraceni or Ruth." Several of the recruits shifted uncomfortably. Juliet was really pulling and twirling at her ponytail by this point.

"More secrets! You're telling us to trust you and dishing us more secrets in the same breath. That's it! I've had enough," Juliet snapped. She rose and threw a water bottle across the room. She pressed against the door, which was locked and then began kicking with all her force against the windows, leaving size 7 footprints on the clear surface.

"Juliet, c'mon!" Gabriel tried to reason with her. She really let loose and started kicking twice as hard, with an occasional pounding of her fist. Running Wolf moved closer as if he might grab her from around the waist and restrain her, and he glanced sideways at Gabriel as if seeking permission. Gabriel shook his head, took one step back, and flung both of his hands away from his body emphatically.

"Just let her go," he said more quietly. Everyone watched as she continued her tirade against the imprisoning walls. After two minutes or so, she fell onto her hands and knees and stared at the floor. Wood had seen this on the monitor and came flying into the room. Juliet did not sob, she just stared at the floor in complete silence, devoid of all energy or even mental capacity to absorb more. She just wanted to go home, back to her ranch with wide open skies and mountain views. She had a brief image of riding her horse across the plain, wind flying through her hair. Suddenly, she had an image of her horse now, smaller than the size of a cell and her shouting after him "Run, Oskadis , Run!" and she started to giggle. Escalating slowly at first and then exponentially, her giggle grew to a full laugh and then hysterics as she began laughing uncontrollably. Wood knelt next to her body, still on all fours, on the ground, but did not touch her.

"That girl's done lost her mind!" Chandra exclaimed. This struck Juliet even funnier, that out of everyone's mostly calm, cool reactions over the last weeks that she should somehow be the crazy one for reacting normally. What kind of genetic freaks were these people? It struck her so funny she now rolled onto her back and started howling with laughter, pointing at them-

"Genetic freaks!" she said, pointing and laughing, "Oh, Dr. Frankenstein, I wonder how a quantum computer is built. Oh it's simple, I just attach these jumper cables to your neck and pow!" she roared. It should've been funny. On any other day, it would have been. They'd have all joined in the fun. Not today. Kyle then spoke to Stone as two parents discuss a child as if she isn't even there.

"I think I'll have to call Saraceni out of the project meeting," Kyle said to Wood. Wood was assessing the situation when Juliet sat up, slowly reigning in her laughter, and responded amidst slowing giggles,

"Oh, calm down, Poppy. I'm fine. They can stay in their precious project meeting." She looked at Wood to back her up and leaned toward him slightly. His training had replaced his feelings and he assessed her with the discipline with which he was trained.

"She's fine," he said to Kyle, helping her up of the floor. The rest of Molior relaxed slightly- Jack's shoulders, David's jaw, Gabriel's fists, all relaxed. Jane stopped biting her lip. Juliet returned to a chair and tried to speak very authoritatively, directly to Kyle,

"Yes, and then what happened, Frankenstein? Continue!" she said very seriously, knitting her brow as if concentrating immensely, and then she giggled again. Gabriel rolled his eyes for lack of any other reaction, but then she sat quietly awaiting a response. As if stepping onto a frozen lake to test his weight on it, Kyle began,

"Well, we decided to build the quantum computer, an exact replica of our universe within it, and to create a series of tests for the souls there, so they could go through a gauntlet of trials preparing them to be worthy of being selected to come here."

"Because here is so great!" Juliet, motioning grandly at the room, roared without a hint of sarcasm, and broke out in a brief laugh. She was clearly just entertaining herself at this point, but they were happy she wasn't acting out.

"I always read that a quantum computer copy would be an exact match-size, shape, everything, how can it be a copy but not the same size?" Mr. Aquila asked. Juliet was genuinely interested in the answer and listened attentively.

"You were to the point of learning in The Cupel where we thought that was true, originally, but we eventually learned there are some ways around that rule that allow scale to be manipulated without interfering with the integrity of the environment," he continued.

"It's not an exact match, though, anyway. You said you created tests, and it's clearly not the same as here," Jack reflected.

"Right," Kyle paused, collecting his thoughts, "Right, that's where I was headed. So, we deliberately broke the system up into seven sub-pieces. Seven cultures, separate languages, separate religions, so we could execute some discreet testing but also to test the ability of the subjects to vertically and horizontally integrate information," he said.

"Like Ruth mentioned," Gabriel confirmed.

"Yes, she was mentioning how the goal is to process information. Well, to learn how to process information, you have to have a wide array of it to process," he said.

"It's like those block puzzles for babies," Jack deduced," First, you have to spread the blocks out all over the floor, far apart. Sure, you could just give 'em to the kid, or put them close together, but what would he learn then, right?"

"Good analogy." Kyle praised the man who towered over him. Juliet looked at Wood.

"Were you there? For this grand spreading out of the blocks, the breaking up of the totality of knowledge so us simpletons could evolve?" she grilled.

"No. I was born in The Cupel and moved through my lives there until I came here, just like you," he replied, suddenly conscious of how much he wanted her trust and respect. "Just a few circles earlier, that's all," he added.

"What's a circle?" Gabriel queried.

"Like Ruth mentioned earlier about the expansion and contraction of the universe. The time it takes for one occurrence of the universe expanding from a point to apogee where it's fully expanded and then back to a point again is called one circle. We also use the term to reflect levels of progression."

"There or here? Whose revolution time determines how long the circle is- I'm assuming they're not the same length of time since you said before some years here is an aeon there?" Gabriel dug for deeper understanding.

"Um, both," Wood responded reflexively, surprised by the question. It wasn't really his role to teach, but nothing about this class had gone exactly as planned, or as needed, so he didn't see the point in maintaining the false distinction now. "Each has their own respective cycle. Like a day on the earth, vs. a day on Mars, vs. a day on Saturn. They are all different lengths of time, but they all represent one revolution around the Sun for that entity and they are all called a 'day'."

"So when it shifts to a new circle, is it just like going to sleep on New Year's or does something actually happen, like the world burns in fire each time or something?" Juliet asked.

"Nothing like that, but it is spectacular. It's just like a gate that opens up to the next circle, and everything resets, and all the collective information from the prior circle is downloaded."

"Wood!" Kyle boomed in a reprimanding tone.

"Kyle, they'd get this tomorrow anyway."

"You don't know that," Kyle retorted.

"Well, I do know they need to sleep, and they need some answers in order to do that, or have you forgotten what it's like to be human already?" Wood responded.

"May I remind you that you are a circle 2 and I do still outrank you. Quite considerably, in fact," Kyle chided.

"Yes, sir," Wood checked himself. Circle 2's always had trouble forgetting the face in front of them and remembering the soul behind it. At this level, they weren't able to read souls by sight yet, so it required a constant inner reminder to stay in check. Then Kyle surprised Wood, by continuing the explanation he began. In a tone that acknowledged that Wood was right, Kyle explained.

"So, the gate opens, the information collected downloads to the master plan, and everyone gets promoted to the next circle," Kyle continued.

"Wait, I'm confused- here or there?" Jane asked.

"Both. So you guys are called circle 1's, it's your first revolution," Kyle explained.

"Wait, but I thought we did a whole bunch of lives in The Cupel- how can I only be a circle 1 if I already did a bunch of circles there according to what Saraceni said?" Juliet asked.

"You're a circle one *here*. You were some other circle in The Cupel. I don't know them, I'm afraid," Kyle said.

"I had observation duty for this class. She was a circle 28 in The Cupel," Wood reported. Juliet crossed her arms uncomfortably at the thought that Wood had been observing her and the others for months, or years, and Wood looked down.

"What was I?" asked Running Wolf.

"You were circle 30," Wood answered.

"And me? " Gabriel asked.

"I can see where this is going. Gabriel, you were a 33, Jane a 26, Alexander a 32, Enam a 32, Chandra-". He stopped abruptly realizing where he'd just led.

"What am I?" Chandra asked. Wood paused and looked at Kyle.

"Well, you can't not tell them now." Kyle said.

Stone resumed, "Chandra, you're an 8, and Jack you're a 19." The team appeared confused.

Juliet replied: "Why did they get to come so much earlier? We had to do all these lifetimes we don't remember."

"There are many reasons someone might be brought early," Wood attempted evading as he had seen Saraceni do many times. The recruits were wise to this move, though, and Wood learned why teaching assignments aren't given out for many, many circles.

"Yes, but why were they specifically brought early?" Gabriel pressed. Wood opened his mouth as if to speak, but Kyle abruptly cut him off.

"They were needed. And that's all we are permitted to say. Ruth and Saraceni will discuss this very soon, but we may not." Kyle looked pointedly at Wood to reinforce his words. Wood remained silent.

"It's the DNA matches, it's got to be!" Running Wolf said to his fellow recruits.

"Hey Dad, I'm older than you!" Gabriel broke his first smile of the day and put his arm around his father's shoulder.

"And I'm the same age as you, Alexander!" Enam added.

"Actually, Enam, you and Alexander are the same number of circles because you were brothers originally. In your first life, I mean. You've been tied together in many of them," Wood advised.

"Is that common?" Jack asked. A gnawing feeling had been building within him and this just might explain it.

"Actually, yes," Kyle continued, "To some extent it's a natural occurrence. There's a certain natural binding between some souls, like electron pairs, but we also learned to engineer that, so we will attach souls together if it suits the greater learning, or once we know you are being recruited. It helps to come here having formed workgroups already, to know how to work in established teams. It's like the difference between a military unit that is freshly recruited and one that's been together for three years. You operate better; You can read each other. It's an advantage we cannot afford to forfeit." Kyle expounded so matter-of-factly regarding the manipulation of their lives and souls that some of the recruits, Chandra in particular, were disturbed by it.

"Can we tell?" Jack continued, "I mean, can we feel the difference if it's someone we've known before vs. not, natural vs. engineered?"

"Most people can. In The Cupel, only some can, though most everyone there can recognize their binary soul match. Here pretty much everyone can." Kyle responded.

"Binary soul match? Is that like your detached way of saying a soul mate?" Jane queried.

"That's a primitive view. The scientific relationship between the souls is much more complicated than that, but for ease of understanding, yes." Kyle affirmed. Wood looked at Juliet, who registered and looked back at him, then casually stepped away slowly.

"I should check on George," Wood said flatly and left the room.

"Typical guy," Chandra muttered under her breath.

"So, we live all these lives learning all these lessons you have preselected for us, gathering this collective intelligence that who uses for what we don't know, but why all the cloak and dagger? Why the monitoring of us, our families- do you monitor everyone?"

"We monitor those with promise. We monitor your families because they are tied to you and, as such, have been assigned as a future workgroup member. They will be recruited," Kyle responded. His plain tone was really grating on Chandra.

"When?" asked Gabriel. He thought of Lela, Gretchen and Caleb.

"When they are ready. When they have completed their missions within the Cupel. When they are needed here, or, sometimes, if it's otherwise necessary. " Kyle responded.

"Otherwise necessary?" For what?" Gabriel asked

"Their protection." Kyle conceded.

Chapter 19

Molior assembled the next day, hoping to hear news of George and from the project briefing. They finally knew they were brought here for some very specific reasons and were eager to learn more- their fates, the fates of those they left behind, in particular. Ruth and Saraceni stood outside the door.

"I issued the collection order on George's adjuvant as you instructed," Saraceni reported to Ruth. She nodded briefly, still seemingly distracted by thoughts of George's health. Her laser focus was what made Ruth, so Saraceni knew without it that she was less at ease than she was letting on.

"If he's not up to par, the adjuvant may provide the extra boost to allow the mission to be completed," she confirmed. "If we're lucky."

"Theoretically based on the other missions where we've used adjuvants as a booster, it should work." Saraceni actually thought about patting her shoulder as he would with any other colleague in this situation, but withdrew his hand without detection, deciding better of it.

"When will she arrive?" Ruth asked.

"I just put in the order for her collection, but obviously the highest priority. Clara herself is doing it. There's no way to tell whether it's today or tomorrow though." He paused and then added reflectively, "If it's tomorrow it should be in the earlier part of the morning, however."

"If George simply doesn't wake up today, and we have to ship him to core medical, we could always try it with her in his place. It would be better than the otherwise gaping hole he will leave in the mission team. God, I wish we could just put an experienced operator in there." Ruth grinded her teeth a bit as she spoke.

"I know, but if we could've done that, we wouldn't have recruited about half this team at all yet. They have the Pheres configuration in their soul maps. No substitute," he concluded as they walked into the room. The recruits did not scramble to their seats as they usually did, but instead merely shifted their attention to Saraceni and Ruth. Juliet looked calm, almost placid, as if the outburst had done her good.

'Perhaps they all should try it' Stone mused to himself, thinking if they could just get past this part and focused on the mission, everything would pull together. He'd worked many missions in his last years of Circle 2 training where things needed to gel just right in order to be effective. Monitoring in The Cupel showed that, too- it was all about timing. People would wait and wait for a breakthrough, frustrated because they are unable to force things forward, and then suddenly the breakthrough would come. Not always without assistance, he knew, but sometimes.

"How's George?" Enam broke the silence.

"The same," Saraceni confirmed. He looked at Ruth who again displayed the briefest flicker of a distant look in her deep blue eyes, so he added, "but we have reason to hope he may wake up today." The recruits nodded in assent, welcoming what seemed like promising news. Thirty seconds of quasi-optimistic calm spread over the group, the gentle glow of the orb pulsating in rhythmic waves.

Suddenly, Wood raced into the room, knocking over a stool at the lab counter on the way. He was flicking all the monitors on as fast as he could, one after another, until every display was lit up. He tried to show formal courtesy to Ruth by looking at her, but interrupted with bursts of attention toward the monitors, this looked odd.

"Ma'am, they are after the adjuvant!" he shouted.

"How do they know?" Saraceni asked.

"They intercepted our communication to Clara," he reported. "I don't know how."

Ruth knew the answer. She turned to Saraceni, "The decoherence. It must be compromising the encryption." Next she turned her attention to the monitors.

"How long?" she asked.

"Five minutes, maybe ten," Wood added. For the first time since his assignment had been split from Wood, Stone felt a pang of regret that he'd not been monitoring with him.

"Okay, I see Clara. She's already en route." She punched a few buttons and the screen magnified. A small girl of four years old was reading with a flashlight in her bed. Her mother was asleep in another room. Ruth pulled up a side-by-side view of the house layout next to the video. The girl's room was at the front right corner of the house, and the mother's room was at the back left corner of the house. On the video, an apparent burglar lurked outside her window, while a second worked near the power grid for the house.

"There they are. Damn, how'd their agents get there so fast?" Ruth muttered. She pulled up the implantation program and focused it on the tiny girl.

Phoebe Jacob was quietly reading "Geraldine Belinda", a book her father had left her. She quietly whispered the words to herself as she read, not yet having mastered the art of reading silently. She was, after all, four years old.

"Her pigtails danced," the small high voice whispered and Phoebe looked at the accompanying picture of Geraldine's pigtails dancing in the air when she was instantly filled with dread. Inexplicably, the worst feeling she had ever known came over her and she was terrified. For a moment, she was so scared, she couldn't even move. Ruth adjusted the controls downward slightly and typed some instructions into the command. Phoebe then had the idea she should turn off her flashlight. She did so, and slid out of bed and onto the floor. Her very first thought, her own, was to run to her mother's room, but she suddenly had the idea she wouldn't make it that far. Next she considered climbing under the bed, but knew that would be the first place they would look. She finally crawled as quietly as she could to her closet and opened it as slowly and quietly as she could. The burglar was now peering in her window, but he did not see the door close slowly as it was nestled against the corner most in his peripheral vision.

"How far is Clara? His guys are getting close." Ruth shouted.

"Two minutes, maybe three still," Saraceni responded, having taken up residence at the opposing bank of monitors, following the project architect as she raced to the scene.

"Thank God we sent the master soulweaver," Saraceni confirmed, "can you imagine if that assignment had gone to someone else? They'd never make it."

"She'll make it," Ruth muttered desperately, but her tone was less certain, "She has to."

"What's going on?" Juliet asked.

"No time," Saraceni answered, "just wait."

"Kyle, Stone, feel free to narrate but just don't interrupt," Ruth added, punching more buttons, changing the view on the display to the closet interior. Phoebe was there, breathing very fast and louder than she wanted, but she didn't know how to keep herself quiet. She wanted to cry, but restrained, knowing this would not help. She thought if she stayed as quiet as possible, maybe they wouldn't find her. The girl wriggled her small frame behind some of the hanging clothes, pulling an old bathrobe over herself for concealment.

Outside, the other emissary snipped the wires to the alarm system. True, it would trip an indicator at the alarm company, but the delay in time was all they needed to grab the girl. He nodded to the second man in black who then cut the window glass with a circular cutter and flipped the window lock as simply as a light switch. 'Not even cube locks' he thought to himself, amazed at the stupidity of these people in the suburbs. He knew who the family was, had read about them in the paper, and marveled at how it had never occurred to him before that day to nab the girl and hold her for ransom. 'Easy money' he thought. A career criminal, he frequently felt compelled to commit various crimes, some so violent he tried to forget them afterwards. His gloved hand slowly slid open the window.

"These are assignees of the dark forces." Kyle whispered, "They don't even know it wasn't their idea, not really."

"Why do they want her?" Juliet asked, concerned. Jane held her hand over her mouth as she watched the screen.

"We have to help her!" Jane squeaked.

"We are. We have our top architect on the way. THE master weaver. She's almost there, see Saraceni's screen." He explained, "They want her because we need her and they found out about it."

"Is she one of you returned?" Gabriel asked, assuming this small girl was a friend of theirs.

"No, she was to be a recruit, later on in this life, but now we had to issue a collection order for her, because of George," Kyle answered hurriedly. The masked man climbed in the window and snatched back the covers to the bed that Phoebe had left in a rumpled mess when she gently slid out from beneath them. The bed was empty. He dropped to his knees and looked under the bed. The second man appeared at the window, standing just outside waiting to be handed the girl. The first man looked at him and shook his head. Gabriel's monitor showed a ball of light racing to the location. It turned down the main street of the young girl's town.

"Why does she need to be collected- because of George?" Juliet asked Stone as they watched.

"She was his daughter, in The Cupel I mean, a complementary soul who we engineered into the daughter placement to further her learning. But he had to come back early, and now she'll have to be recruited early, too," Stone whispered to the recruits, who had moved to be almost huddled together.

"Phoebe Jacob," Gabriel said loud enough for all to hear. "She was there with the Governor, I mean, George, at the Africa project kickoff." The group was silenced as the intruder finished looking in the attached bathroom and made his way toward the closet. He took one step and heard a creek on the hardwood floor in the hall. He stopped in his tracks on the carpeted floor of Phoebe's room. He heard another creek. He withdrew a gun and stared intently at the doorway. Jingles, the cat, appeared and hissed at the man. He closed the door silently and continued toward the closet. He opened it swiftly and saw nothing, but the involuntary draw of breath that Phoebe took was audible. She then remained silent, trying to trick him into thinking she wasn't there. His eyes adjusted and he could tell where the silhouetted shape of the girl stood behind the bathrobe. He leaned in, knowing if he was fast enough, he could cover her mouth before she could scream. Tears began to stream down Phoebe's tiny face, but she did not cry out loud. She didn't think she could scream if she wanted to, but she had no time to find out. The man descended on her like a falcon, pressing his hand against her mouth, the bathrobe in between, in one swift motion.

As he dragged her out of the closet, her arms and legs flailed about, but were too short to really reach him or do any damage. Jingles the cat started meowing an eerie meow on the other side of the closed door, like a banshee call. In 5 seconds, he was handing the girl off to the man outside the window. The streak of light on Saraceni's monitor turned down the street toward the Governor's mansion, where Phoebe and her mother still lived until a permanent replacement would be named. The man ran across the lawn with the little girl still kicking and flailing, but he had her firmly in his grasp. As the second man exited the window and moved to catch up with him, a dark figure appeared by the truck in Saraceni's monitor.

"What the hell is that?!?" Running Wolf exclaimed.

"Dark Janae," Kyle answered, riveted on the screen. The ball of light appeared and passing right over the men and the little girl, the kicking and flailing suddenly stopped. Phoebe's body went limp. The dark shadow figure retreated and the first man put Phoebe's body in the truck and they both hopped in, crouched down out of sight.

"What did you do- suffocate her?" the first man barked.

"No, I didn't, I mean," the second man stuttered as he removed the tangled robe from Phoebe's body to get a look at her, "She must've passed out or something." They examined her body. It was lifeless.

"I swear. She was breathing. She must've had a heart attack or something." The man felt a pang of guilt. This wasn't even his type of job. He wasn't sure why he even accepted it when it was changed from the originally-planned robbery, and now he really felt badly about it.

"Whatever, we were going to kill her anyway," the other man responded without any hint of inflection in his voice, "let's dump the body before dawn and then we can hit the Mom up for the ransom money." Saraceni shut off the monitor.

"What happened?" Jane cried out. "That poor little girl! To die so horribly! She was terrified!"

"She won't remember it," Stone reassured her, "We won't download that portion of her memory."

"So we got her, that light-thing, it's bringing her here?" Juliet asked.

"Sending her here," Kyle corrected, "but yeah. We got her." They breathed a collective sigh of relief. These dramatic outbursts were becoming more common. Wasn't this supposed to be this peaceful, enlightened place? It didn't feel like it. Ruth turned off the monitors and pushed herself back, pausing a full moment in silence before turning to the recruits.

"That was Clara," she explained, "She is one of our three master weavers. No one else but her could've pulled that off. We are so lucky Phoebe is out of peril."

"Is she human?" Chandra asked.

"Phoebe? Of course!" Ruth answered.

"No, the other one. The light-thing, Clara? Is she an angel?" Chandra pursued.

"No, not an angel, but she's not human right now. She is just her soul, her energy alone, no body. We have an order of architects who can work in The Cupel without bodies due to their experience. The rest of our people need bodies when we are there, same as anyone," Ruth explained.

"So, you have people that are there that are from here, going through to learn, and then you have these souls without bodies- do they all just impose their will on everyone else?" Chandra seemed concerned. Saraceni intervened.

"Chandra, there are three levels of our beings in The Cupel, and then the people that are first born there. We have people who have returned to reset, who usually have a higher task and purpose, though it is not known to them because they don't have overt memory from here, then we have the order of the Janae, who may visit in pure soul form and actually weave and shape outcomes there. From here we can only influence, not actually weave. Lastly, we have the order of Kajika." Saraceni explained.

"Walks without sound," Enam translated the phrase. Saraceni turned toward him.

"Yes. The Kajika are given human bodies and live lives among the people in The Cupel, but they are not there for resetting and they retain their full memory. They help guide in a more overt way, as friends, coworkers, messengers," Saraceni continued.

"So George wasn't one of those Kajika because he didn't remember who he was, what his assignment was?" Chandra sought to clarify.

"Yes. George was there to be reset. After a certain number of lives here, we are required to complete one cycle in The Cupel. It serves to cleanse our souls of certain buildups and reset our ability to upload the collected information at the end of a cycle here," Saraceni explained.

"So every so often we have to go there and not know who we really are in order to keep our souls functioning properly." Kyle added.

"Shouldn't our souls work in a way that they don't need to be forcibly reset?" Juliet said skeptically.

"And so they did," Ruth clarified, "before The Cupel, but introducing that quantum subsystem introduced some additional complexities here, and that's one of them. It is worth the tradeoff, I assure you." Juliet said nothing further, but she wasn't so sure. The Cupel sounded like a huge compromise to this world, the real Earth, and as far as she could see, the arguments against it were as strong as those for it.

"So these Kajika, if they know they are there for a reason, do we ever know it or are they always in stealth mode?" Jack asked.

"They are often quiet, unobtrusive individuals who go unnoticed. Occasionally their assignment is to directly teach," Saraceni answered.

"For example?" Gabriel prodded.

"For example, Ghandi, Kant, DaVinci," Kyle relayed proudly. Saraceni provided a slight warning look to proceed no further. Though accurate, these were not the examples he would have chosen.

"And the reset ones, they have missions and don't know it, how do they ever succeed?" Jane asked.

"Each person's soul guides them. We are preprogrammed. We don't need a lot of guidance and cajoling to reach our destiny, just a clear path. If a soul has a particular talent, it will materialize over and over again, out of their very DNA. We help steer with our monitoring and influencing techniques, or the occasional assignment of a Kajika or Janae in very critical times, as you saw today, but you are speaking of less than one hundredth of one percent of all forward motion." Saraceni answered.

"Like who, give me an example of that kind." Juliet pressed.

"Galileo and Tesla, same person- reset through different lifetimes," Gabriel turned to Stone.

"I thought you said that dark shadow after Phoebe was called a Janae? If Janae are people's souls without bodies from here, why was it trying to harm her?" Saraceni jumped in, resuming his finesses for teaching which far outweighed the explanations Kyle and Stone had been trying to distribute.

"There are Dark Janae and Light Janae," Saraceni began, " The Light Janae are from our teams, for the most part, except for a few we see occasionally that seem to have no known origin."

"They're just there, but no one knows why?" Gabriel pursued

"Yes, but they are always helpful, so we do not mind or question their presence, but welcome it." Saraceni responded.

"And the dark? Who sent them? And why didn't they just go into Phoebe's room to get her?" David Running Wolf had an eerie feeling even just asking the question. He had seen things like the shadow on the monitor in his dream-state and with his grandfather, a Shaman, as a boy. He once walked into a room where a baby had died and knew that it had just been there. Just seeing it again made the hair on his neck and arms stand up.

"We had protected that residence- they could not enter directly, so manipulated the men to achieve their end. As to who controls them, some are independent, so to speak. As you've seen from your soul maps, each soul is born with certain proclivities. Well, souls with a disproportionate amount of dark matter DNA are, by their very nature, driven to deconstruct rather than construct. Some of them don't even know why they do it. Those are exactly the sort who became disruptive thinkers in our world and brought us to the edge of destruction." Saraceni paused, taking a sip of water. He noticed how tired the group looked. They would need to begin mission training very soon and he had a fleeting thought of failure in looking at them before he continued. "Most of them, however, are aligned with a group with no name. We call their group collectively the Duister, and they are led by a man named Valswak. They have the same levels of operators as us- their Dark Janae operating without bodies, agents on the ground with memory and bodies, and then agents in bodies with no memory, but missions to destroy. They intercede into the system, marrying others only to destroy the family, starting unnecessary wars, leading others astray, committing abuses on children. Some are afflicted to a lesser extent and merely seek to undo what we have done, but they don't hurt others proactively. They just lack any faith, or drive to serve the greater good, which is present in most people. They operate solely for themselves."

"Their leader, why does he do it?" Juliet asked.

"Some would argue because he must, but I don't believe that. I believe his choices led him to where he is now," Saraceni responded.

"You know him," Gabriel surmised. This was not a question.

"Yes. He was one of us, our friend and comrade," Saraceni reported.

"What happened?" Gabriel asked.

"He never really agreed with The Cupel in the first place. He argued against it, but in the vote he lost, so he participated in the project teams on the original creation. He is a brilliant scientist and programmer. When we started having problem with The Cupel and realized we each had to do a cycle there to reset, he was furious. He said we were playing with fire and he knew we never should have built The Cupel."

Juliet looked at the floor, exactly what she'd been thinking.

"But we had to go. The consequences here are dire if we don't so he went. The problem was, when it was time for him to return here, he did not pass the minimum standards test to return, so he was brought to this holding area and advised he would have to do another cycle in The Cupel in order to return. He became furious and refused to go," Saraceni continued.

"Wait, I thought for those of you here originally, you had screened for disruptive thinkers in the first place. How was he let in originally and then not back through?" Jack wondered.

"His choices. He made some questionable choices in his lifetime in the Cupel and tested at a level of morality below acceptable here by a small fraction. He barely passed the disruptive thinker test initially, but he did. And we all knew his level of brilliance came with a bit of eccentricity. He was our friend, so barely passing was still passing as far as we were concerned and we thought nothing further of it."

Ruth interrupted, "In retrospect, had we been more advanced then, we would have put him on restricted duty and area assignment until he further proved himself, until we were sure."

"Like quarantine," Jack absorbed.

"Yes, that is why new recruits are separated for a time. Privileges must be earned, not freely given, plus you do need time to calibrate," she responded.

"So, he refused to go back, then what?" Enam prompted, eager to get back to the story.

"After about a week here, he began to degrade physically without recalibration. Our council met and decided we would put his soul back into The Cupel, but provide him his own team of Kajika to guide him, and 24 hour a day monitoring. No one else had ever not been cleared to return," Saraceni added.

Kyle interrupted, "or has since."

"Or has since," Saraceni agreed, "So, we knew we had to do all in our power to make sure to bring him home again. So, we reinserted him."

"Little did we know, while he was here, he used the equipment and freed himself from all monitoring or guidance while in The Cupel, and made himself retain his memory, as if Kajika, when he was really a reset. So after he returned, we were unable to help him. He thought he could complete it himself, but he couldn't. He viewed our reinserting him as a betrayal, as if we were not his friends. He thought the fact he only missed the test by a small margin that friends should allow a small margin of error."

"Was he above the level of Chandra, or Jack, or Phoebe?" Juliet asked .

" What?" Saraceni stepped back, off guard by the bluntness of her question.

"Was his test less than theirs? You've made exceptions in emergent times for some people to come here before they were really ready. Could you have done the same for him?" she asked. Everyone looked at her as if she were arguing pro-Hitler and she reacted.

"I'm not saying I agree with the guy, I just want to know if he had a point. You can't fight an enemy you don't understand," she clarified.

"No," Saraceni answered slowly, "his test was not less than theirs. By today's standards for emergency situations only, he would have passed."

"Those standards didn't exist at the time," Kyle defended, "we only relaxed them when it became a matter of life and death for everyone in both systems."

"Right. When it was important to you, you made an exception, but when it was important to him, you did not," Juliet concluded.

"It's not so easy, Juliet," Ruth leaned in, sitting right next to the woman, "The test picked up proclivities in him that are dangerous here. We will loosen standards on ability, or insight, but not on morality, that one is not flexible, and for good reason."

"Which did play out; He came close the first few times, but with each cycle he became more and more bitter and farther and farther from passing. Now he is so opposite of what he once was. He decided if he couldn't be here, he would prove all the errors in The Cupel that he claimed from the beginning: Ding all the chinks in the armor, pull at all the loose threads, just to prove he was right. He dedicates his time solely to being destructive, destroying the environment and recruiting others to do the same."

"But you made him like that! You had someone who was basically good, but a little conflicted, and instead of helping him, you kicked him aside and let him slide into being wholly evil and self-loathing," Juliet accused.

"We didn't! We were going to help him! He just cut all ties to our help and then chastised us for his decision."

"Because he didn't think he could trust you. I wouldn't go in there with ties on me in that situation," Juliet added.

"Juliet-" Gabriel gently grabbed her arm in brotherly fashion, "If you were going to die unless you reentered The Cupel, you're saying you wouldn't trust us to monitor and guide you, if that's what was needed?" He motioned to the rest of Molior.

"Or me?" Wood added, bolstering the argument. Juliet stood in pensive contemplation, on the edge of her answers. Ruth made a note on a chart and knitted her brow slightly.

"Well, if it was you guys," Juliet peeled back each word one at a time, "but, I haven't had a reason to mistrust you guys. If you had ignored me, or not listened to me, or if it were them instead," she motioned to Stone and Saraceni, "I can't say for sure."

"Hindsight is perfect, "Saraceni concluded, "and I personally will wonder until the end of time if I had handled it differently if things might have been different, but it is moot now. He is so far beyond redemption there is no hope for him now."

Chandra was vexed by this, "Aren't we all allowed redemption? Isn't there always a chance- no matter what?" she asked.

"Alexander!" Saraceni prompted, jolting Alexander Aquila to attention from the intent listener he had been, "Does energy always have potential?" Alexander thought for a moment.

"Well, conservation of energy says it is always preserved, but that doesn't mean it is potential energy in every case."

"Right," Saraceni was a bit more forceful than usual, "and when dark energy becomes too destructive, where its destructive potential is hundreds of times greater than any constructive use, that dark energy is just cast out into the universe, with no potential to be born. It just is."

"So, if people go through so many cycles and don't progress, you cut them loose?" Juliet pressed.

"Not if they are not destructive," Ruth added quickly. " If they just fail to progress, then they won't be born here, but can continue to exist in The Cupel quite comfortably, just as organic, just as real, just no upper-level soul development." Juliet stared at Ruth coolly, expecting her next sentence.

"If, however, they are actively destructive for multiple cycles and can't progress, then their energy is relegated outside of an organic body and their destructive influence not empowered any more than it has under its own existence. Regular dark matter is required to maintain balance. They are necessary."

"The Dark Janae?" Gabriel asked.

"Some of those that are actively destructive are Dark Janae," Kyle explained, "They only become Dark Janae because Valswak empowers their bodyless souls. Without him, they would just be free-floating energy, with very minor abilities to influence, but nothing dramatic."

"You've created all your own enemies. Maybe they wouldn't be so destructive if you didn't treat them so," Juliet nearly spat the words.

"You are mistaken, my dear. We have given them every chance and tried to help them. They are what they are," Ruth answered.

Chapter 20

"Stone, please check on Phoebe. She should be in the holding area, ready to be assimilated. I'd prefer you stay with her, even though she's not yet with body or conscious," Ruth instructed. Stone departed soundlessly, with a nod to Gabriel on the way.

"I'm going to check on George, and stop in to make sure the project team is on task. You don't need me for this," Ruth relayed and then she, too, exited soundlessly.

"It's time for this team to learn monitoring and guiding souls," Saraceni began,

"Gabriel, let's start with your connectors. Wood?" Wood flipped on the two monitors again, but this time Lela and the Africa crew, in the cavern, appeared on the monitor on the right, and two unshaven, dirty men appeared on the monitor on the left. Gabriel watched for a moment, taking in the scenes. Lela was sleeping, as most in the cavern were. It looked to be late afternoon there, perhaps just prior to sunset. The unshaven man was punching away on a waterproof computer resting on his knees as he lay behind a rock in what appeared to be an environment out West, or at least somewhere very dry. He snapped the computer case shut and spoke to his partner in a language Gabriel did not understand. It was the voice Gabriel recognized, for the man before him did not look like James at all. Though he'd met the man several times through Lela, Gabriel wouldn't have recognized James if he passed him on the street. His hair wasn't long, but not short either. Bleached out by the sun, it appeared nearly platinum blonde and the sun had etched lines into his face Gabriel did not remember. Add to that a pile of dirt, a 12 o'clock shadow and about a 20 pound weight loss, and the thin man with dark circles under his eyes just barely resembled the inner shell of James Matthews.

"Geez, he looks like hell," Gabriel muttered mostly to himself. Wood, being the only other person close enough to hear him agreed.

"Yeah, the Dark Janae have been after him for a while. He's strong, though, he won't turn," Wood reassured him.

"What do you mean 'after him'?" Gabriel asked.

"You know, making life seem hopeless. Nudging the variables so all his challenges and lessons hit him at once rather than spaced out over time. They have limits to what they can create outright, but there is no end to the manipulation." Gabriel nodded understanding, crossing his arms slowly in front of his chest as he leaned back slightly and shifted his attention to his sister. She slept completely sprawled out, shifting around frequently. Definitely not the cute little kitten-like sleeping he loved so much about Gretchen. Gabriel remembered how he loved to watch Gretchen sleep and then chuckled a bit as Brett Davies stepped over his sister's sprawling form to gather a backpack from against the wall.

"Do we have any ability to impact that manipulation? Push them away or anything?" Gabriel asked.

"We can't outright push them away. The only person who can directly manipulate from outside is Valswak. We can introduce countermeasures, though, and provide tools, encouragement – ancillary things mostly, but they do seem to make a big difference sometimes."

"How come he can manipulate directly?" Gabriel said incredulously. It hardly seemed fair; the rules should at least be even.

"Because he wrote the code," Kyle supplied. "He secretly gave himself full access and no restrictions in the very program itself. It can't even be rewritten; he locked it." Gabriel sighed deeply, realizing they were not in as good a position as all the surrounding technology made it seem. Wood pressed a button and the controls to the monitor slid out of the space beneath the screen. He tilted them down at a slight angle toward Gabriel.

"Okay, let's give him some help." Wood said. After a few taps of the keyboard, the field radio at James' hip beckoned and he answered.

"Red Wolf 2," James droned in rote fashion. He was barely awake, coasting on fumes.

"Red Wolf 2, return to base. You and 1 there have a 24 hour sleep pass. We need you fresh before tomorrow. Head out in 10."

"Yes, sir," James affirmed, marveling at his good luck as he shared the news with his partner.

"Gonna take a lot longer than 24 hours for us to be fresh again, but I'll take it!" he replied. "Real food!" the man added as he shoved the MRE he had just withdrawn to eat back in his pack. Reflexively, they continued scanning the horizon as the ten minutes passed before they could leave. Wood showed Gabriel, who then held the controls. After a moment of silence between the men on the screen, Gabriel managed a small guidance.

"You gonna call your girl?" Red Wolf 1 asked.

"What girl?" James said. He had given up hope of that at least a month ago. He could barely survive, how was he supposed to keep someone an ocean away in consideration?

"The one in the picture that's so worn her face looks like my Grandma," Red Wolf 1 replied. "You better get a new picture or she'll be like 90 by this time next month!" he teased.

"I don't understand," Gabriel said plainly, "We're supposed to be helping. Certainly there is something more important we could be working on than my sister's love life."

James rubbed the back of his neck and barely even considered the question. He almost didn't care at this point. Of course he cared, but not overtly. It just seemed an untenable situation to him in his present circumstances.

Saraceni explained, "First of all, he is her binary soul match, which means they will work closely here and need to prepare for that there." He adjusted the controls so that each person on both screens reflected in a series of colors, much like heat-sensored photography, but with distinct color signatures and patterns. "And secondly, we need him to help convince her to complete her mission there." Gabriel focused intently on the screen , noticing that Lela and James had color patterns that matched identically: bluish toward the top, magenta in the middle, yellow to the center left and green at the bottom part of the body with a thin red line right across the knees. Quite distinct from everyone else. The other people showed as their own unique rainbow mixtures of varying colors, but each very distinct from one another. A couple pairs looked very close, but none as identical a match as James and Lela. It was then they noticed one figure in the cavern in Africa was solid gold light from head to toe.

"Who's that?" Alexander pointed at the man on the screen, worried his daughter might be in danger from one of those creatures.

"That's a Kajika." Kyle explained. They flipped the screen sensor back to the regular picture view. The Kajika was an African guide hired to assist the team, the one who had spoken to Lela on the bus, in fact, though Gabriel did not know that. He sat in the dirt in native clothing and no shoes eating rice.

"He is protecting," Saraceni informed. "We assigned him to her when you came here and we made the decision to leave her there."

"You decided to leave her- Why?" Alexander asked softly, "Why couldn't she just come here with us?" Saraceni patted him on the back, much like he had seen Alexander do to Gabriel.

"I'm sorry, Alexander, I know it is difficult. She wasn't ready. If we bring her here too soon, she will be unsuccessful and frustrated, and hold back the others. Besides, she is the only one we trust in position where she is to complete the assignment there. It is imperative and we needed someone of one of the highest levels within The Cupel, which she is." Saraceni attempted to lessen the blow. Alexander looked at his daughter asleep on the screen and suddenly became overwhelmed with thoughts that she had been left all alone and now she'd have an assignment to complete on her own. Gabriel returned to the controls on James' monitor. He pressed the final stroke and nothing happened. He looked at Wood.

"Here, you forgot the suggestion," Wood said, making the adjustment.

"How can you tell when there's one loaded and not?" Gabriel asked, "I thought there was one in the holding box thing over here?" He pointed to a box at the bottom right of the controller.

"No, that's for direct suggestions. Indirect suggestions are up here." Wood adjusted and a smaller banner box revealed at the top.

"Oh, the decagon design, I see," Gabriel then moved the controller to see the indirect suggestion at the top banner and in a moment it was gone. Red Wolf 1 turned to James.

"I really think you should call her while we're on sleep pass, or at least email her." James did not respond. "You might not think you want to now, but you'll regret it later and I don't want to be the one dealing with you crying in your beer and sobbing hysterically in front of the women I'm trying to pick up when we're in a bar back home." James smiled slightly. As if he would ever publicly cry in his beer- or privately, for that matter. The two men rose and began to run at a measured pace back toward the base. Wood muted the volume on the monitor and shifted his attention to the cavern monitor.

"What- that's it?" Gabriel queried.

"Yeah, he's good, he'll think about it a while and then do it," Wood confirmed.

"How do you know?" Gabriel wasn't convinced.

"This indicator here. See, it's gold now. It was grey before." Pausing upon reaching for a third monitor, Wood glanced at Saraceni who nodded. The third monitor showed James typing an email in a cramped bunk back at the base. Gabriel looked from that monitor to the muted one, where the men were running in time, and then to Wood.

"Which one is right?" Jack asked, puzzled. The entire team was huddled around the monitors, learning throughout the entire exercise.

"Both are right," Saraceni responded.

Wood clarified. Pointing to the one where the men were running, "This one is now..." and then he turned to the one where James was back at base emailing, "and this is the future." The team reacted in surprise.

"Why am I not surprised?" Juliet asked, "But if we can see the future, why can't we just see the outcome of all this?" she asked earnestly, seeming for the first time like the curious young woman who had arrived on the first day.

"Well, it can only see into areas that are not grey. Plus, it's a future picture of the thread or strand that exists right now. It can change, though," Wood answered.

"The bike spoke thing again," Gabriel muttered. "So if we stay on the current path, then this is what will happen, but if we change things, we can change that future, jump over to another thread, so to speak?"

"Right," Saraceni confirmed, "it's wet design, Gabriel. You're all familiar with that. In fact the entire Cupel is wet design work. It was created, yes, but that is not a one-time historical event that is complete. It is presently and continuously being created." The team nodded in assent. They grasped the concept, not unlike specific scientific projects they had each worked before, only on a grander scale- all of space and time.

"Well, can you tune in on their future?" Alexander turned the attention back to Lela and those in the cavern. Wood adjusted the controls and as soon as the picture emerged, Saraceni was quick to speak. A brutal war was going on between villages on the future screen.

"This is the main future thread related to their activities at the moment. It doesn't mean these particular people will be in the war," Saraceni reassured, lest Alexander think Lela would be battling it out in the Continent Civil War. Alexander looked at Lela still sleeping as one of the other people (Rachel, the intern) performed some tests on the DL mineral. It was a rare opportunity to test such a large amount and Lela had files full of incomplete test scenarios.

"So, how does their thread become that battle?" Alexander asked. The Civil war picture changed to a different village.

"That's near my hometown," Enam exclaimed, "very far from where we were just looking, which is closer to the sea."

"Enam, that is a continent-wide civil war that will embroil all of Africa in 30 years of bloodshed," Saraceni advised. Enam slumped in his chair. "*If* Lela doesn't complete her assignment, that is." He turned to Alexander before adding, "Now you see how important it was she stay behind and how much faith we do have in her. The assignment should also help her learn the remaining lessons to pass her test after this cycle, if she does all she should."

"How does it start?" Enam asked, still a bit off-kilter at the idea of it.

"Events have already set in motion which, left unchecked, will produce this result," Saraceni advised.

Kyle interjected: "It's the Africa project- It must be stopped."

"But that project is bringing malarial medications, and schools- fresh water!" Jane had worked on the project team as they all had and was very invested in the benefit they could bring to so many needy people.

"Yes, Jane, and the deliverables aren't the issue. The compromises made to get those deliverables are. The funding came from multiple corporate sponsorships, many of whom are seeking land and mineral rights. The short-term benefit is clear, but in 6 years, each of these corporate sponsorships will evolve into zones involved in border wars. From there, sides are chosen, alliances are made, and 30 years of fighting will follow. The majority of the people they will heal and educate will be killed. Soldiers arriving from distant lands will be killed. Nearly everyone involved will be killed. It is the result of a thread we started to bring you all together; we can't allow this," Saraceni reported.

"How can *we* stop it?" Gabriel queried.

"Lela has to sabotage the project, so it never gets fully off the ground," Saraceni responded. Gabriel shook his head at Saraceni. There was no way she would do that, he knew. He knew her better than anyone.

"She'll never do it," Gabriel advised.

"It may take longer and more prompting, but I think we can steer her in the right direction," Wood said to Gabriel directly.

"So is this what you do all day? Monitor and guide?"Gabriel asked.

"Pretty much," Wood confirmed, "It is my present assignment, and I think if we do the right things in the right order, we can get her there." He tweaked the controls and the screen changed from the cavern view to a fuzzy picture of the mountainside, with the bus going over the guardrail.

"Why are we watching this?" Chandra asked, still somewhat upset by the image on an emotional level though on an intellectual one she understood no harm resulted.

"It's Lela's dream. You can suggest directly into dreams. Clearer and more effective overall." Wood switched down to the direct suggestion box at the bottom of the screen and handed it to Gabriel. "Talk to your sister."

"Directly to her?" Gabriel confirmed.

"Sure," Wood answered.

Gabriel spoke, "Lela, it's Gabriel." In her dream she saw his hand at the edge of the cliff. He struggled to pull himself back up from the edge and then sat on the edge, feet dangling, with the smashed bus in the ravine far below. Lela rushed to him and slid on her knees.

"Gabriel, oh my God, you're okay," she said and hugged her brother.

"We're all okay, Lela. Me, Mom, Dad, most of the others on the bus," he advised. She looked over the edge and saw no one else hanging on the cliff face, the bus flames still billowing smoke far below.

"That's not possible," she said, "but I'm so glad you're here. I thought I was all alone."

"You're never all alone. I'm not really here, though, I'm there, and so are Mom and Dad, but I came to tell you that and give you a message," he said. In her heart Lela knew the truth and the sky around Gabriel turned a purple hazy color with a surreal quality.

"I'm dreaming, aren't I?" she slumped and looked down at her folded hands, dejected.

"Mostly," he said, "but I am really here, I promise. The people we're with have been trying to help you, and now I will be helping you. I promise I'll send signs whenever I can and we are always there." Gabriel adjusted the controls to keep the frequency aligned and Wood tapped the clock in front of him. Gabriel nodded and resumed.

"Lela, I know this project has the best of intentions. You know I believed in it, but the corporations will break into zones, start border wars and a 30 year continent-wide war will be the outcome. You have to end the project," he said.

"They have acted so greedy. I know the motives of all the investors aren't pure," she conceded, "but we can get them to pay for so much good here." Her brother's face became ghostly in front of her.

"They will all die. Find another way. Dismantle the project," Gabriel said, and then he was gone in the dispersion of a mist. Lela sat on the edge of the cliff, elbows resting on her knees, looking out across the mountain. On the other side she saw a wolf rise from a rock cropping, stop at the ledge and stare directly at her before letting out a loud howl. She jumped and awoke abruptly, still on the floor of the cavern, remembering every detail of the dream as if she lived it. She shivered.

"Are you okay?" Brett asked.

"Yeah. I just had the most realistic dream." She shrugged it off, not wanting to look upset at seeing the bus go over the rail or seeing her brother. Deep in her gut she had a feeling they were alright, though, but she couldn't fathom why.

"Waking dreams," the African guide interjected, "This cavern brings you messages from beyond." He pointed with one long, outstretched finger cuffed in a Lobi iron snake bracelet toward the small skylight rock opening in the cavern. Suddenly, a wolf appeared and stared directly at her. The wolf was smaller than a North American wolf, red in color with a black-and-white tail and white blazes on his chest. The white fur on his throat, contrasting with the predominant red color, swept in a curve toward his eyes, a look that would have seemed almost amused but for his intent stare.

"Jesus, is that a wolf?" Kye asked Brett, who had more prior experience in this region.

Brett nodded. "Brought by breeders long ago. Some have survived." Lela stared at the animal and had a further wrenching in her gut, like the feeling she would have when knowing not to go in a certain direction in the city. It was then she noticed the Wolf staring at her intently had one brown eye and one blue eye. Stunned by the coincidence, she stood up abruptly.

"A sign, I think," the guide said quietly directly to Lela.

"I don't believe in signs," she said flatly, though internally she was not sure. If she hadn't met Phillip Harriman, or had such a strange feeling, she would easily have dismissed it. Still, her academic brain told her that her grief was driving her to grasp at straws. Textbook reaction, really. She felt confused and instantly thought of calling James. He was her litmus test in uncharted waters. He could help her navigate this. She discarded that idea as easily as she had embraced it. 'He barely even speaks to me. No way am I playing damsel in distress.' she thought to herself.

Gabriel shook his head back in the control room. Her stubbornness always had hurt her more than helped her, but the companion traits that accompanied that stubbornness like loyalty, determination and a puritan work ethic served her well.

"She'll never dismantle a whole project based on some dream," Gabriel said to Wood and the Molior team. "She's too pragmatic for that."

"True," Saraceni responded, "but we've planted a seed." Wood withdrew his work plan for Lela's guidance and handed it to Gabriel.

"I think if we execute these steps the right way, we can lead her there." Wood said, proud of his plan and truly confident in its' potential for success. He was slightly anxious to hear Gabriel's thoughts since he knew Gabriel was right- he did know his sister better than anyone. Gabriel intently reviewed the plan. Twice.

"Maybe," he said slowly as he handed it back.

On the monitor, a loud series of noises could be heard outside the cavern. Lela, Brett, the entire Africa team stood perfectly still and listened as what sounded like voices approaching from the distance.

"We need to assess," Brett whispered, looking at Kye.

"I will inspect," the guide said to Brett. Brett knew a native guide would be much more likely to go undetected, blend in with the forest, and not be harmed if found, but he was worried about the departure from the thoroughly-hidden cavern opening.

"I think they may see you exiting. We should just wait here," Brett responded, for once not entirely convinced of his own decision.

"I walk without sound. No one sees me," the guide responded.

"Okay," Brett said, approving the action, and in a moment the man who walked among them that was really Kajika was gone.

"Isn't he her protection?" Alexander asked, concerned.

"Yes, and he's doing his job," Saraceni reassured him.

Chapter 21

Lela and the others sat with a stillness approaching perfection, surrounded by the gentle amethyst glow of the sun cascading through the small rooftop opening and bouncing around the mineral walls like electrons within an atom. The vague distant noises drew closer and coalesced into shouting voices and the sound of many footsteps running quickly around the river's edge. Mako looked at Lance, still clutching one of his colored cubes as if it were a security blanket. Rachel, who had been in the middle of mineral readings, gently flipped off the equipment and sat down next to her brother, Brian, rather than Kye. Brett, Kye, and the three other soldiers gathered around the only entrance in semicircular formation, ready to pick off anyone who entered. That was the one, and only, advantage of their position, aside from being concealed- that if they were discovered, the entrance was so narrow that enemies would be forced to enter one at a time.

The remainder of the science team picked up the assorted weapons they had gathered earlier. At least ¾ of them had large hunting knives, and those who did not held either pieces of metal or sharp-edged hunks of the DL mineral. Tina pulled out a 9mm sidearm and joined the soldiers by the doorway. Brett didn't move a muscle, but looked at her inquisitively. She shrugged, aware she had flounced the rules of declaring weapons to the head of security- a surly, stout man who worked for Brett while he was temporarily assigned to the camp with Lela. Lela reflected briefly on the fact that less than thirty-six hours earlier she had been comfortably ensconced in her parent's home, sorting through boxes and taking conference calls on speakerphone with a large glass of iced tea.

The voices drew closer and gunfire could be heard, though it sounded like random shots into the jungle to see if they might hit someone, which was exactly what the rebels were doing. They were firing at random hoping to hear a gasp or moan or shriek that might tell them in which direction the arrogant intruders had fled.

"It looks like they went into the river!" Kye heard one man shout in a local dialect, and whispered the translation to Brett and the others. Lela's heart skipped a beat, suddenly exhilarated at the prospect of remaining alive. She closed her eyes tightly and thought to herself 'If we get through this, God, I promise I will never mope around or take my life for granted again.' she thought intensely and then continued praying to herself with her eyes closed. Many in the room were also praying, in 12 different languages and 6 different religions, all inwardly focused, and all silent, the force and energy of their conviction was almost tangible. In fact, the light of the mineral walls even seemed to grow just a shade brighter.

For a long time, the group heard nothing, but Brett knew it would require several hours and subsequent reports from his scouts before he would even consider relaxing. They continued to sit quietly, but the overall postures did seem to relax. A few people even went to sleep, fueled by their belief that the threat had passed. Just when their relaxation was near complete, they heard a noise outside the entrance to the cavern. Lela wrapped her hand more tightly around her hunting knife. Mako awoke abruptly and appeared alarmed. A few rocks tumbled away from the cavern entrance. Brett and team were poised to strike.

"It is me, the silent one," the native guide, the unknown Kajika, called out to them. His foot appeared first, followed by his body and finally his head as he contorted his body to move through the narrow partial entrance.

"Quick, replace the entrance cover!" Brett ordered one of his men.

"They are gone. They have moved to the land of the rift valley," the guide advised.

"Thank you," Brett answered, truly grateful for the information, "but I would prefer to make sure they have left no individual scouts behind. Our team will sweep the area before anyone from the science team will exit." Three of them left, replacing the entrance cover, and three remained with the weary camp members.

"Everyone please remain quiet. We will do a sweep of the area and if that's successful, we can move out to the riverbank."

"Calls of nature will certainly be easier out there," Tina added jovially. Lance smirked and waved a jar back and forth to her.

"No problem here! I just scoot around that corner of rock over there and I'm hoooome freeee!" he taunted with his Texas twang.

"Oh, yes, if only I were male- an homage to utilitarian construction," she quipped back. Rachel laughed quietly, once again retrieving her monitoring instrumentation from the floor of the cavern, where she had placed it neatly on a jacket and covered it as if a delicate infant.

"What have you found so far?" Lela asked her, and the young intern was all too proud to present her project findings to the project lead. Still a freshman in college, Rachel already knew she wanted to do graduate work in geology and thought this project might help boost her credentials for one of the competitive spots at the University of Colorado, one of the top geology programs in the country.

"The readings are very high in the electromagnetic spectrum," she pointed at the instrumentation, "and look at this- it's almost 6 times higher in here than when I conducted independent readings of mineral samples back at the camp. Did they come from somewhere else?"

"No," Lela crinkled her eyes at the data, "those samples came from here."

"I knew you had found something in this zone!" Lance exclaimed. He turned to Mako and nudged him, which Mako bristled at slightly, not because he didn't like the man, but because the gesture was too familiar for his taste. "Didn't I tell you, Mako! That she found something out here?" Mako nodded affirmatively.

****

Back in the training room, Wood asked Kyle, viewing the monitor, "Did you get those mineral readings?"

"Yes." Kyle viewed them and materialized a graph with a wave sin with an occasional peak. He pulled out a small metal clip from the machine and handed it to Wood.

"Would you like me to analyze this?" Wood asked Kyle.

"I just did," Kyle responded. Wood looked surprised for only a second.

"How?" Wood responded, not grasping how Kyle had just skipped about fifty steps of the process he knew.

"I'll show you sometime, but right now please take this to the project team. Ruth and Saraceni will be interested to see it, I think," the teen ordered the hulking man.

"Yes, sir," Wood responded reflexively, more to the tone than the individual.

"You need data from The Cupel?" Jack asked, "Why don't you just pull it yourselves?"

"We can't access everything we need directly, or impact everything we need directly. That's why we have Kajika and future recruits with assignments there- to get to what we can't," Kyle responded.

The camp team stepped one at a time gingerly out of the cavern into the open area near the river's edge by the cliff's face.

"You're clear to come out here, but we need to hug the cliff face for a while and not spread out any farther," Kye relayed Brett's instructions to the others. They were relieved to be outside and able to walk around after being huddled inside the cavern for so many hours. The guide sat next to Lela as she assembled the radio equipment, now that they would be able to get a clear satellite line of sight.

"I am thinking the rebels will not stop. They do not like the corporate invasion into their lands," he reported.

"Don't they realize we are bringing critical medicines, cleaner water into the interior, and education?" she asked.

"Perhaps the price is too high," he mused, "They will not give up." Lela reflected somberly, recalling her dream. She just wanted to help these people, not cause a civil war between those who agreed with the assistance and those who didn't.

"Those companies do not care about these people." He was stern. Lela sighed heavily, nodding. She turned to grab an antenna and when she turned back, he was gone. She completed the radio setup and set it aside so it would be ready when the reconnaissance team returned with information to relay to the main security base back in town. Next she turned to her waterproof hardbook computer and was thrilled to see she had two bars of satellite network available, enough to send some email. First, she typed a short paragraph to Pfister back in the states:

Have fled base camp with all camp team members except those remotely stationed. Rebel activity all around. Dangerous. All present here are safe now. Status of remote team members unknown, but security detail is gathering more information. Brett Davies advises we will likely take a boat out of here. Portable equipment with us. Some mineral samples and all project data are with us. All else is left behind at camp. Will call you when we are in the clear -Lela

Lela noticed her incoming mail. Three messages down was JMatthews. 'James!' she thought. Somehow, no matter how long it had been since they had spoken, he always knew when she really needed him. The message was not what she expected, though. He seemed to be having a hard time himself, something that he didn't often share, so she knew it must be troubling indeed for him to admit even a shred of it. James closed the email with, "I miss you and I want to talk to you. When will you be back in the States?" Her heart tugged in a way it only did for James and she realized how much she missed him as well. She knew she couldn't admit her own circumstances- that she wasn't sure when she'd be back in the States or if they'd even get out of this mess, though she was more optimistic than earlier, or in fact than she had been since her family had died. She couldn't worry him when he was already under such heavy stress, though she did not know the details. Lela decided to merely relay that she would find out the schedule as soon as possible and tell him, and that she missed him too. She flipped the keyboard shut with a sense of relief. She wanted to see him. If only their lives could ever be in the same place at the same time.

Brett returned.

"We're getting out of here. The boats will be here shortly," he clipped, out of breath from the run back from the scouting. He turned to Kye, "Call in all our men in the area. We're escorting them to the city and the rest will return to home base."

"I set up the radio," Lela reported.

"Thanks," he replied, "but I used an alternate one." In four hours time, the boats arrived and the camp members boarded. Lela hesitated.

"We left a lot back at camp. Do you think there's any chance we can retrieve it?" she asked Brett.

"No," he said, taking her arm gently and guiding her toward the boat, "The risk is too high." The boats cruised along the river and Lela was surprised at how choppy the ride was. The river looked more placid from the bank than it actually was, and after some time passed they entered some gentle rapids. The bottom of the boat could be heard scraping over rocks as they navigated some of the more narrow passages between rock formations.

"Everybody hold on tight!" the captain yelled, 'We're about to head into the roughest part, and you don't want to fall in or those hippos by the banks will be very interested in meeting you!" He pointed toward the bank where several hippopotamus sat in the water, just the tips of their heads and nostrils peering out. If they'd not been pointed out, Lela wasn't even sure she would have seen them. Everyone grabbed a tight hold on the center line rope woven through some metal eyes on the boats decks. Brett and the other soldiers wrapped the rope around their left forearm three times, and continued to brandish their rifles in their right hand, constantly scanning the area for any signs of rebel threat.

The boat hit the rapids and bounced at least four feet in the air. Lela felt her body leave the deck by about a foot for an instant and then descend, not exactly slamming into the deck, but not a gentle replacement either. She spread her feet to the left and right slightly, distributing her weight and pressing the side of her right foot against the inner wall of the boat.

"Do this!" she yelled to the line of people to her left and pointed at her feet. Those on the left side of the boat secured their weight in similar fashion and pressed their left feet against the boat's inner wall, and then all those present pressed against each other shoulder to shoulder toward the center of the boat. None too soon, because the boat hit a hard rock edge and bounced very high, and the camp team inside the boat bounced 3-4 feet in the air. Two near the outer edges almost bounced out, but their feet caught on the top lip of the inner wall, and those nearest to them grabbed their inner arms and pulled them back to the deck. This continued for 5 minutes or so, and then the boats entered more placid water. Everyone was soaked, and the water was colder than expected, but otherwise fine. They relaxed.

"Any more like that expected, Captain?" Brett yelled, not wanting them to relax too much if the respite was merely a temporary one.

"There are more in the waters far east of town, but we'll be docking before we hit the next set of large rapids. There may still be a bit of chop, so stay secured, but it shouldn't be too uncomfortable. The boat bobbed up and down repetitively, almost a perfect cadence in a dance with the surrounding wildlife. One of the scientists became seasick and stood up, racing to the edge to vomit overboard.

"Get away from there! Vomit in the pail!" a crewman yelled, but it was too late. The boat hit a smaller bump which otherwise would have been uneventful, but with the man leaning far over the edge, the slight pitch sent him overboard. He was in the water and they were 200 meters past him before they could even cut the engine. The man was being swept in the opposite direction by the downstream current quickly, and they lost sight of him briefly before his head popped up and he instinctively grabbed a nearby branch, flailing for a grasp at anything. The second boat, nearly hitting into the back of the first, managed to steer to the side enough for the first boat to move in reverse to the left of it, but there was insufficient room to actually turn the entire boat around due to the narrow width of the river where they were in comparison to the boat's length. They moved in reverse steadily, but the man was at least 400 meters away. Brian noticed the hippos open their mouths wide and tapped his sister. Rachel grabbed Kye's vest and pointed. The entire boat watched as two of the hippos then turned around toward the man in the water. It was a race between the boat and the hippos and from the present speeds of both, it appeared the boat would lose by a narrow margin. Brian jumped up abruptly.

"How long is this rope?" he shouted to the crewman.

"One hundred meters," the crewman responded.

"Count to twenty and then start reeling me in." he told his sister and Kye, and jumped off the right side of the boat, closest to the shore and the hippos. He swam toward them and started waving his arms and making noise as the boat moved lateral to him to reach the man in the water. The hippos, realizing he was slightly closer due to the angle of approach, turned instead toward Brian.

"Brian!" Rachel yelled. 'Pull him back! Pull him back!" she yelled to Kye. It hadn't been the full twenty seconds, but Kye and Mako, the closest to the rope, began pulling it as quickly as they could toward them. Others joined in and soon Brian was flying toward the boat, the hippos now fast on his heels. Simultaneously, the boat reached the downed scientist and several others pulled him in at the back of the boat as the central crew pulled Brian in at the side. The first hippo snapped into the air and let out a rumbling, guttural sound.

"That was stupid, you moron!" Brian's sister yelled at him. He put his arm around her shoulder, seeing that she was shaking.

"Sorry, Rach, but it just came to me in a flash. All that swimming training, I guess," he said. She was still mad and shoved his arm off her.

"Outswimming hippos? Moron. More- onnnn!" she said forcefully, and then hugged him. For the remainder of the trip, no one spoke, and no one went near the sides of the boat. In another hour they docked smoothly and deboarded. Once in town, Lela reached Pfister by phone and was told the entire project was put on hold until they could be sure the area had stabilized and no threat existed from the rebels.

"That'll be a while," Brett confirmed when he heard the news.

"I know," Lela said. "Our flight is back in the morning. I can't wait to get a shower and some food." Brett looked at her long frame, caked in dirt and mud, the dirt on her face making her green eyes stand out even more brilliantly than normal. She pulled her hair off of her neck.

"Want some company?" Brett asked, and the implication was that for either the shower, the food, or both would be acceptable. Lela, who might have accepted just a few days earlier, now felt a renewed feeling of loyalty to James.

"Brett, I'd love to, but I'm just really tired. Long day, ya know?" she said. He looked slightly dejected for about half a second before resuming a stoic front.

"Of course. Yeah, long day. I'll see you tomorrow," he mumbled and then disappeared quickly. She felt bad for a moment. Lela liked Brett. Very much, but if there was any chance that she and James could finally be together, to get on the same page at the same time, she wanted nothing more. She hoped she wouldn't regret the rebuff later. It wasn't everyday a guy like Brett Davies came along, either.

Lela's shower at the hotel was far from luxurious. The spigots had to be cajoled into balancing just right to keep a moderate blend of the cold and hot water flowing well enough to neither scald nor freeze her. The space was so tight, she banged her elbows repeatedly while shampooing her long hair twice to get all the river water out, and she had to use a local organic paste as there was no real shampoo or conditioner available, but as far as Lela was concerned, she felt as if she were in a 5 star hotel, surrounded in luxury.

She sat on her bed in some dry clothes she had gotten from Tina, who had thought to wrap her extra clothes in her pack in plastic. Lela used her only plastic bag to wrap her passport and documents tightly. Her wet hair dried quickly in the hot air that streamed in the open screened window and she ate a sandwich. She thought of Gabriel, all they'd been through in the last few days, her dream, the mineral test results, her parents and the decision of what to do about the Africa project. Without reaching any conclusions at all, she closed the window sleepily, turned off the light, drew the mosquito netting over her bed, and instantly fell asleep.

Chapter 22

Wood slept also, in the chair in George's room. He had fallen asleep monitoring George as instructed by Ruth and now had his lengthy body maneuvered sort of diagonally in the chair, his arms tucked tightly across his chest and his head rolling to one side. One foot was on the floor while one stood propped up on the bed. In the hallway, the screen, with no one watching at the time, silently rolled up one percent to read 94%. The alarm sounded yet again, filling all buildings with the screaming sirens they had dodged only a week ago.

Wood's body straightened reflexively and he twisted in the chair, catching his foot into the edge of the bed frame as he attempted to rise. The result was a dramatic bellyflop on the cold, hard floor, his foot still hung upward behind him as he lay face down. For a moment, the wind was knocked out of him, but the continued alarm jostled him back to reality. Withdrawing his foot carefully, and with a slight groan as he pressed his weight off the ground, he rose to see George awake in the bed before him.

"You're up!" Wood exclaimed over the alarm.

"So're you," George replied. Rubbing his head, he added, "Can't they turn that off?" As if on command, the alarm ceased

"They reset it." Wood stepped closer, "How do you feel?"George looked a little weak and displayed the faintest hint of disorientation, but answered.

"I'm okay, I think," he said. Wood strode purposefully to the wall unit and pressed the indicator for Ruth. He was sure she was busy with the alarm, but George's awakening was a huge plus for the mission.

"What percent are we up to?" George asked.

"94%," Wood answered.

"Hell," George said quietly, still holding his head.

Kyle held his head also, back in the training room.

"You still seem off," Saraceni said to him.

Kyle, knowing this was true, also knew he couldn't afford to be pulled to go through medical screening. They were already down a person.

"I'm fine," he lied.

"Why does that alarm keep going off?" Chandra asked

"It can't be shut down above a certain threshold. It's a failsafe so no one may shut it down and then allow progression to go unnoticed," Saraceni responded.

"But what's its purpose?" Enam asked.

"It's warning of our state of decoherence. We're at 94% and if we don't prevent it, it will be 100% in about a week, give or take."

"Decoherence, as in tied particles disentangling like we discussed in training?" Juliet jumped in.

"Yes."

"And if this decoherence thing gets to 100%, then what?" Jack asked. Saraceni paused and Gabriel had a sinking feeling and reflexively took two steps backward, looking at his father. Alexander knew as well and sat swiftly, pressing his palms against his thighs. Jack cocked an eyebrow at the reactions of the others.

"What?" he said louder.

"It's all destroyed," Gabriel said quietly

"What- The Cupel? How can the whole thing be destroyed? What about my family, all the people?" Jack registered the gravity of the situation.

"Well," Chandra began, vehement and forceful, "y'all are just gonna have to bring them here. Perfect society or not, you got them into this now you're gonna get them -" Gabriel cut her off-

"Not The Cupel, Chandra. Everything. Here, there, everywhere- all decimated." Juliet turned a quick heel toward Saraceni

"How on Earth could you let this happen? You, Ruth, the others, look what you've done."

"We didn't do it all," Saraceni relayed. "A certain amount of decoherence is expected. The cost of doing business, so to speak, but as soon as Valswak saw the process had begun, he began aggravating it, assigning Dark Janae to hit critical juncture points so it would unravel all that faster. Not even our own project teams know this. They think it's happening at a steady rate, a fully natural process."

"Then why are you telling us?" David Running Wolf asked, "You must think we can help or we wouldn't be here." It dawned on Molior that though they were specifically recruited, they hadn't since their arrival thought that there might be a reason why, other than to come here and be a member of this "advanced" society. Now they could see there had been signs along the way that their role was somehow bigger. They were cordoned off from even the rest of the recruits, all flooding over the hills that day, allowed to interact, all in different colored uniforms, none matching their own.

"You were recruited now," Saraceni pulled up the screen as he spoke, "because you have a mission. We think you, and you alone, can open a gate to the next circle, relieving the pressure on the current system and providing us time to solve the problem of decoherence."

"The circles that we move through- the ones that keep escalating?" Jane queried.

"Yes, as Ruth explained, after a full interval, a new gate opens and we ascend as all the gates below remain open as a ladder to that top circle," Saraceni explained.

"If the gates open on their own, why do we have to open it?" Enam asked.

"Because we passed the data saturation point where a new gate should have opened, and it didn't," Saraceni continued, "so information is being gathered by those in The Cupel, and those here, to contribute to the Overall Purpose. Some of those particles, each element of matter holding some amount of data, are entangled with one another and some are not, but they are approaching the point of every particle being full."

"And when that happens, there's nowhere else for the data to go, so it starts acting completely as a free agent, decoupling links, decohering the very ties that preserve the boundaries. Think of collective dephasing. Observation equals decoherence, and because every particle is 100% full of data, all count as being observed, so when some room is freed up, the extra decoherence ceases." At that moment Wood burst into the room.

"George is awake! He's awake!" Wood shouted. The others cheered and clapped lightly, happy for the good news.

"Thank God," Saraceni tipped his head back and closed his eyes, "now he'll be able to complete the mission. I have to update the project team." He turned to Wood, suddenly reverting to the former task-master he had been before things began falling apart. Hearing that George was awake was just the morsel of hope Saraceni needed to renew his own drive.

"Wood, please return to George and stay with him until Ruth arrives. And you," he said to Molior directly, "will have a lot to do in a very short time, so while I'm gone, finish these exercises. You have to be able to do them perfectly, so keep going until you have at least ten perfect trials." With that, he left the room and Molior had no choice but to focus on the tasks at hand. Just seeing Saraceni's confidence rise had somehow settled them as well. Surely, if he had the impression things would be alright now, then they would be, they each thought.

Saraceni entered the project room with renewed authority in each step. He had to believe this could be done. He had to believe it would work. He had to. For if he did not, no one else would have the faith necessary.

"Status report!" he commanded.

"Sir, we can't figure it out. The decoherence was supposed to have two more weeks, but it seems to be accelerating. It's beyond all comprehension," Elizabeth Hallowell relayed.

"I told Molior about their mission. Please mark that off the project plan," Saraceni responded.

"How did they take it?" Elizabeth asked with trepidation.

"Let me clarify. I didn't tell them all the details, just the primary objective."

Ruth entered the room, barely noticing them, and walked straight through on her way to George's room. At the last moment, as if awaking from a dream, she nodded to Saraceni in passing, a subtle acknowledgement he had everything under control. Saraceni gave a subdued nod in return. He hoped George was well and would check on him soon enough himself, but Ruth clearly wanted first crack at her son. With a few flicks of Saraceni's wrist, the double-sided display screen emerged vertically from the table and in moments the mineral readings were displayed.

"These don't look right," he assessed efficiently.

"We ran them twice, Sir," Elizabeth responded. Saraceni noticed how perfect the data was, and her reporting of it could not have been any more thorough. When this was all over, he would tell her that she had run as tight a project as anyone could have, that they knew they were giving her impossible targets, but had to push for maximum gains in an untenable situation. Used to always being at the top of her game, Elizabeth was clearly flustered by the feeling that she was somehow not managing the project well. She knew she wasn't as good with people, which was not that uncommon in the middle circles from 5-8, but her analytic and calculation skills were top notch. The middle circles tended to focus too much on the technical and physics aspects of their new world. In the struggle to integrate their humanity, they often left it behind and were too laser-focused on the analytics of it rather than the meditative balance.

"The harmonic frequencies look right, but the cumulative wave functions are too low. We must not be counting some," he advised.

"The broullian zone energy widths are much smaller than expected based on the data we have. Perhaps when we receive the new data we will discover something useful," Elizabeth offered.

"Precisely my thought," Saraceni agreed, " When will the new data analysis be ready?"

"Two days," she reported, "maybe late tomorrow if we get lucky."

"Ma'am, I thought George already analyzed it?" an assistant inquired.

"Preliminary analysis, yes. He assessed enough for us to know a detailed analysis is required, but that detail will take some time because it is so comprehensive," she clarified.

"Please run another test scenario. And add the interaction components for energy levels, conductive ability and manipulation of broullian zone widths. Perhaps we can figure out why it's an electric siphon at the same time. If we could figure out a way to get the choppers up to that mountaintop, it would be a huge coup."

"Yes, sir. I'll add that to the testing orders now," the assistant said, happy to have been included in core team activities.

"And lastly, what are the Dark Janae up to?" he asked

"Still after key targets from a balance perspective," the assistant answered, "and they seem to have a flurry of activities in the following areas." He highlighted the map in yellow, "but there don't appear to be any Kajika or key recruits there, so we're not sure why."

"They still don't know about the girl, or her Kajika, and they haven't actually won any of the others they are after...yet," Elizabeth added for context.

"Okay. Keep recording their activity on the map, and definitely use all countermeasures to keep the targets and recruits safe," Saraceni ordered.

"Yes, Sir."

"Call me immediately if they go into any new zones without targets nearby."

"Yes, Sir." Saraceni exited and the alarm went off again, to be stopped after just a second or two, so he shouted over his shoulder, "and have someone monitor that round the clock and press the stop button immediately every time it starts. "

Ruth entered George's room with each step dripping in the gratitude of a mother who had been given her child back. So accustomed to being able to fix bodies easily, true worry over another's welfare was infrequent in this world. But if their mind was gone, even with good engineering, it felt like they were doctors using leeches in trying to repair the damage. With decoherence involvement, the risk to even try would have been great and likely resulted in George's death, so every ounce of relief poured into the hug Ruth gave George.

"How do you feel?" she asked.

"Okay. A little strange, Mother, but I guess, considering, that I am pretty well. I've tried a few simple harmonic alignments while lying here, though, and I don't think any of them worked." Ruth's concern moved immediately from her Son to the mission. She gave a forced smile.

"You are so out of practice with lying," he chided. Unaccustomed to it, Ruth gave a weak, but genuine smile this time.

"Yes, well, I suppose that's a good thing," she reflected "that we're fortunate enough to not have to deal with that regularly."

"Indeed," he concurred. Ruth forced back a lump in her throat at the thought that after all these centuries he might actually all die, if the mission were not successful. She was resigned to it herself, and were she a lone operator she would have not minded as much, but the intense ties between family and senior team members made the thought of all those people dying nearly unbearable. Knowing what she was thinking, George squeezed his mother's hand.

"The mission will work," he reassured her, "I really believe that." She nodded.

"What a role reversal," he added, "You're always the one reassuring everyone."

"Well, don't tell on me." She patted his hand as she rose, "Speaking of, I'd better get back to it. Please rest. You still look wan and we need you ready soon."

"I know." he said, "I should like to meet with the recruits when it's convenient."

"Okay", she said, and closed the door behind her. She could hear Saraceni speaking with the recruits in the common area as she left and decided not to interrupt just now. Saraceni was breaking down the mission into its components for them and they had just been advised they would need to practice with climbing gear tomorrow.

"I know how to climb," Jack piped in, "I had to learn it for this spy movie, and just fell in love with it. I go climbing every chance I can on my downtime."

"That will be a huge help," Saraceni added, knowing this fact already.

"Me too," Jane added, "I live in the mountains. My friends and I rock climb on the weekends. I mean, before."

"Anyone else very comfortable with climbing?" he asked. Chandra and Alexander raised their hands. David, who Saraceni knew to be an excellent climber, did not.

"I've never seen you climb, Dad," Gabriel commented to Alexander.

"There's a lot you don't know, but I'll fill you in later," Alexander reassured.

"So this is the top of Mount Jarib. It's just a few hours from here by air," Saraceni instructed, displaying the topography on a program monitor, "We'll land here, and then have to hike to this ridge. From there it is a climb to reach the top, but only about half a day of climbing."

"That ridge has a huge, flat field. Can't we just take a few smaller planes and have them drop us off one at a time at that point?" asked Enam, who had flown small aircraft during the war in his twenties.

"That would normally be an excellent idea," Saraceni agreed, "but nothing electronic works within about 3,000 feet in any direction from the mountain's peak. We've had planes cut power and barely able to restart before hitting the ground before. We won't try that again. We have to land in the lower safe zone and then hike on in."

"Wow, it's like the Bermuda Triangle!" Chandra chimed in.

"Something like that," Saraceni sanctioned the analogy.

"So, we know we can all hike, and handle some surprising terrain," Kyle interjected. "We proved that in the course exercise. The climbing can be tricky, though, so we'll have to practice it."

"Saraceni, why does it have to be at that mountain top? Can't we just do whatever we need to in order to open the gate from somewhere else?" Gabriel asked.

"That location has particular qualities in relation to this planet, and the universe. The lay lines are perfect, and the very things which likely make it unsuitable for electronic activity make it perfect for our mission."

"Why? How will we open the gate?" Gabriel asked. Saraceni launched into the lecture-like explanation:

"Our theory is that each circle functions, among other things, like a layer of quantum storage and since these are naturally occurring and self-producing, we believe if we can jump-start or kick off the process, nature will take over from there. So, we'll start with a quantum system and minimize the decoherence effects as much as possible by insulating the system from the environmental effects. That's why we do this from the top of the mountain where decoherence effects appear to be operating at a fraction of what they do away from that location. We start with quantum dots, which are just semiconductor nanocrystals, and we've already perfected the creation of those. Each dot has an encoded coherence time, so we make those as large as possible by using quantum dots of the maximum allowable diameters. We will arrange the quantum dots linearly and apply a laser (battery-powered in our case) and that will create the gate. We've done this before in testing, so we know that much will work. The problems we've faced in trials so far that have kept us from going farther are few. First, the gate we can create isn't nearly large enough. Second, once the gate is opened, it only stays open so long as we continue to apply lasers or radiation. As soon as we turn it off, the gate returns to ground state and it ceases to function. This is from the effects of decoherence, no matter how small, the gate is still interacting with the environment to some extent in our trials and that prevents it from becoming self-propagating. Only in the zero decoherence environment around the mountain will that be possible. Third, once we open the gate, even if we could get it to be self- building, the information needs a swapping operation to be transmitted to the new system. This is where you come in. You already know, even in The Cupel, that you can do this by ion implantation or through DNA-based self- assembly. What I'm here to tell you is that your particular structure of DNA, and particularly your unique configuration of dark matter and the way you interact with one another, can be manipulated to create a swapping operation capable of transmitting that volume of information. You just need to learn to manipulate your dark matter in that way."

"Simple enough; let's get started!" Juliet was elated to finally learn how it all fits together, and a way they can help.

"Not simple," Kyle brought her down to Earth. "It will be hard. Usually people aren't expert at those types of manipulations until they are Circle 4 or 5 here."

"So, we have one week to prepare?" Juliet asks.

"Well, really six days, because we must leave here on the 6th day," Saraceni responded.

"Maybe we could be ready to leave earlier," David Running Wolf interjected enthusiastically, "Sounds like we'll be cutting it close."

"That would be nice. We'll see how quickly the team gets through the preparation exercises," Saraceni responded diplomatically, knowing that the ideal timeframe would give them a couple weeks and even six days was amazingly ambitious. However, he saw no reason to dampen their enthusiasm. Intangibles like motivation could impact mission success.

George came wobbling around the corner. Clearly struggling with each step, he made his way into the training room.

"George!" Jane exclaimed. Wood, surprised to see him, rushed to his side, and David to the other. They helped him to a chair.

"Hey guys. I got bored in there all by myself. Thought I'd come say hi." George managed a small wave, "though I think I felt stronger lying down."

"You should be resting," Saraceni directed. His worry grew. George would need to be much stronger to make the journey. Gabriel exchanged a look with Saraceni- he was thinking the same thing.

"I know, I know, I'll go in a few minutes."

"Let's take a very short break," Saraceni suggested, and the group disbanded and surrounded George with pats on the back, filling him in on what happened while he was in the coma. They brought him water, and food, and he did seem a bit brighter just for the company, Wood observed.

"And they showed us the Kajika, and the Dark Janae," Chandra told him, "Then when they were trying to get Phoebe, that weaver just sweeps in and-
"

"They were after Phoebe?!" George bellows.

"They didn't get her," Wood interjected quickly.

"What happened? Where did they hide her?" he asked.

"They didn't hide her, George," Saraceni strode to his side, "The weaver sent her here as an adjuvant." Seeing he was upset, he added, "If she had stayed there, the Dark Janae would surely have her."

George's upset was exaggerated by his frail condition, and his body started shaking, "Oh my God, poor Jillian. How will she ever recover?"

Chapter 23

Jillian Jacob was in shock. Police permeated her house and news crews covered her lawn and most of the block. Every room seemed to be hub of a different activity center. In Phoebe's room, the detectives gathered evidence-footprints, photographs, fiber samples and other clues to help them discern who had abducted the small girl from her own bed in the middle of the night. On every TV station, 'The disappearance of Phoebe Jacob blared as the lead story, with the media talking for hours about nothing significant, as they often did in cases like this. One camera from the street zoomed in on the trampled flowers beneath Phoebe's window as the reporter's voice commentated.

"Well, folks, as you can see, those trampled flowers say it all. Something delicate, beautiful and fragile destroyed by the thoughtless monsters who took this little girl. We can only imagine what her poor mother is going through. Just as a reminder, Phoebe Jacob is the daughter of the late Governor Jacob, both survived only by the late Governor's wife, Jillian Jacob. At this point, none of the authorities are commenting on the speculation that the child's disappearance is somehow related to the mysterious bus accident, still under investigation, which left Governor Jacob and 54 others dead just 2 months ago this week. Stay tuned for late breaking coverage as we bring you all the unraveling details as this tragedy unfolds."

Fortunately, inside, the televisions were off as Jillian attempted to cooperate with police. The police asked Jillian question after question, but she answered in a fog, not even sure of what she said afterward. Less than 2 months after the death of her husband, she was almost numb to the disappearance of her daughter. Only her innate training as the dutiful Governor's wife kept her maintaining a semblance of cordiality when she wanted to tell them all to leave.

"Mrs. Jacob, I know this is very difficult, but everything you can tell us about last night might help us find Phoebe," the lead detective pressed. Jillian looked at Phoebe's picture on the mantle, her toys on the floor, and immediately knew her daughter was dead. Somewhere deep in her inner core, she just knew Phoebe would never be found alive. She turned and left without answering anymore questions, crying the entire way as she had done for hours.

General Peter Charles arrived shortly thereafter, and found D.A. Felix Lee.

"What do they have so far?" he queried. "Does it seem in any way linked to the bus incident? Any ransom demand yet?"

"No demands yet," Felix Lee informed, "and too soon to tell if the incidents are related." He walked the Colonel through the crime scene, explaining each detail they had found. The phone tap team completed their setup on the dining room table. The Colonel saw Brett Davies walk in the front door, looking worse for wear and carrying a large rucksack on his back, which he instinctively dropped right inside the front door.

"Brett, thanks for coming, I heard you ran into some trouble down there," the Colonel said. "I expected it to be a babysitting assignment when I asked you to do it; now I'm really glad you were the one there. Is Lela okay?"

"Yes, she's fine. We handled it, Sir. I heard about Phoebe Jacob in the cab from the airport and had him bring me straight here. Any word yet?" he asked.

"Not yet. No calls and we haven't seen any signs it's related to the bus incident, but we can't rule that out. Where's Lela?" he asked. Brett's mind raced as he realized if these were related she may be in more danger than he initially thought.

"I left her at the airport," he responded slowly, registering late due to his tiredness, "I'll call a team in for her right now."

"Yes. If this is related to Alexander's classified research as we suspect, they may yet go after her." In moments, Brett was on the phone with Lela. She was tired from her trip and almost didn't answer when she saw the caller ID, but he had gotten them out of there, so she felt compelled to put aside her own desire for sleep.

"Hey, Brett." she said, wondering if he was calling to smooth over the awkward goodbye at the airport.

"Lela, where are you?" he said quickly.

"In my house, I just got home," she reported.

"Lela, Phoebe Jacob is missing. She was taken from her own room without a trace in the middle of the night."

Lela, who had not even turned on the television yet, responded, "Oh, my God! Mrs. Jacob must be completely distraught. What can I do to help?"

"Nothing really. Well, stay put, I mean. We need to assign a team to you. We still don't know the results from the crash investigation, but this does make it look more like that may have not been an accident. We'll have to secure your perimeter and have a team on you for at least a few weeks."

"Brett, I still have a lot to do at my parent's house, and more digging through files that might help this investigation. If anything I find could help find Phoebe, that needs to be my number one priority," she said.

"Okay, but if you set up there, you need to stay there a few weeks. We can't cover you in both locations. We don't have the manpower for that," he said, a little annoyed due to his own tiredness. He was hoping she wouldn't put up her usual fight. He had bigger things to do right now.

"I understand," she said compliantly, "I'll head over there now."

Brett hung up the receiver and received a case briefing from the D.A.

"Not much to go on," he surmised.

"Yeah," Lee agreed.

"And none of the neighbors saw anything?" Brett inquired.

"Not in this town. This sleepy suburb closes up shop at like 9, or 10," the D.A. replied . Brett looked around a bit as the gumshoe jabber continued around him. The drone of meandering fact accumulation was interrupted by the very loud ring of the phone and the teams bolted into action. Three men appeared as if materializing from nowhere at the kitchen table, leaning into the recording equipment, reflexively checking the setup that had already been checked several times. Felix Lee took Jillian Jacob by the arm, speaking quickly while ushering her to the phone.

"Don't forget, Mrs. Jacob, the list of questions you should try to be asking is right here. Try to keep them as long as possible and ask to speak to Phoebe. If we can hear her voice, that would be best. Ask her how long she drove, that'll help us define the radius. " His words peppered her like rapid machine gun fire. Jillian lifted the phone from its cradle tentatively.

"Hello?" Jillian ventured.

"Mrs. Jacob, we have your daughter." Jillian began to cry.

"Please, please don't hurt her," she said while crying, reading from the sheet the words she didn't entirely believe. "What do you want?"

"We're going to want two million dollars, with no smoke and mirrors. We'll be calling you back with where to drop it, but you just go ahead and get it."

"That's a lot of money. I want to talk to Phoebe. I need to know she's alright," she read.

"You'll talk to her when I say you'll talk to her, and if you don't get my money, you won't be talking to her at all!" he yelled. Jillian's crying increased.

"Please. Please, I'm worried sick. Surely you have a mother. Please let me talk to her!" she managed to get out between sobs. She lengthened her sobs so the words took longer, trying to take up more time.

"I'll call you tomorrow. Get my money!" and with that the assailant hung up.

Jillian broke into hysterics and fell to the floor as one of the officers attempted to console her.

"Forty-five seconds," gumshoe #2 said to Felix Lee, "but he's still in the state."

"Increase the timing on the amber alerts on all the major interstates within the state borders, and notify the adjacent states," he ordered.

Lela saw the amber alert for Phoebe Jacob as she neared the exit for her parent's house and shook her head. She couldn't believe the child had been taken without a trace. It was already getting dark, and she'd told Brett she'd be to her parent's house by dark so the security detail didn't start having fits about not being with her. Suddenly, she was struck with the idea that Phillip Harriman could find Phoebe. She blasted past the exit as she dialed his number on the cell phone.

"No answer," she muttered to herself as she upped her speed to 75. Just fifteen minutes later she pulled into the driveway of his Victorian home. The front half of the house, the portion containing his offices, was dark, but the back half was lit. Instead of knocking on the front door, she walked around the side of the house, her shoes crunching on the tiny gravel pebbles beneath her feet. She swung open the screen door to the wraparound porch and knocked instead on the small side door leading to the kitchen and courtyard area. The last bit of light left the sky at that moment and she was standing in the dark. After a minute, the porch light flipped on and Phillip opened the door. He didn't appear surprised though he was attired in sweatpants and a worn Georgetown t-shirt.

"Sorry to bother you," she began, feeling intrusive. Phillip's lab puppy lolled its way up to Lela and began jumping at the bottoms of her legs until she reached down and petted his ears.

"No bother. I expected you, just thought it would be in the morning," Phillip advised. He started banging the side of his head dramatically, "Gotta get this thing checked out." Lela chuckled and the puppy yanked a toy from the porch and started repeatedly ramming it with all of his might, which wasn't much force, against her legs, beseeching her to play.

"This is Jules," Phillip said, picking up the dog's leash from the side table. "He wants to go play in the yard, do you mind?"

"Of course not," she agreed, and the pair plus one rambunctious Jules pup ran to the small side yard.

"Did you hear about Phoebe Jacob?" Lela asked. Phillip looked grave, feeling something was very wrong as soon as Lela said the name, but he'd seen none of it prior.

"No," he said.

"She was abducted from her room last night without a trace," she informed him. As Phillip heard the words, he felt nauseated, his heart began to race, and a subtle burning sensation entered his ears. He sat quickly on the weathered outdoor patio set.

"I didn't see this when I met with him last," he conceded, "which usually means it wasn't set to occur at that time. They must've decided spur-of-the-moment."

"They?" Lela urged.

"The men that took her," he reported flatly.

"Can you see where they took her?" she asked, hoping he was as good as she thought he was.

"I see them. The faces are really dark, though. Almost obscured by something. Very strange," he revealed. "Your mineral helps me get a better frequency- Let me go in the house and get some."

"Oh, I have some with me," Lela said. She'd been carrying her backpack since she hadn't time to switch back to a purse for her keys and such since returning from Africa.

"Sorry," she said, brushing it off the table, and digging in the pack. She pulled the Ziploc bags from the bottom, removed a large chunk of DL mineral and handed it to Phillip. Jules the pup, suddenly curious about the pack, propped up on his hind legs, paws swimming at the pack's edges unsuccessfully trying to grab hold of it as his nose sniffed and sniffed the foreign scents. Phillip held the mineral in both hands like a pitcher with an expectant baseball and breathed rhythmically as he focused his energy.

"I see them better now," he said, "Clear faces.... no sign of Phoebe."

"Can you see where they are?" Lela asked. Phillip suddenly saw a map of the state in his mind and a dot on the city of Greenville.

"I think they're in Greenville," he said.

"Really? Can you see the house? The number- or the street?" she pursued.

"They're in a hotel room," Phillip answered slowly, robotically. He searched the room in his mind for a sign of the hotel name. Looking for stationery, on the phone, everywhere he could think of, but the surroundings were unclear. As he focused his attention on the desk in the kidnapper's hotel room, he noticed a picture of Phoebe. As soon as he saw it, his mind flashed an image of the men digging a shallow grave in a remote area full of brush. They picked up the tiny girl's lifeless body, slung it carelessly into the grave and began to cover her with dirt.

"What hotel? What number?" Lela asked.

"I left the hotel," he explained, opening his eyes and looking at Lela solemnly. "Lela, she's dead. I saw them burying her." Lela recoiled.

"She's gone just today. Aren't they going to ask for ransom or something? Don't they usually wait at least two or three days? Are you sure- maybe you're seeing the future." Lela hoped she was right.

"No, I'm sure, she's gone." Lela's cell phone rang, and it suddenly occurred to her that she was at least an hour overdue at her house. It was Brett.

"Lela, are you okay? My guys said you're not at the house yet."

"I'm fine. Sorry, I got sidetracked," she replied.

"Lela, Phoebe was kidnapped- by people who may or may not be after you or others involved, so you can't be taking off without letting us know, alright?"

"Yeah."

"Where are you?"

"I'm at Phillip Harriman's," she rose and took a few steps away into the yard, turning her back to Phillip, "I was thinking he might have an idea where Phoebe is, so I came straight here."

"I learned to get the bad guys the old fashioned way. CAG teams never really use psychics much," he chided.

"Brett, he says the guys that took her are in Greenville, in a hotel, but he can't tell which one." Brett weighed the information. They had absolutely nothing to go on. Perhaps a small chance of a Hail Mary pass was better than nothing.

"How many does he think were involved?"

"Phillip, Brett is asking how many guys you saw," Lela relayed.

"Two," he replied, stroking his dog's ears, still trying to calm himself from the disturbing images, which impacted his sensitivities more than the average person.

"Two," she reported back to Brett, "and Brett, he says they killed her already, and buried her body in an area full of brush."

"Well, we received a call here just a while ago demanding ransom. Pretty bold move if she's not even alive. Nice hotel or a cheap one?"

Lela turned back to Phillip, "He's asking if it was a nice hotel or a cheap one."

"The furnishings weren't very nice, but definitely had that corporate cookie-cutter feel, so probably a low to mid-grade chain, not a local motel or anything." Lela relayed the information to Brett.

"Okay, not sure what we can do with that, but thanks. And please get back to your parent's house." He hung up, mulling over the limited information. One of the officers gathering evidence appeared.

"Lee said to give this to you. It's the make and model of the van used by the kidnappers. We found a tire track in the soft dirt near the edge of the road matching their factory-issue tires, so it's probably a late model," he told Brett.

"Get me the names and addresses of every mid to low grade chain hotel in Greenville. We'll drive there and start searching parking lots for the van. I don't want the locals stomping around too loudly and scaring them off. I don't trust to farm this out to them," Brett requested, the General overhearing as he approached.

"You're going to Greenville now? How long has it been since you slept?"

"I slept on the plane, plus I'll sleep on the way, let the officer drive." The General nodded and Brett rolled his shoulders back fighting his own tiredness.

Lela, too, was completely exhausted when she finally did reach the safe haven of her parent's home. She had begun the day in Johannesburg, her stopover from the regional airport, and was grateful to be home. Eager to dig into files she had been thinking about on the plane, she switched the light on in the office after dropping her things at the door. She flipped on the computer and began to read through files casually, one foot on the floor and one in the chair, not sure what she was looking for. She had been through these files before and had the gnawing feeling that there was something there she needed. Like a person who remembered they had a dream, but couldn't recall the dream itself, her memory grasped for the one piece of information to trigger the recollection. She removed pictures of Baby Girl Dossler and the infant's mother, no doubt taken by Lela's own mother. Why couldn't she remember the baby's name? Why had her mother not recorded it?

"Gabriel would remember," Lela muttered to herself. She pulled out some maps from the file and potential living arrangements. One was circled. That must've been where they went. The small town was one Lela had been to as a child, but not since then, and only an hour and a half away. She made a mental note to consider taking a ride out there.

Her computer chimed at her softly as an email arrived in her account. She smiled widely upon seeing it was from James. It read: EXPECT TO BE HOME WEEK AFTER NEXT (BUT PLANS CHANGE). I'LL LET YOU KNOW WHEN I HAVE FIRM DETAILS. CAN'T WAIT TO SEE YOU. Lela answered the email quickly, hoping to catch him so they could have an actual conversation, but he was already gone. She left the files out on the desk, flipped off the lights and computer, and headed for the shower.

Brett awoke when the car stopped moving. They were in the parking lot of the first hotel and the officer with him exited the vehicle.

"I'm gonna ask the front desk if they've seen two men with a small girl." he explained.

"Okay, but fly low, and instruct them not to speak openly about it, in case the kidnappers should overhear."

"Right."

Brett himself exited the vehicle and began casually strolling the parking lot. He pulled his keys out of his pockets, carrying them in his hand, as if he was walking to his car. Around the back of the building, he spotted one van of the correct make and model. He took down the license plate and met the officer at the front desk, handing it to him silently and then pretending to read the rack of travel brochures nearby: Dino-park, alligator wrestling, the largest tree in this hemisphere.

"A thriving metropolis," he said under his breath. The officer joined him.

"That license plate is on the check-in forms for an older couple, a man and woman. He remembers them checking in and says they've been here for three days, out by the pool all day. They haven't even left since they got here. Brett felt a bit foolish even going through the exercise, but any chance was better than no chance and he had some friends who said they had used psychics for some investigations before. Still, he didn't expect a positive outcome, but knew it would gnaw at him if he didn't at least try.

The next hotel they visited, the eighth on the list, was the most remote in town. Far from the interstate, the winding road to get there was pitch black with no street lamps to guide the way. As soon as they pulled in, Brett spotted a van in the far corner and had a strong feeling this might be the one.

"Park over there," he instructed, "then we can look like we're checking in." As the car pulled into a spot just three spots down from the van, he noticed a flash of light as a curtain moved aside in one of the windows.

"We have no luggage," he said, handing the officer one of his bags as he grabbed his backpack. Inside, the clerk confirmed the name of the man who had checked in.

"Just one man checked in, earlier today" the clerk explained, providing the name, which the officer promptly called into Felix Lee at the base location. He confirmed he hadn't seen any children. Brett's heartfelt heavy and he hoped with all hope that Harriman wasn't right that the little girl was dead, but, of course, had no intention of mentioning that suspected fact to anyone.

"I'll bet you he's got his friend with him-probably snuck him in the stairwell door," Brett said, checking his weapon. The officer hung up quickly.

"Guy's got a sheet of priors a mile long, and we're in luck! There's an outstanding warrant for him, so we can pick him up now. I told them to send some plainclothes local guys for backup ASAP. They'll be here in fifteen minutes."

"Okay, I'm going to go get line of sight on their door directly so there's no way they can slip out a back stairwell while we're down here. I'm putting my cell on vibrate. Text me when you're on the way up."

"Will do," the young officer responded, excited at the potential of getting a collar this big and hoping to save the little girl. This is why he joined the force-to save lives. Brett hung out unobtrusively by the ice machine until he felt the cell phone alert in his pocket. In moments, the other officers arrived and together they stormed the room. The assailants were shocked to see them, and the leader managed to fire a shot off before he was tackled, but he missed. He'd been drinking for hours since making the ransom call, celebrating his impending fortune. Once in custody, the men would admit nothing, and there was no sign of the little girl anywhere. There was a bent picture of her on the table next to the phone, and that evidence would be plenty to hold them as long as they wanted while they searched for the girl. Brett looked at the beautiful little girl's beaming smile in the picture, whose pigtails were framed with purple barrettes that matched her flowered dress. 'Please be alive,' he prayed silently with all his might.

Chapter 24

Ruth knew, as everyone did, that George and his condition were some of the biggest question marks of the mission. The project team met briefly to greenlight the next phase. Though tight on time, the team had instituted these tollgates to be sure that no critical steps were missed and, thus, they would hold a quick meeting at each project tollgate before moving forward.

"And the last of our risks is George's recovery time," Elizabeth Hallowell completed her briefing. Stone and Wood were present, but no longer stuck against the back wall. Less people in the room and the level of their involvement since the recruits had arrived warranted them chairs at the main conference table.

"Mitigation ideas?" Ruth punted to the team, "We're already doing everything medically possible to improve his medical condition. He should stay on light duty as long as possible until he has to climb. It's his mental state that's a concern. He hasn't seemed himself, but he's only been out of his coma a little more than a day."

"When can he see Phoebe?" Elizabeth offered, "That should help."

"Her acclimation steps are progressing well, but she won't be physically acclimated enough to participate in the pretest today. We could bring her by for a short visit," Stone reported.

"Okay, mark that as risk mitigation 1 on this sub issue," Ruth ordered.

"He's also very concerned about Jillian. I think that is affecting, very slightly, his concentration here," Wood interjected. "Could we assign someone to her?"

"Every available person is battling the Dark Janae, either by monitoring their heavy and escalating activity, or as assigned Kajika. We don't have anyone to even assign to monitor her, much less assigned for unnecessary guidance," Saraceni responded. Stone shared Wood's assessment that her situation needed more attention than it was receiving, but being a Circle 2 meant knowing when to listen instead of speak. He was thoughtful in his additions to the conversation.

"Perhaps we could just assign a promising Circle 1 to monitor." Stone began, "Wood and I did some monitoring as Circle 1's. The individual just needs to monitor- they don't need to know how to adjust or intervene, just observe and report. This would make George feel more secure without pulling a more experienced person from a critical assignment."

"Good," Ruth agreed, "Hallowell, please assign someone."

Shortly after the meeting broke, all parties broke up to tackle different tasks. Saraceni went to collect the recruits. Stone went to set up the next learning assignment for them. Wood went to collect the Circle 1, show him the post and teach him how to monitor and report properly. Ruth went to get Phoebe to take her to visit George. The rest of the team returned to decoherence analysis, dark Janae countermeasures or excursion prep for the mountain voyage. The entire training facility was energized with activity. Every so often, the decoherence alarm would go off for two seconds, but the assigned Circle 2 would immediately hit reset to stop the noise.

After they changed into athletic uniforms, Saraceni gathered the recruits into the common area. George was the only recruit out of athletic gear, but he sat on the sofa and listened attentively.

"All of you will be undergoing some mountain terrain and climbing training today in preparation for the climbing we will do next week," Saraceni explained. "Fortunately, George is already an experienced climber, so his absence is of no concern to the mission. The others of you who have climbed before, please help those who haven't. There are no points for excelling. If we don't all make it up that mountain, then there's no purpose in any of us going because the mission requires everyone."

"What about Phoebe?" Gabriel asked.

"She can't possibly climb, obviously. We'll have to harness her to someone for most of the trip," Saraceni responded.

"I still think we should do it without her. She's supplemental, not a critical participant," George protested.

"Let's see how the trial run goes today," Saraceni humored him, knowing Phoebe's effects as an adjuvant, no matter how slight an advantage, were needed in a mission where the outcome was so questionable. Just then, Ruth walked into the room happily holding Phoebe's hand. Seeing George, Phoebe broke away from Ruth and ran directly to him.

"Daddy! Daddy! Daddy!" she cried, flinging her arms around his neck and squeezing tightly. She giggled. "You look funny, Daddy!"

"How did you know it was me?" he asked curiously, playing with her pigtail braids, clearly brightened by the exchange.

"You look just the same on the *inside* silly!" the tiny voice responded, as if he were insane to ask such a question. George glanced at Ruth, already knowing this would mean advanced testing for Phoebe after they returned. 'If we return' he thought. The skills to view intrabody without monitors were usually not acquired until Circle 5 or 6. She wasn't the first, of course, but the cases were rare and those candidates trained and assigned differently.

The group took a break, all enraptured by their small visitor. She clearly won the hearts of the team. Seeing her Dad talking to Chandra and Jane, Phoebe started to look around the room.

"Where's Mommy?" she asked. George glanced around to the others and then crouched down to put his arm around his daughter.

"Mommy is still her old self, so she still lives in our old house in the old place, but she'll come here to be with us probably around the time you're getting as big as this guy here," George said, pointing to Kyle. Registering that 16 was a relatively distant time away, Phoebe added,

"That's a long time. I'll miss her." She looked sadly at her shoes.

"I know. Me, too, but we can play and you'll have lots of friends and be going to school, so it'll go by faster than you know."

"Okay, let's go play." She began pulling on his arm.

"Lucky me, I get to go play with this little gem while you guys do climbing training." George then added to Gabriel, quietly, "Don't forget, this team really relies on your leadership more than you realize. They take their cues from you. They feel more secure if you seem at ease, so please capitalize on that." Gabriel nodded, compliant in receiving the instruction.

"See you guys back here this afternoon for the trial run," George said to the group before leaving.

"I'll come get Phoebe in an hour," Ruth said to him, wanting to make sure he could sleep before the trial run to be at peak performance for the test. Saraceni took Molior through parts of the building they'd never been to before. As they left their secured quadrant, they entered a vast room with 30-foot floor to ceiling picture windows framing a beautiful cliff view.

"I had no idea we were so close to mountains on this side. I thought there were just those we can see from the back patio view!" Jane exclaimed as they entered the room. Jack leaned to see the view sideways as far as he could from the building's interior. There was a beautiful valley with a river and deer grazing nearby. As they exited the building, inhaling deeply the clear, fresh air, the view expanded and he could then see a whole herd of buffalo on the very far side of the river from the deer.

Making their way down narrow and winding dirt paths single file, the recruits arrived at the base of a cliff face where Wood already stood with some others and various ropes, hooks, pulleys and other assorted equipment.

Each team member climbed the cliff face twice, once with assistance and once by themselves. Everyone managed it, but some had more difficulty than others. Jack and David Running Wolf clearly were the top climbers within Molior, but Jane was surprisingly strong as well. The team focused on the last team member's descent, Chandra's, with cheers, and a side conversation began with Running Wolf, Saraceni, Wood and Jack.

"I'd really like to carry Phoebe," Running Wolf offered to Wood and Saraceni.

"So would I," Jack jumped in, then directly to Running Wolf, "and you've already helped with that genetics and science stuff. I'd really like a chance to help out more."

"Okay," Running Wolf responded, fully agreeable to relinquishing the task to him in the interests of teamwork.

"Not so fast," Saraceni corrected, "I'm sorry, Jack, but we have to operate at maximum performance. That has to go to the one with the highest skill, not the one who wants it the most."

"I did just as well as David," Jack defended.

"You did, but that was without a pack," Saraceni advised.

"How about a competition!" Wood suggested, recalling a similar event during training between himself and Stone. In no time, the two men were hooked up to parallel paths and battling it out in the ascent with a fully weighted pack equivalent to the harness plus Phoebe attached to them. Their teammates cheered them on from below, alternating between shouting Jack's name and David's. The two ran neck and neck for the better part of the journey, but about two thirds of the way up, Running Wolf pulled slightly ahead and stayed at the exact grueling pace as Jack fell behind and then became slower and slower. David Running Wolf reached the top and waited for Jack to arrive, impressed that he insisted on finishing the task.

David hung almost in mid-air near a shelf, but was able to rest his back into the supporting curve of the rock behind him. Jack finally got within a few feet of him.

"Welcome to my outdoor furniture set," David said, extending his hand to Jack, who strained just to reach it. David helped him up, and Jack moved into position to also rest in a semi-reclined position next to David.

"Don't feel bad," David encouraged, 'I grew up with cliffs for my back yard and my brother and I used to do climbs almost this difficult without any equipment. You've come closer than anyone else I've seen- you're really good!"

"Now he tells me!" Jack laughed.

After a meal and one hour of rest, the team returned to the training room ready for their trial run of creating the gate and supporting the information transfer. Wood and Juliet were speaking quietly as Gabriel entered and he noticed they both took one giant step backward from each other, and Gabriel smiled subtly to himself. Next entered Kyle, looking less exuberant than he had as of late, followed quickly by Alexander and Enam, deep in discussion on quantum mechanics. Chandra and Jack entered with David Running Wolf, the three still finishing lunches as they walked. Only George and Jane were still missing when Saraceni and Ruth arrived.

"George is in the monitoring room," Wood advised, and left to retrieve him.

"I'll get Jane," Chandra offered, and jogged down the hallway with a bounce in her step to Jane's room. She knocked lightly and then opened the door. Jane sat on the bed, elbows on knees, staring at the floor. Chandra could tell she had been crying. She rushed to her side, sitting next to her on the bed.

"Jane, what's wrong? Are you okay?" Chandra asked, her deep southern drawl emphasizing her concern in a way that would have sounded sugarcoated to anyone that didn't know her genuineness.

"So sorry," Jane began, with her British accent punctuated by sniffles, "Yes, sorry- I must look a fright. I don't know what came over me, really. I'm fine." She tried to brush off Chandra's concern with a wave of her hand.

"Darlin', I know it's hard. It's okay to be upset. We're all away from our families forever, or at least for a good long while, and there's all this pressure and no real downtime. It's no wonder. We're all here for ya, though, girl," Chandra continued.

"I'm just so silly. I just realized everyone here has someone, or misses someone, but I didn't have anyone there, no husband, no kids, just my fieldwork, and I don't have anyone here. It's almost worse, I think," Jane confided.

"Well, you have us! And I am serious as a heart attack- you need anything, you come to me!" Chandra said as Jane arose and started toward the door.

"Thanks, Chandra. Now, let's just go get this test done." The two walked down the hall like school girls. Saraceni could tell Jane had been crying, but she looked to have pulled herself together now. Still, he made a mental note to record it on the project status record later. Wood had already returned with George, who actually seemed to have more color in his face than the day prior, and was setting up the apparatus of the tenth platform. Seeing a platform, the team again viewed it with trepidation. Saraceni also made a mental note to reassess the future training curriculum since the first platform experience seemed to have soured them completely.

"So, is this one going to hurt?" David Running Wolf asked, deciding that he would rather be prepared than surprised.

"It shouldn't," Saraceni responded candidly, "but you might have less energy afterward."

"Now, this test will approximate the effects around you when we open the gate, and this," he said, pointing to an indicator on the side of the screen's display, "will show you how high you are elevating the frequency. It won't get to the top today. As we described yesterday, it's not possible outside of the zero decoherence area around the mountain. So, let's just see how high we can get it today." Saraceni knew, as did Wood, that if the team could achieve level 8 out of 10 in this environment, they should be able to achieve the level necessary for mission success when it came time for the real thing.

"Maybe even 7.5, considering Phoebe's not here to act as adjuvant today, so anything 7.5 and up we'll count as success," he instructed Wood on the side, who made a note of it in the project log on the flat tablet screen he carried with him.

"Team, please stand in a circle in the order we assigned," Saraceni instructed, which they did. "Once the machine is turned on, you will need to concentrate as you did in your meditation exercises. You are to focus all your energy on elevating your own natural frequency as high as possible. If you all do this, your dark matter DNA will operate in unison at the necessary frequency and should act as a control switch to transmit information in a direction upward."

"That's why we're in the order we are," Kyle added, " because by being in ascending order counterclockwise, the flow moves upward. If we were in ascending order clockwise, it would flow downward." They all nodded.

"Everybody ready?" Saraceni asked, and they all assented. Wood turned on the machine and as its gentle whir built to a full hum and then a steady noise the volume of a large roomful of conversation, the team members of Molior began to feel the effects. Jack felt disoriented for a second, but then remembered his breathing techniques. Gabriel, being in the first position, felt a heat sensation and a small vibration throughout every cell in his body, as if he were lying flat in the bed of a truck as it rolled across rhythmic ridges in the road. As the exercise progressed, the heat became more intense, but did not rise to the level of pain. Saraceni watched the monitors closely, which the team could not see, as the team members struggled with adjusting to the effects. After a few minutes, when he felt like they were adjusted, Saraceni gave the nod to Stone who increased the machine up to its full capacity. Wood did so, watching Juliet closely for a response, but she continued her breathing exercises with her eyes closed and did not seem to react to the increased intensity as some of the others did. David Running Wolf's long hair moved away from his body slightly, full of static charge.

"Good breathing exercises. Now focus on your meditations," Saraceni talked them through the exercise as they had done in some practice sessions in the early weeks of their training. Though they didn't know why at the time, the focus and effort they paid to the task then would certainly help them now. As they meditated, the frequency clearly raised on the monitors. Easily at first, and then more slowly until it seemed the team was exerting intense effort for the smallest fraction of gain in the level. Wood recorded the overall level of the group at 5.8, and noted each participant's individual level achieved. With all of Molior's eyes closed, Saraceni gave a look of concern to Wood and shook his head, pressing his lips together in dismay. He could feel a hair on the back of his head turning grey. He pointed to two scores, Juliet's and Gabriel's and raised his eyebrows in approval. Saraceni was very surprised to see Juliet at the top of the pack, at 8.2 individually, with Gabriel not far behind at 7.9. Wood gave a smile of approval, briefly displaying his pride in her. They noted that George's level only reached 4.5, the lowest of the group, and Saraceni furrowed a brow in concern as Wood made the note. They let the exercise run just a moment longer to be sure they wouldn't achieve any higher frequency. The faintest glow of an illuminated circle of light running parallel above the recruits' heads began to appear -spanning nearly the width of the room. When the machine results stayed flat and the light did not grow any further in intensity, Saraceni cut the power. As soon as it turned off, most of the team either doubled over as if they had finished a marathon, or fell to the floor. They looked weak. Exhausted, in fact. Kyle looked woozy again.

"Saraceni," he said in a weak voice, and then passed out. George did the same. Saraceni and Wood rushed to their sides.

"He's just out- he'll be okay," Wood reported of Kyle.

"I think George is the same, but call medical. Let's get him back to his room to be safe. Are the rest of you okay?" Saraceni looked around the room, assessing the condition of the other recruits. None looked close to passing out, but they didn't look well either. He hoped they could recover in time for the mission.

"You're all on rest status for the rest of the night. Everyone, when you feel ready, get back to your rooms, or to the common area at the farthest."

"How did we do?" Juliet asked, barely getting out the words.

"Well. You did well." He didn't consider it a lie, since he was responding to Juliet. His coolness betrayed his true belief. Saraceni knew at that moment the mission was likely to fail, and it terrified him for the first time he could remember.

Chapter 25

It was a sunny Saturday morning, the kind of day perfect for picnics. Lela was making coffee when outside the window she witnessed the "changing of the guard" as her night shift protection team left in favor of the day shift. Bianca's car pulled into the driveway, ten minutes early for their Saturday morning coffee, but, then again, Bianca was always early. Her datebook had noted reminders to be early in front of the standing appointments, in contrasting colors. Bianca could make a trip to the County Fair organized, but since Lela had been her friend since childhood, she barely noticed anymore. Lela heard her knock at the door.

"It's open," she yelled. An irony, given that it was left unlocked so the protection team could come and go freely into the front part of the house for the kitchen and the powder room. Bianca bounded in, datebook in arm and a Coach bag slung over her shoulder, her ponytail perfectly pulled back, her designer sunglasses perfectly matching her outfit and her makeup already done at 9 am on a Saturday. Lela was in light cotton sweat pants, a tee shirt, and bare feet. She had combed her hair at least, not that it mattered much. Bianca was like a sister and didn't require any formalities. The two women hugged and flopped on the cushy chairs in the back porch sunroom with their coffees.

"Soooooo….. are you glad to be back?" Bianca launched.

"Yeah," Lela responded in a mellow tone, "but I wished I'd had more time in Africa."

"More time getting hunted down and shot at? What are you, crazy?" Bianca scolded.

"No, not that part, but more time for research. And to help people."

"Well, maybe you can go back, once it's safe." Lela mulled this over and raised an eyebrow, giving a noncommittal noise. She thought about the dream, about the prospect of the corporations launching zone wars over resources and ruining what was left of peace there. It was almost impossible to imagine, yet the idea nagged at the back of Lela's brain. She knew there was a grain of possibility in it. She had seen Richard Currier's behavior in the meetings with Pfister. Those people cared about nothing, literally, but the bottom line. Almost caricatures, she doubted they could be persuaded by reason or human rights arguments.

"Anyway, I'm glad to be here. I can finish stuff with the house. I think I've decided to rent it out instead of selling. I might want to live in it when I'm older, but right now my apartment is fine, and besides, I might want to do some traveling, or need to for work." Lela's explanation rambled on until it sounded more like a desperate justification.

"You don't need to convince me," Bianca chimed, "I don't think you should be shuffling around this big house all by yourself, but you might want it later." Then Bianca broke into a wide, teasing smile and leaned in toward Lela, "besides, never can tell if you might want to go see James." Lela smiled slightly, but said nothing.

"So, heard from Captain America lately?" Bianca continued, not for a second intending on letting Lela get away from the topic that easily. Lela laughed.

"Yes," she conceded," He's coming this week. I think he wants to talk about seeing each other more often."

"Well, hallelujah! It's about time."

'Now, Bee, don't make a big deal out of it. He still lives about 1,000 miles away, so who knows what might work." Lela dampened her own enthusiasm.

"Yeah, yeah," Bianca waved her off, "but at least you're talking about it. Ready to give it a real try?"

"I think so," Lela answered slowly, not for lack of conviction in the idea, but for the fact that it had been a long time coming.

"Well, keep me posted. Now, find me an honorable Captain America type, and we'll both be good to go," Bianca joked. There was a knock at the door.

"It's open!" Lela and Bianca yelled in unison, their voices harmonizing in a way that sounded as if they actually were sisters.

"Lela?" Brett's voice echoed tentatively through the house. He couldn't tell where she was from all the sound bouncing in multiple directions in the foyer.

"Back here!" she yelled loudly, and then whispered "Brett" so only Bianca, who nodded knowingly, could hear. Brett appeared in the doorway freshly scrubbed, looking tan and exuberant, a stark comparison to the exhausted, pallid, sickly-looking version of Brett Lela had last encountered.

"You look better," she complimented.

"So do you," he responded, but wasn't looking at her, at all, but Bianca. After a moment, Brett realized he was staring and pretended to see something out the window. He pulled up a chair and became less casual in his carriage.

"I'm here in a more official capacity," he confided and glanced hesitantly at Bianca, as if to question whether he should continue. Lela stiffened her posture, rising at least eight full inches in the chair in the process, curiously.

"Bianca's like a sister, Brett. There's nothing she doesn't know, " Lela advised.

"Okay," Brett began, "Well, they found Phoebe Jacob's body."

"Oh, my!" Lela exclaimed, reflexively clasping her hand over her mouth.

"Yeah," Brett shook his head in dismay, "she was buried in an area with some brush." He looked pointedly at Lela, but did not elaborate further on the correctness of Phillip Harriman's assessment.

"Did they catch the guys who did it?" Bianca interjected.

"Yes, we did." Brett added a slight inflection to the "we" but not enough to be arrogant, just enough to clarify. "In fact, I interrogated them myself for hours. That's how we found the body. One of them had a conscience about it and I kept reminding him that the child's mother would be hunting indefinitely for her. He finally caved."

"I still can't believe this. So, did they say why they did it?" Lela's gaze rekindled an old intensity she had right after the bus accident. Brett knew she was wondering if this was related.

"They just wanted ransom money, believe it or not. We investigated thoroughly and there really is no connection at all between this and the bus accident," he added, not sure if she'd be glad or sad that the two were unrelated.

Lela became angry. "Then why did they have to kill her if they just wanted ransom money! Her poor mother is already grieving and they could have just gotten the money and returned her."

"I know," Brett consoled her, "the one who told us where the body was said it was an accident. I believe him."

"Yeah, "accidentally" dragged a four-year-old out of her own warm bed and killed her. I hope they get life in prison."

"I say death penalty," Bianca added, taking a sip of her coffee.

"Me too. Or at least the one- he was cool as ice. No remorse at all," Brett commented. Lela refrained. She didn't believe in the death penalty.

"Anyway, it's in Felix Lee's hands now. Which reminds me..." Brett pointed to the front door, " ...those guys are being removed today. They declared the bus incident an accident. There really was no foul play. They're sure." Lela was relieved, and felt a sense of closure in the knowing of it, behind her sadness.

"Well, I suppose that's better, that it was just a random accident and not someone intentionally taking my family away," she said quietly. How much better it was, she wasn't sure, but however slight the improvement, she did feel it.

It renewed Lela's desire to close out all the existing mess, both in the house and in her life. She wanted to start completely fresh, and in order to do that, she had to tie up loose ends. After Brett and Bianca left, Lela dug back into the office. Her guards had left and she felt a sense of peace at finally being able to be alone, after weeks in the company of others. Since the investigation was no more, she did not pick up with her mother's old notes and files, but instead focused on closing out the Africa documentation. She would be presenting to Pfister, Currier, and other company representatives this coming Monday for the assessment of the future viability of the project.

It occurred to Lela that the precious mineral would be a sought-after commodity once the location of the cavern, and the mineral vein, was known. Surely they'd want to start testing, and mining, as soon as possible. She had managed to keep it secret, deferring the moment when she'd have to decide how much to tell them, and now she had fifty or more other people who also knew the location. Fortunately, only the core team would be on location Monday to present their findings to the committee. She read through her emails and was finally jolted from her indecision by one line from Pfister: "Currier is continuing the project on their dime. He'll be sending his own team." Lela's body shuddered in a way that reminded her of when she and Gabriel were children and they would say "someone walked across your grave". Every bone in her body screamed out that Currier's men going in without any buffer from a truly scientific team would lead to disaster. She knew they would be callous. She knew they would be ruthless. She knew that the dream was right- they would start a war.

Lela dialed Tina's number immediately, as she reached for the list of who else would be presenting Monday. Lela, Tina, Mako and Brett were scheduled to speak, but Lance and four others from the project teams would be in attendance to assist with technical detail if needed. 'Nine people' Lela thought to herself. She and Tina agreed they should call together that small team of 9 for a meeting that afternoon to decide how to handle the situation.

"I have a huge empty house," Lela offered, "We won't be bothered here and it's very private." Tina advised that Brian and Rachel were already in her garage lab cataloging samples from the trip, and that she'd bring them as well.

"Good," Lela added enthusiastically," Rachel has some data I never got to see. Can you please ask her to bring it?"

"Sure," Tina replied, and hung up, leaving Lela wondering if she could convince the entire rest of the team to do something so against all of their natures, as well as her own- lie. She finished with her emails and was halfway through creating her PowerPoint presentation before she once again heard a knock at the door.

"It's open," she yelled in a rote manner, realizing that the door was still wide open though her security detail had left. She'd spent nearly her whole life in that house, never wondering about whether a door was locked or unlocked, now to have it spring to mind all too often. She hoped she wouldn't feel this jumpy about security forever. She just wanted to feel safe without having to think about it, the way you do when you're a little kid. In walked Gretchen, arms overflowing with a pile of files.

"Here are those files of Gabriel's you asked for," Gretchen stood in the doorway, stiff and still holding them. She still did not feel very relaxed in this house. Plus, everything here reminded her of Gabriel, which she hoped someday would be a fully good thing, but for now it still was not. The grief was too great.

"Thanks! Please, put them here." Lela cleared a tiny corner of the desk off.

"I'm so glad you can use them," Gretchen added sincerely, "I wasn't sure what to do. I wouldn't want to destroy any of Gabriel's research, but I can't do anything with it either. I hope one of these weekends you can come over and help me sort through what's needed from his lab and what can go."

"Of course. Someday we'll be done sorting through piles and piles of hard memories," Lela added in an attempt to console Gretchen. She felt closer to her now that the family was gone, like a war buddy almost, and was hit with her intense remorse for not having been nicer to her sooner, while Gabriel was alive.

"Someday," Gretchen sighed, glancing downward. A picture on the desk caught her attention abruptly and she grabbed it up without hesitation, without even thinking.

"Where did you get this?" she was almost frantic.

"My Mom had it," Lela informed her, "It's a woman and a baby she helped before I was born."

"No, it's me!" Gretchen corrected, "And my mom. I've never even seen this picture. I wonder if Gabriel found it and somehow it got mixed in with your stuff."

"No, Gretchen, this picture is taken in our upstairs back room. See the trim on the window? It used to be a nursery." Lela began sifting through the rest of the file for the two other pictures that were within it. She pulled them out. One was of the two mothers standing together, and one was of Gabriel, about three, sitting and carefully holding the baby, Gretchen, in his arms. Gretchen saw it and pulled it gently to her face, examining every detail. She began to weep softly.

"He knew me. You all knew me- and my Mom. I barely remember my Mom. I wish I'd known. I could've asked about her. Your Mom would have had stories. My Dad never likes to tell stories about her, especially after he married my step-mom." It was as if someone were pouring lemon juice over the already-existing wound within her.

"Gretchen! We have all those home movies. Remember when Mom did that huge project converting everything on film or VHS to DVD last year and then bored us to death with old vacation footage? Well, there are like hundreds in there! C'mon." They raced out of the room and upstairs to the storage closet. Lela whipped open the top of the box to reveal hundreds of DVDs, each marked clearly by year and color coded as to type of activity.

"Typical Mom," Lela smiled, pulling out a large stack of twenty or so from the year Gabriel was three. She rifled through them, but there was no real way to tell which footage might be helpful and which would not. She handed them to Gretchen.

"I can borrow all of these?" Gretchen asked, knowing these memories were precious to Lela, too.

"Of course. Just make copies of what you want and please bring them back eventually." Gretchen looked as if she had been given the Hope Diamond.

"I will! Thank you so much. This is so exciting."

Lela hugged Gretchen as she left, glad that she was able to help in some small way atone for the prior treatment of her. She knew they would always keep in touch and feel connected by the deep loss they had shared. As

Gretchen departed the front porch, Tina pulled up in her Jeep and jumped out with a springing motion.

"Grand Central Station, welcome!" Lela said, noting how good it felt to have the house bustling with activity again after shuffling around in silent solitude over the last months.

"The interns are right behind me. Brian and Rachel followed me from my house. The rest will be here in about half an hour." When Brian and Rachel arrived, Lela immediately began reviewing the mineral data Rachel had gathered with her while Brian and Tina prepared the sitting room for a meeting. She wanted to get the data review out of the way before the others arrived.

"This is what I thought was odd," Rachel, commented, pointing to the unique crystalline structure of the mineral. It was comprised of what seemed like thousands of very tiny decahedrons all tightly packed in a beautiful array.

"Hmmm, strange." Lela mumbled.

"Yeah, and watch this!" Rachel withdrew a tuning fork and struck it gently on the desk. The pure tone emanated from it and then seemed to level off at first, instead of fading as was usually the case. Then, when Lela started to think of the continuance of sound as inordinately long, it actually began to increase, becoming slightly louder at first and then building. Lela looked at it with surprise, and then realized the sound was now coming from the crystal itself, not the tuning fork.

"Wow! Well," she patted the stack of file folders Gretchen had brought over of Gabriel's, "I'm really gonna have to dig into these files and see- hope, rather- that my brother was ahead of me."

"Yeah, my brother and I help each other like that," Rachel said, then stopped short, not sure if she'd made a social guffaw with Gabriel having died so recently. Lela smiled warmly, reassuring her no misstep was made. The others arrived soon thereafter and the meeting was brief, with little debate over how much detail they should provide the sponsoring corporations. Lela shared her concerns about the corporations' misuse of the information and seemingly bad intentions regarding the villages, and Tina followed with an eloquent speech regarding the duty of scientists to preserve pure science and not allow good discoveries to be used for ill purposes. Not that they needed much convincing, but any trace of doubt held by the team members in attendance vanished in the face of Tina's conviction and they all agreed to near silence on their findings regarding both mineral and other resources catalogued.

Monday morning Lela marched into the presentation room and did exactly what she thought she would never do. She blatantly lied. She, Tina, Mako and a few others described how few resources were found, the difficulty in retrieving them and the instability of the area. Mako even added a comment about how it was clear people wouldn't live that poorly if they had any other choice, and unless the investment motives were purely altruistic, they shouldn't expect to yield any benefit. Lela added a pitch for continuing on purely altruistic levels to help the education, fresh water in malaria treatment in the region, and mentioned that she was sure there would be some great tax benefits to it. She masterfully painted herself as a scientist so embedded in the pure research of it that she didn't understand the harsh economic realities and that the tax benefits were negligible. A brilliant performance, by her and by all, and a successful one.

All the corporations pulled support and Richard Currier, who had intended on continuing with his own people was so disgusted, he stormed out, declaring, "This is the biggest damn goat rope I have ever seen. Don't ever call me for anything again. Ever!"

As the huge conference room cleared and the others walked the remaining guests who had not stormed out to the entryway, Lela stayed behind with a twinge of guilt. 'It's for the greater good' she reminded herself, mostly convinced she'd done the right thing. She knew herself well enough to know she'd wrestle with it for the rest of her life, whether she had done the right thing. She glanced out the giant floor to ceiling picture windows at the canyon, where her family had died, remembering how she couldn't even look there before she left for Africa. She was filled with a deep sense of tranquility and calm. She knew deep down she had taken the proper course of action. Regardless of how much she would wrestle with herself in the years to come, she would always remember that in the immediate wake of the action, it truly felt like the right thing to do.

After the guests left and Lela had moved down to her office, Pfister entered as she was packing a small box of personal items.

"Ms. Aquila, I'm so sorry they wouldn't pursue the project. There is so much good work to be done. We just can't afford to keep you attached to this facility when your skills don't match any of the other chartered projects. I do hope to work with you in the future." Pfister was obviously deeply concerned for her, and the sincerity of his message was felt.

"Thank you. I know it's all about the numbers. I have some other standing offers to consider, so don't worry about me," she advised. Pfister was visibly relieved, his slight shoulders dropping a few inches as he adjusted his glasses.

"Well, that is good to hear. Still, if Governor Jacob were here, he'd have replacement funding in no time," Pfister commented.

"Yes. I'm sure we would," Lela agreed, then added, "Have you heard how Mrs. Jacob is doing?"

"No, I have not," he replied. "We sent our condolences and flowers, but didn't really wish to intrude. I can't imagine how distraught she is. I just can't imagine."

That was the truth. No one could imagine how badly Jillian Jacob was doing- how deep the sorrow cut. She had lost her soul mate and her only and young child in the space of so many weeks. With the finding of Phoebe's body, all the police teams and investigators had left the house and Jillian was left alone. Unanswered messages piled up on the machine. She went through the motions of making herself a sandwich now and then, or watching the television, or sitting in the garden, but the lack of joy was unbearable. Painful moments were borne more harshly by those who were truly blessed- because they knew joy, they knew what they were missing. Jillian felt an emptiness that she could not even conceive could ever be filled. She felt as if half of her body and soul were gone, and she was dragging herself around the world by one hand and one arm, bleeding emotion all over the carpet like a slug leaving a trail of slime as she did. This was her mental image of herself moving through life, and she found it unbearable. She thought of helping others hunt for their missing children, but couldn't imagine being around grieving families reflecting her own pain. She thought of starting an orphanage, or a camp, in Phoebe's name, but shuddered at the prospect of seeing smiling children every day when every space between two children standing next to one another would be the place Phoebe should be standing. She thought of working on another campaign, and found all other candidates infinitely paler imitations of her husband's conviction and genius. She couldn't envision a life where she could contribute without being a burden.

Jillian looked at the grandfather clock. It read 9:00. Her own breathing took on a surreal quality as it echoed through the house with heavy thuds. In. Out. In. Out. Thud. Thud. Thud. Thud. She heard the water dripping from the faucet 2200 square feet away in the kitchen. The water dripping competed with the heavy echoes of her breathing thuds. Thud- drip. Drip, drip, thud. Out of sync. Her mind tried to wrap around it, yet could not. Out of sync. Jillian took a bottle of sleeping pills and lay down. Thud-drip. Drip-thud. Thud. Drip. Thud, thud. Drip- drip. Drip. Drip. Drip. Drip, Drip. There were no more thuds.

Chapter 26

Wood was still training the additional technician on the finer points of monitoring when Saraceni entered the monitoring room with Gabriel and Alexander Aquila.

"Just reroute according to this sheet, like I showed you yesterday, and I'll check it in a bit," Wood advised. Turning toward Saraceni and the Aquila men, he added, "I'm glad you're here. I earmarked the portions of Lela's monitoring that referenced the research as you requested.

"Excellent," Saraceni praised, "Gabriel, Alexander, I'd like you to review anything we find related to the research up until the time we leave tomorrow, both of you. We can afford every advantage possible- I've asked that it be consolidated, so you can make the best use of your time and not be in here continuously."

"If we're leaving tomorrow, I'd still like to see my wife before then. Ruth had said it would be acceptable," Alexander prodded.

"That's right!" Saraceni remarked, "Tell you what- Wood, cue them up the excerpts we need them to review and Alexander, I'll go get your wife. You can visit with her as soon as you are finished until meal time." Alexander brightened. He'd been married to the woman for 40 years and hadn't spent any lengthy time away from her since Lela and Gabriel were small children. He had really been missing her these last few weeks. Saraceni left and Alexander exuberantly turned his attention toward the monitor where Gabriel's attention was already focused. The monitor displayed the scene from a short time earlier when Lela was reviewing the unique crystalline structure of the DL mineral with the grad student intern, Rachel. When Rachel appeared, the Circle 1 monitor trainee broke attention for a second, glancing over at the monitor upon which they were focused.

"Hey! Eyes on your own screen, Cowboy!" Wood joked, and the Circle 1 snapped back to his own work.

"Had you ever seen that before?" Alexander asked Gabriel of his own research.

"No way," Gabriel chirped, quickly adding, "of course, I didn't get that far before I was so insensitively torn away from my work." He looked pointedly at Wood, clearly joking.

"Hey, I just follow orders around here. I'm just a Circle 2," Wood responding, having relaxed to the point of feeling as close to Molior as to his own training class.

"So, if it has a harmonic building capability, maybe that suggests it is isolated from external environmental influences as Saraceni suggested of the mineral here," Alexander analyzed.

"Do you think they're the same?" Wood asked. He raised an eyebrow in the way that Stone hated, and Gabriel mimicked his expression in an exaggerated caricature, making Wood laugh boisterously.

"I think if it's not the same, it's very close. Very similar properties, perhaps." Gabriel ideated. "Wait! She referenced a conversation earlier in the morning- can we go back to that?"

"Sure. I wasn't the one recording this morning, but I'll estimate. Let's go back to when she woke up and then forward about an hour and start there." They did, and realized Lela had had some minor phone conversations regarding the mineral, set up a meeting with some of the project team members, nothing really useful. Just then a knock at the door got their attention.

"Perhaps that's someone with the information she referred to," Gabriel hoped.

"They didn't earmark this section," Wood added skeptically, almost suggesting they skip it, but then Gretchen arrived and plunked a stack of Gabriel's research files on the desk as they watched the tape.

"Jackpot," Wood said, thinking for a moment the night shift had missed an important section.

"No, there's nothing in there. I know, they're my files. So, unless Lela is going to comment on how they might relate to the findings of the project team in Africa, we got nothing," Gabriel replied. They all listened in intently to hear what comment Lela might have. Gretchen grabbed a picture of the desk. "This is me" the image showed her saying and in the next few moments the entire story unfolded before Gabriel and Alexander of how Gretchen and her mother had lived with them when Gretchen was a baby.

"I remember that baby," Alexander said in amazement, "Your Mom was insistent we act as a sort of assistance house until the girl got on her feet. She never did anything like it before or since, and I wasn't crazy about the idea, but you know your mother- once she gets an idea in her head, there's absolutely no arguing with her." Lela pulled out the other pictures, including the one of Gabriel, three, holding Gretchen as a baby.

"I remember that," Gabriel said slowly, "That was Gretchen?" His wheels were visibly turning and he spun to face Wood, "It was you guys, I mean this place. It must have been. That's just too much of a coincidence."

"I wasn't here then. Before my time," Wood advised.

"Well, how far back do these tapes go? I mean, do you have a tape of that moment? I'd love to see it," Gabriel said. Wood could see how important it was to him. Gabriel had done a fairly good job masking his own grief over the separation, but Wood had been monitoring him for years and knew his mannerisms very well. He could tell leaving Gretchen and Caleb behind really did bother Gabriel more than he was letting on.

"I don't know the date. Let me check the weaver's log. That should show an intersection of your and Gretchen's threads during that time frame." In a moment, Wood returned with the data and had narrowed the time frame down considerably. Next, he checked the index by subject name and found the segments where both Gretchen and Gabriel were present, which were fewer than expected. He narrowed it down and finally the proper sequence materialized on the screen.

A toddler Gabriel was being handed the infant girl and took her in his arms as if she might break, emphasizing his special care so the adults could see how responsible he was being.

"Support her head, Gabriel," he heard his mother's voice from off-screen. He looked down at the baby Gretchen and she was staring directly up into his face, completely fixated on him, the way babies get, studying every detail. Then she smiled.

"She smiled! That's her first smile!" Gretchen's mother enthused in an elevated and speedy voice. "Gabriel, honey, try to get her to smile again."

The adult Gabriel was happy as well, "That was her very first smile. For me," he said to his father, who was happy to see his son fully happy again, even if for a moment. On the video, baby Gretchen started wriggling and toddler Gabriel wasn't doing a very good job of managing her movements. Mrs. Aquila's voice could be heard off-screen,

"Here, Gabriel, give her back to me, sweetie." Five seconds later Athena Aquila came into view, leaning over to take baby Gretchen from toddler Gabriel and her entire body appeared illuminated in shining bright gold light. She was even brighter than the other Kajika they'd seen in the cavern. 'The *other* Kajika,' Gabriel registered internally.

"She's Kajika," Gabriel whispered. Wood lunged at the monitor and hit the stop button.

"I forgot," Wood interjected hurriedly, "I'm so sorry."

"It's alright, Wood," Athena Aquila said seriously from the doorway where she leaned against the frame, apparently having been there for a few moments. Alexander Aquila faced her in his swivel chair and looked at her as if he were looking at her for the first time. After a moment, he rose and gave her an earnest hug, but not the kind of jubilant swinging around he originally pictured as he'd thought of this moment over the past weeks. She took his hand and Gabriel rose to follow, but Alexander asked him to please remain so he could speak to his wife privately.

The training room was empty and they sat in the nook beneath the paintings, just feet from The Cupel. "You're Kajika?" he sought to confirm it, but his tone sounded as if it were a rumor he'd heard from an enemy.

"Yes, I was," she answered softly, squeezing his hand.

"So, I was just an assignment to you?" he said, bordering on accusation.

"Of course not!" her tone was still soft and sweet, and she was smiling at him,

"Alexander, you're my kindred. I came back for you."

"Look, you know that I more than anyone understand when you have a job to do. You had an assignment. I understand that."

"Alexander," her tone became slightly more firm, "you have no idea what it's like to be here and find your binary soul match in The Cupel, and have to watch for hundreds of years as they move through circle after circle and they still aren't here yet. Yes, there is solace in knowing that they are on the way, but it doesn't alleviate the empty feeling. I watched as you progressed through circle after circle and as you reached the point where they said it would be anywhere from one to three more circles, I grew anxious. Then, when this problem arose, and the Dark Janae increased activity, it was determined a Kajika would be sent to protect the souls of you, Lela and Gabriel. I wasn't scheduled to go back for a normal resetting cycle for ten more of my circles here. I saw the opportunity to not only go back to be with you, but to go back as Kajika-with full memory- and to not only protect you, but to guide your choices in the hopes this could be your last circle in The Cupel. I took the chance. Would you have done any differently?" she asked.

"No, I wouldn't. I still don't like that you've had this secret from me for all these years. You could have told me."

"It is forbidden. Then I would have had to stay extra cycles in The Cupel to remediate, and no way am I doing that. Plus, I'd be away from you even longer and not even know it. I'd feel lonely and separated and not even know why. I've seen people go through it and it's torturous. This was the only way," she explained.

"I understand," he conceded, "I don't like it, but I understand." After a moment's hesitation he added, "This is why I had the job I did? So I'd understand the necessity of keeping secrets."

"Yes," Athena Aquila admitted, "I placed you in that career because I knew you wouldn't like it, but at least having been exposed to similar difficult dilemmas, you'd understand. I just wanted us to all be together."

He moved toward her, finally giving her the sort of warm embrace he had dreamt. Athena was truly elated, to finally be with her kindred without having any secrets from him. Even during their marriage, she always loved him with all her heart, but always had to hold something back, to make sure she could maintain the emotional walls necessary to achieve the tasks at hand. Now, those came crumbling down, like the destruction of an old building to break ground on a new one.

"Oh, Alexander, you're going to love it here! It's so different, much better, in so many ways. We'll finally all be together, living here as you and Gabriel learn all about True Earth."

"What about Lela?" Alexander queried.

"Lela has probably only one more cycle. This might have been her last, and may still be if she really steps up and develops in her time left, but either way, it's only one more cycle!"

"We won't be able to see our daughter for years and years. Doesn't that bother you?" He didn't understand how Athena could be so jubilant.

"The monitoring helps with that. That's why it's allowed. You'll be able to see how she's doing in this life, and the next if necessary. You can even help guide her. After a millennium of waiting for you, it does seem less to me. I'm used to it." With that, Alexander Aquila truly appreciated a small glimpse of how hard it must have been for her to wait for him. He was glad the situation had not been reversed.

"You always were the strong one, Athena." He tucked her hair behind her ear, "Let's go see Gabriel." Alexander and Athena walked into the monitoring room holding hands, and Gabriel knew instantly all was well. Every child knows when their parents are really getting along and when they are pretending. He was happy to see them so happy. They were both beaming.

"Kajika, Mother, really?" Gabriel asked. She hugged him tightly, doing the mother's involuntary scanning of her child for injuries.

"A mother's work is never done," Athena repeated one of her favorite quotes to her son. She motioned to the screen, which showed Lela meeting with the Africa team regarding the sabotage plan, "Case in point."

"Mom, why did they have to leave her behind? I feel terrible about it," Gabriel finally admitted to his mother what he would not to anyone else.

He trusted her to be honest, where he had not fully trusted anyone else from True Earth since he arrived in it.

"She's not ready yet. Plus, she has work to finish. Don't worry, we'll help her." Her response was succinct, but reassured him in a way no one else could have. Wood turned off the monitor.

"They'll bring us any additional footage about the research for you two to review later," he said to Gabriel and Alexander.

"Sir," the Circle 1 trainee at the far end said quietly.

"And Gretchen?" Gabriel said to his mother.

"She may be a bit longer, but I did all I could to be sure she was taken care of while I was there," Mrs. Aquila replied.

"I saw. Thanks, Mom." Gabriel smiled.

"Sir!" the trainee said louder to Wood. He pointed at the screen looking disconcerted. The subject he was monitoring was dead.

"Oh, this is grave," Athena said, seeing Jillian Jacob's dead body on her sofa, the empty bottle of pills next to her, and the top perched neatly in the crystal dish on the coffee table.

"Won't she just come here, or do another cycle?" Gabriel asked.

"No, Gabriel, she will now have to do several more cycles. She has shown she can't support the greater good over her own pain and concerns. That is one of the primary lessons to master before coming here. George will now have to wait hundreds of years for her." Athena's tone was very serious. She knew better than anyone how her friend would feel. Plus, there was a stigma to the suicides that never fully went away, even after they reached True Earth. They weren't treated poorly, but it was like a permanent black mark that could prevent them from getting the top assignments, or the most responsible positions- never eligible to be an elder, never allowed to teach any circle higher than a 13, the list was considerable. George would be devastated.

And he was. Upon hearing the news, George calmly walked out, went to his own room, and broke everything in it.

"Not the best state of mind to start the mission," Ruth said to Saraceni, "We should have waited."

"He'd have been twice as mad when he returned if we withheld it from him," Saraceni defended his decision. "Besides, if he knows she's in the between while we do the exercise, he will be more motivated for success."

"George doesn't work that way. He'll be concerned that she is between, more susceptible to the decoherence effects for not being grounded anywhere. It will distract him."

"I'm sorry, Ruth," Saraceni apologized, though he was still not entirely sure his decision was the wrong one. He did, however, defer to the fact that Ruth likely knew her own son better.

Chapter 27

The morning of the mission, Wood entered Juliet's room silently. He stood watching her sleep for a moment before she realized someone was there and shuddered awake. He quickly moved to sit at her bedside.

"I'm sorry. I didn't mean to startle you," he said.

"It's okay," Juliet responded, acutely conscious for the first time that no other person had been in her personal room since she arrived at the training compound.

"Is everything alright?" she added, not understanding why he was there.

"Yes, yes, of course," he seemed nervous. "I just came to bring you something." Wood removed from his pocket a beautiful, large piece of a polished mineral that looked something like a diamond might if it were more silver in color. It was attached to a leather cord, a stark contrast to the way such gems were customarily presented in The Cupel.

"Is that the mineral where we're going- the one Saraceni keeps talking about in the mountain?" Juliet asked.

"No," Wood responded quickly, still nervous, both for his own discomfort and in his own underlying concern for Juliet's safety in leaving on the mission that day. He knew it was dangerous. He knew chances of success were good, but not great, and certainly not guaranteed. He knew he might never see her again, for, if someone died in the enigmatic region around the mountain, their soul was lost to True Earth forever. The souls lost there could not be reengineered, redirected, or passed through The Cupel, because they were gone- beyond retrieval, and where they went, no one knew for sure. The presumption was to the Divine- by most, anyway.

"No, this is not that mineral. This comes only from a small island on the far side of the planet. It is thought of as holy by the Derexi. It is said to invoke the protection and guidance of the path to unity. The technical name is azimuth but everyone calls it Godstone."

"What's a Derexi?" Juliet asked, looking at the morning light reflecting off the necklace.

"They are spiritual leaders, like if in The Cupel you were to combine a Native American Shaman and an Australian aboriginal spiritual leader, something like that. Thought that's still not the best explanation, it's the most you can understand right now with your training," he confided.

"Well why didn't we learn about this?" she asked, a bit perturbed that something this important hadn't even been mentioned in the weeks and weeks she'd spent at the facility.

"We don't talk about things like that here. It would be like opening up into gospel songs in the middle of a military briefing to pray for the success of the mission. Everyone prays, of course, but it's a silent thing, not socially acceptable in this context. It's private," he explained. Juliet took the necklace from him.

"Well, thanks, Wood, I can use all the help I can get, divine or otherwise," she joked, holding the necklace casually. Wood clasped both his hands around hers to protect the necklace, almost reflexively. He looked directly at her.

"Juliet, any stone like this is very rare. They are powerful," he continued quietly, knowing that she didn't fully understand, "and this particular one has been in my family for many years." She understood, and looked at him apologetically. She opened her hands gently, stressing the fact that she was being extra careful with the stone, the way Gabriel had done at three with baby Gretchen.

"Oh, Wood, thank you so much. I don't know what to say. I don't want to take something so important to you," Juliet's tone was soft.

"You are important to me, and I want you to have it. It will help protect you. I believe that," he said, taking the necklace to tie it around her neck. "See how the leather strap goes straight through the tiny hole drilled through the stone- no hooks or clasps, and then- we triple tie it back here with a series of Gideon knots. Affixed this way, a stone like this has never been lost. This is the strongest cord there is."

"I will treasure it always," Juliet said, and then she hugged him. The two sat with their foreheads pressed together for a full minute before moving.

"We'd better go," Wood said, standing up abruptly. He turned to see her, the necklace shining around her neck, twinkling in the morning sun, and immediately felt a great sense of relief. He knew in his heart she would be protected.

They joined the others in the staging area as the crew did flight pre-checks on the two helicopter-like crafts nearby. All of Molior were checking their packs, adjusting their gear, or reviewing the maps for the difficult terrain they would face once they landed. When Wood and Juliet arrived, Stone saw the necklace around Juliet's neck and gave Wood a reproachful glance, knowing he was courting a reprimand. Ruth walked across the concrete staging area with a pair of metal blocks with stone, crystal, laser attachments. They looked like something from a seventh grade science project, not slick or sleek like all the other technology at the facility.

"Team, this is your one and only communication device. Everyone on the mission must protect it at all costs," she advised them.

"How about a tin can phones and some string," Gabriel joked, and his mother gave her old standard look instructing him this was not the time for his humor.

"I thought we couldn't communicate in the mountain ring zone?" Jack queried.

"That's right," Ruth responded, "no traditional electronics or communication equipment will work there. However, this is different. It doesn't have any conventional pieces. Think of it like a hard land line. It works on the spiritual plane, and therefore it may only be used by kindreds. It's the same way kindreds sense each other in the physical world without ever meeting. They have a direct connection to one another that cannot be created or duplicated. It just is." She handed one device to Alexander and one to Athena Aquila. "Alexander and Athena, as binary soul matches, can keep our communications open."

"Alexander," Saraceni jumped in with an instructional tone, "In that zone, this will take a fair amount of energy out of you to use, so no phoning just to chat. Necessary communication only, and then as short as possible or it will wipe you out, and we can't afford that."

"Understood," Alexander responded, taking the device from Ruth. Athena did the same. With just a few minutes left before departure, a project team member brought Phoebe to the takeoff area. She ran to George.

"Daddy! We're going on the big bird! Up in the sky!" she squealed.

"I know, honey," George scooped her up in his arms, and smiled mildly at how much easier it was than with his 42 year-old body as Governor Jacob in The Cupel, with the bad knees and shrapnel in the shoulder.

The two metal birds became pregnant with possibility as the team divided and entered their bellies for transport to the mysterious mountain zone. The doors were about to close when the messenger brought Ruth the latest report.

"The fifth earthquake over 7.0 in The Cupel this week, Ma'am," the messenger reported. Then after a moment, "Shall I take it to the mission chief, Ma'am?"

"No, thank you," she responded slowly. "They have enough to worry about." She looked up at the craft. Saraceni saw them hand her the tablet, and saw her face upon reading it, but the craft were waved onward and took off, leaving him wondering what the message contained. He quickly put it behind him, and looked to the arduous task ahead. After an hour of flight, the team was relatively quiet, the initial nervous chatter having died down. They would be landing within half an hour.

"Now on approach, we may get a little bumpy, but we will keep sufficient capabilities to function adequately and land. We've done it many times. That's how we know this particular spot is safe." Bumpy turned out to be an understatement. As they approached the clearing in which they would land, the last five minutes were bordering on sheer terror. The aircraft would abruptly descend 15-30 feet or more, be corrected only to repeat it again. Pitch to the left, drop, hard pitch to the right. Now they understood why each person was strapped in at both shoulders. By then end, they all sat with eyes closed, just praying for it to be over. Ironically, in the final moments the birds set very gingerly on the ground. When the passengers emerged, it was a surprise to see the beautiful, clear sunny sky. The crafts had been forced to pitch and yaw by unseen forces.

The area immediately surrounding the clearing was dense with forest, but the red cliffs could be seen protruding upward behind them, or the tops of them anyway. The team walked through the forest, and Phoebe was the first to regain her composure following the flight, being spellbound by the trees and forgetting all about the preceding fright.

"Look how big they are, Daddy! I've never, ever seen trees *that* big before." the small voice was nearly lost in the volume of foliage.

"Me, neither," George agreed, staring himself at somewhere near a thousand trees averaging 118 feet tall and 17 ½ feet in diameter. More striking, they were all branchless all the way up the height of the tree until very near the top, where each branched into 2, 3 or 4 branches.

"Yes, these are about 3500 years old," Saraceni informed, clarifying, "True Earth time measurement." Soon they left the shade of the forest and were in the open sun, walking across a wide swath of land approaching the cliffs. The heat intensified notably and a few people removed their jackets, rolling them up into their packs. Juliet and Kyle walked side by side in perfect stride, having been a hiking pair in several of the prior missions. They communicated nearly wordlessly and handed items back and forth as needed as if reading each other's minds. After a while, they spoke as they walked, as many of the team had small sidebar conversations going.

"It's funny I think of you like a little brother. How much older than me are you, anyway?" Juliet asked Kyle.

"Several centuries," he laughed, "but you can be my unofficial adopted little sister if you want. My parents would be so proud."

"You know your parents? How does that work, exactly? How can people have parents here if some of them were born the first time in The Cupel?" she asked.

"Well, we've obviously taken the whole "parent" part out of being a parent in that we engineer the bodies and don't give birth the old fashioned way. Still, if some come here as children to avoid the mental shock of it, like Phoebe, and then grow up here, or if they had a parent-child relationship in their last lifetime, like Gabriel and his parents, then they maintain those titles here. For others, they go through a soul selection process to select their "children", but not everyone does. Since being a parent here entails nurturing and educating the child, some people prefer teaching or mentoring opportunities to help in the same way without being labeled a "parent". It's really a matter of choice," Kyle explained.

"Do most people choose to, or choose not to?" Juliet was curious.

"Mmmm, about half and half, I guess," Kyle appraised.

The group reached the cliff face and stared at the first vertical climb with some trepidation. It was about twice as tall as the one they practiced on.

"Now just remember, it's no more difficult than what you have already done, just longer. So, you will have to spend more time doing the climb, but it's the same skills for the top half as for the bottom half, and you can stop for a good sized break halfway up if you wish." Saraceni advised.

Phoebe was strapped securely to David Running Wolf's back. He did not feel the additional weight as much as he felt the hindrance of movement. As the next strongest climber, Jack carried Running Wolf's pack in addition to his own and they started first, both to set the pace for the others, and as a safety measure in the unlikely instance Phoebe should fall, there would be others below to catch her. With the unequal burdens, Jack and David moved at the same pace and climbed side by side most of the way, occasionally moving into singular position when the terrain called for it. They reached the first ledge and stopped to take a good water break. Looking down, they saw the remainder of the team paired off, straining on the climb beneath them. Chandra and Jane were next, then Gabriel and George, then Juliet and Kyle, then Alexander and Enam, and lastly Saraceni and five equipment team members brought up the rear.

"Daddy's really far down there," Phoebe commented fearfully. It was clear she was worried her father might be hurt.

"He is. Just like we were!" Jack replied brightly, "and now we're here, and he will be too. See these straps?" He tugged hard on one, "See how he has them, too?"

"Yes," she replied, trying to be brave, but she still didn't sound convinced. David Running Wolf, a father of four, tried a different tactic.

"Wow, look at Juliet's necklace. It's shining into my eyes even way up here." Phoebe looked.

"It is very shiny," she seemed to be distracted for a moment.

"Well, I heard there are other shiny rocks like that in these rocks we're climbing on. You should keep an eye out for them while we're climbing. Maybe you could find one!"

"Really?" Phoebe responded, her eyes brightening. She began scanning the rock face for signs of such a miraculous treasure. "Then I could give one to my Mommy when she gets here." Jack and David both knew what had happened to Jillian, but they agreed anyway, though with slightly less enthusiasm. They would live here a long time and know this tiny girl long after she was grown. No doubt they would work with her in the future and they didn't want her to feel misled someday. After another forty-five minutes, they made it to the next ledge. Starting to feel the intensity now, they knew the others must be even more worn out.

They agreed Jack would pull himself over the top first, having the lighter load, and then help pull David up to help keep Phoebe's positioning as upright as possible as David pulled up. This worked pretty well, except for Jack had to drag David a few feet away from the edge, face down in the dirt, so he could have room to pull his knees under him and rise to his knees so Phoebe was standing vertically behind him.

"Gee, thanks," he said to Jack snarkily.

"Don't mention it!" Jack grinned in his charming and affable way, detaching Phoebe from David's back. She skipped around the flat mountaintop area, turned a cartwheel, and looked at Jack.

"You look like Prince Charming," she said, examining him as if she had met him before in her living room.

"Well, I was. Were you ever in a play in school- where you pretended to be a part that was somebody other than you?" he asked.

"Of course. I was Eleanor Roosevelt in the history pageant," Phoebe said as if it were common knowledge.

"Right, but you weren't really Eleanor Roosevelt, right? You were just pretending to be her. Well, I was just pretending to be Prince Charming," he explained. She thought about it earnestly for a moment and then added.

"Well, that's good. I was thinking you don't act very much like a Prince. I mean, you're nice and all, but you don't bow, or wear a crown, or like dance around and stuff." David and Jack laughed and then saw a hand come over the edge, reminding them they were there to help the others. They pulled Jane and Chandra up the last few feet over the edge with ease and waited on the others. Before long, all of Molior and the equipment were up over the edge. They sat taking a break in the field, and Alexander communicated with his wife on the device.

"We've arrived at the top of the mountain. Confirming 3:48 PM," he spoke into the microphone. His body felt strange as he communicated, tingly all over and sort of warm with a slight sense of being disoriented for a moment. Athena copied and then they moved to radio silence. Saraceni wanted the entire team to rest at least a full hour before they attempted to open the gate. If they could succeed before sundown, they could camp there for the night and then climb down in the morning, when it was less dangerous. Night climbing was insane, and they had brought plenty to keep warm with when the dusk air turned cool.

Molior lay in the grass forming a circle, staring up at the clouds and sunny sky. They could feel their energies aligning in this place. The mountain's properties were almost palpable. The equipment team worked to set up the necessary elements into a configuration matching the one they had tested in the training room, only this time they did not have the benefit of monitors to tell how close they were getting. Saraceni surveyed the group, assessing that several of them should be a half point or full point higher than in trials since they had rested the last couple days. George seemed to be much stronger than in the first days after coming out of his coma, and Gabriel and Alexander both seemed brightened by the visit with Athena Aquila. Overall, he thought their chances were much improved.

Just when all were very relaxed and focused solely on the mission at hand, they felt the ground shake beneath their backs. Fortunately they were at the top of the mountain, for a wide array of rocks began crumbling down on all sides. If that had happened while they were climbing, they would have been pelted by small rocks and probably lost their handholds or footholds. The ground rumbled softly. It was a small quake, but it still unnerved them all.

Saraceni grabbed Alexander and moved away from the group with him and the communication device. He didn't want the others to hear the exchange. Their mental state needed to be as positive as possible.

"Whatever we talk about, it's confidential," he said to Alexander.

"Yes, Sir," Alexander said in rote fashion.

In the communiqué, they learned that there were multiple earthquakes happening in The Cupel, likely the beginning of the more serious decoherence effects. There had been one tsunami and Mt. Rainier in Washington State in the U.S. had started smoking. Out in the universe, new black holes seemed to be popping up, or so said the media conjecture since patches of sky where stars formerly twinkled were now dark. Solar flare activity was up 11% overnight. Alexander thought of Lela.

"So, we can expect more of these earthquakes here, too?" Alexander relayed Saraceni's words to Athena, who took her responsive cues from Ruth.

"Yes," they heard back. They also learned the earthquake was much stronger in the areas away from the mountain. It did seem they were buffered from the external physical effects some, but not completely, since they were coming from deep within the planet. Time was crucial, and in moments, Saraceni had the group arranged in a circle around the equipment just like in the training room test run. This was the moment they had trained for, and the world was literally breaking apart with every moment they delayed. The sun was still fairly high in the sky, but had just begun to tip its hat at them.

The apparatus began to work and the gate seemed to have the possibility of opening. The space in the interior of the circle between them became fuzzy, almost opaque. Each team member focused on achieving the highest frequency, so the data could transfer from the current circle to the new one they were trying to open, and they watched for some sign the automatic natural processes were taking over as expected. Phoebe held her father's hands and focused her energy with her eyes closed. George could feel the difference added by her tiny presence over the last trial run, and knew that she as his adjuvant did have an additive effect to his abilities. They focused with all their energy, but after a few minutes of the effect seeming to build, it began to level off and they could hold out no longer. The energy in the circle broke and they fell to their knees, or to a laying position. A comet streaked by in the sky and though it was outside the immediate mountain zone, they could hear its shrieking noise as it tore through the atmosphere. 'Please let that have burned up and not impacted anywhere' Saraceni thought to himself, looking around at the beaten team before him. They had failed.

Chapter 28

In a few moments, they arose.

"We have to try again," Enam said.

"What went wrong?" Gabriel said to Saraceni.

"I don't know," Saraceni responded and all were silent. "We have to call this in."

"Let's just wait a minute. We need to try to figure out what might have gone wrong. We should call it in when we have a plan. Otherwise, everyone will freak out," Juliet said.

"Okay, let's break it down and see what we can come up with," Saraceni began.

"Alright," Enam started, "We need a quantum gate, and for that we need a very long linear string of quantum dots that are raised from ground state."

"Check," Saraceni said, motioning to the apparatus.

"And we needed a low-decoherence or no-decoherence environment," Enam continued.

"Right, we hauled our cookies all the way to the top of this mountain cause y'all said it was low decoherence," Chandra commented.

"And we needed a swapping operation, which we were to create by raising the frequencies of our dark matter," Enam progressed. Saraceni did not check this item so quickly. Juliet sensed his hesitancy.

"Saraceni, how close did we get in the test?" she asked.

"Pretty close," he was deliberately vague, "but you weren't right there. However, you've all improved since then."

"I think we found our problem. We just aren't getting it done," Juliet said.

"Maybe," Gabriel interjected, "but let's not make any assumptions. What was the fourth thing?"

"We were counting on the natural occurrence to kick in," Alexander offered.

"Right, well that was a big assumption. I mean, we could do everything right and maybe this natural occurrence doesn't just catch on. Maybe you can't force it," Gabriel said.

"All our tests show it should be able to be artificially begun and then self-propagate from there. It is the same as other fields where we've had similar theories that have turned out. There's no reason it shouldn't work," Saraceni said.

"Well, let's attack this scientifically," Gabriel began, "Where have these gates been witnessed to open before- are they always in the same location?"

"They happen so fast, we can't really tell where they originate, but no one has ever witnessed one opening before," Kyle explained.

"No one? Ever? Well, that's something. Sounds improbable," Juliet said.

"Unless the location was invisible, or the occurrence itself was invisible," Jane thought aloud.

"Or hidden," Gabriel added.

"Maybe the coherence time is just too short," Enam said, "Even if we were 100% successful, if it can only be maintained a fraction of the time it needs to stay coherent before decoherence disassembles the assemblage, it wouldn't catch."

"Do you know the coherence time? I mean, the exact calculation?" Gabriel asked Saraceni.

"No. Those calculations were prebuilt into the equipment settings, but I think Ruth does," Saraceni responded.

"Okay, let's call it in, and get some other information," George suggested.

"Agreed," Saraceni said.

Alexander reached Athena on the communication device and after a few moments the team learned the coherence time, and had the answers to all the other questions they could think of.

"Lela and the team found some additional info on the mineral. The team is pulling up the monitors to replay now. It'll be just a minute," Athena said. Alexander leaned over struggling for breath, and Saraceni feared he was using all his energy to communicate. It wasn't designed to have lengthy conversations like this. Juliet's necklace, and some of the purple mountain mineral started carrying a small light within. He was surprised, but before he could think about the property itself, Juliet herself gained his focus. He motioned to her to come over and instructed Alexander to ask Ruth if Wood was there.

"Yes, he's here," Athena responded.

"Put him on," Alexander advised, at Saraceni's instruction. Saraceni handed the communication device to Juliet. She looked at him curiously.

"I thought this only worked for kindreds," she said, confused.

"Right," he answered, "Ruth wouldn't confirm it for me, but she didn't deny it either, so let's see if I'm right." He looked at her intensely, hoping. Juliet had more strength to start with, 8.5 on her own. She could afford the depletion more than Alexander could at this point. If they were to get another shot, he needed to stay at least with high enough energy levels to carry his weight.

"Wood?" she said into the device, feeling self-conscious speaking to him in front of the others.

"Juliet?" he responded slowly, not sure if she could hear him and somewhat dazed that it might work for them.

"I can hear you!" she smiled.

"Great! Listen, decoherence is at 98%. You must work quickly. Lela's team found that the mineral takes on the frequencies of many properties, not just sound. Many properties would self-build within that mineral, independently of the environment," Wood repeated Ruth's words one by one.

"Of course!" Gabriel said. He looked at his Dad, "Nothing happens without a reason. Saraceni, where is this mineral from?"

"It's found all around the mountain. We find small pieces every now and then. We've built up a decent amount over a long time," Saraceni responded.

"Are there any caves around here?" Gabriel asked.

"There's one, about a quarter way down the mountain on the far side, opposite of the direction we came up, but I've only seen it in photos. It's not near any steppes or decent rock trails," George said. Gabriel turned to Saraceni.

"Saraceni, I think the mineral is inside the mountain. Like a giant geode. Like in Africa. If I'm right, we should be doing this from inside the mountain, not on top of it. The interns tests in Africa showed results were amplified a thousandfold when they were inside the cavern. It must protect itself from decoherence somehow in the mass or continuity or volume of it," Gabriel said.

"Gabriel, you're asking me to take a huge risk. Take all these people down the treacherous side of a mountain- at night- and redo the test from inside when all our data shows open fields are needed," Saraceni said.

"I think Gabriel's right," Alexander jumped in, "Think about it. The mineral self-propagates properties. What if- just what if- it has naturally-occurring quantum dot nanocrystals embedded in the mineral itself? You wouldn't need to create them artificially- they'd already be there. Everything else needed is already in nature- why wouldn't this be? And if that were the case, with a whole mountain full of them, inside the crystal lattice the quantum dots could give rise to a vibration which, instead of competing and canceling out each other's amplitudes, just pile one on top of the next creating a huge tidal wave of oscillation at the same frequency. That's why the sound didn't diminish. In effect, it did become self-propagating."

"It's the only plausible explanation," Gabriel said, "and besides, it's better than anything we've had so far. It has to be worth a try." Saraceni paused, looking around the group.

"You've asked us to trust you- all this time," David Running Wolf added, looking at Gabriel for support in his argument to Saraceni, "Now you need to trust us."

It seemed Saraceni had succeeded. Gabriel was now a leader, and everyone was following him. Saraceni just hoped they weren't following him to their deaths, to the deaths of everyone. Another tremor shook the ground. The sky smelled of ozone and a lightning storm without any thunder or rain could be seen on the next ridge, coming their way. The barely perceptible sound of lightning alone moving through the distant air was eerie.

"Okay, let's do it," Saraceni said. Juliet sent in the communication of their plans as the others moved quickly to the mountain's edge.

"I'll go down to the cavern first and make sure it has the crystal walls we expect. No point in all of us going down there if it's just a dirt floor and rock walls," Running Wolf said.

"I'm going with you," Jack added.

"What about Phoebe?" Jane asked. If they both went, whose back would carry the little girl?

"I'll take her," Enam said, "I felt pretty strong on the way up. I can handle it."

Running Wolf and Jack descended into the dark. The sun had been gone for some time now. The lightning in the sky from the storm nearby, though threatening, actually did help them to see, plus the moon was almost full. They blazed the trail and set the anchors as they descended which would give the others a more secure path to follow. Just feet from the top of the cave, David grabbed a handhold and let his foot dangle, searching for the next stepping stone. He thought he had it, but his large size 12 foot had more out than in and he lost his footing, hanging only by one arm with much slack in the rope. Jack grabbed him and helped pull him back to a position of safety.

"Thanks, man," David said, breathless.

"Well, ya know, I do mountains tons of times bigger than this with my superhero brother back home," Jack deepened his voice to mimic Running Wolf.

"Funny," David responded sarcastically, not entertained with the impression, but smiled briefly anyway at Jack's ribbing. They pushed their legs out from the cliff face. Letting out some slack on the rope, they swung into the cave with enough momentum to grab onto an edge and pull themselves in, first David and then Jack.

"Wow! Amazing!" Jack exclaimed looking around. The cave was huge, easily ten times bigger than they expected, and entirely encrusted in the crystalline mineral. It was photoflourescent, emitting its own soft light glow of gentle purple light.

"Well, at least we don't have to worry about trying this in the dark," David said, sticking his head out of the cave and giving a long, loud whistle to let the others know that they were correct and to head on down.

Chapter 29

As quickly as they could, the remaining team members made their way into the cavern. David Running Wolf helped each and every one, pulling them in, removing their packs. As he continued with the second half of the recruits, the first to arrive began setting up the equipment. Running Wolf took Phoebe from Enam, who barely seemed out of breath.

"You're strong!" she said. Then, looking around the cavern for the first time she added, "Oooh, pretty, all the little crystals are talking to each other!"

The cavern held a mild purple photo-fluorescence generated from within the mineral walls themselves. Though made of a different mineral, it was reminiscent of the cavern in Africa, but for being entirely closed in. No open sunshine could have streamed in even in the daytime. The mineral was more densely packed and sparkled more brilliantly, almost as if it were a substance foreign to the region. As the recruits arrived, the glowing intensified very subtly. When Gabriel, the last, stepped in, the presence of all the recruits triggered the room to light up to the luminosity of a regularly lit room.

"Well, that's helpful," Gabriel commented. The ground shook mildly. A few rocks, having come from the short distance of cliffs above, tumbled by the cavern opening to the starry sky outside

"It's worse everywhere else," Saraceni reminded, "and in The Cupel."

Word had spread about the earthquakes, volcanoes, tsunamis and meteors in The Cupel. The decoherence was at 98%, and while that applied to both The Cupel and True Earth, the effects were felt sooner and more acutely in The Cupel because of its' small scale. A small ripple of energy on True Earth represented a cosmic blast in The Cupel. As they finished setting up the equipment, Jane and Jack, closest to the entrance, noticed a meteor shower outside. Hundreds of meteors streaked across the sky.

"Okay, let's do this," Gabriel announced, confident that this time the Gate would open to the next circle. The recruits stood in a circle- this time, Phoebe right in front of George holding his hands. They all concentrated intensely. Saraceni monitored as best he could and adjusted the equipment when he thought it would help. Otherwise, he felt helpless. He had taught them to this point and now had to just sit and watch the fate of himself and all living things unfold. The large, halo-like circle of light began to form over the collective arrangement of the recruits almost instantly this time. In a few short minutes, it grew to an intensity that surpassed anything they had seen in the trials.

Alexander felt his entire body filled with flowing energy as it warmed up. Each recruit felt the small vibrating sensations, except Juliet. Her necklace emitted a beam of white laser light directly out from it which then reflected around the room 16 times in a geometric pattern. The crystals under their feet brightened with luminosity, which spread out from the crystals under the feet to those next to them, and those next to them, in a chain reaction that spread throughout the entire cavern, then the entire mountain, until every tiny nanocrystal was lit up with energy. The recruits concentrated their energies toward their dark DNA and raised their own frequency. As they did so, the entire mountain was transformed into the switch to convert the data from the present circle to the new one.

In a blinding flash, the circle above their heads spread outward, beyond the cavern, beyond the mountain, past the horizon and into the distant edges of the universe. In an instant, the gate was created and the new circle opened up. The circle of light provided a beautiful contrast against the falling meteor shower and a planet full of cheers could be heard faintly, as if listening to a stadium of people from miles away. All the recruits fell to the floor and the room went nearly dark, back to the gentle ambient glow intrinsic to the crystals in their natural state. The recruits were not exhausted, sick or ill this time. Instead, they felt energized. They turned to Saraceni.

"Did we do it?" Juliet asked. Saraceni smiled.

"No instruments in here, so I'm not sure, but I daresay we did," he replied, truly relaxed since the first moment he had received this assignment. The recruits cheered and hugged one another. George spun Phoebe around. Chandra started to do her victory dance, not seen since the day of the last footrace. They looked outside and saw the beautiful starry sky, silent and still, restful and reassuring.

Success was confirmed when they returned to the training facility.

"Decoherence is at 2%," Ruth reported as they departed the chopper, "That's the normal range of background effects that is always present."

Wood was waiting there at the landing zone's edge, and when Juliet arrived, he took her aside, kissing her for the first time.

"Oh, is that all I have to do to win your affection. Well, I'll just have to go save the world again tomorrow." She blushed.

"You may regret saying that when you get your next assignment," he said.

"There's a huge celebration in the main ballroom of the Central Palace Union. Everyone is so looking forward to meeting you all," Wood reported.

"You mean we finally get to go somewhere besides the training facility?" Jane said, "Well, hallelujah, I thought we'd never leave here."

Athena Aquila took Alexander's hand and walked back toward the training facility.

Gabriel stopped into the monitoring room. He knew thousands of such monitoring rooms were afire with activity, still battling the never-ending efforts of the Dark Janae, but this one was empty. He adeptly started the monitor and tuned the frequency to see Lela, Gretchen and Bianca, packing boxes at his parent's house. He quickly learned that Gretchen and Caleb were moving into his parent's house, and Lela was leaving her own place.

"Lela, thank you so much for letting us stay here while you are gone. We'll take great care of it," Gretchen said. She unpacked a beautifully framed picture of her own mother standing next to Athena Aquila, the first item she wanted to place on the wall in her new home. Lela smiled.

"I couldn't imagine it going outside the family, and since I won't be here..." she grinned.

"Now, how long will you be there? When does James get new orders?" Bianca asked.

"I'm not sure when he gets new orders, but I'm getting a one year lease at my new place. It's about five minutes away from his. It'll be so exciting to launch my own research team. I've had this idea for a decade, and I can think of no better time to finally dig in and see what we can do to help people," she said.

"I can't believe you two are finally going to be able to give it a real try," Bianca said. "I bet I'm a bridesmaid inside of a year. Maybe I'll bring that Brett along as my date."

"Let's not get ahead of ourselves! Let's just see if I can stand the guy a week straight," Lela reprimanded, laughing, knowing the truth.

"They'd be really proud of you," Gretchen said, grabbing Lela's hand. Lela felt small tears rise up, but took a breath instead. She knew she would always miss her family and only hoped she could honor their memory with her own contributions to science. Gabriel smiled, looking at Gretchen one last time, and turned the monitor off.

"You'll see her again," Saraceni said as Gabriel cut across the training room, "and Gretchen, too-in a few hundred years," he added half-jokingly. Saraceni exited in his dress clothes toward the transport.

"I know," Gabriel said to the empty room. He turned off the light and the gentle amber glow of The Cupel held steady in the corner. He looked at it and exited toward his room. A week later, walking down the same long corridor, the night of the celebration seemed it had been long ago and his memory of it was only in flashes of images:

-The men in pressed outfits of navy, white and silver. Jack had tied his silver cord into a double-wrapped bowtie-style, very old-school Hollywood, while David Running Wolf had used it to incorporate a braid pattern into his long hair with the silver accent.

-The women had appeared in gowns of either white or silver, each with a sapphire bodice. The only one who seemed at ease was Chandra, having grown up in the land of debutante balls.

-Phoebe shouting "I look like a princess!" as they all rode the transport to the central palace, passing the point where the old world stone structure architecture gave way to the futuristic glass city as the white cherry blossoms lining the streets were punctuated by a carpet of bluebells.

-Most of all, he remembered the gratitude of his True Earth colleagues over Molior's success in opening the gate and his discovery of the latge door behind which was a small lake of iridescent light-infused water.

"This was the place I always used to see as a kid. I dreamt of this!" he exclaimed to his parents. Athena had taken his arm on one side, and his father's on the other.

"Of course you did!" she replied with a knowing smile.

Now he stood next to the Cupel in a dark room, his stare of growing concern barely illuminated by its' amber light. Saraceni arrived and, too, looked at the Cupel.

"It's not safe, you know," Saraceni confirmed, " Valswak and the Dark Janae won't stop. We're in for a lengthy battle."

Gabriel sighed, "I know."

"We're handing out new permanent team assignments tomorrow. You will be one team Captain." Saraceni held out to Gabriel the small silver bars to affix to his collar indicative of the rank. Gabriel paused.

"And what will I lead?" he asked.

"The charge against the Dark Janae." Gabriel then accepted the silver bars, feeling the full heft of their weight in his hand as he did so.

In a distant corner of quantum space, Valswak watched the exchange between Gabriel and Saraceni on his own surveillance monitor. Alone, he smiled to himself.

"You'll lead a whole lot more than that, Gabriel. The Aquilas will lead a revolution."

The End

Visit wolfpawmedia.com for details on book II in The Cupel Recruits Series, The Soul Trials, as well as other Wolf Paw authors and titles.

Acknowledgments

For the thousands (and I do mean thousands!) of hours of science fiction "education" growing up, I wish to thank my Mother first and foremost. In addition to the unending belief in me, encouragement, instilling a deep love of reading and the old adage to any question, "look it up", I will forever be grateful for your love and support. If we could categorize some of those as grade "Z" science fiction films, though, I would say there are a few I could have done without. (Anyone need only ask my sister for confirmation on this). Thank you to my capable and wonderful daughter, who has endured years of my own lectures on scientific concepts, research principles, and philosophy. You are a BA terminatrix who has shown amazing resilience and will always be the shining star in my life. You are destined to follow a beautiful path. I appreciate your dedicated editing, but more so your mere existence, fun energy during hiking expeditions, and just being you. Likewise, I must thank Dad for having been Dad, and this book has me hoping he has found himself hanging out there somewhere with the other good guys. My sincere gratitude to my good friend and author, Brian Bailie, Jr., for the joint editing process of our books and to his family for tolerating our occasional need to micro-analyze ad nauseum. (We know when we're being like that). My best friend, Tina, who is more like a sister to me, thanks for knowing all the history back to age 11 (and appropriately keeping it to yourself!) and for having three beautiful children and allowing me to be a part of their lives. Thanks to Kevin for the encouragement early on, without which I probably wouldn't have started this book, for helping me grow up, and for your unique outlook. Kate Wyman, thank you for having the artist's vision of what I could only see in my head and producing the cover art. To all my other friends and family who have been wonderful people for the many years I have known them, too many to name, I am happy to say, a huge collective thanks and looking forward to some serious fun in the near future. Thanks to every Starbucks on the planet, but especially the crew at 30th and Arapahoe in Boulder. Lastly, to all the teachers, scientists, soldiers, artists, writers, historians, adventurers, dreamers and everyone who gets out of bed in the morning and makes it their aim to contribute something to the greater good- we inspire each other.

www.ingramcontent.com/pod-product-compliance
Lightning Source LLC
Chambersburg PA
CBHW071133170626
46809CB00002B/596